The Architectural Record Co.

Architectural record

July - September 1899

The Architectural Record Co.

Architectural record
July - September 1899

ISBN/EAN: 9783741198977

Manufactured in Europe, USA, Canada, Australia, Japa

Cover: Foto ©Andreas Hilbeck / pixelio.de

Manufactured and distributed by brebook publishing software
(www.brebook.com)

The Architectural Record Co.

Architectural record

Vol. IX. (WHOLE No. 33.) No. 1.

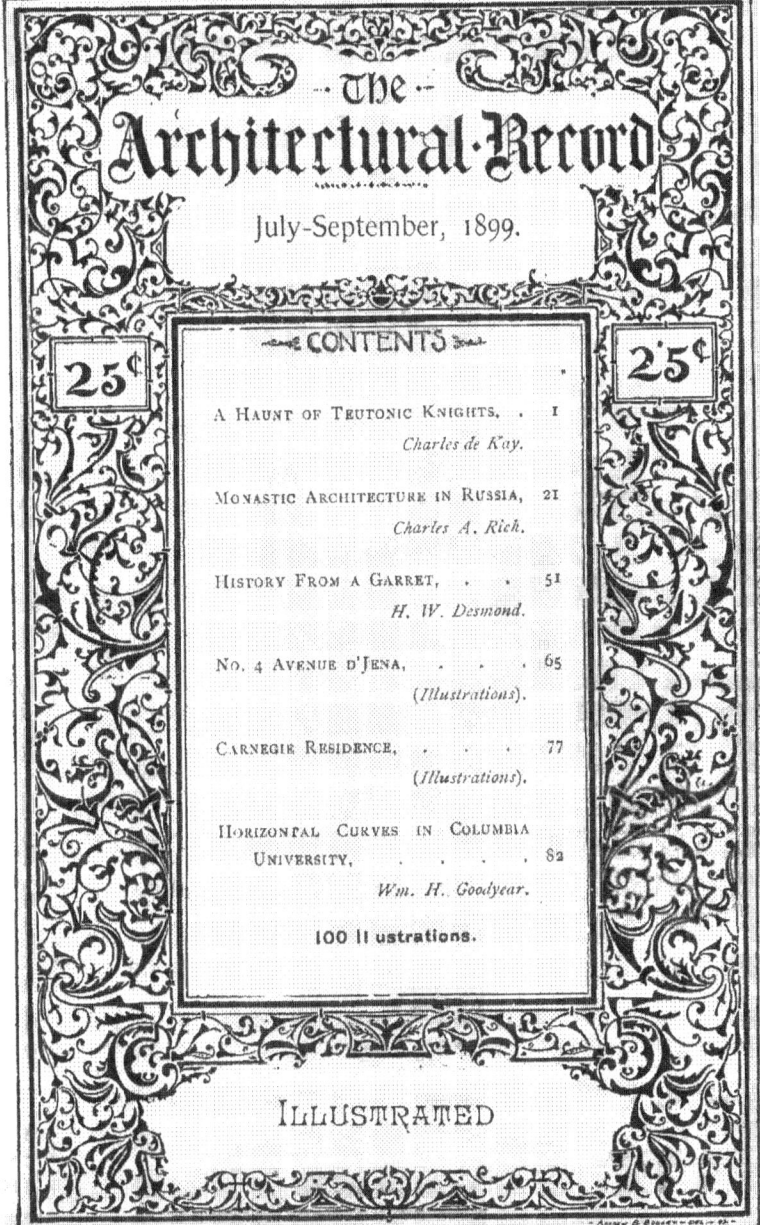

··The··
Architectural·Record

July-September, 1899.

25¢

25¢

❦ CONTENTS ❦

100 Illustrations.

ILLUSTRATED

ADVERTISERS' DIRECTORY.

Vol. IX.   (WHOLE No. 34.)   No. 2.

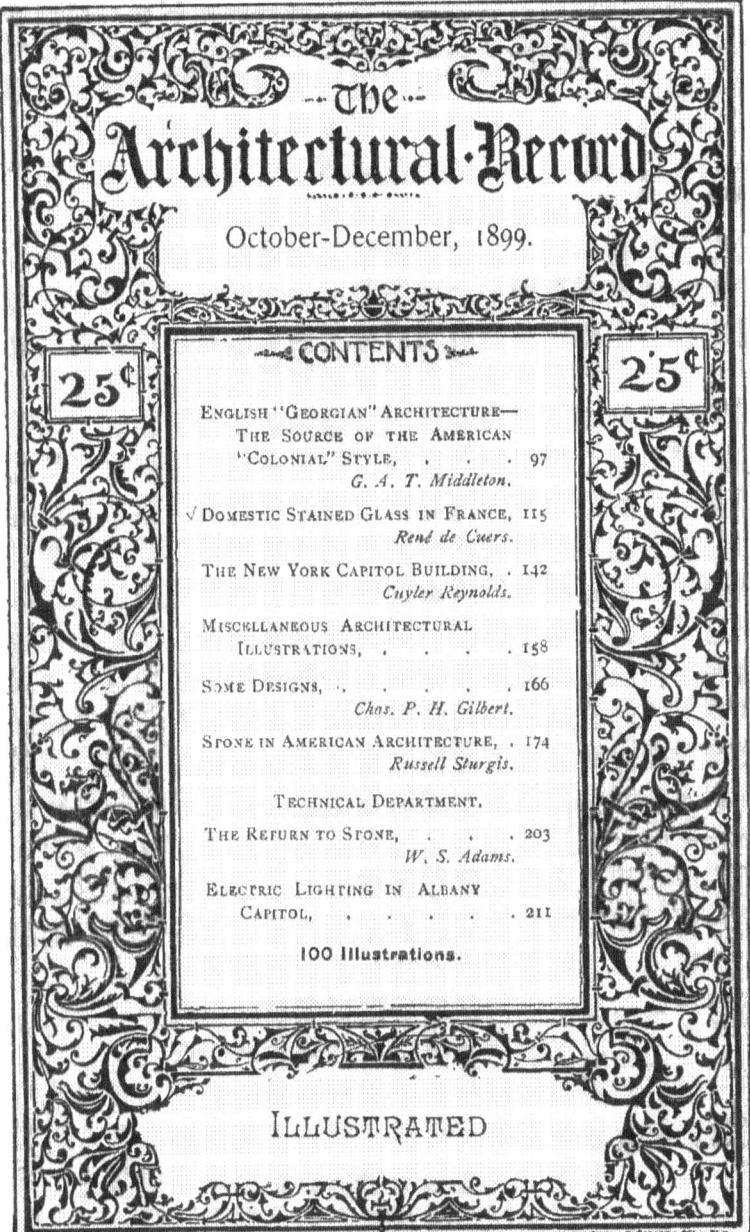

--·The··--

Architectural·Record

October-December, 1899.

CONTENTS

25¢   25¢

ILLUSTRATED

ADVERTISERS' DIRECTORY.

10

Vol. IX. (WHOLE No. 35.) No. 3.

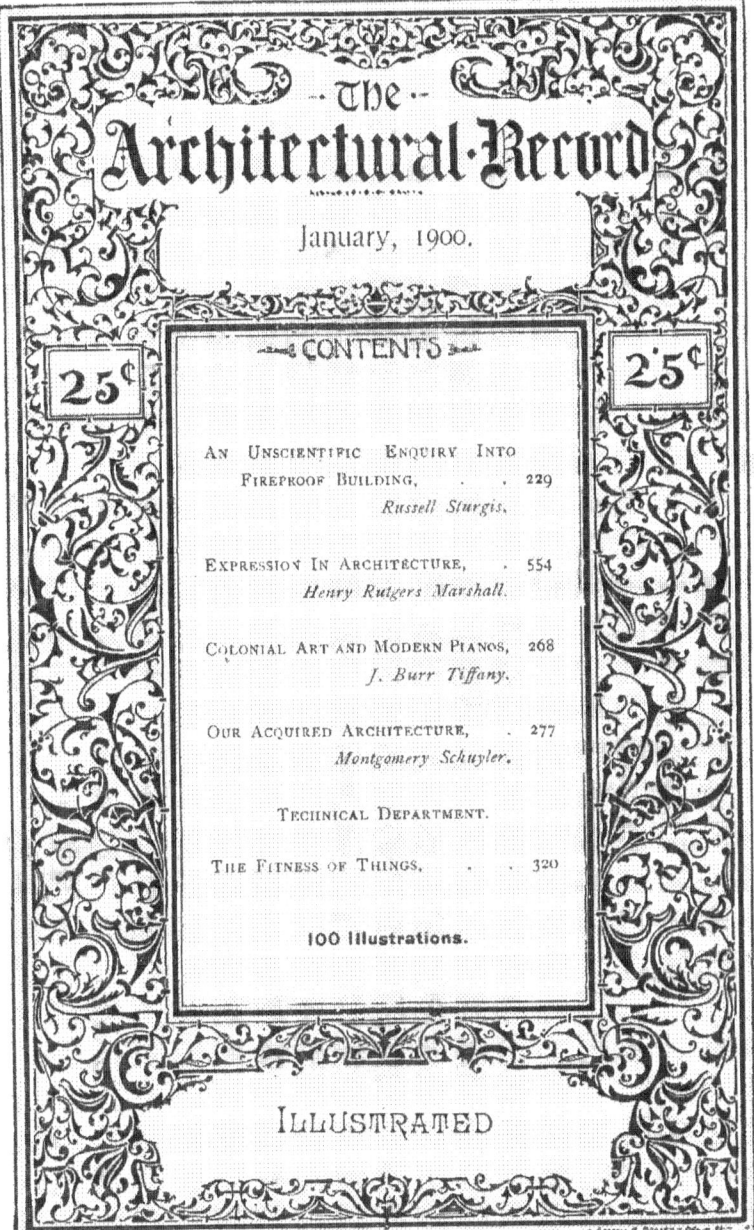

--The--
Architectural·Record

January, 1900.

CONTENTS

25¢   25¢

100 Illustrations.

ILLUSTRATED

ADVERTISERS' DIRECTORY.

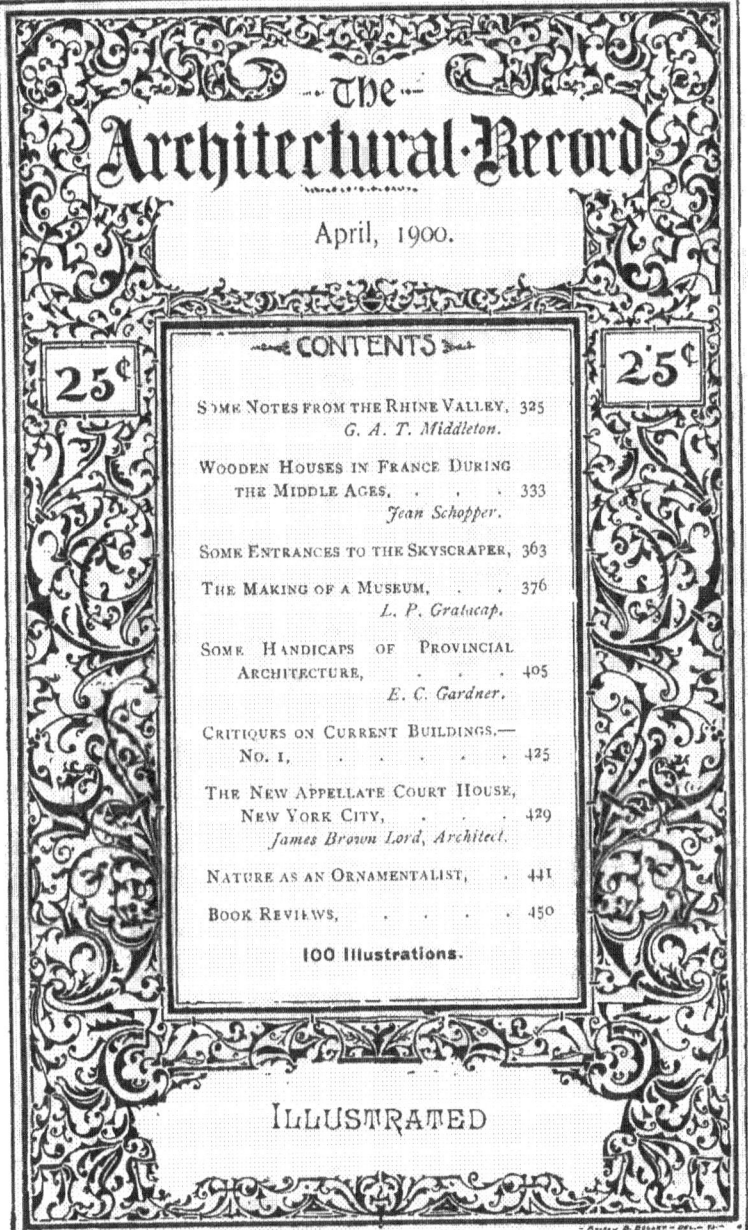

...The...

Architectural·Record

April, 1900.

25¢   25¢

CONTENTS

100 Illustrations.

ILLUSTRATED

ADVERTISERS' DIRECTORY.

6

The

Architectural Record.

VOL. IX.   JULY-SEPTEMBER, 1899.   No. 1

A HAUNT OF TEUTONIC KNIGHTS.

WHAT a difference it does make, he may have said to himself, whether you are a heathen with no rights to anything but hell-fire, or, on the other hand, a champion approved by society and licensed by the Christian church—an exterminating angel, in fact, with vested rights not only in your own person, property and land, but in the land, property and persons of the heathen!

Thus may have mused Kynstud, chief of pagan Lithuanians, as he sat in his cell at Marienburg on the Nogat with two sentries just outside the door, a prisoner of the Order of Teutonic Knights after one of the fiercest battles in the Baltic crusades. As if it had been the nineteenth instead of the fourteenth century, and the plains of the Oder, the Vistula and the Memel had been Central Africa—on the plea that their enemies were heathen the pious brothers of the Order had for the past century and a half levied war on the Russians, Pomeranians, Livonians, Lithuanians and Poles, killed or driven off their cattle, ruined their crops, cut down their orchards, burned their villages and towns, and forced the captives to build castles and fortify seaports in order that German settlers should be protected against the earlier owners of the land.

And what land was it? Well, it had a respectable antiquity in the middle ages, for it had been known, hazily 'tis true, to the Greeks and Persians and Phœnicians.

It is the broad land of water courses, forests and swamps, of swans, storks, cranes and falcons. In classic phrase it is the region where Kuknos the doting friend watched Phaëton scale the sky in his father's chariot, saw him fall from heaven, and grieved thereat so greviously that Apollo changed him into the dirgeful swan, whilst his sisters, struck with a double sorrow, turned slowly into poplars or willows, and their tears falling into the waters of the Eridanus of the North congealed to drops of amber.

It is the great and only amber country. The old legend of the

Italian stream Eridanus as a source of amber was but a mistake for the river that falls by several branches into the Baltic, instead of that which enters the Adriatic. Up the Weichsel, or the Nogat if you will, for they are different branches of the same stream, passed the ships of the Phœnicians on their way back from the north, bearing the amber of the Baltic strands to Greece and Persia and India. But a greater, weightier trade than that of amber throve then, and throve in the middle ages, up and down the great rivers of Russia—the trade in slaves. And this trade in human beings was flourishing still when

MARIENBURG.
General View from the West.

Prince Kynstud the Lithuanian, in the year of Our Lord 1360, sat pondering how to escape from the Marienburg, chief chapter house of the Teutonic Order in Prussia.

The combat between the Order and the wild Lithuanians seemed a very unequal one, since the knights were in possession of all the ideas as to military matters new in Europe, ideas which had been learned or learned afresh in the last crusades, after the Order, along with other crusaders, had been thoroughly drubbed and driven out of Egypt and Palestine by the Saracens. It was then the brethren sought easier victims on the Vistula.

Moreover the Order had been long in Venice, where it had watched the statecraft and commercial polity of the Venetians. Its chapters met in Sicily and France. They were merchant princes of great weight. At the courts of the Pope at Rome or Avignon they were powerful through their ready cash; they were not less strong at the court of their suzerein, the Holy Roman Emperor. As knights hospitalers in the crusades, founders of leech houses and caretakers of wounded crusaders, they stood in great repute during most of that sinful, grasping, most Christian fourteenth century. French knights dying of wounds or the plague in Egypt had deeded them many

MARIENBURG.
St. Mary's Church.

farms, mills and chateaux, or they produced wills and deeds which purported to be such gifts and saw to it that their claims were allowed.

But they were also favored in other ways. Venturesome men and noble youths longing for the spurs of knighthood flocked from England, France, Germany and Austria to the standard of the **High Master** at Marienburg. Numbers, experience, discipline, the **most** perfect armor and at last the death-dealing blunderbuss with its infernal racket and leaden hail put the Teutonic Knights far above the pagan Prussians and Lithuanians, armed for the most part with long and cross bow. Still, each year the latter managed to issue pretty regularly from their forests, swoop down on the farms and towns, carry castles by assault, and grappling with armies of knights, destroy them utterly. Then, as likely as not, they would go into camp without following up the advantage, heavy with booty of women, wine, food, horses and harness. Being prone to forget themselves in debauch, they would often be caught napping and put to the sword by a rally of the crusaders.

Fortunately for him, Prince Kynstud could not speak German, so they gave him as an attendant by day one Alpf, a baptized Lithuanian. Many were the talks they had together in that peculiar language, so unlike German or Italian, and even Polish or Vendish, still less like Esthonian or Finnish. One fine frosty night, after Alpf had left him and all in the castle save the sentries were asleep, Prince Kynstud moved aside a wardrobe in his cell, disclosing a great hole in the wall which he had gradually excavated. The remaining bricks on the outside were soon removed and he swung himself down through the opening into the moat by a rope which had been thoughtfully introduced. Beyond the moat was someone—no other than baptized Alpf, who, to the dismay of the knights, had taken literally the injunction of the gospel to succor those in distress. He held two horses, one of them the High Master's gray stallion; nay more, he had that august man's gray mantle with the black cross, and even his sword! Mounting quickly, thus disguised, Prince Kynstud and his savior rode to the east gate; Alpf gave the countersign and they were let out. Then Kynstud turned and on the point of the sword reached up to the sleepy gatekeeper a letter, bidding him deliver it next morning to the Marshall of the Order. Then they put spurs to their steeds.

The letter in Alpf's German read:

"To His Illustrious Highness, the High Master Weinrich von Kniprode, greeting:
"This is to thank you for the hospitality shown me at Marienburg, and to say that if ever I have a chance to return the kindness, I shall see that you are more carefully watched than I have been.
                                        "Kynstud."

Oddly enough, a similar escape had been successfully planned just 33 years before, namely in 1327, from the castle in Dublin, Ireland, by a native prince named Donall McMurragh. He had been elected provincial king by some Irish tribes in the hill country near Dublin and was surprised by the British while flaunting his flag within two miles of Dublin castle, on which at the time the banner of Edward, king of England, was displayed. An Anglo-Irishman named Adam de Nangle supplied him with tools and a rope, but, less lucky than the Lithuanian, de Nangle was caught and promptly hanged.

In other ways the parallel between Prussia and Ireland was sufficiently remarkable. There was the same hatred and intriguing of the
clergy directed against the Teutonic Order in Prussia as against the
Templars in Ireland. Although nominally the Poles and Prussians
were Christians like the native Irish, yet pretexts in both countries
were found to treat them as heathen. Their lands were parcelled
out and they were expected to thank the knights for introducing to
them the beauties of feudality and slavery. So to this day there is

MARIENBURG.
Entrance to Lower Castle with Statue of Frederick the Great.

great indignation in England that the native Irish did not welcome
the Anglo-Norman civilization when they came to understand its
working, but stuck to their Keltic laws, ways and tongue as pertin-
aciously as the Lithuanians and Old Prussians to theirs.

When Weinrich von Kniprode (1351) was raised to the high mas-
tership at Marienburg, he held an eight-day festival. Among the en-
tertainments was a recital in Old Prussian verses by one Rixel, a native bard, who sang the deeds of a heathen hero, Waidewul. The recital, I regret to say, met with jeers, because none of knights and
burghers understood Old Prussic. In Ireland the descendants of the
first conquerors had learned Irish; for, about a century and a half
after the conquest, namely in 1329, the greatest bard of Ireland was
killed in the train of the Anglo-Norman leader John de Bermingham. His name was Maolruanad mac Carroll, his nickname Cam-

shuillech or the squinter, which misfortune did not prevent him from being termed a "phœnix" in his art. As this bard was killed at the head of twenty disciples, it is plain that John de Bermingham had become a native chief even to the point of having with him his Irish poet-laureate with a tail of twenty minor bards.

The fertile but dreary lands to the east of Marienburg were seized, settled and defended as lawful property with the same imperturbable effrontery that the invaders of Ireland showed when they took the lands of the Irish. Prussia had been a province of Poland in the eleventh century under Boleslaus, first Christian king. I have not observed that modern English writers whose word carries weight are greatly proud of the deeds of the first conquerors of Ireland or seek to cloak their villanous performances with the terms religion, culture, reform. It is different with some German writers, who expatiate on the heroism and nobility of the Teutonic Knights in laboring so hard and so long to Christianize the heathen, without reflecting that a less selfish mode of imparting the truths of religion might have made the Lithuanians quickly converts, while enslavement, seizure of lands and cattle, killing with sword and spear, burning of captives alive and such mercies often roused doubts concerning the real meaning of Christianity in ingenuous pagan souls.

Originally the Teutonic knights were called into the lands near the Baltic by a certain Duke of Masovia, vassal of the Polish King, who were unable to subdue the pagan Lithuanians and Prussians. Soon they made themselves so powerful that they refused allegiance to their Polish suzerain, just as the Norman-Welsh adventurers called into Ireland by a petty king discovered that they might as well set up for themselves. At first the Order obtained the aid of Duke Svantepolk of Pomerania; it was with his aid that the Teutonic Knights in 1326 destroyed a fort near a place on the Nogat called Alyem; here Marienburg was built later in the century. But in 1338, twelve years later, they had quarreled with Svantepolk. They demanded for themselves the strictest obedience on the part of all conquered tribes, but when it came to obeying the same feudal rules on their own part, they set up claims to self-government which pleased neither the superiors of the Order in Austria, Germany and Italy, nor their religious chief at Rome. In Venice the Order was regarded askance, because it still had a foothold in the Levant. In France and at Rome the clergy found the knights inconveniently popular and rich. Rulers coveted their possessions; nor were they without violent rivals in Austria and Germany.

At first the Order treated the conquered Prussians with gentleness, demanding few taxes and posing for men of virtue beyond the ordinary, anchorites who had parted from the pomps of the world and the allurements of the flesh. Very soon, however, people awoke to the fact that they had become slaves like the commons in France and Germany. In 1240, when they were asked to build castles, they rebelled. In that year, supported by their old enemy Svantepolk of Pomerania, they rose against the oppressors, introduced paganism once more and sacrificed the captive Germans to their old cruel gods of war, gods to whom unblemished men and women were agreeable, whether directly captured in battle, or seized in a raid, or bought in cold blood from the slave merchants for the purpose.

MARIENBURG.
Dormitory, Upper Castle.

More than half a century had elapsed since the advent of Teutonic knights under leaders of lower rank; yet no High Master had appeared at the head of the bands. The raids were directed from Venice or some German city; their chiefs were a Landmaster or a Marshal. Not till 1274 did Marshall Thierburg begin to build a castle at Alyem on the Nogat; in two years it was finished; but it was not till 1296 that Conrad von Feuchtwangen as High Master so much as visited the place. It was dedicated to the Virgin Mary and received the name of Marienburg. The Order had been driven from Acre in Palestine just five years before.

Six years later the High Master Gottfried von Hohenlohe came from Venice to organize victory and reform the Order; but the insolent knights soon taught him that they did not choose to be reformed. It is supposed that only in 1306 did a High Master take up his abode at Marienburg, near which a small town had grown up for safety of the citizens against raids from Poles and Tatars, Lithuanians and Prussians, pirates from the Baltic and wild horsemen from the Russian steppes. Doubtless this Hochmeister would have delayed yet longer to take possession, had not the accusations of Popes, Kings and commons directed against the Knights Templar for paganism, tyranny and hideous crimes, begun to be transferred to the Teutonic Knights. From that time forward the Order showed no little skill in playing off the Dukes of Poland against the Dukes of Lithuania.

Lithuanian folk stories recently collected by Leskien include a fable that fits very well the Order of Teutonic Knights in its dealings with Christian and pagan princes.

A farmer (aina gaspadorius) finds a dragon (smákas) caught under a fallen tree. The dragon promises him a fine reward if he lifts the tree. He does so, whereupon he is informed that he is to be devoured. To his expostulations the dragon answers: Uz géra padáryma (for a good deed) tai vis (there's always) szlektu uzmóka (evil paid). But the farmer begs to refer the case to three judges.

Having met and appealed to a dog, the latter answers:

"When I was young I kept the swine from my master's crops. Now I am old and useless my master has driven me away. Good deeds are always repaid with evil. Dragon, devour him!"

They meet a horse and the horse gives the same advice. Finally they meet a fox, who privately asks the man what he will give him if he saves his life. The man promises a fat goose, whereupon Master Reynard leads them back to the fallen tree, and on pretense of wishing to know exactly how the matter happened, induces the silly dragon to place himself as he was before. "Now," says Reynard, "your life is saved; where is my fat goose?"

The farmer takes the fox home in order to deliver to him the promised reward; but when he enters the house and tells his wife, the latter whispers: "You fool, take your gun and kill the fox!" As Master Reynard expires under the shot he has breath to say: "Uz géra padáryma tai vis szlektu uzmóka"—"a good deed is always repaid with evil."

That misgovernment which has been the lot of generations of Lithuanians in Russia, Poland and Prussia seems to have crystallized into this cynical little fable—a variant on well-known stories in the Arabian Nights and other folk tales. Some Lithuanians maintain that it reflects the situation to the present day.

It is five hundred and thirty-nine years since Prince Kynstud fled by dead of night from his jailers and by swimming a river escaped their sharp pursuit. Marienburg stands yet, cleaner, larger, sharper-edged, more brilliant in the sunlight than then. It is true that the bridge of piles with a draw in the centre is not there, and the bridge gateways are not complete. There is no tête-du-pont over on the west bank. But there rise the high roofs and strange gables which tell the presence of the castle church with the big statue of the Virgin on its apse; there are the oblong square tower beside it and the middle castle advancing toward the river. Lancet and pointed-arch windows tell of the spread of Gothic from the valley of the Seine to this distant spot. Seen from the town or land side, the big Virgin on the apse looks stolidly out across the deep moat; her draperies and the niche in which she stands glitter with gold and colored mosaics of glass. The tall windows to right and left show that the choir is

MARIENBURG.
General View from the South across the Nogat.

lighted with stained glass of modern make. The moat runs about the upper, middle and lower castles, binding them together; yet the upper castle with its church and tower is cut off from the rest by a transverse dry moat in case the enemy should gain possession of the lower half.

At the northwestern end, down stream, is a green park before the principal entrance to the lower castle, where stands a bronze statue of Frederick the Great, the pedestal having at its four corners the figures of four High Masters. Little enough, however, did Frederick do for Marienburg. At the southeastern end, beyond the upper castle and its deep moat, begins the old town. Its main street.

called the Market, faced with arcaded house-fronts, runs broad and parallel with the river to the old town gate. All the Market is a delight to those who relish the picturesque, but especially the Rathaus and the "arbors," square enclosures before each shop or private dwelling, are pleasing to the antiquarian.

A very curious Catholic church, with a low, cut-off tower, its three equal naves showing separate in three low, arched roofs side by side, stands close to the north moat and turns the gables of its triple back to the river. It may be detected in the general view of Marienburg from the west bank, on the extreme right of the castle.

The west front of the castle, with its gables flanked by turrets, remind one of churches in Prussia, such as at Pasewalk and Stargard; indeed there is an odd ecclesiastical touch to the architecture of Marienburg which fits very well the anomalous position of the knights in the body politic. Among them were strictly religious members for the celebration of the offices; the majority, however, were not priests, but fighting men, who professed chastity, obedience and poverty, and while omitting to practice the same, expected the people to hold them in reverence as anchorites, whilst they indulged in war and commerce, plunderings and feasts, luxuries and the excesses of the camps.

In its architecture, however, the world carries off the palm from religion. The church does not count for much more than does the chapel common to royal palaces. The great lower castle shows its original purpose of stabling and lodging for hundreds of horses and pilgrims, as well as for granaries and hay-lofts. The round towers by the waterside, once guards of a vanished bridge, are for defense, and the battlemented advanced portion of the middle castle, questionable as its restoration in some regards may be, indicates well enough the sumptuous life of the oligarchs who feasted and played their games of chess behind its front, with royal and ducal guests to keep them company. In fine, Marienburg is the place of opulent rulers rather than the castle of stern converters of the heathen. The old Schloss at Berlin may offer a more imposing single mass; but it would be hard to find between the Rhine and the Memel a pile more varied and interesting its architecture than this haunt of the Teutonic Knights.

In certain account-books rescued from oblivion, we learn that the Tresslers or treasurers of Marienburg were thrifty, laborious souls. In the early days of the castle, say from 1300 to 1400, its hospitality was not so much called upon as later. On the other hand, it was only then that sagacious Hochmeisters had begun to realize what a mine of profit there was in the fame the Order enjoyed as a promoter of knighthood. Not only did men flock from western Europe, but gifts of money and arms came from the faithful. Notwithstanding expensive raids and regular wars by land and sea, outlays for hosts of guests and princely sums spent in buying lands, the Order presently grew rich and peace-loving. The Hochmeister lent money to Polish and German nobles, gaining many enemies thereby. He made treaties with the Hansa towns; his galleys destroyed the pirates of the Baltic who levied tribute on commerce with Holland and England. His gifts went not only to Pope and Emperor, but foreign Kings. He even went so far, by hoarding grain, as to offer

MARIENBURG.
View of Lower Castle from River.

a very pretty mediæval precedent to modern capitalists who "corner" the grain market. It is true that German writers have much to say about the culture and civilization the Order brought to the benighted banks of the Vistula; it is also true that later on, when they were rich, poets and singers were encouraged, and schools were even founded at Königsberg and Marienburg. But it needs the robust optimism of a native to believe that the Teutonic Order did anything in the line of education which would not have been done much earlier and better had they never infested eastern Prussia with their particular form of piety for profit.

It is a singular and suggestive fact that during the ages which belong to chivalry, the knights at Marienburg entirely lacked a place for knightly exercise with arms. Nor in the surviving account-books is there mention of tournaments or feats of arms. They had commanders of experience and hired soldiery, but there is no sign that swordsmanship flourished; even strategy seems at a low ebb. The wars were often mere plundering raids from either side in alternate years. Some real armies met—horse, foot and artillery; but they usually hammered away at each other until one got a panic and fled. An exception was the famous battle at Tannenberg, which practically ruined the Order.

Nor is there any sign that chivalry improved the position of woman. On the contrary, the Order was based on a low view of woman.

The pagan populations, which offered no great obstacle to the intrusion of the crusaders, perhaps believing that men with such professions must bring them relief from the constant strain of war, became restive when they found the nature of the civilization they really brought, and contrasted the acts of the cross-marked knights with the professions of their forerunners, the missionaries. What seems to have impressed them was the haughtiness of the Knights which sprang from the twin roots of godliness and feudal rank, and next to their haughtiness, their cruelty and lust. It is probable that cruelty and haughtiness were useful in keeping the half-civilized men of the plains in awe up to a certain point, until the overtaxed bow snapped.

Reminiscences of the Baltic crusaders can still be detected in the dramas or popular ballads of the Lithuanians. One runs thus:

1. Five brothers left on the meadow green,
   To-morrow in the crusaders' hands.
2. When they captured us young men
   They laid on our ankles the iron bands.
3. The iron bands they laid on our feet,
   And drove us footsore to Tilsit town.
4. The crusade leader most unkind
   Ordered them bring the green, green rods.
   *   *   *   *   *   *   *
6. And when they beat us, began to flow
   Our blood to the ground, and quaked the earth.
   *   *   *   *   *   *   *
12. Thanks, O mother, for all your love,
    And you, O father, for white loaf-bread.
    *   *   *   *   *   *   *
14. But on the street a call is heard:
    Protect the corpses of your sons,
15. Who lie unburied upon the ground,
    Where dogs are tearing them foot and hand.

The Order was elaborately organized under a Hochmeister, who at one time ruled over the whole of Prussia as well as the settlements in Austria and Germany. Next came the Grosskomthur or Count-General, who attended to the finances of the Order and received reports from chapters, castles and farms. At Marienburg itself the affairs of the castle and town and district villages and farms were managed by a Hauskomthur or Count of the House. Under him was the cellarer (Kellermeister) who watched the fermentation

MARIENBURG.
View of Upper Castle from the North or Town Side.

of wine in hundreds of casks; for at the time there were many vineyards in Prussia planted with choice Italian stocks that yielded a wine whose fame reached England.

Then there were the armor master (Trappier), the millmaster (Korn or Mühlmeister), who saw to the harvesting and grinding of grain; the gardener (Gartenmeister), the stablemaster (Marshall), the fishmaster, in whose purview were the carp ponds and fisheries; the cattle-master and the smith. A curious hint of the Oriental origin of the Order was the Karwansherr, manager of caravans, who had charge of the camels—but owing to the climate he did not occupy himself with the care of just those beasts of burden. Finally there were in time the Büchsenmeister, who cast guns and cannon, and the Glockenmeister, who cast bells. Originally the name of the Order was La Maison de l'Hospital des Teutoniques dans Jérusalem, so it is not strange that an officer called Spittler should survive; it

was he who looked after the sick and wounded. At Marienburg
there was also immediately below the Hochmeister a Burgmeister
who saw to the defences and sentinels, as commandant of the fortress.
Ranking with him and the Grosskomthur was the Tressler, already
named, who had charge of the finances, the fruits of peace and the
sinews of war.

In each castle the clerical members, distinguished by a special
dress, performed mass and shrived the dying, much to the disgust of

ST. ANNE'S IN MARIENBURG.
Crypt with Tombs of High Masters.

the clergy round about, who were subjected to taxation for the bene-
fit of the Order, just like ordinary men; therefore they complained
bitterly to Rome. But an order which had so many clerical and
secular enemies found it necessary to have its own paid diplomats
in the Eternal City to defend its rights and usurpations. We know
all these facts, because some of the books of the Order have survived,
including the private book defining the duties of officers, which was
handed down from one Hochmeister to the other. Two household
account-books, covering the period 1410 to 1420, have also escaped
destruction.

The organization at Marienburg was in fact a very elaborate man's
club, in which it was difficult to gain membership and where no

woman was supposed to set her foot. Still, distinguished ladies like the Queen of Denmark and the Duchess of Lithuania, coming on solemn visits, were admitted to the castle, but lodged outside the upper castle. They were permitted to visit the church of St. Mary and the chapel of St. Anne underneath. But at times the rule for the complete exclusion of women seems to have been relaxed; how are we to account otherwise for stories of inroads of milk-maids on Easter morning into the very bedchamber of the Hochmeister, where, in

MARIENBURG.
Dining-Room in Upper Castle.

accordance with mediæval ideas of jollity, they attacked the master in bed and forced him to ransom himself with gifts of money?

Such things happened under the peace and commerce-loving Master Ulrich von Jüngingen, whose jester did not scruple to act as the spokesman for the young knights, impatient to win glory and booty in war, furious because the Master was for commercial treaties and the peaceful heaping up of riches. The likeness of the Order at Marienburg to a club will seem greater, if we reflect on the original meaning of club as some have defined the word, namely, as a contracted form of the German word Gelübde, vow. A club would, therefore, have meant, if we accept a doubtful etymology, a band of men knit together by a vow, exactly as were the members of the Order of Teutonic Knights. It is denied by others, however, that club comes from Gelübde; they regard it as a specialized meaning of club as a clump or crowd of people.

The coat-of-arms of the Order bore two crosses, one applied upon the other; a slender gold on a thick black cross. According to Venator, a German authority of 1670, the original was the black cross on a white or gray mantle, said to be Pope Celestine's grant. At Jerusalem King Henry granted the right to apply on this black cross the golden one. The first, second and third High Masters quartered this double cross with their own device. But Hermann von Salza, a master who was never in Prussia, proves himself so useful an intermediary between the Emperor Frederick IV and the Pope, that the former granted him the right to place the imperial eagle on the cross, while the Pope made him an hereditary prince. He was a man from Meissen on the Elbe and became High Master in 1210. He it was who persuaded Gregory IX in 1236 to preach a Baltic crusade. Forty years later King Louis the Pious of France, in honor of the services of the Order at the seige of Damietta, gave them the right to decorate the ends of the gold cross with lillies. The arms of the Order are, therefore, a composite granted by two Popes, two Kings and an Emperor. Here again we see the international character of the Order, which was continued down to the 15th century, when Poles, Hungarians, Danes, Britons, Flemings, Scots, French and Italians fought for the spread of German culture, so-called, among the warlike peoples on the Baltic.

MARIENBURG.
Interior of the Church of St. Mary from the Altar.

The other divisions of the Order made it their business to urge the adventurous to pilgrim eastward to the Vistula in order to win their spurs in battle with the heathen. Thus in the first quarter of the fourteenth so vast an army was formed that 70,000 Poles and Lithuanians were captured and set to work building towns and castles. Again in 1354 a crusade was preached and soldiers hired. An army of 60,000 men set out for Lithuania, but was stopped by a great fall of snow, followed by floods, tempests and the pest. Another crusade was preached in 1384, this time against Jagjiel, a Lithuanian prince by a Polish mother, who united Poland and Lithuania under one crown. Still another call came in 1390, when Henry, duke of Lancaster, responded with 300 knights from Britain and Ireland.

The next year a fine army of Germans, French, English and Scots plunged into the woods of Lithuania and besieged Wilna when an army of Poles and Lithuanians fell upon and destroyed the besiegers. The blow of this defeat was more than the Hochmeister, Konrad von Wallenrod, could stand. His mind gave way and he died.

Jagjiel determined to make an end of the rule of the Order, and for that object collected an army said to have numbered 163,000 men, among whom were 21,000 hirelings from Bohemia and Hungary and 40,000 Tartar horse. On the 15th of July 1410 the army of the Teutonic Order, 83,000 strong, drew up in three lines of battle at the village of Tannenburg. There they waited through the long hours of a broiling day, cased in iron and weighed down by their armor; but the shrewd king never budged till he knew they were hungry, thirsty and worn out with the heat. Then he attacked.

"ERHOLUNGS REMTER" IN MARIENBURG.
Upper Castle.

After three hours of combat the first line of his troops gave way, but when the Order moved forward they were caught between two converging masses of reserves and crushed. With his body-guard King Jagjiel fell upon the centre, while the wings that had given back returned to attack the flanks. Brothers of the Order, 5,000 in number, all the banners and guns, and countless horses and weapons were captured; 600 knights and 40,000 soldiers lay dead on the field.

Jagjiel moved on to the siege of Marienburg, where a brave Saxon Komthur, Heinrich von Plauen, had hastily collected 5,000 men and provisions. The pest broke out in the camp of the besiegers; after eight weeks of attacks and repelling sorties, Jagjiel had to retire. He was not provided with a siege train and his troops were undisciplined.

But the days of the Order were numbered, nevertheless. Its downfall occurred as much from internal decay as from the envy and hatred of its rivals. According to the rules of the Order the nobles of the country were not allowed to become members. They formed themselves into a secret league called the League of the Lizard, choosing a reptile as their fetish as other leagues of nobles chose

the falcon or the swallow. These symbols were echoes of heathendom,
I believe, coming down from the practices of the old pagans, who
worshipped bird and beast and dragon gods or human figures bearing
a bird or beast in their hands or on their heads. The League of the Lizard was aided by the citizens of towns, who formed guilds; and the
farming class and country clergy were also enraged at the exaction
of taxes and tithes. In 1440 a new League was formed at Elbing, not
far from Marienburg, the Prussian League, which was prohibited by
the Emperor at the complaint of the Teutonic Order. But in 1454
the Prussian League defied the Order, and, with the aid of the towns,

MARIENBURG.
Market Street, Townhall, and Old Towngate in Distance.

took all the castles, until Marienburg and Stuhm alone remained
faithful. Then they called for help from the Poles and Kasimir IV
was able in 1457 to enter Marienburg without opposition, the Hochmeister having been plundered, beaten and driven out of the place by
his own hired soldiers. Six years later the citizens of Danzig fell
upon the Baltic fleet of the Order and destroyed it. It was not till
the iniquitous division of Poland between Russia, Austria and Prussia that Marienburg fell to the share of Frederick the Great.

The story of the Teutonic Knights in Prussia is that of many other
organizations which were so rigidly safeguarded from possible
changes for the worse that they became fixed in certain ruts and incapable of adapting themselves to new conditions. In 1369 when

they retook a castle from the Lithuanians they burned all the captives alive. A century later a satirical verse sung to their discredit accuses them of loafing and luxury, not fiendish cruelty:

> Kleider aus, Kleider an,
> Essen, trinken, schlafen gahn—
> Ist die Arbeit so die Deutschen Herren ha'n.
>
> Clothes off, clothes on,
> Eating, drinking, going to bed—
> That's the work the German masters have to do.

And another, directed at the easy morals of the Teutonic knights, runs : "Where the German masters are, a man who has a pretty wife, a bushel of corn and a back door—will have plenty to eat for a year."

The Order was impossible after it had fulfilled its purpose ; it could never have maintained itself ; but what hastened its downfall was not the jealousy of the Polish king, nor even the undying rancor of the clerical party, but the vices of its own members. It was useless for Kniprode to send presents of wine to Edward III of England, or start a Latin school in Königsberg as well as Marienburg, or send for grammarians and jurists to lecture to the knights. It was he who introduced the sport of shooting at a jointed wooden bird on a pole with the crossbow, still a popular game in country parts. The virtues of individual Hochmeisters could not stem the torrent setting against the Order, and when the reformation began, the last clutch of 'the Order on northern Germany was loosened. But it still exists as a grand survival with chapter houses and occasional festivals. After the Hohenzollerns had used it as a political tool it retired definitively into Austria, where it still exists, exhaling not so much breath as an odor of parchment. It is a fossil club for royalties and hereditary princes.

Marienburg was neglected but not actively ruined under the Poles ; the kings of Prussia turned it into a granary and were about to improve it off the face of the earth when a poet's protest, followed by the efforts of an amateur antiquarian, put a stop to vandalism and turned the tide. The early years of the century saw such a change in favor of restoration that the architects held high carnival over the ancient burg. Now the restorations are nearly complete. The original or Hoch burg stands solid and rejuvenated. The master's house and the refectory are in order ; work is still going on in the later portions of the castle the extension which has suffered most by being torn to pieces inside for the storage of grain and hay. The present emperor has given special signs of favor to Marienburg, even to the point of promising to make it one of the stopping places on his constant flittings to and fro. The state as well as private individuals have endowed it with mediæval collections which will soon render it yet more attractive to pilgrims.

The castle belongs to the transition between Romanesque and Gothic. Its foundations are built of the rocks found erratic about the country, but the absence of quarry stone caused brick to be used elsewhere.

SUMMER "REMTER" IN MARIENBURG.
Middle Castle.
(Modern Glass Windows.)

The massive wine cellars and lower stories with their vaulted ceilings and round-arch windows, the upper stories with their elegant central columns supporting vaulted roofs and their lancet-shaped windows, the various "Remters" or refectories for Knights and guests, the chapel in the crypt with the tombs of High Masters, make Marienburg a place of interest to architects. Here the antiquarians have a rich feast in criticising the restorations and telling each other how they would have done it, if the task had been entrusted to them. Halls with a single central column which is generally an eight-sided granite pillar with capital of limestone or brick are a special feature. These are found also in the Rathaus of the town, in the Artushof of Danzig now used as the exchange and in the castle of Lochstadt. The claim that this is peculiar to Prussian architecture is of course without foundation, but it is true that there is an individual stamp to the architecture of these Baltic regions, as there is to the human beings there to be found. The gradual growth of Marienburg, its decay and restoration, with its final period of glory as a museum for the antiquarian and the people, constitute an example of the life of many other famous edifices in Europe; it is all the more notable because of the poverty of Prussia in buildings on such a scale, seized and possessed of such an historic past.

Charles de Kay.

ANCIENT GATEWAY TO THE KREMLIN.

MONASTIC ARCHITECTURE IN RUSSIA.

AN entrance into Russia must always be interesting to the stranger because of its unknown character. Stories of red tape flood the mind and one instinctively reckons how he may properly prove to the expectant guards that he is neither a nihilist, a brigand, nor a disturber of Russia's peace of mind. But anticipation is worse than reality: one expects more trouble than he finds.

It was my good fortune *last* summer to receive a commission in far away Russia, and having been interested somewhat in the curious systems of monastic life in that country, it opened before me the opportunity of seeing many of those interesting establishments, and more particularly to study the curious architecture whose history is shrouded in the mists of the Eastern Church systems, whose architects were generally *not* Russians, and whose worth depends more on picturesqueness than any intrinsic artistic value.

As I have said, the introduction to Russia is interesting. While yet a great way from the border a Cossack enters the train. He wears the conventional high black boots with trousers tucked into the tops. His cap is a huge bell-crown, and below it are huge black whiskers of the ferocious type calculated to bring the chills to any evil doer. His coat also is a huge affair drawn in at the waist, so that he has really the appearance of an animated Russian bell. He seizes the precious passport, gives a sharp look and is gone. We see no more of him until hours have elapsed, and hope about the passport has grown dim. Meanwhile, we have crossed the border, have imbibed many glasses of the ever-present hot clear tea, and become quite Russianized. Then another official appears, quietly looks over the compartment, speaks a name, looks for "brown eyes, oval face, straight nose, curly hair," and after a sharp, piercing look soberly hands back the document.

During this time, as I afterwards found out, it was known in Moscow that an American, five feet, eight inches tall, with brown eyes, straight nose and curly hair, had entered the Royal domain and come under the official eye of great Russia. It was rather mysterious, and I suppose intentionally so, for nothing is truer than the Russian idea of scaring one into the belief that he is watched at every step. It is only carrying out the proverb of the country: "The

SCENE IN RUSSIAN LIFE.

gates of Russia are wide to those who enter, but narrow to those who would go out."

The country traversed is terribly depressing; long distances, huge marshy prairies, log cabins or turfed-up houses and muddy roads, which lead apparently to nothing but a wilderness of desolation. To intensify this, the mind receives a cold chill as we pass a grave-yard where not a house is visible and only the few bare black poles stand, with cross awry, desolate and decaying, around whose tops fly great droves of crows, black and gruesome. Poverty, ignorance and hopelessness seem to be an everlasting impression after the brightness of Italian life.

Only the little railway station seems like an oasis in the midst of this drear waste, for it is bright with flowers and fresh paint; the starlings make their homes in baskets hung from totem-like poles around the house, and the clear hot tea always simmers in the huge samovar. But the groups around the station seem to belie any happiness in life, for they are a sad apathetic crowd, who look as if no joke could ever move their epidermis. Their very costume is funereal, lifeless and unchanging, and you hardly know a man from a woman since both are covered much alike. I speak, of course, of peasant folk, who seem the only inhabitant for miles around, and I

SPASKI GATEWAY, MOSCOW.

think it is this *general view* that gives that hopeless sort of a feeling, as if there never could be any possibility of rising out of their hard lot. It is depressing to say the least.

And so at last we arrive at Moscow—"brown eyes, oval face, straight nose and curly hair," and we are allowed by the grace of God and his Majesty to enter, but if we change from room 16 to room 25 of our hotel, we do so through the kind permission of the Chief of Police, and our poor passport is again reddened, or blackened, or blued, by mysterious markings.

When one reads of Athens it is a line to Athens, and a page to
the Acropolis; and much the same might be said architecturally of
Moscow, for the Kremlin is the veritable Acropolis of the city, and
looms up with the high walls of the palace and the shining pinnacles
of many churches. In the centre is the high bell tower, and around
the walls are picturesque towers of different forms and sizes.

As we approach the great square which flanks the Spaski Gate,
one of the most curious pictures of Russian architecture attracts
the eye. It is the Church of the Protection of the Virgin, or St.
Basil the Beatified. As an architectural creation it baffles descrip-

THE KREMLIN, MOSCOW.

tion, and must have been the outcome of a bad dinner and a disor-
dered digestion. It is a total refutation of the general idea that the
exterior form should be an index of the interior arrangement, and
no architectural nomenclature springs to the pen in description.
Basil was an idiot—a holy idiot—one who in stark nakedness was
free to roam at his own sweet will, and given a liberty to speak as
he listed. But do not for a moment lay up this church to his charge,
for while he was buried there, the church itself was built by Ivan
the Terrible, in 1555, who sent for German architects, placed in their
hands Tartar designs and demanded of them that they be carried

out. It demands no description, but a view of it is sufficient to show its incoherences and grotesque irregularities.

We enter the Kremlin through the fine Spaski Vorota, known as the Redeemer gateway, the work of a Milanese architect, Pietro Solarius in 1491. Over the archway is the famous picture of the Redeemer of Smolensk, so famous as a factor in the defence of the city and brought there by the Tsar Alexis in 1647. Against it no hand is ever raised, and under it no one passes without removing the hat,

ST. BASIL.

under fear of punishment. The Russian adds to his reverence by bowing three times, and crossing himself three times, a procedure which at first moves the visitor, until he finds that the life of Russia is made up of bowing and crossing to such an extent that the action seems involuntary. A count being instituted he will probably stop after several hundred impressions per morning, and assumes that the muscles and bones have made an agreement between themselves to act upon the slightest emergency.

And so we enter the large open hilltop of the Kremlin and can understand how Mouraviett should graciously feel that Rome with its Pincian Hill reminded him of Moscow. but as he sagely adds: "Moscow without the Kremlin."

PLAN OF
CATHEDRAL·OF·THE·ASSUMPTION
·MOSCOW·

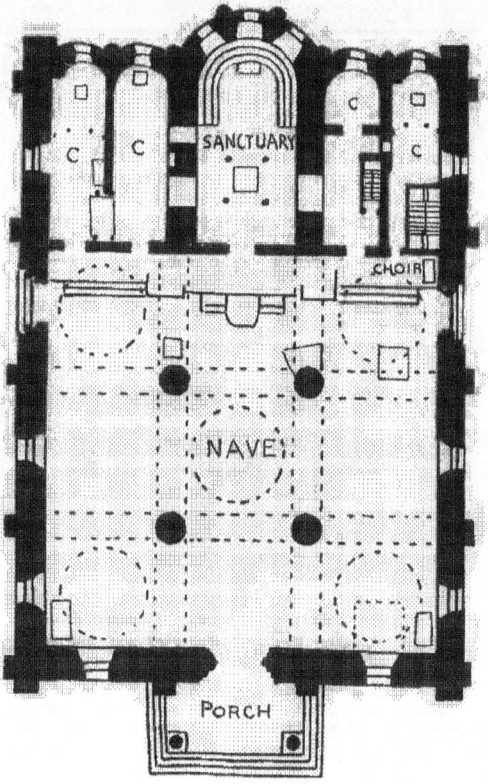

And so it is, a fortress hill, from which is seen a vast city beneath the eye, a conglomeration of domes, spires and glistening bulbs, the campagna stretching away towards the west. and the river winding itself away in the distance, lapping the foot of the Sparrow Hills, from which Napoleon first viewed the city.

"Ah!" said my good Russian friend, "when Napoleon he see Moscow, he fall down and expire at its beauty." "Ah, no," I replied, "he could never have done that; much more like his impetuous selfish nature to have shouted. as history says he did shout, "Ah, and that is Moscow at last: it is high time!"

We find ourselves before a high iron gate, which upon entering is found to surround the many churches near at hand, as well as the Terem and Synod, while the general plan shows besides these the Chudof Monastery, the Convent, Palace, Treasury, Senate and the Arsenal.

I think one is rather surprised at the modest appearance of the little square white-walled church that confronts us, and which, bear-

THE CATHEDRAL OF THE ASSUMPTION.
(Where the Czar is Crowned.)

ing the name of the Cathedral of the Assumption, is the Coronation Church of all Russia. An uncompromising, square white-walled structure, with copper gabled top, it is surely lacking in any architectural beauty. The most interesting feature is the east side wall with buttresses on the ends, and the side wall filled by five apsidal chapels, the centre one being the Bema, or Sanctuary. The bays only run up one-half of the height, and then receeding are hooded over with three circular copper pediments, and the wall enriched with decorations. Above are the four corner cupolas with a

central one higher than the rest, and all with bulging tops shining
in gilded metal and surmounted by the ball and cross, across the
lower part of which is a second crooked cross-bar, the latter peculiarity arising from the Russian belief that our Saviour was de-
formed, with one leg shorter than the other—"He hath no form or
comeliness, etc."

INTERIOR, CATHEDRAL OF THE ASSUMPTION.
(Coronation Church.)

I entered the small, insignificant entrance one Sunday morning
when the church was full of people—so full, indeed, that not a foot
of space was left, and one was obliged to push and crowd his way
along. The whole interior was a blaze of gold and color, and the
mass of worshippers, all standing, bowed and crossed continually
with a restless, feverish enthusiasm. The Church is small, and the
four huge circular columns, covered with frescoes on a gold ground,
rise to a low-toned ceiling which divides into five domes. The
church has no other architectural feature, save the many tombs
which line the walls, and thus depends on the absolute simplicity of

form and richness of wall color effect. But the *ikonostas* adds the crowning glory, for like a huge rood screen it reaches across the church and runs nearly to the ceiling, a blazing mass of gold and precious stones, covering the *ikons*, which show through with a perfect wealth of richness. When one considers, however, that here have been crowned all the Tsars of Russia, from Ivan the Terrible to the present Czar the interest is increased tenfold.

Singular as it may seem this church was built by an Italian architect, Fioraventi, of Bologna, in 1473. I say "singular" because there is not the least Italian feeling in it. The same may also be said of a large proportion of the Russian churches built by Italian and German architects, which shows that the architects sunk their own training in nearly every case, and studied the Byzantine models, as illustrated in such churches as the old Cathedral at Vladimir, which had been the former cathedral of Coronation. I think it is a fair statement to say that there is little architectural beauty in any of them. Byzantine in model, they have seemed to loose nearly all the richness of detail that is found in the churches of the East and South, for the continual early warfare with the Tartars tended to introduce a stern and unyielding spirit even to the walls.

In most cases the only attraction to the eye are the curious high bulging cupolas, enriched by golden tops, and the oft-times interesting wall decorations under the cornices and pediments. Even in these architectural details there is seldom any effort at design ; the mouldings, string courses and ornament being exceedingly crude and often bizarre. The size, too, of the churches in general is extremely disappointing, rarely being larger than the term "chapel" would best express.

As we enter, however, the effect is not uninteresting and a general plan of one answers for all. Totally different from any but the Eastern interior, they differ in every way from our European Church. Imagine, for a moment, a large, square hall with four huge columns, high in proportion to the church, rising to the roof and supporting a ceiling pierced with from five to nine domes of such small size as to be absolutely worthless as architectural features. A little slanting light enters and serves to lighten the effect.

The columns remind us of Egypt. There Anubis, Osiris, or Amen-Ra, in flat relief, forever march in stately array. Here Christian saints march from side to side and from floor to dome. On the south side are the Seven Councils ; on the north the pictured life of the Patron Saint or the Virgin ; and across the church and·dividing it into two parts, is the high screen of the *ikonostas*, a mass of architectural design, filled with *ikon* upon *ikon*, from whose golden surface peer saint and sinner from their masks of gold and silver with only their faces, hands and feet exposed. Behind the *ikon-*

ostas no woman may go. It is the holy of holies, the Bema or Sanctuary from which the Metropolitan thunders the law. I say "thunders" for I have never yet heard such voices as these, which, beginning in a low and moderate tone, increase in volumn till the
whole church rings with their intonation.

Picture this scene to yourselves and you can see the interior of
the Russian church.

A step takes us to the Archangel Church, the burial place of the

ARCHANGEL CHURCH.
(The Kremlin.)

Tsars, which is so much like the Coronation chapel. Likewise a
step more brings us to the Church of the Annunciation, in which the
Tsars were baptised and married. It is also of the same general description, but is honored with nine domes. All these churches are
within a few feet of one another, indeed, are so close that they almost hide from view the little ancient Church of the Saviour in the
Wood, which is the oldest one in the Kremlin, and was founded in
the Thirteenth Century. It is a tiny edition of all the others.

In the midst of this group is the Bell Tower of Ivan the Great, built by the Architect John Villiers, in 1600, and 269 feet high. It is a sort of pulpit tower for the Sovereigns who deign to address the people, and, while not particularly architectural in itself, together with the adjacent mass of buildings makes a picturesque group. It brings into prominence, however, the bells of Moscow—those glorious bells, which have been seldom equalled in tone and never surpassed. You see in the photograph the central opening

CHURCH OF THE ANNUNCIATION AND RED STAIRCASE.

with its great bell. Imagine its sound! Think, then, of the square below on such an occasion as Easter eve; the whole city around a blaze of light; the towers hung with lanterns from the cross to the ground, row upon row, hung on the ropes seen dangling from the cross above; the square crowded with a solid mass of worshippers with tapers, and the clergy and Metropolitans in their gorgeous official robes. The church doors swing open and they enter behind the Sanctuary; the solemn chanting begins and the Metropolitan in purple robes makes a tour of the church, crawling on his knees and kissing the *ikons*, while the great bell, and every bell in Moscow, peals out the grander anthem which announces that Christ is risen!

If you look down from this tower you see the Great Palace, the Treasury, and the Arsenal, with row upon row of great brass cannon which were left by Napoleon, and on the other side, the Convent and the Chudof Monastery. One would think as he looks down on these churches encircling the top of this hill—these churches with their golden domes and cross-topped minarets—that naught but unity and good will could be an active agent below, but probably no place has ever been more fruitful of intrigue and bloody deeds.

Directly under your eye is the beautiful staircase, so red with the

IVAN'S TOWER.
(The Kremlin.)

blood of its victims that it is called the Red Staircase. Broad and restful in its architectural surroundings, it is rightly named, for the annals of Karamsin run with intrigue and blood, and as we look down upon this old Kremlin hill, every stone is stained with its fearful color.

It almost goes without saying that the Palace is much like other palaces, interesting historically, containing some charming old rooms, and in this case, three noble halls of colossal size, making up a pile of varying architecture and containing seven hundred rooms.

The Hall of St. George, the military order, founded by Catharine, in 1769, is an enormous hall, 200 feet by 70 feet, and 60 feet high. It is a vast barrel-vaulted room with penetrations dividing the sides into alcoves, flanked by columns of the Corinthian order, and supporting Victories above. But around the wall surfaces are panels of white marble, with the names of the illustrious order in gold. The effect is grand indeed—pure white and gold in ceiling and wall, and

THE LITTLE CHAPEL, CHADUF MONASTERY.

all the furniture in the colors of the order, black and orange. I confess to a feeling of disgust, however, in finding out that the beautiful carving and capitals are of zinc. Thus are one's idols of fitness thrown to the ground.

Alexander Hall, and also that of St. Andrew, are no less grand in proportions and decorations—the former being in pink and gold, and the latter in blue, the color of the order.

And after all this grandure, upon which the peasant looks with awe as he scuffles along the polished floors, one is carried to the home quarters of the Tsar and Tsaritsa, which show that these monarchs did have a bit of home-like notwithstanding the terribly honorous duty of bearing a crown and guiding the destinies of their nation.

The Terem was the nursery of the Palace. Here the rooms are small and charming in their curious decorations. Odd tiled stoves gave heat, and the rooms starting with a large one gradually grow smaller as we ascend, till at last we are in a sort of a tower room; in

ST. GEORGE'S HALL, MOSCOW PALACE.

these rooms it may be supposed the little Tsars could kick around, play with their silver and golden toys, and possibly—possibly howl and kick and scratch their patient nurses just like any other bit of humanity. I confess that these quarters appealed strongly to me. The crushing weight of the crown was absent; the black whiskered sentinel was unseen; the toys of childhood and innocence filled the walls and cases, and the shadow of distrust and danger had not seemed to reach this abode. I thought of the Coronation of the last Czar, and his beautiful companion, as he solemnly fitted the crown to her shapely head, and wondered how there could exist in the whole of Russia a soul so black who could wish them ill.

I was strongly moved also by another point in the grounds of the Kremlin.

As one turns around to go out by the Spaski Gate he passes the Convent and Chudof Monastery. I stepped into its garden, which faces the brow of the hill and came to the little square church which is a good example of the simplest architectural form of the Russian Greek Church. A high, square box of red brick; its walls divided by heavy white architraves forming three arches, and sub-divided into smaller arches in the middle section with circular arches above, filled with rich decoration on a gold ground. The roof itself is

THE DINING-ROOM IN THE PALACE, MOSCOW.

perfectly simple and from the centre springs a single high turret, with glistening bulging top and heavy cross above.

It was evident that some ceremony was being performed, for the grounds of the little garden were filled with children and a hum of expectancy seemed to pervade the groups. This was shortly explained by the procession of priests who entered bearing with them sacred dishes which held the *chrism* of a baptism to be performed. The *chrism* is the sacred ointment or oil made but once in two or three years. An interesting legend is connected with this sacred oil, a few drops only being taken from the great copper vase called the Alabastron, in which was the *chrism* sent to Russia from Constantinople when Christianity was first introduced. Thus is represented the perpetuation of the ointment made sacred by the love of Mary Magdalene, for while a few drops have been taken every few years, they have been replaced by an equal amount of the new oil, prepared in great solemnity by the Metropolitan of Moscow, and after preparation sent to the several bishops of the Church.

Stepping into the church a most beautiful spectacle presented itself. Scores of little ones were being presented; the priest dipped a little brush into the *chrism*, and with great solemnity crossed the hands and feet, then the eyes, ears and mouth—"the eyes in order that the child may see only the good; the ears that they may admit only what is pure; the mouth that he may speak as becomes a Christian; the hands that they may do no wrong, and the feet that they may tread in the path of virtue." And then was each little one taken, and the whole tour of the Church made, while the little one kissed the sacred *ikons* within reach, bowing its little head and crossing its little body three times.

The night before leaving Moscow I again went up through the Kitai Gorod and passed through the Resurrection Gate with its charming little Iberian Chapel, dear to every Russian. Here again one is moved by their veneration. The little chapel is only a few feet square, yet containing as it does an *ikon* of the little Iberian Mother of God brought from Mount Athos in 1648, the platform outside is constantly crowded and every Russian speaks lovingly of "the little mother."

The virgin wears a brilliant crown and a string of pearls, but the right cheek is noticed to be scratched; scratched at one time by an infidel, and from the wound of which exuded blood. Note the love which springs into the face of every Russian peasant as they kiss the *ikon* and bow and cross themselves. No dearer drop of blood was ever shed by the infidel hoards, for the sight of this *ikon* has caused the sword to spring from thousands of scabbards, as well as shed blessings on thousands of sick to whom in their distress it was carried. Thus has superstition, love, and devotion, ever joined in moving mankind to action, whether in war or peace. One can hardly but feel its influence and be strongly moved as he sees the love of the Russian for the little Iberian Mother.

As I remarked at the commencement of this article, the monastic institutions of Russia have always interested me, and I determined to see something of them. The very reason of their existence was in different forms of superstition, of course, but the root idea of all was in retirement from society in search of some ideal of life which society could not furnish, and which they believed could be attained by different forms of self-abnegation. Poverty, chastity, obedience, seclusion, perpetual adoration, study and prayer—these were the ideals, but the results of centuries showed the frailty of human nature. Poverty gave way to an itching palm and a disregard to the rights of others, as exemplified by the idea that the world owed them a living. Such severe asceticism also led to all kinds of abuses which ran from the ravings of a naked monk, forever bearing a heavy chain (as in the case of Basil of Russia), to the austerity of such idiots as Simeon, a Syrian monk, who spent years on the summit of a column sixty feet high. Comments to be sure record the fact that these actions gave rise to strong objections from the brother hermits themselves, one of the writers remarking in regard to the former—

"Of this kind there are not many, because it is a very hard and cold profession to go naked in Russia, especially in winter."
Verily so!

The very extent of such life, however, led to lavish expenditure, and often to interesting architectural examples. But it must be admitted that no architecture in Russia has ever held a high place, as it consists of the most extravagant forms of all the Eastern countries, subservient to no well-understood laws, classed, of course, among the Byzantine orders, but even then perfectly lawless in its expression of forms and details, and enriched with barbaric colorings. Thus it is interesting, but never very instructive.

We started out from Moscow one bright morning to spend a couple of days at Troitsa Monastery, a few hours from the city. It was six o'clock in the morning, and the drosky rattled along at a terrific pace through the long uninteresting streets, lined by low structures, dull, dirty, and unkempt, where little patches of green and blue paint were the only enlivening influences.

Arriving after a couple of hours at a little country station we found a dozen dilapidated affairs, known as tarantas, hitched to horses by ropes. We chose one which carried with it a diminutive specimen of driver with a long cast-off Russian coat and boots and cap that made him all top and bottom. The boy was connected to his rig by strings, and the rig in turn was connected to the vehicle by other strings, and nothing but Providence seemed to stand between us and the total destruction of the whole outfit.

If the boy and his rig were picturesque, the sight that greeted the eye after a few moments ride rivals even that of the far East. I do not remember to have seen anywhere a more beautiful picture than this old monastery, with its white walls, studded with peaked red brick towers of different styles, and surrounding the little fortress made up of checkerboard refectory, glorious old bell towers, and the domes and cupolas of its twelve churches and chapels covered with bright metal and glistening in the sun-light.

Troitsa dates from 1342, and was started by Sergius of Radoneg who was a hermit and first built a small church, which, added to

TROITSA MONASTERY.

year by year at last became inseparably connected with the destinies of Russia. Legends of Sergius are endless, but possibly one
having more truth than fiction is that which relates how when the
Tartars advanced to annihilate the Russian forces, Dmitri of the
Don was strengthened by the war-like strength of Sergius and his
monks, who urged him forward to victory, and themselves led the
way, dressed in coats of mail, upheld by the mysterious power of
their huge *ikons* to which ceaseless prayers were offered. At any
rate they conquered the invaders and drove them out. From that
time the Troitsa Monastery rose in power, added to its buildings,
and surrounding itself by huge walls became a fortress of defence.
Its last defence was in 1615, against the Polish prince Vladislaf, who
sought to userp the power of the Romanoffs, but was unsuccessful.
From this time the monastery has been often a place of refuge, and
became in some way connected with almost every important event
of Russia.

Ivan and Peter, best known characters of Russian history, spent
most of their time here, and Napoleon knowing its power intended
to destroy it, but was captured, it was said, by the charm of the Virgin of Troitsa and the spirit of St. Sergius. Which of the two had
the most influence is not stated, but Napoleon seems always to
have had a most susceptible heart both in reality and fiction. To
Peter the place was much beloved, for it had sheltered him several

times against political influence, and as a boy his life was preserved in one of its churches during a terrible strife, when he was crouched behind the sacred screen with Natilia.   On the outside were the fierce soldiers who sought his life. "Drive him out," they cried. "No, Comrade," replied another, "not before the alter." But hardly would this appeal have sufficed had it not been for faithful cavalry who rushed in at the moment and drove out the invaders. Thus the place has been so full of thrilling scenes as to make a history in itself; strangely enough, however, its pages would be full of blood and intrigue, but very little love.

From my observation of Russian monasteries they are nearly all on the same general plan : the fortress walls, the outlook bell tower, the monk cells, the school, the generous refectory, and the many churches.

We approach through an open square filled with peasants and visiting pilgrims, all clad in a seeming superfluity of garments, huddled into all shapes, the limbs simply bound with rags, and the long, unkempt hair and whiskers surmounted by the big visered Russian cap. Here were a hundred men and women, pilgrims from the north, who had tramped hundreds of miles, grim and dirty, hungry and thirsty—all lovingly looking towards the Mecca of their religion, all anxious to kneel and vow their allegiance to the *ikons* of this curious shrine.

Entering the huge gateway we look up and observe that the walls are double in thickness, and contain a covered walk all around. Thus was the place a castle as well as a monastery.

The interior view is full as entrancing as the exterior, for one no sooner emerges from the entrance tower than he sees a vista of shady paths through avenues of lime trees, paved pathways leading to palace and dwelling, and all around great groups of ravens that find repose in the picturesque wall-nooks and greet you with welcoming croakings.

You proceed and ere long come to the picturesque porch of the Church of the Assumption, built in 1583, over which hangs a great tree with sheltering care. Architecturally it is a good example of Russian Byzantine. The very porch has the hanging pendants between the columnated arches, and the entrance is enriched (or shall I say rather defaced) by a heavy, ugly, ornamented roll moulding. The church itself is square in form, and surmounted by five cupolas, high and picturesque, but of no earthly good as far as interior effect is concerned, as the churches themselves being small, the domes have to be supported by the four columns which still decrease the apparent size of the interior. All the surfaces are ornamented by pictorial decoration, rich and effective. If you observe also the exterior walls you will find them also decorated with designs of much value. But the important feature, as in every Russian Church, is its *ikonostas*, which, in this church, is extremely impressive. Built up with columns, frieze, pediment and panel, filled with paintings of the saints of the church, the life of Christ and incidents of their faith, surrounded by ever-glistening light, it stands out resplendent, a mass of gold, silver and precious stones. It is thus the important architectural feature of the interior, and as in all cases represents the most important adjunct to Russian worship and adoration. Even in romance the victorious warrior enters the presence chamber, bows to the sacred *ikon* before recognizing the princes, and even the Czar himself vies with the peasant in his love for the mysterious bit of art. This feeling throughout Russia seems unchanged with time as far as my observation goes, for as far back as Ivan, George Turberville wrote—

> "Their idols have their hearts, on God they never call,
> Unless it be Nichola Baugh that hangs against the wa'l.
> The house that hath no god, or painted saint within,
> Is not to be resorted to, that roofe is full of sinne."

To the left, standing on a slight rise of ground and approached by a wide flight of steps, is the refectory, of noble proportions. It is in reality the church of St. Sergi Radonejski, but a part of it has been given up to carnal lusts of the body, for even monks must eat. A wide exterior gallery runs all around it, and is most interesting.

We stood looking from this point of vantage when a multitude of frowzy-headed, dirty and unkempt monks shuffled across the open space and gathered for their noon meal. I confess to a strong stomach, but of all smells I ever smelt, concentrated essence of cabbage and dirty Russian may be said to hold the palm.

I would like to have examined the roof and ceiling of this building, which are interesting from their peculiar iron construction, but nature could not stand the strain and we were forced to retire.

If we cross over now to the bell tower, built by Rastrelli in 1769, and 290 feet high, we pass through the little cemetery around the church, and crossing a heavily shaded road look directly into the garden of the Ecclesiastical Academy, which was founded in 1749. It is really the most important part of this monastic system, but it is hard to see how the youth can over-look the terrible condition of superstition and the low tide of morality of the monkish clergy who surround them. The retreat, however, is beautiful—the building itself of good proportions, and a sense of quiet and repose fills the place as we walk through the little gardens over whose walks the sun casts ever-flickering shadows. And as we leave it we pass out by the walls, masses of shady balconies, old staircases, broken by brick towers, some with steep roofs, others with bell tops, and the whole a very cobweb of picturesque beauty.

Everywhere are the pigeons flitting about with perfect freedom. They are sacred in Russia and may not be molested, for are they not the representation of the Holy Spirit?

We pass the palace entrance, of no particular interest, and reach the Cathedral of the Trinity. It shows possibly better than any of the others the favorite method of general construction. The form square, with numerous circular apsidal bays and the side walls divided into arched sections, the spandrils of which are covered with exterior paintings. A high central dome covered with gold surmounts the whole. From the main body grows an apse, square, with triple

TRINITY CHURCH—THE TROITSA MONASTERY.

divided side walls and surmounted by a smaller dome, projecting into a huge bulbous top shining in metal.

The whole is extremely characteristic of Russian architecture and as such is interesting. Within one is charmed also with the *ikonostas* formed of ancient *ikons* of marvelous beauty, many of them in old silver facing, whose colors have softened with age, and from whose richness glistens gems of all kinds. Here, too, are *ikons* hanging from the walls, which in time of battle were carried to victory by Peter the Great and later in the Crimean war.

Retracing our steps we go through one of the tower arches and sitting down start to make sketches of the beautiful bits everywhere visible. To the lover of the picturesque it is a most beautiful sight to sit beneath the lime trees and among the brilliant gardens rich with flowers.

It is June, the white clouds chase one another through the skies and the sun shines brightly on the red brick walls, with their cool recessed balconies. Gardens surround you on every hand; flocks of pigeons fly hither and thither; they alight on the rustic seat and bill and coo at you as if perfectly aware that since they represent the quieting influence of the Holy Spirit you will not harm them. And, indeed, who could molest these lovely creatures? Great hives of bees also stand under the walls which are covered with sweet smelling flowers, from which the little insects sip the honey and never once threaten you with danger. The box hedges lead hither and thither, and priests slowly pass in their long robes and high caps, looking terribly religious, but if stories are true, are far from it. One is obliged to admit the truth of the old line which assures you "that only man is vile." Here you are, bound in by huge sheltering walls, picturesque towers, a veritable haphazard plan of church and tower, from whose recesses may be heard the drone of the priests, the soft tinkle of a bell or the big, rich and melodious stroke from some tower around you.

One can get into a reverie of the past of this old fortress monastery very easily, and if you would add to this the presence of the rightful owners, those whose lives have been associated with its life, you could conjure up before your eyes the visit of Alexis and his Court in 1675, as given by its own Secretary, Adolph Lyseck:

"Immediately after the carriage of the Tsar there appeared from another gate of the palace the carriage of the Tsaritsa. In front went the chamberlains with two hundred runners, after which twelve snow-white horses, covered with silk housings, drew the carriage of the Tsaritsa. Then followed the small carriage of the youngest prince—Peter the Great—all glittering with gold, drawn by four dwarf ponies. At the side of it rode four dwarfs on ponies, and another behind, etc., etc."

Verily a bit of a charm of the coronation just ended.

You awake from this reverie and the scene is exactly the same with the exception of the Tsar and his Tsaritsa. Your mind, which has been led into a semi-religious turn, is startled as you behold the same old monks, blear-eyed and sensual of face, and see the slight stagger of old vodka apparent. 'Tis wise not to investigate the present day life of idleness and superstitious uselessness, for the presence of the grand old Metropolitan Plato is no more.

But bless my heart, the churches, the tower, the doves, the bees, the flowers are there, and the beautiful sun shines on the just and

NOVO DEVICHI MONASTERY.

the unjust, all of which cannot blot out from our minds the beautiful picturesqueness of the whole scene.

It was not only the monks who sought seclusion from the world, looking for an ideal that ended in the general desire to avoid work. The Russian sisters also took upon themselves religious vows and founded convents which have become famous. Away upon the outskirts of Moscow lie the white walls of Novo Devichi Convent, at which I spent a day. We approached it by way of Sparrow Hill, made famous by Napoleon. The walls are well preserved, lined with machiculations curiously wrought, and enriched by red brick-topped towers, circular and square, and the whole mass of churches, bell towers, and other buildings springing from the architectural mass. A lofty, square bell tower with three arches and picturesque wings gives entrance, and a most beautiful view greets one. Directly in the centre of the convent space is the large cathedral church, with circular gabled roof line and surmounted by the usual central dome, covered with gold, with four corner cupolas on the angles, painted in blue. The entrance is very picturesque, surrounded by the graves of the sisters and is approached under a heavy columnated arcade and staircase. Over the entrance in a circular pediment is a beautiful *ikon* in rich colors and gold, and representing one of the most charming wall decorations I remember seeing. Here were gathered the sisters for service. Shall I say sweet-faced sisters? They certainly were so.

Richly endowed, the convent was originally opened in 1524 in commemoration of the capture of Smolensk, and was a refuge for Tsarinas, who renounced the world. It is still a retreat for those who finding no chance for happiness in married life, give up their life to the education of noble girls. And this leads me to digress sufficiently to say that it was easy indeed to see how Russian ladies of good birth and education should choose to spend their lives here rather than in the pitifully desperate plight of waiting the appearance of the decent, educated, and refined lover to woo them into the sea of matrimony. To the traveller such chances seemed few and far between in the thousands of miles of desolation that seemingly made up the country known as Russia. And so, I say, it was with feelings of sympathetic interest that we watched these sisters as they entered into their devotions in this little cathedral. We saw a service in which only one man was admitted, and he the Metropolitan who only could approach and pass the lofty and magnificent *ikonostas* which led to the holy of holies; a service where all chanting and all the curious offices were performed by nuns, in long black robes and high-peaked hoods, with only their faces visible. And as one after another came forward, and on her knees chanted the litany and responses, the remainder incessantly bowed and crossed themselves, the two first fingers only and thumb being used as the mystic symbol of the Trinity.

Beginning in a low, sweet response the voice grew stronger and stronger, till after some mystic sign from the Metropolitan, the last response increased in a long drawn out sound which died away in a wail of penitent anguish. And then from some part of the Church which we could not see came the sweet, soft music of a women's choir, weird but ineffibly sweet chords, which brought to mind a long drawn out Sheherazade of old. And so the service ended and the nuns returned to their little one-storied cells, before each one of which was a garden patch full of sweet peas and zinnias, from which they gathered nosegays and possibly lamented that in all Russia there did not appear a knight for whose love they might throw off the black and assume the white and orange blossoms.

A thrilling story is told of these sisters at the time of the French invasion.

Napoleon to emphasize his retreat went directly past this convent, and not content with the havoc which his miserable ambition had caused his sister nation, he sought to blow up the convent which had given him shelter. But he counted out the heroic sisters, who not only repulsed his attempts at entrance, but fought royally and put out the flames which Napoleon caused to be ignited so as to reach the powder concealed in the church. Such conduct was worthy the wretch to whom nothing was sacred!

The bell tower is interesting, and one of the sisters gave us the key, so that we might ascend the five stories, from which height a magnificent view is obtained of the old city of Moscow with its winding river and the Sparrow Hills covered with little pleasure booths. It was the first point from which Napoleon saw Moscow, and also from which he started his welcome retreat.

Historically, this convent, founded by Varili III., in 1524, is interesting as being the home of Irene, widow of Theodore I and

DONSKOI MONASTERY.

daughter-in-law of Peter the Terrible, and also Sophia, the sister of Peter the Great, who governed Russia from this retreat during the minority of Peter. For, although Irene and Peter were declared joint sovereigns, he was incapable of rulership, and the power was vested in Sophia.

Other monasteries in and around Moscow are also very interesting. Donskoi, founded in 1591, was once of great size, endowed with seven thousand serfs. It has a most peculiar circular bell tower in five retreating stories besides five churches.

Novospaski also is still more interesting, and its enormous white·

walls, its glistening domed cathedral, its picturesque towers and magnificent bell tower 235 feet high are seen from afar. Indeed, this whole mass makes a most picturesque grouping, in which the architectural detail is remarkably fine.

Several miles from St. Petersburg is the monastery of the New Jerusalem, full of associations of the monk and afterwards the Metropolitan Nikon. A whole article might be written on this picturesque spot which "is as beautiful as Jerusalem itself."

And the same might be said of Kieff, the most important monastery in Eastern Russia. Its point of architectural interest is its

NOVO SPASKI MONASTERY.

church of St. Sophia, the prototype of its Moslem brother in Jerusalem. Memories of Yaroslat and Vladimir haunt the place, and the sight of this wonderful place, filled with a motly group of pilgrims, is like Troitsa, except that being further removed from what the traveller calls civilization, it is full as interesting and bazarre. No better description can be given than that by Hare when he looks around and sees—

"Cossack men in a single garment of sheepskin or sackcloth; women in turbans, short, brilliant colored petticoats and jack boots. Most strange at first is the bowing, curvetting and prostrating figures, never making their obeisance at the same time, but just when the impulse of the moment prompts them; and yet no one can help being touched by the reality of their reverence which is seen here, the absorption unconscious of all surroundings; often the wrapt attention. At night, near all the churches, rows of sheepskins may be seen lying on the ground. These are men and women asleep under the stars, sheepskins being at once the dress, beds, carpets and tents of the peasants."

I will speak of but one more monastery, and that shall be Simonof. It stands like a jewel in the midst of the desolation of the outskirts of Moscow and is approached through what might once have been a charming grove of trees, but which seems now to have

SIMONOF MONASTERY.

taken on the forlorn and poverty-stricken look of the neighborhood. Why it happens that the original entrance under the bell tower has been closed and one is forced to sneak around to some other gate, I do not know, but I could not help thinking of the Biblical injunction as we went around between the cliff and the wall by a sandy path and at last entered a small archway. Then it is, however, that the dirt and squalidness of Moscow is forgotten, and a vista of enchanting beauty lies before us. There are four paths leading into charming retreats of shady walks through which the warm sunlight breaks across the path in showers of flickering light.

Directly in front but away down the avenue is the central church porch, above which you can see the white domes and golden coronets almost dying away into the azure blue of the sky. To the left is the great bell tower and the shrubbery is so full that only glimpses of its beauty are seen, and yet it is a monster, both in size and height, and is surmounted also by its golden crown. And to the left one sees the checker-board refectory church. I remember that I wondered if that form of decoration was a particularly good stimulant to the digestive apparatus, for my monks in plaster on my book case almost look down upon me rather gauntly, while those whom I see in gown and hood soom to have a preponderance of paunch. But the shrubbery hides them as they pass, and I see bit after bit of picturesque towers and walls and balconies, which leads one again to remark that all the monastic establishments of Russia seem to be laid out exactly alike in plan and feature, and only vary in detail. Scattered around also are other churches and the cells and outbuildings of the monastic life. The monastery was founded in 1370 by St. Sergius, who, it will be seen from Russian monastic history, was a most important factor.

Here we had a glimpse of the regular life of these monks, a glimpse that threatens approaching dissolution, I think, for certainly no moral or intellectual good could ever result from the daily life and devotion of such monkeries.

As we entered, the place was seemingly deserted, but upon approaching the central cathedral, men were noticed at work on the structure. The cupolas were being repaired and the interior *ikonostas* was being regilded and a new panel added.

The old church is of Byzantine feeling, with five cupolas, which shine in the morning sun, and its *ikonostas* is now being restored as of old. Here is an *ikon* missing, and we are told that it is one on which St. Sergius blessed Dimitri of the Don, when he went out to conquer the Tartars. The old monk, who turned out to be the Metropolitan, leads us around with unctious grace, evidently speculating as to the amount of his fee. Suddenly the huge bell in the tower nearby rings out and with many apologies he leaves us for some service. Following him, we entered the old church in the rear of the larger one, and here were three old women awaiting a service for which they had paid several roubles. The monk has changed his robe for a richer one, and advancing to the *ikonostas* with ill-concealed carelessness, mumbles away the forms, which answer to the litany. The old women bow and cross repeatedly. Suddenly another monk crosses the church in the distance and the older monk shouts out to him to come and continue the service. He advances, starts off at a rattling pace on the Epistles known to him as the Minacon and Octoechos. Meanwhile the older monk has broken off with what seems very scant pietic propriety, and shuffles off to us to ensure his fee. The great bells in the tower keep up their solemn tolling, which tells of a service being performed, and just as we are about to go out we hear another monk, who with changed voice and glorious intonation, rings out the service of the Trisagion, in which the word holy is thrice repeated with ever-increasing tone. The old women increase their genefluctions and crossings until the last re-verberations of the voice have ceased, when they arise and, making a complete tour of the church, kiss *ikon* after *ikon*, all the time bow-ing and crossing, till they conclude their devotions for very fatigue. I ask to whom their many roubles go, and my guide, turning with an expressive gesture, simply answers "Vodka." This rather sweep-ing answer seemed harsh, but I think the general impression is the same, the true monastic feeling as handed down from the saints of the church has disappeared, and the great sin of Russia is stamped even on its monastic life and those who support it—whiskey.

Around the walls we walked, sketching the curious old towers, balconies and architectural bits of picturesqueness until the setting sun warned us of approaching evening.

The quiet walks seemed deserted; the monks slept within their little cells; the bees buzzed feebly in the syringa, and as we went out under the archway the old walls became enriched by an after-glow; the shadows of the willow grove cast long shadows upon the fast-fading brilliancy of the green meadows, and the great tower frowned down darkly upon our pathway, as one of its huge bells tolled out the requiem of a departing day.

Chas. A. Rich.

New York City.

PRESENT CONDITION OF THE CATHEDRAL OF ST. JOHN THE DIVINE.   Heins & La Farge, Architects.

HISTORY FROM A GARRET.

I RENTED recently for the summer an old house long uninhab-
ited in a certain dormant New Jersey village. Everything about
this hamlet has the air of by-gone times, except, indeed, that lately
macadamized main road, which nothing traverses but an occasional
farm-wagon and some stray meandering bicyclist, who invariably,
as I have observed, slackens his pace to discover some sign of his
whereabouts or some indication of life amid the unexpected surroundings. There is little of a public nature to enlighten him. So seldom
is there anyone astir that he might reasonably wonder whether the
village was not a lost survival of a hundred years ago, which the
affrighted inhabitants had suddenly evacuated upon his approach.

A hundred years did I say? Some few of the houses must surely
antedate a century, though we dare not accept the local tradition
which erects them near the year of Queen Anne's coronation. The
greater number of the buildings, I judge, are of quite modest antiquity. Probably they were constructed within the twenty years
whose meridian was eighteen hundred and twenty-five.

The house that I have rented is one of the earlier. There still
clings to it that air of quiet gentility, that certain charm of homely
urbanity which distinguishes, and is, indeed, the secret of the
"Old Colonial." I wonder greatly where the Jersey country carpenter acquired the lightness of touch and the refinement of taste
which removes from modern work by much more than seventy-five
years that dentiled and box-columned porch in front of my door and
that festooned cornice under the steep, weathered roof! I wouldn't
exchange his simple doors and casements nor his even plainer stairway for any amount of "hardwood" trim. And this—the stairway—
leads me to my point—the garret.

On my first tour of inspection, after our household was settled,
this garret was the last spot I reached. It contains no rooms, but is
open over the entire area of the house. It is roofed by heavy oaken
beams and visible shingles, which slope almost to the floor. But not
quite. On the floor line of the longer sides are four windows, mere
semi-circular lunes, through which the evening sunlight was
streaming when I entered, and the yellow radiance blending with
the reflected tones of the weather-stained timber colored the atmosphere gold and brown. The dust was so thick under the feet that it
was like velvet. Around the two brick chimneys which intruded
from the rooms below were accumulations of finely disintegrated
brick and mortar. Cobwebs, mostly untenanted save by the almost

ghostly fragment of dead insects, were everywhere. Clustered along the rafters were deserted red clay hives of colonies of hornets. The place was so still and forgotten, so apparently unattached to any memory that I felt an uncanny sense of intrusion, as though by some necromancy other than the payment of a small monthly rental, I had been permitted to really enter the past and step physically into the atmosphere of by-gone days. I would not have been surprised had shadowy forms advanced to meet me, and I can imagine how beautifully the faces of a departed generation might have grouped themselves in the sunlight and the shadow at that moment. The sentiment of the place compelled me to step lightly as I moved about.

In this cautious manner I had almost completely circumambulated the garret when I discovered in the darkness of one of the low corners an old iron stove. It was only a fragment. It was powdered thickly with rust. I might have passed it by without examination had not something in its make attracted me. Its surface was covered with elaborate arabesque ornamentation exceedingly well cast. In order to inspect it thoroughly I drew it into the light and then I noticed, hidden in what was the fire-box, a number of discarded volumes. Some of the covers were missing. The pages of all were discolored and stained as though water had leaked in upon them from the roof. Perusing them one by one I found they were fragments of the literature current when the house was still new. They were, moreover, of a dull domestic type, save three, which did, indeed, bespeak the scholar and his interests—a new testament in blinding, crabbed Greek text, entirely unsuspicious of Porson, a French version of Catullus, and a leather and linen covered volume of "The Architectural Magazine and Journal of Improvement in Architecture, Building and Furnishing and the Various Arts and Trades connected therewith," published in London in the year 1835, by Longman, Rees, Orme, Brown, Green & Longman, of Paternoster Row.

Here, then, I had alighted by chance upon the predecessor of The Architectural Record, and—another instance of there being no new thing under the sun. I ran hastily over its contents: "On the Studies and Qualifications necessary for an Architect," "Thoughts on the Origin Excellencies and Defects of the Grecian and Gothic Styles of Architecture," "A General Survey of the Present State of Domestic Architecture in the Different Countries on the Continent of Europe," "Further Remarks on Palladio," "A Waterproof Casement." "Designs and Description of a Double Door for a Room, So Contrived that one Door cannot be Opened until the other is Quite closed," "Observations on the Comparative Advantages and Disadvantages of the Various Systems of Heating by Hot Water now in Use, and on the System in General," "Remarks on Competition Plans with another Instance of Partial Decision," "On the Discrepancy which often occurs between the Sum charged for the Erection of a House and that which the Gentleman building expected to pay for it." So slowly do we move in some matters, I thought, that even to-day, nearly three-quarters of a century later, the Architectural Record might take these very titles as texts for articles for a later generation!

But two articles especially attracted my attention because they related to New York City, and I have ventured, therefore, to present them to the readers of this magazine, believing they will be as much interested by them as I was when, after my descent from the garret, I read them carefully.   *H. W Desmond.*

Art. VI.   Street Houses of the City of New York.

By William Ross, Esq., Architect.

In my former communications [which, unfortunately, never reached us] I only alluded to the general principles, as it were, of the buildings of this city: in the present paper I intend to go more into the details. Of the general sameness of design (or rather want of design), in the street fronts of the houses, I have already spoken (in the lost papers); and I likewise mentioned that the new houses are built much more substantially here than they are about London; but, on further acquaintance with the subject this remark must be taken with great latitude. A much greater quantity of timber is, indeed, used in the joists and roof than in England; but the want of consideration which is shown in its application, as well as of scientific skill in its distribution, more than counterbalances this advantage. The fire law requires, for the prevention of fires, that no wall be built less than one foot thick; and the builder takes too good care of his bricks (which are here 8 ins. long, 4 ins. wide, and about 2 ins. thick) to make them any thicker (i. e. than a brick and a half). When we consider that some houses are six stories high above the street, and two below its level for cellars and basement, it is evident that the practice of loading the walls with timber does not add to their stability.

While writing this paper an alarm of fire was given in the neighborhood, in a large house of four stories above the ground. The side wall has fallen, crushing the roof and considerably injuring the adjoining house, or rather store, which was at least 12 ft. distant from the one on fire, and would othe.wise have escaped damage, as the wind was in a contrary direction. By the way, fires are so frequent here that they excite no alarm (except in strangers, for the first night or so); and the rule is, if the alarm is given during the night, to put the hand on the wall at the head of the bed, and, if it feels rather warm, to get up; but, if otherwise, to turn about and go to sleep again.

To return: many of your readers may not be aware that the streets of all the cities in the United States are laid out in parallel lines, crossing each other at right angles, or nearly so, and at nearly equal distances apart. This will, in some measure, account for the sameness and monotony which I formerly alluded to in their appearance.

> "Street answers street, each alley has a brother,
> And half the city just reflects the other."

Each lot or building site occupies, as near as may be, 25 ft. frontage, and 100 ft. in depth. Of this depth the house occupies from 45 ft. to 55 ft.; the remainder is used as a court, at the far end of which are two Greek temples, dedicated to Cloacina; the only access to which is through the open court, exposed to all the rain and snow, and to the view of all the back windows in the house. These temples are placed immediately over the cesspool, into which, also, all the waste water from the house is thrown, and the whole surface exposed to the air when the flaps are left open. I leave to your pen to point out the effect of this arrangement, as it is more able to do it justice than mine. Yet there are officers styled "Inspectors of privies and cesspools."

I have already said that the greatest difference of design consisted only in the number of stories in height, and in the height of the stories themselves; so that I will now say something of their arrangement in plan. The lower, or second, story down from the street is intended for cellars, and need not be particularly described; the one over this is called the basement. (Fig. 210). In this plan there are the entrance, a; passage, b, which is in length the whole depth of the house; staircase, c; kitchen, d; oven, e; and in the front is the large room, f, the windows of which look into the front area, and where the family live, except when they have company. There are four closets, g; two entering from the passage, and one from each of the two rooms.

The rooms are all divided by quarter partitions, seldom, if ever, trussed; the sides are all battened out from the walls and lathed; and to this circumstance is attributable the oversight I committed in my last, when I said that the houses here were built more substantially than in London.

On the principal floor the arrangement is much more simple than on the basement, there being only two rooms, communicating by folding or sliding doors, and the hall or passage, which likewise contains the staircase. These rooms, called the dining and drawing rooms, are, generally speaking, only used for company; the family usually living in the basement, as before observed. On the next and all the upper floors, the arrangement is the same as on the basement;

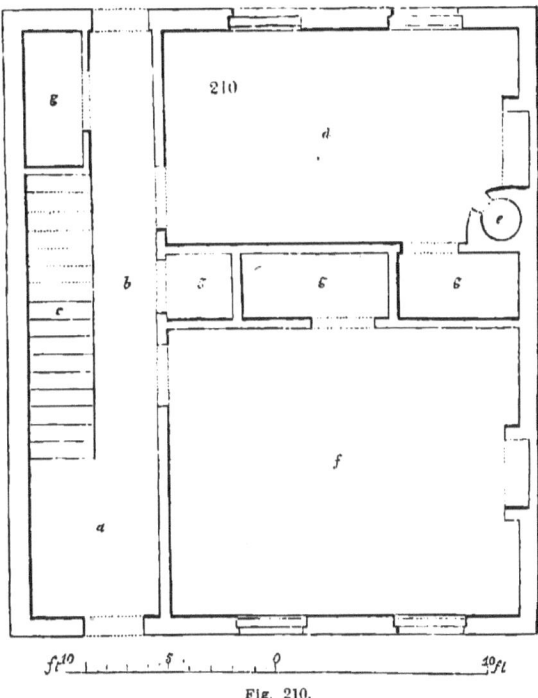

Fig. 210.

that is, there are only two rooms, a front and back bed-room with closets in each.

Such is the arrangement of one private house, and the same description will apply to five hundred of them; the same plan being almost invariably adhered to, and varying little throughout the whole city, save in the dimensions of the rooms, and perhaps a few inches in the height of the stories.

In the elevations of the houses in New York there is considerable apparent variety, but it consists solely in a little difference in height, and sometimes in the size of the windows. The doorcase to the principal floor, which is always four or five feet above the street, is in the better and middling class of houses, decorated with two columns, either triglyphed or voluted. The proportions of these columns are as various as are the builders, each having a proportion of his own; the triglyphed from seven to twelve diameters high, and the voluted from ten to eighteen; yet each are pure Greek. The Greek mania here is at its height, as you may infer from the fact that everything is a Greek temple, from the privies in the back court, through the various grades of prison, theatre, church, custom-house, and statehouse. There being no taxes here upon windows, each door has side-lights, as well as a fan-light; so that the hall is as well lighted as any room in the house. The bricks of which the front is built are painted of a glaring red; while the doorcase, window sills, and lintels, or su-percilia, are of white marble: the contrast to an American is very pleasing; though doubtless, few Europeans will fully sympathize with him in this respect.

I had intended to send you an elevation to accompany the plan (Fig. 210); but I neglected to prepare it till it was too late; for which I must apologize, and promise to be less remiss in future. I will, if possible, send it with my next. The roofs are now generally covered with tin, as lead will not stand when exposed to the great difference of temperature which occurs here between the winter and summer; it is about 118°. There are few or no parapets; those that exist being only boards over the cornice, which is also of wood, and generally consists of an entire Greek Doric entablature, nailed on the front of the house; having the gutter formed in the upper surface, and the rain-water pipe, which is likewise of tin, carried down the front of the house. The entablature of each house returns on itself, so as not to overhang the adjoining property; and the decorations, including the mutuli and guttæ, are all painted white, to harmonize with the door-case, etc.

You will think I have drawn no very flattering picture of the archi-tecture of New York; but, like London, there are a very few struc-tures which may command considerable praise; but then, they form the exception, and not the rule.

The New York University is a mountain of white marble and brick, with Italian details, more incongruous than those of Wren's towers of Westminster Abbey; it is more indebted to the woodcutter (Mr. Mason from London) than any work I have ever seen. In London it would be termed "Carpenter's Gothic;" but even that can give you no idea of its hideous abortions and monstrous absurdities. With such a specimen as this before their eyes, no wonder that the Greek, "the classic and simple Greek," is preferred by the people, who will not be gulled into admiration of anything so outré as this university.

New York, Dec. 31. 1834 (received April 17, 1835).

Original Communications.

Art. 1. Plan, Elevation, Section, etc., with a descriptive account of the Improvements lately made at the Custom-House, New York.*

By William Ross, Esq., Architect at New York.

The whole of this building, which is now in the course of erection in the City of New York, is to be of white marble, and your readers may, therefore, fancy that it must be splendid; but, were they to see it, they would have no hesitation in saying that Bath stone is much to be preferred, as the marble is left rough from the chisel. The value of marble here is chiefly in the fine polish of which it is susceptible; and, when it is not polished, it is no better than any other stone.

The windows in the exterior are in two tiers; they are each 10 ft. high, and 5 ft. wide, and set in a space of 7 ft. 9 ins., which is the clear of the pilasters: the latter are 4 ft. 10 ins. on the face, and project 3 ft. from the wall. The mode of forming the vaults of the apartments q q. in the section, is the same as that employed in forming the ceiling of the rooms next to Pine street. This mode I shall particularly describe at a future time, as it is peculiarly adapted for London or other shop fronts. The long flight of "shelf-like steps," to the Wall street front, I proposed to arrange in the same manner as those of the portico of the London University; but this proposition was overruled, as that manner was considered "not to possess dignity enough."

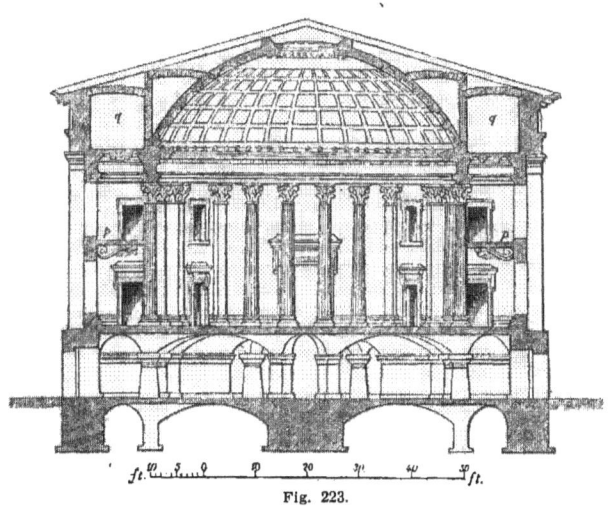

Fig. 223.

Fig. 222 is the principal plan of the building.

Fig. 223 is a transverse section through the great business-room,

*Now the Sub-Treasury, on the corner of Wall St. and Nassau St.—Ed. Architectural Record.

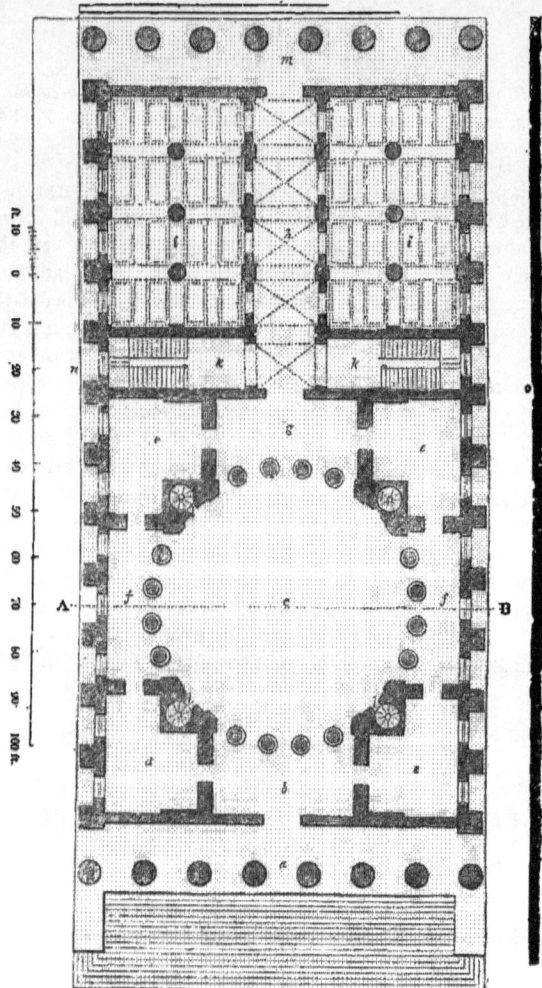

Fig. 222.

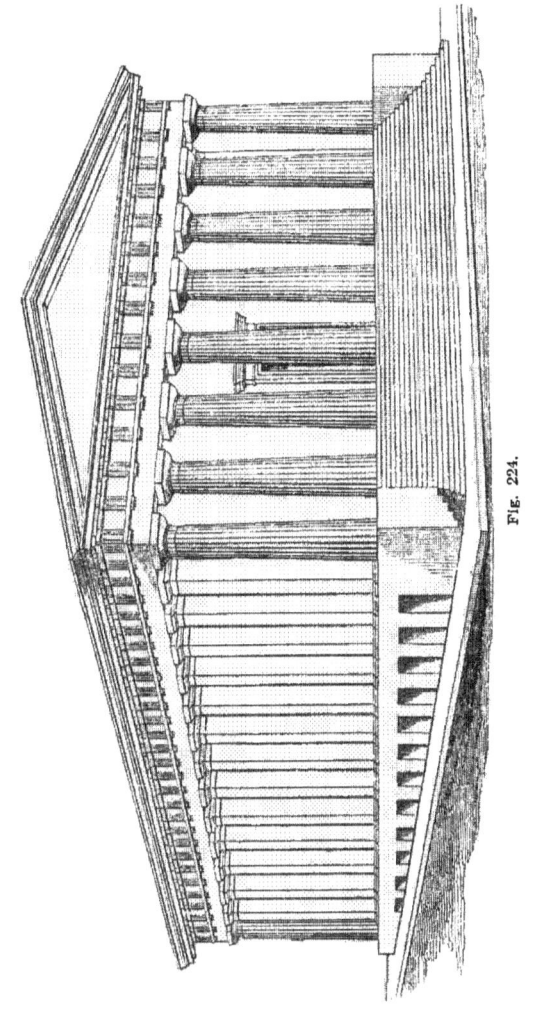

Fig. 224.

on the line a b, Fig. 222. In this section are seen the vaulted apartments under the principal floor; the galleries (p p), supported by
trusses; and the apartments (q q) in which the papers are to be preserved.

Fig. 224 is a perspective view of the building.

Fig. 226 shows the interior finishing of the two large doors entering to b and g.

Fig. 225 is the profile of Fig. 226.

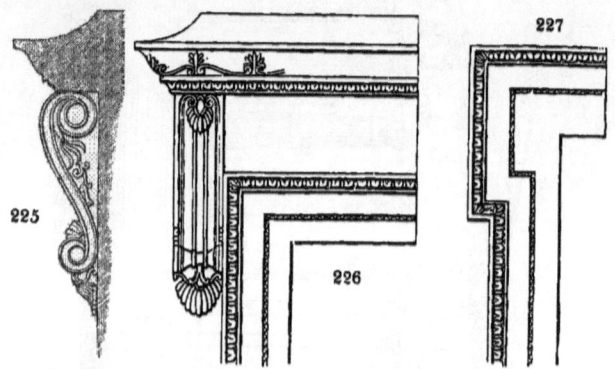

Fig. 227 shows the tracing round the windows which open into
the great business-room, and light the winding staircases.

In the principal plan (Fig. 222), a is the portico and principal entrance from Wall street; b, the hall or vestibule; c, the great business-
room; d, the collector's private office; e e e, three private offices; f f,
recesses, over each of which there is a gallery supported by trusses,
forming a communication between the rooms of the upper floor; g,
a vestibule uniform with b, which leads to the arch corridor h: i i, offices: and k k, principal staircase leading to the floor
over these offices. In the large piers of the cupola there are four winding staircases, l l, two of which lead to the roof, and the other two to
the vaulted garrets under the roof, in which papers are intended to
be preserved. The portico m forms the entrance from Pine street;
n is a sunken area, and the front to Nassau street; o is the United
States Bank.

The original design for the Custom-House was selected from a
number of competition plans; and, in order that your readers may
judge of its merits, I send you the original plan (Fig. 228), and the
perspective view (Fig. 229). In the latter figure, the details, and a
part of the basement, are omitted, as they are the same as those of
Fig. 224, and are not necessary to be repeated. In looking over the
plan (Fig. 228), your readers may, perhaps, be able to perceive what
it has puzzled me to find out; namely, the supports and abutments

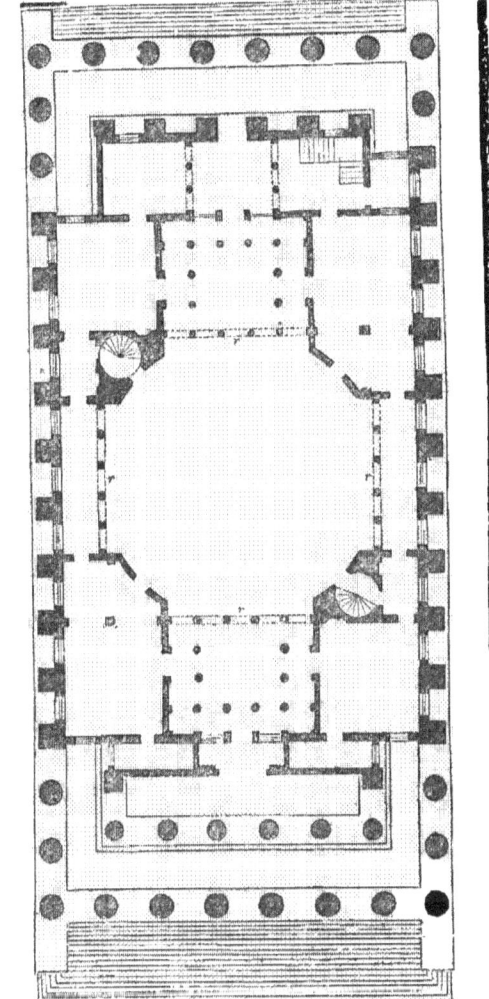

Fig. 228.

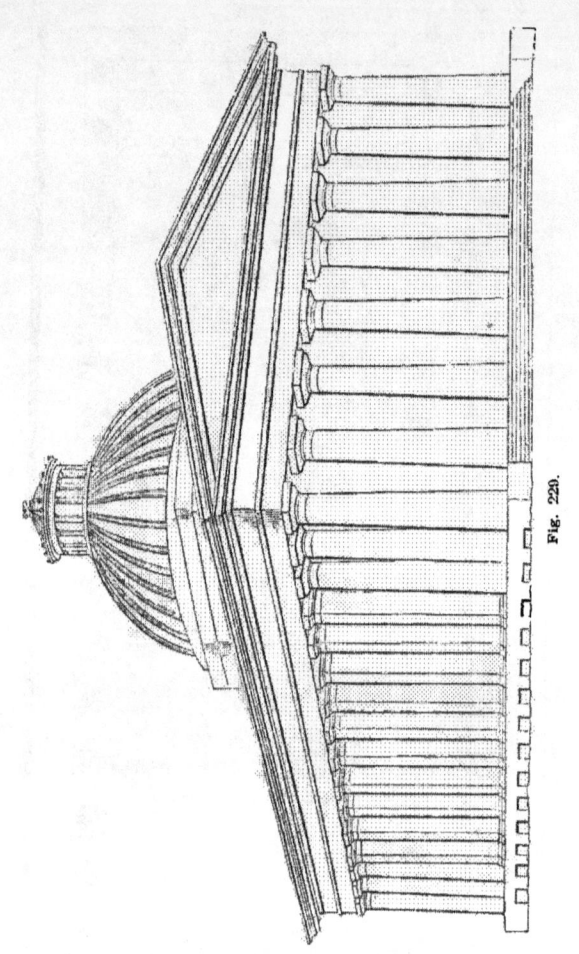

Fig. 220.

of the double-vaulted cupola, which rises so majestically on the ridge of the roof of the temple. (Fig. 229). In doing so, it will strike them that the columns, which are so profusely used, cannot, from their situation in straight lines (r r), carry any part of the pressure; and, indeed, they were not so intended; they were to carry nothing but their own entablature, the ceiling being arched like that of a church, with transepts; and the hemispherical and spheroidal vaults over the intersection, to rest on 16-inch brick walls (a brick here being 8 ins. by 4 ins., and by 2½ ins.). Your readers will, perhaps, imagine that the designer of this cupola intended the arched ceiling to be formed of timber, and lathed; but this was not the case. There was not an inch of timber to be in the edifice, for the whole was to be of stone, iron, and bricks: even the roof was to have been of marble, and so were to have been the cupola and lantern! A description of this approved design may be seen in the "New York Mirror," to which I refer your readers.

By the arrangement of the desks on the plan (Fig. 228), the greater number of the columns are concealed to about 4 ft. from their bases; and, this being the case, one can hardly conjecture their use at all; for an arched ceiling, with a cupola on the intersection, would not be incapable of a very pleasing effect, unless, indeed, the Parthenic exterior might have spoiled it by its associations in the mind before entering. But what would be said, if double rows of columns were placed between the sides of the nave, choir, and transepts of St. Paul's, London, with their entablatures running longitudinally and transversely from each column, and forming a species of network, with the space between the top of the cornice and the apex of the arch, having the appearance of a naked floor, when looking up through it? Notwithstanding the length of the foregoing remarks, I have not pointed out one-half of the absurdities of this original design: for, like Hogarth's perspective frontispiece, new ones are discovered every time I look at it.

After the drawings had been selected from among the other competition plans, and adopted, they were sent from Washington to three gentlemen in New York, who were appointed commissioners for the erection of the building (one of whom was the collector of the Custom-House). On these gentlemen examining the drawings minutely, as to the accommodation afforded, they found that it was quite inadequate to the purpose intended; and even this was not discovered until the foundations of the external walls were laid. It therefore became necessary to have the drawings revised, and I was applied to for this purpose. What I have been able to make of the building will be seen by comparing my plan (Fig. 222) with the original plan (Fig. 228). My instructions were to preserve, as much as possible, the appearance of the original plan and elevations; to provide more ac-

commodation, and to keep the long, or business, room of the cruci-
form shape, as before, with the cupola at the intersection. These instructions have been complied with, as far as practicable, as may be
seen by comparing the plans, etc. No part of the building is my design ; at least, no part of the exterior. To it I have done nothing, except what was necessary to increase the accommodation within, and
to get rid of the Italian cupola, which I was only permitted to do after a long discussion. In the interior I have provided supports, for
the hemispherical vault over the middle of the large room to rest
upon, as may be seen by Fig. 223. I have arranged the columns so
as to be of some use ; and I have also reduced the inordinate projection of those external lateral excrescences, which, to call buttresses,
would be to profane the term ; and what other name to give them I
know not ; the section will show the form of ceiling behind the columns. Behind the columns, at the sides or transepts, are galleries,
which communicate with the rooms on the upper floor that are next
the portico in Wall street, as the winding stairs in the large piers are
not intended for the public. These galleries are supported by iron
trusses, as shown in the section. (Fig. 223). Another section, showing the mode of forming the level ceilings over the large rooms next
Pine street, will be sent at some future time, and will form a communication by itself, as the method is entirely unknown here ; and, if
it be known in London, it is not practised ; at least, so far as it has
come under my observation, or else the "Bishopgate bressummer"
would not have made the noise it did in the "Mechanic's Magazine,"
in 1830. .

The mode which I proposed of warming and ventilating the
building has been set aside ; there is now to be a stove in the cellars
for every room that is to be warmed, and ventilation is left to chance.

New York, March 14, 1835.

No. 4 Avenue d'Jena,

Paris.

M. Schoellkopf, Architect.

"Dekorative Kunst."

VOL IX.—1—5.

No. 4 AVENUE D' JENA, PARIS.

No. 4 AVENUE D' JENA, PARIS.
(Rear View.)

No. 4 AVENUE D' JENA.
(Stable Entrance.)

No. 4 AVENUE D' JENA.
(Stable Entrance.)

No. 4 AVENUE D' JENA.
(Detail of Façade.)

No. 4 AVENUE D' JENA, PARIS.
(Salon.)

No. 4 AVENUE D' JENA.
(Staircase.)

No. 4 AVENUE D' JENA.
(Dining Room.)

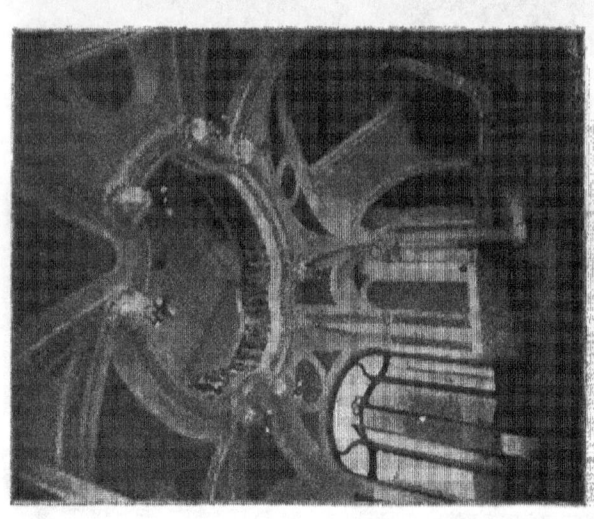

No. 4 AVENUE D' JENA, PARIS.
(Views of Staircase.)

No. 4 AVENUE D' JENA.
(Dome over Staircase.)

No. 4 AVENUE D' JENA.
(Mantlepiece.)

No. 4 AVENUE D' JENA.
(Mantlepiece.)

No. 4 AVENUE D' JENA.
(Mantlepiece.)

No. 4 AVENUE D' JENA.
(Mantlepiece.)

Carnegie Residence

Fifth Avenue, New York City.

Note.—These illustrations show the elevations of the competitive drawings, which have been modified in many particulars since the work was committed to the architects.—Ed. A. R.

Babb, Cook & Willard, Architects.

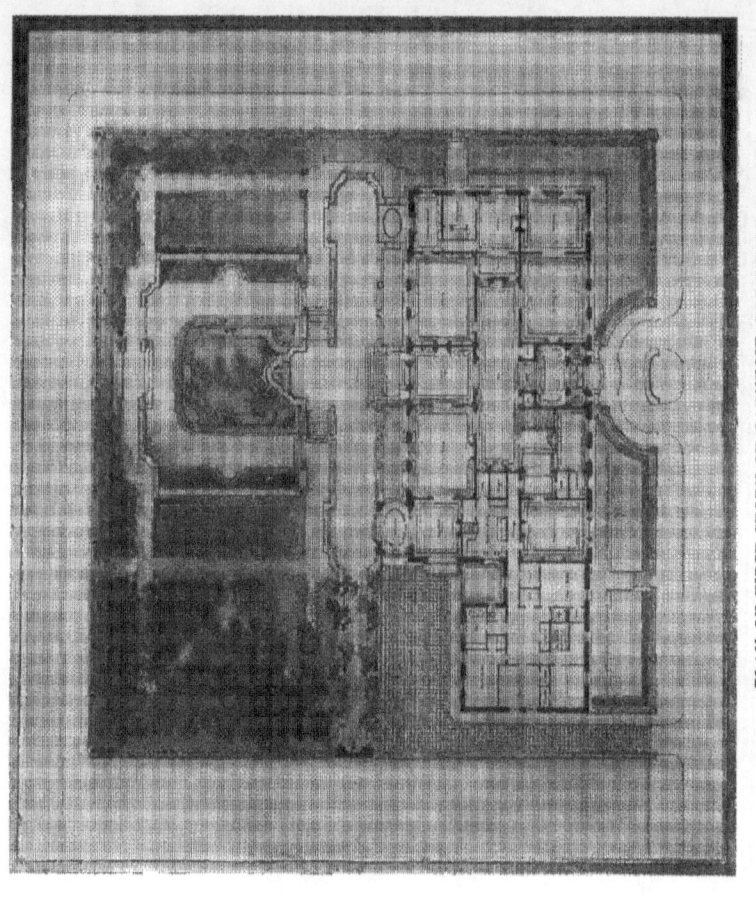

PLAN OF FIRST STORY OF CARNEGIE RESIDENCE.

Fifth Avenue, 90th and 91st Streets, N. Y. City.　　Babb, Cook & Willard, Architects.

NORTH ELEVATION, CARNEGIE RESIDENCE.

Fifth Avenue, 90th and 91st Streets, N. Y. City.

Babb, Cook & Willard, Architects.

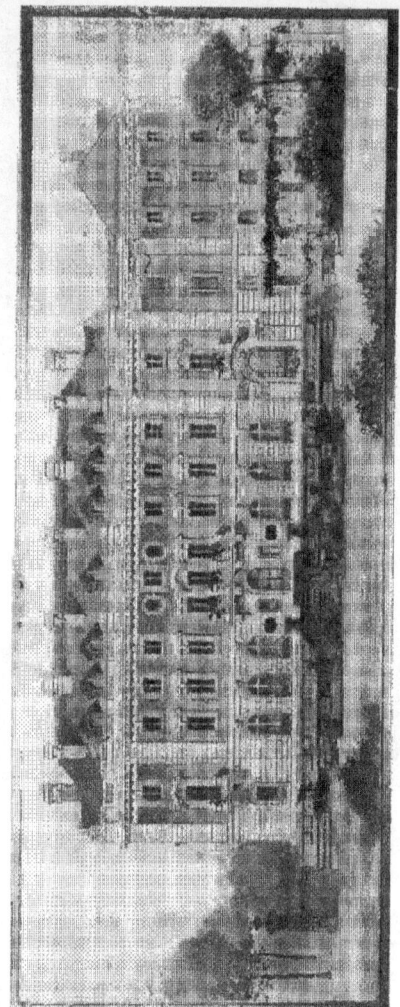

SOUTH ELEVATION, CARNEGIE RESIDENCE.

Fifth Avenue, 90th and 91st Streets, N. Y. City.

Babb, Cook & Willard, Architects.

WEST ELEVATION, CARNEGIE RESIDENCE.   Babb, Cook & Willard, Architects.

Fifth Avenue, 90th and 91st Streets, N. Y. City.

I.

IN their designs for the Columbia University Library and University Hall, Messrs. McKim, Mead & White are probably the first among modern architects to make the experiment of using the Greek horizontal curves on an extended scale. With one interesting exception in Boston, in the work of Mr. C. H. Blackall, to be mentioned later, it appears likely that the Columbia University buildings are absolutely the first modern structures to which the Greek horizontal curves are applied.

Mr. George Oakley Totten, Jr., of Washington, was the first to advise me of the curves of the Columbia University buildings. He considered it highly improbable that they could be due to any cause but intention, and this was my own view after inspection. But the imputation of discovering curves in the art of the Middle Ages, which were not intended, has been occasionally laid to the charge of the writer, and it seemed wise to forestall such a disaster, inside the limits of modern work and of New York City, by a letter of inquiry to the firm. The quotation below gives the substance of the answer received, which was most politely illustrated by complete prints of all the original plans on which the curves were laid down:

* * * "We beg to say that the curves to the steps and South Court of Columbia University were intentional, and were intended to counteract the apparent deflection in horizontal surfaces and lines of great extent.

"The curves are arcs of circles, that of the lower flight of steps having a rise of eight inches in the centre.

"It was not our purpose to make the curves perceptible without a close examination; but, on the other hand, should there appear to be a slight upward tendency, we should consider it beneficial, as conducing, with other causes, to draw the eye towards the Library, as the centre of interest. In general, we may say that it was the intention that the curvature be felt rather than apprehended, as in the Parthenon and other classic buildings.

"We send herewith, prints of the South Court in front of the Library, and of the University Building behind it, with the lengths and rises marked thereon. In the University Building, the curve will reappear in the lines of the entablature of the finished building.

"Yours truly,

"McKim, Mead & White."

In the general view of the Columbia University Library from 116th street (Fig. 1), we see next the street sidewalk a portion of the

FIG. 1.—THE LIBRARY—COLUMBIA UNIVERSITY.

McKim, Mead & White, Architects

FIG. 2.— PLAN OF COLUMBIA UNIVERSITY.

McKim, Mead & White, Architects.

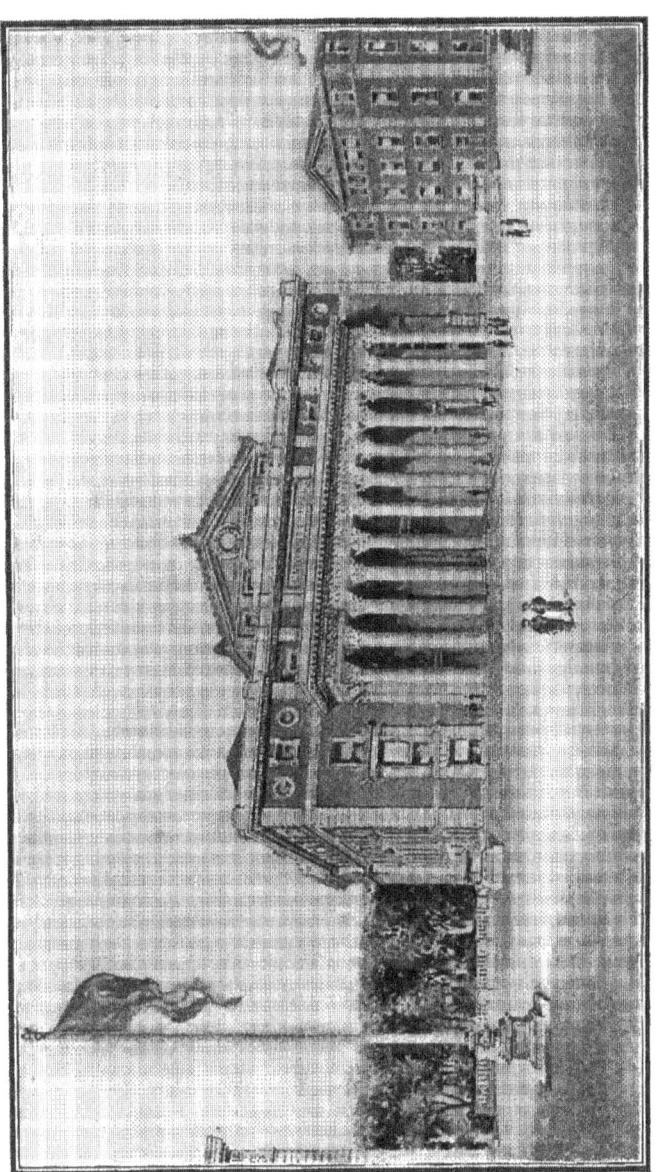

FIG. 3.—UNIVERSITY HALL—COLUMBIA UNIVERSITY.   McKim, Mead & White, Architects.

long line of steps forming the approach to the South Court. (Compare the ground-plan, Fig. 2.) These steps are all built with a curve in elevation; of 8 inches in a whole length of 327 feet. The entire platform of the South Court curves in a corresponding line from East to West, i. e., in a direction corresponding to that of the steps. From North to South, i. e., in the line from the street to the library, the South Court is built with a very pronounced but not especially noticeable upward slope toward the steps leading up to the Library. Beyond this Court the first of the two flights seen in Fig. 1 has a rising curve in elevation of 3½ inches in a whole length of 134 feet, and the second and narrower flight, rising to the colonnade of the Library and including its platform, has a curve of corresponding delicacy. No curve has been applied to the entablature, but on account of the greater length of the colonnade of University Hall (not yet built) its entablature will also have the curve. So far, only the platform and substructure of this building have been completed. Here, the steps directly in front of the portico and its platform have rising curves in elevation of 2½ inches in a whole length of 107 feet; to be repeated above as observed.

An interview with a representative of Messrs. McKim, Mead & White is authority for the advice that this upper curve is considered a necessary consequence of the curving platform on which the columns are to stand, as the central columns would otherwise be shorter than the outer columns in a too conspicuous degree. It is to be very carefully noted that the illustration of University Hall (Fig. 3) represents a building which has not yet been erected above the level of the platform, and that the curve of this platform and of the steps which rise to it is confined to the length and extent of the colonnade. At the angles of the portico the step line breaks backward and is thence carried on with straight horizontal lines to the angles of the building. The gentleman interviewed is also authority for the statement that the Greek refinement of horizontal curving lines gave the suggestion for the introduction of this refinement in these buildings. The amusing experience has been made that several gentlemen have directed the attention of the firm to the said curves as a defect of construction, or as an accidental occurrence of which the firm was ignorant, and they are explained by one of the guardians of the University grounds as an expedient for carrying off the rain.

II.

During the early part of our century, when copies of Greek temples and Greek porticoes were very widely built, and when they were, aside from traditional Renaissance forms, the exclusive and only admitted style of ornamental architecture, the discovery of the Greek

temple curves had not been made and the experiment of using them
in the modern copies was consequently not dreamed of. This experiment seems, therefore, to call for serious comment and widespread
recognition. The only parallel known to the writer is found in the
work of Mr. C. H. Blackall, of Boston, and the following letter from
Mr. Blackall will show what this parallel is:

"Dear Mr. Goodyear: The building to which I referred in conversation with you was Tremont Temple, which was built by me in conjunction with Mr. Geo. F. Newton, with whom I had a partnership
under the firm name of Blackall & Newton, during the greater portion of the time of the construction of the building. I enclose herewith a photo-print which, while not a particularly good photograph,
will illustrate in a measure the necessity which I felt existed. You
will notice that the façade is divided into three distinct portions; the
lower part, which corresponds to the stores and entrances to the
building proper, the central portion marked by a plain diapered wall
surface corresponding to the large auditorium, and the upper portion which corresponds to the superimposed office building. * * *
The plain wall surface is crowned by a level string course, and the
whole building is capped by a low pediment. Our feeling was that
the horizontal line of the belt course beneath the crowning colonnade, also the lines of the pediment, would look out of level and depressed in the middle unless these lines were slightly crowned, and
we, accordingly, attempted to arrange for having all of these crowned
on a slight curve with a rise of, if I remember rightly, about 4 inches
in the center, the total width being 91 feet. This would be sufficient
to correct the apparent concavity of the line and would have given
the appearance of being absolutely level. Unfortunately, we found
this involved much change and expense, necessitating that each piece
of the terra-cotta, very nearly, should be made on a different bevel,
and the builder interposed many practical objections, not the least of
which was the delay in completing the building. We were therefore
obliged to abandon the plan, very much to our regret. An inspection
of the photograph which I send you will show that the lines have the
appearance of sagging, and every time I look at the building I regret
that we were not able to at least try the experiment. I certainly shall
attempt it, if an opportunity comes within my grasp.

"I wish to state further that in the construction of a warehouse in
this city some years ago I was enabled to crown slightly a long stone
belt which was immediately over a row of columns in the first story.
The crowning started accidentally by the settlement of an end
column but I continued it purposely, and though the crowning is
very slight, I think only about 1½ or 2 inches in a front of over 70
feet, it is sufficient to entirely counteract the sagged appearance which
is so common with a long horizontal line. This is a warehouse on
Purchase street.

"Yours very truly,

"C. H. Blackall."

The illustration of the new Tremont Temple kindly sent with this
letter fully corroborates its remark that the gable gives a sagged ef-

fect to the line beneath it, and this downward deflection of a line beneath a gable is the most generally recognized of all optical illusions. But Mr. Blackall's letter contains another passage of still greater interest, relating to a line with which no gable interferes. This reference to a "sagged appearance which is so common with a long horizontal line" duplicates and repeats the observation in the letter from Messrs. McKim, Mead & White, that the curves of Columbia University "were designed to counteract the apparent deflection in horizontal lines and surfaces of great extent." Such personal observations on the part of practicing modern architects are a most valuable addition to those which have been made by archaeological writers on the theory of Greek curves, none of whom mention any such general appearance in straight lines.

Our one solitary surviving reference to ancient curves by an ancient writer is the celebrated prescription of Vitruvius directing the construction of curves in an *elevated* stylobate, which gives the explanation that its lines would otherwise be "alveolated" or depressed at the centre. Only one modern optical expert* has attempted an explanation of the reasons why both the stylobate and upper flank lines of a temple should be thus affected, but this tentative explanation does not include the observation that horizontal lines are so deflected under other conditions.. Penrose, who is practically the only English authority on the subject, has wholly ignored the explanation of Vitruvius, and has moved from the modern observation that a gable deflects the straight line beneath it, to the theory that the Greek curves began with the correction under the gable and that the upper flank lines were an afterthought—thus assuming the stylobate curves to be the final afterthought or necessary corollary of the upper curves, whereas Vitruvius conceives the stylobate to be the point of departure in the matter of explanation. The most important passage among the brief remarks of Penrose in the line of explanatory comment is one which conceives of motives for the curves on the temple flanks which are wholly apart from purely corrective purposes. Penrose expressly says of these side curves:

"We may attribute the use of this refinement to the feeling of a greater appearance of strength imparted by it, to the appreciation of beauty in a curved line, and to the experience of a want of harmony between the convex stylobates and architraves of the front and the straight line used in the flanks of the earliest temples."

To mention still other modern writers who have slighted the explanation of Vitruvius we come next to the name of Burnouf. Burnouf has also evolved a modern theory from a modern observation

*Thiersch. Optische Täuschungen auf dem Gebiete der Architectur; in the *Zeit schrift* für Bauwesen. Vol. XXIII., Ernst & Korn, Berlin, 1873.

which has no special reference to the stylobate, and which supposes the Greeks to have corrected effects of concavity due to the influence of the horizon (in the case of the Parthenon) and due to the spherical appearance of the sky.[*]

Finally, we have the modern writers like Jacob Burckhardt and Schnaase, who have ignored both the corrective explanation of Vitruvius and the corrective explanations of modern optical experts in favor of an æsthetic preference on the part of the Greeks for delicately curved lines as æsthetically preferable to straight ones. It will be noticed that Penrose has advanced both classes of explanations for different cases.

We thus see that a number of modern writers who differ more or less among themselves unite in slighting the explanation of Vitruvius, sometimes by implication and sometimes as in the case of Boutmy by direct assault. (See Le Parthénon et la Génie Grec.) Boutmy has most palpably given voice to the feeling common to those who have ignored Vitruvius, viz.: that his directions were borrowed from Greek authors whom he had imperfectly understood or that among various explanations he had chosen the one which best accorded with the matter-of-fact and utilitarian point of view of the Roman, as opposed to the more artistic temperament of the Greek, overlooking other æsthetic explanations of greater importance and wider application.

The revived use of horizontal curves in actual modern buildings enables us to add to these various opinions of archaeologists and of experts, debating the problematical purposes and views of the ancients, the more valuable testimony and authority of practising modern architects as to their own feelings and experience about modern construction. The remark of Mr. Blackall about "the sagged appearance of a long horizontal line," therefore, tempted me to draw him into farther correspondence. A second letter from him contained the interesting remark that:

"In case of a flight of steps I should perceptibly bow them from preference."

This was such a striking corroboration of the feeling which had found expression in the Columbia University buildings, to which no allusion had been made by my letter, that a third letter was addressed to Mr. Blackall. This letter mentioned the Columbia University buildings, and its purport is otherwise apparent in the answer given below:

[*] *Revue de l'Architecture* for 1875, p. 146.

Boston, June 16, 1898.

"Dear Mr. Goodyear:

"In reply to your two questions in regard to bowing a flight of steps: (a) I cannot recall a single flight of steps that is bowed horizontally.* The other day at Albany I was interested in noticing the large exterior stairway which leads directly up to the centre of the Capitol building. These steps are broken up into several flights, one of which, the central flight, is slightly bowed outward in plan. Looking up at the steps from below, this bowing out, which is I should think not more than 3 inches in a width of about 50 feet, does have a slight corrective effect and it certainly helps to keep the whole flight from looking hollowed in, in plan.

"(b) My reason for perceptibly bowing a flight of steps would be simply because I have never seen a flight of steps which was dead level which did not look depressed in the centre. This is exactly the reason which actuated the old Greeks, as far as I understand the subject. Also, a straight line is not as pleasant to the eye as a curve, and the bowing not only obviates the appearance of sagging in the centre, but it also by its optical perspective makes the steps themselves seem wider.

"I should add to the answer to first of your questions that I have noticed the steps to which you refer on the front of the Columbia College Library.

"The effect of sagged lines, which my reason and sometimes my observation have told me were perfectly true, is very often noticeable in interiors. Last Thursday I was at the Mountain House, in the Catskills. I happened to meet the original proprietor, who has been there since 1845. He took me into the big parlor or ball-room and took a great deal of pride in explaining how he had crowned the whole ceiling in order to prevent the appearance of sagging. I consider this quite essential in a large room, especially if prominent girders are crossing it, and in every such case, if it could be worked in, I should try to curve all the lines slightly. Of course this is entirely experimental, and I should have nothing to guide me as to the exact amount of curvature and I would probably make mistakes; but I think mistakes would be more apt to come from a level ceiling than from one which is curved too much. I do not believe that carpenters crown their floor beams from any other reason than to prevent an actual sag, but when it comes to a ceiling, I quite agree with the Catskill Mountain House proprietor that the centre ought to be decidedly higher than the sides or it will look wrong.

"You are perfectly at liberty to quote me in any way which you see fit. I should be interested in knowing what other people have made up their minds to regarding such subjects. Perhaps I haven't expressed myself quite rightly. I do not feel a desire for a curve in horizontal lines, considered as a curve, but rather as a corrective of the depressing, dead appearance of an absolutely level or, for that matter, vertical line.

"Yours very truly,

"C. H. Blackall."

*i. e., excepting the Columbia University Buildings as subsequently specified.

The final sentence of Mr. Blackall's letter is so comprehensive that nothing could be added to it from the standpoint of the expert. But it suggests some reflections as to the present and future attitude of the public of intelligent laymen on whom all artists are so dependent for encouragement and support.

We are reaching a point, but have not reached it very long since, in which the knowledge that the Greeks curved their horizontal temple lines is becoming diffused among the educated public; but chance conversation with members of this public will reveal the general impression that these lines were curved in order to make them appear straight. This explanation is simple, is matter of fact, is easily remembered and exactly accords with the previous prejudice of the intelligent layman that the lines of a Greek temple ought to be straight. But the intelligent layman ought to be warned why the artistic sense objects to a sagging line. This is not due to an æsthetic preference for mathematically straight lines, but to the appearance of weakness in a building whose lines sag. Conversely it holds that the delicate upward curves of the Greek temples tend not only to correct effects of sagging but also positively tend to contribute to an appearance of vital strength and elasticity about the building.

In face of the classic buildings of Washington we do not so much rebel against an effect of sagging lines, as we rebel against the insufferable coldness and monotony of the general effect. In face of the Neptune temple at Pæstum the eye does not weary of looking at it, but it is not likely that this is because the horizontal lines appear exactly straight. In face of a classic portico at Washington the eye is bored, but it is not likely that this is because the main horizontals appear to sag. The fact is that no consideration of the distinctions between ancient and modern classic architecture is satisfactory which stops at the curves. We ought rather to include in one view all the refinements, i. e., leaning verticals, deviations from the parallel, irregular incolumnations, and irregular dimensions of all kinds. It is true that most of these things have been disposed of by Penrose as correctives, but it is also true that Mr. Penrose has in express terms called attention to the "dryness" of modern copies of Greek temples as due to the absence of these irregularities. By some other writers all these facts have been treated as positive rather than negative refinements, but their existence has been greatly ignored in favor of the curves, and they are almost totally unknown to the intelligent layman.

It is believed that a more general familiarity with all the Greek deviations from mathematical regularity, considered in mass, will minimize the tendency of the general public to treat the Greek curves as exclusively corrective expedients. The point of view which is so generally accepted for the entasis seems to apply equally well to the horizontal curves. The entasis is recognized not only as a corrective to an appearance of concavity in a column but as a positive and perceptible addition to the delicacy, vigor and beauty of its outlines. There is no reason why the views of so many Continental writers on the æsthetics of Greek architecture, which take a similar attitude to the horizontal curves, should not have a wider circulation and more general recognition. We bear especially in thought at this moment the remarks of Jacob Burckhardt, in his world-famed "Cicerone," on the curves of Pæstum, as "expressions of the same feeling which demanded the entasis of the column and which sought everywhere to manifest the pulse beat of interior life (Pulschlag inneren Lebens), even in apparently mathematical forms."

But above all, let us come back to the utterance of the man who alone has thoroughly measured the Greek curves and whose book on the "Principles of Athenian Architecture" will infallibly remain for all future time the classic authority for the existence of the Greek irregularities. Penrose is undoubtedly indirectly responsible for the notion of the intelligent layman that the Greeks curved their lines in order to make them appear straight. Out of a number of explanations the intelligent layman has seized on the one which he could best understand and most easily repeat, and this is the explanation of the correction of the gable illusion, reduced to simple terms, and leaving out the mention of the gable. But Penrose has also said, and it may be well to quote him twice for the flanks of the temple.

"We may attribute the use of this refinement to the feeling of a greater appearance of strength imparted by it (and) to the appreciation of beauty inherent in a curved line."

The above reflections and quotations are inspired by the very remarkable revival of the Greek curves in the Columbia University buildings Artists are notoriously prone to work from feeling, rather than from definite abstract principles or theories, but the public is prone to quote the easiest practical explanation out of a number which may be offered, and to lose sight of other explanations which are vitally allied to the feeling of the artist, but not so easily expressed in words. As long as only the buildings of the ancients are in question the purpose of their curves will naturally be debated only by the archæologists. As soon as modern buildings are in question it is important that the standpoint of the artist should not be obscured by the very prejudice against which he is really taking his stand, viz.: that mathematically straight lines are the only tolerable ones in architecture. This discrimination is all the more important because horizontal curves must, in the nature of the case, be an infrequent and unusual resort in the work of the modern architect, whereas other deviations from mathematical formalism are more easily practiced and may very probably become an habitual and constant feature in modern buildings—provided the public taste which calls for and approves such deviations, be cultivated and encouraged by a proper study of the works of the ancients.

In case the innovation of Messrs. McKim, Mead and White should find would-be followers, these may be glad to be referred to the simple and inexpensive method of building horizontal curves in elevation which is described by Burnouf. The article in the Revue de l'Architecture, 1875, p. 146, is easily accessible in architectural libraries. The description of this method undoubtedly settles the long contention about the *scamili impares* which are mentioned by Vitruvius as the means of constructing the curves. To Burnouf alone, of all modern writers on the passage, belongs the credit of a clearly true and simple explanation of this passage and of the simple mechanical expedient by which curves in elevation may be constructed without great difficulty or expense, but we are not familiar with a single other writer who has adopted, or even mentioned, the solution of Burnouf. This becomes highly important, on account of the cost, as soon as the modern construction of curves is attempted. It would not, however, apply to the difficulties involved in the use of terra-cotta, which are mentioned by Mr. Blackall.

It need hardly be said that the use of the curves in the Columbia University buildings has no exact counterpart in Greek architecture. As far as we are advised at present, curves were not applied to flights of steps apart from buildings, as in the first two flights of steps approaching the Library. Nor were they used in porticoes which were adjuncts of other buildings which in themselves have no relation to the Greek temple form, as here in both cases. Nor have we any advice of a curving stylobate whose line was not repeated in the entablature. This is the case with the Library, but will not be the case in University Hall. These points of distinction are natural results of the difference between the old Greek temples and modern buildings.

Wm. H. Goodyear.

VESTIBULE IN RESIDENCE NO. 90 AVENUE HENRI-MARTIN.
Paris, France.   M. F. Vigneulle, Architect.

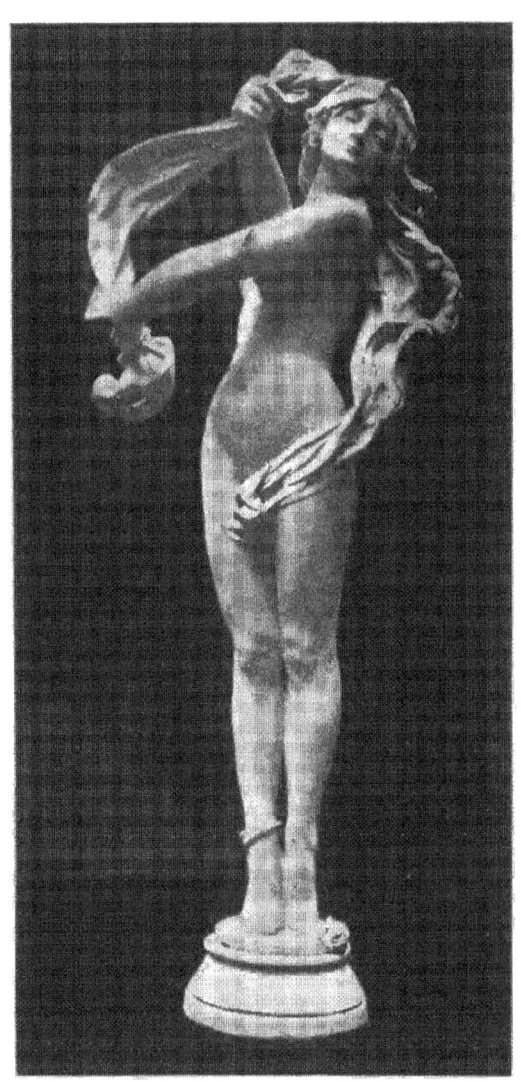

SALOME.
(Bronze.)

Louis Convers.

(Revue des Arts Decoratifs)

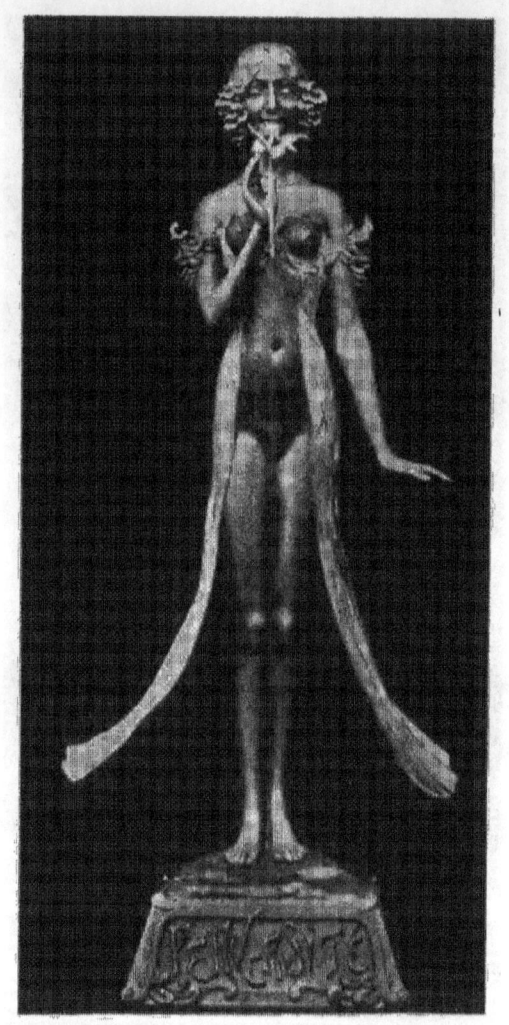

LA PERVERSITE.

L. Chalon.   (Revue des Arts Decoratifs.)

The

Architectural Record

VOL. IX. OCTOBER, 1899. No. 2.

ENGLISH "GEORGIAN" ARCHITECTURE.

The Source of the American "Colonial" Style.

THE identity of the English and American peoples in point of race and language is patent, incontrovertible, acknowledged by all; but that at one time there was an equally evident identity in the style of building adopted in the two countries is by no means so well known. Yet this was the case but little more than a hundred years ago, in the days when the States were but colonies of the British Empire, when their peoples lived English lives upon American soil, and before that energetic development commenced which has made of these colonies a powerful nation, and has been as good for building as it has been bad for architecture, particularly that of the reposeful kind.

Repose had been the principal characteristic of the English "Georgian" work; it was the characteristic of the contemporary, and in fact identical American "Colonial." This is well shown in the illustrations to the articles upon "Colonial Annapolis," and "The Colonial Buildings of Rensselaerwyck" which appeared in the Architectural Record for the first quarter of 1892, and the second quarter of 1895, respectively, and with which it may be interesting to compare a few examples taken from houses of the same date in and around London. They are not isolated examples by any means, but only a few ordinary typical specimens of just that kind of house which was being erected by the flourishing middle-class in London and its suburbs, and in almost every country town as well, a century or more ago.

Whence this style arose, simple, comfortable and homely, essentially domestic, it is difficult to say. Probably it was of native growth, meeting the needs of the times in a natural manner; for no development can be traced from anything which went before. But shortly before its appearance the country had been torn from end to end by the Great Civil War, during the continuance of which all building ceased, and architectural precedents were lost. Even afterwards recovery was slow, and although the Fire of London had necessitated much rebuilding and had given Wren his great opportunity, there

Vol. IX. No. 2.—Sig. 1.

was not much domestic work done until the settled days of Queen
Anne. Possibly the wars in the low countries of the previous reign
had drawn attention to the value of brick as a material for this class
of building; but there is no sign of either Dutch or Flemish influence
in the style which then arose in England and to which the name of
"Georgian" has been given. Two houses, excellent, typical examples,
are known to have been designed by Wren himself during his declin-
ing years, one being at Chichester and the other at Wandsworth—the
latter pulled down some five years ago to make room for rows of

"FAIRFIELD HOUSE," TOOTING.

so-called "villas." It is quite possible that these two were the
first erected, the style thus originating with the great master-architect
of the age.

Whatever its origin, however, it was rapidly and universally
adopted; and it appeared at once as a perfected style, showing no
development, but decadence only, as time advanced. Built in almost all instances of brick, with timber enrichments, such as cornices
and doorways, painted white to represent stone, the buildings commonly took the form of rectangular cubes, somewhat after the manner of the Italian palaces, having deep modillioned cornices propor-

tioned to the total height, and with either a steep roof or a parapet above, the roof frequently having a flat top. The window openings were large and absolutely unornamented; but the doorway, centrally placed in the front, was marked in some way, with order, pediment or hood. Dormers of a plain description were common in many instances hidden behind the parapet; and it is usual to find small horizontal string-courses marking the division of the front into stories.

Such are the usual characteristics of an early Georgian house, of which "Fairfield House," Tooting, is an excellent typical example,

"EAGLE HOUSE," MITCHAM.

departing only from the description given above in having angle quoins in plaster. In this instance, too, the outer door reached by a flight of steps, the principal floor being raised considerably above ground level, and the kitchens occupying a lower and a partially excavated floor—a system of planning which subsequently became general upon the restricted building sites of London and other cities—and the marking of the doorway is accomplished by means of a projecting semi-circular hood, carried by projecting brackets, and enriched with the ornament known as the "Venetian shell." As in the illustration this is partly hidden by the high boundary wall, another example may be seen at Jesus College, Oxford, where the shell-hood is an addition to a doorway in a building of much earlier date.

This type, though basic, was, however, by no means without its variations, of which the earliest, and at the same time the most usual, was the introduction of a pediment in the middle of the front, as a "Eagle House," Mitcham, built in 1704. There, too, the dormers are treated more as architectural adjuncts than is usual, having moulded segmental pediment heads; and the flat top to the roof is utilized as a lounge in summer-time, by the introduction of an open balustrade round it. The lantern is, however, a modern introduction, the house now forming the Infirmary of the Holborn District Industrial School.

THE ALMSHOUSES, WOKINGHAM.

Probably the most noticeable feature of this house is its iron gate, an exceptionally beautiful one even when compared with the many other fine specimens of the smith's art put up in England at about that time. During the entire Georgian period, while the houses them-selves were substantial rather than ornamental, no expense or pains were spared to make the entrances symbolical of the wealth and taste of the owner; and different in character as the light and lace-like iron tracery was from the sombre and sturdy looking houses, yet each en-hances the value of the other and seems so necessary to the other that a Georgian house without wrought iron work about it appears to many to lack one of its most essential features.

It is interesting to compare the large gates of "Eagle House" with the smaller one at "Baron House," now occupied by Mr. J. Boobbyer, which was put up, as testified by the date it bears in Roman numerals, in 1807, or nearly a century after the other (see p. 104). In spite of the lapse of this long period of time there is but little difference in the character of the design, unless it be in a general appearance of greater lightness, and in the absence of any naturalesque leaves or buds.

In the ordinary course of events circumstances would arise at times which rendered even less strict adherence to the general type possible than at the "Eagle House." In such a case a symmetrical plan

Clapham Corners,   "STANMORE" AND "FRANKFORT HOUSE,"   London.

became the one essential feature of the period, others being modified to suit the circumstances, an instance of this being afforded by the Wokingham almshouses, necessarily a long, low structure. The usual plan of the previous Elizabethan period, founded upon the letter E, was adopted, with a slightly projecting central portion marked by a pediment, and two end wings. Otherwise the type will be seen to be pretty closely followed, with red brick walls, tiled roofs of a steep pitch, and with a heavily modillioned cornice. Though little money was expended upon ornamentation, an effect was produced which is suggestive of substantiali'y and of comfort.

Another frequently occurring instance of the modification of the type occurs in a pair or row of houses. Such a pair are "Stanmore" and "Frankfort House," facing Clapham Common, in which the Ionic porches, as also the attic to "Frankfort House," are much later additions. In fact the latter feature, with its plain coping, is as eminently characteristic of the later Georgian work as are the balustered parapet and half-hidden dormers of "Stanmore" of the earlier. The shaped gables of the latter house are noticeable, as also is the gutter between the double span roof, though this is almost as usual in many parts of the country as is the typical flat top. An-

"THE CANONS," MITCHAM.

other change from this type is in the omission of the modillions from, and the consequent lightening of, the cornice—enough to show that erection is not to be dated back so far as to Queen Anne's reign, but at furthest to the time of the earlier Georges; but otherwise all was as usual, symmetry even being carried to the stables of the two houses---those of "Frankfort House" appearing in the photograph--- and to the wide carriage drive, semicircular grass plot, and sunk "ha-ha" in front, all significant of the days of your great, great grandfathers.

Though more nearly true to type---almost absolutely true, in fact, but for recent additions—"The Canons," Mitcham, is of still later date, belonging to the latter half of the eighteenth century; but the only signs of this are to be found in the lesser boldness of the cornice and the plainer character of the doorway. The plain and substantial staircase, too, with its broad handrail and twisted balusters bears out the general impression of homeliness without ostentation, which is invariable; but it is a pity to reflect that the present building re-

STAIRCASE IN "THE CANONS," MITCHAM.

placed others of greater archæological and probably also of greater architectural value. This had been the site of the country dwelling house of the canons of the great church of St. Saviour's, Southwark, possibly better known as St. Mary Ouverie; the fishpond and columbarium (pigeon house) belonging to which still remain, the latter containing a low doorway of the fifteenth century, but with a hipped roof and lantern of the eighteenth.

Later again, much later, and of the present century, is "Wallace Lodge," Balham, the residence of E. Smith, Esq., M. D. (Lond.)— a clever and highly qualified young doctor who has lately buried himself in this out-of-the-way suburb—and by the time of its erection the type had been almost lost sight of. There is still symmetry, for this is one of a pair of houses, and the doorway is pronounced, but the cornice has given way to widely projecting eaves, and the roofs are of low pitch and of slate. The doorway is in fact the only

GATE OF "BARON HOUSE," MITCHAM.

feature in the front, for the proportions are otherwise indifferent, and the general idea of solid comfort present in the earlier buildings is scarcely so apparent now, while even the doorway consists of nothing more than a pair of Doric columns set within the jamb.

With this species of deterioration the domestic architecture of the Georgian period in England gradually faded away to nothingness, to the absolutely commonplace; but America had become a distinct country by that time and causes were consequently at work to produce divergence of custom and of architecture in the two countries, so that there is no necessity to pursue the subject further.

But what, it will be asked, of the contemporary ecclesiastical

FRONT DOOR OF "WALLACE LODGE."

ST. MARTIN'S-IN-THE-FIELDS, LONDON.

CLAPHAM CHURCH.

work? Did that in any way follow the same lines as the domestic? And the answer must be both "yes" and "no." The type was necessarily different, to begin with; and in England, at least, there was not much done, we being well provided with churches, heirlooms from the Gothic builders of the Middle Ages. But in London some few were erected, the type being set by Wren and his successors in the well-known city churches—the well-known St. Martin's-in-the-Fields, by Gibbs, being given as illustration—the prominent features being the classic portico and spire. It was natural, with such

"WALLACE LODGE," BALHAM.

grand examples existing, that the suburban churches should be built upon somewhat similar lines, and in Clapham Church, as in several others, this will be seen to have been done; but it is a deteriorated classic, its redemption being found only in its eminent solidity and air of respectability, while what beauty it possesses is due rather to tones which age has contributed, and to the leafy surroundings, than to any qualities which belong to the design itself.

G. A. T. Middleton.

EXAMPLES

OF

Old Colonial

OLD CITY HALL,

Albany, N. Y.

RESIDENCE,

Portsmouth. N. H.

DOORWAY,
Portsmouth, N. H.

IN SALEM, MASS.

IN THE LADD RESIDENCE,
Portsmouth, N. H.

DOMESTIC STAINED GLASS IN FRANCE.

WE think it necessary, before proceeding with the following paper, to state clearly that we have not the least intention of composing a manual of processes and formulas. We shall not disclose any trade secrets, and only here and there will our descriptions be interspersed with a few technical terms, if necessary. Moreover, special works exist for the use of persons who are desirous to inform themselves as to the manipulation of vitrifiable colors, burning in, cutting and putting the pieces together, as well as upon the progress yet to be made and the imitations to be on one's guard against. Consequently, our present task—we desire to emphasize this at the outset—is merely that of enlightening the readers of this magazine in regard to the present state of the stained-glass window manufacture in general and of domestic stained-glass windows in particular. This paper will, therefore, contain few technical details or references to material causes, but will merely describe effects and results. We shall speak of taste, good workmanship and knowledge ; we shall deal with the decorative part of the subject and the profound science attached thereto—a science wholly devoted to the worship of art and respect for that part of architecture called decoration.

It is scarcely twenty years since the taste for stained-glass windows for private houses took root in France. The cause of this sudden leap into favor must be sought in that great riddle known as Caprice, which, in spite of its seeming futility, has a material influence of wider range than is supposed.

Towards the close of the last century a master glass-maker named Avelin addressed to a learned society a memoir on the conditions of the glassmaking industry, and this memoir ended with this discouraging phrase: "This art has so fallen into disuse that the opinion is generally entertained that the secret of painting on glass is lost."

Such a disheartening view is calculated to fortify the idea held by many people nowadays, who affirm that the present generation of glass makers do not know how to manufacture stained glass— that it is a lost art. This is a grave error against which it is necessary to make a stand. Not only is the secret of stained glass manufacture not lost, but in face of the evidence which we have daily before our eyes we are obliged to admit that it is very well known and has been considerably amplified by the intelligent phalanx of art workers of whom our country has reason to be proud.

There is one fact which is very clear. At no previous period have workers in glass been so abundantly provided with the means of execution. To-day there is not a single difficulty remaining to be overcome. Everything is turned to account by them, and their laboratories—one might literally say their arsenals—furnish them with resources of the most varied, the most unlooked-for, the most delicate and at the same time the most decorative character. There is no longer a single color, a single shade, simple or compound, that has resisted the skilful investigations of chemists. Dumas, Chevreul. Brongniart and other savants after them, have done all that is to be achieved in this direction. The manufacture of glass has now been brought to such perfection, and is based upon such sure methods, that it juggles, so to speak, with its difficult features, which consist in the imitation of ancient windows, inequalities of level, thickness and coloration, bubbles, striae, bunchings and the devitrification which manifests itself sometimes as an acreous haze and sometimes as a disaggregation of the surface, altering the transparency. Without dwelling upon what are at present trade secrets, we may say that the actual state of this industry allows of the production of granulated, crushed, reticulated, undulated, crackled, and other kinds of window glass, obtained by moulding or otherwise. Other kinds are produced into which are sunk filigrane-work, spangles and divers other substances. Others again are opal or milky, with the peculiar feature that they are dichroic; that is to say, they have the curious faculty of changing tint according to the quantity of light they receive, or even according to the luminous jet which traverses them or the point from which they are viewed.

This rapid outline is sufficient to demonstrate that the assertion of the glassmaker, Avelin, was somewhat wide of the truth. But, although what are called the "secrets of glassmaking" are not lost, it is certain that the present excess of manufacture has caused the most important means of execution, the most arduous and therefore the most interesting processes of vitrification to be neglected for the sake of attaining that deplorable but unfortunately justifiable (under the circumstances) result, namely, a large and rapid output.

It is quite certain that there was a period during which the art of glass staining slumbered. The masters of the art delighted in embellishing stately castles and venerable churches. Previous to the last score of years, the only work for which their talent was called into requisition was the restoration of chapels or the completion of the large windows of such manor-houses as were spared by the Revolution. The glassmakers of France, and of every other country for that matter, were few in number. Their skill and talent went to sleep in the stillness of old out-of-the-way castles and ancient cathedrals, upon which they concentrated all their energies and care, as do goldsmiths upon the setting of the jewel which seals their reputation.

But the fever of the busy times in which we live drew them away from their task. Steam, electricity and iron, which have made our epoch an industrious epoch, perhaps, but unquestionably an infernal one, have caused the world to move faster, put life into the fields, noisy traffic upon the roads—in fact, activity everywhere. From the combination of capital have sprung up cities of metal, immense establishments, sumptuous palaces, railroad stations, warehouses, breweries, public edifices, factories, mills, colossal buildings where luxury of decoration, internal and external, has taken refuge.

This was, in a certain manner, the renaissance, by deduction, of furniture and stained glass. But into this, as into every renaissance, false beauties entered by the same door as the true. The sudden demand for stained glass, the desire for large colored bays, brought into the field artists who were such only in name. The master glassmakers disappeared or were swamped by the rush of producers of doubtful taste. Windows were required for the many buildings in course of erection, and windows were forthcoming; a few of superior merit, a certain number passable, but the majority detestable. In short, it may be said that, although excessive manufacture has revived the drooping art of glass staining, it has at the same time called forth bastard productions which have nothing in common but the name with that delicate work which illuminates the great monuments of the Middle Ages.

We have just said that this abundance is one of the causes of the scarcity of fine workmanship. It has killed quality. First-rate work is still done, in order, no doubt, to prove that it can be done, but makers do not by any means utilize all the resources of their art. Neither the necessary time nor the necessary money is bestowed upon it, and instead of working with the aid of these valuable factors, they rival each other in speed rather than in beauty of execution, and they paint the glass in order not to have to put it together.

Formerly, one observed, in all the shades great clearness in the coloring, united to an exquisite softness. The whole arrangement was powerful and harmonious. This was due to the irregularity of thickness, to the non-parallelism of the faces, to the unequal distribution of the color: in fact, to everything that constitutes the art of glass-staining. The old makers knew how to strew in the glass, in order to attenuate its brightness, bubbles, flats, opaque, points, etc., and they attained those marvellous results which all of us are able to admire still, for their handiwork has, among other merits, that of endurance.

At the present day imitation, which has become so clever and penetrates everywhere, has superseded all that, and we think it our duty to borrow from one of our most skillful master glassmakers, M. Felix Gaudin, the following particulars, which will show, more clearly than we could explain, what this imitation is now capable of doing.

"The principal inequalities of old stained glass have been carefully utilized for the creation of new types, which are employed in domestic decoration. Thus, the bosses or roughness of surface, the inequalities of coloration, the veins, cords and threads running through the mass, the pearliness arising from devitrification, etc., have not only been imitated, but by means of clever selection, amplified and improved to such a point as to give birth to positively new kinds, clearly characterized and yet difficult to differentiate, for one is absolutely bewildered by the ingenuity of the inventors, who have hit upon various methods, all of which are good and practical. For example, there exists four sorts of granular glass the aspect of which is almost identical, although one sort is obtained by blowing, another by rolling, a third by engraving and a fourth by powdering."

This shows what our glassmakers are capable of doing. But, without sharing the views of the numerous body of persons who draw too dark a picture of what they consider this abandoned art, we must say that, despite the prosperous condition of the new discoveries, our artists are unwilling to waste their valuable time in applying them. It is all over with the learned, powerful and finished styles of decoration in which our ancestors took delight; all modern manifestations of the glass-staining art suffer from the state of mind of the artists; they are roughly colored, the colors are let go, more regard is paid to the impression than to the design,·to the effect than to finish, to sale than to workmanship. It is certain that to-day, as in the past, stained glass finds its most congenial application in the decoration of religious edifices, and yet, at present, it is perhaps less used for this purpose than for any other. New public buildings and private houses absorb all that is produced. It is true that, here and there, a few ancient windows are being restored, and that with skill; at distant intervals some flat tints and some mosaics have also been manufactured, but all this forms only a small part of what glass stainers are capable of furnishing.

It is, however, in the search for subjects that the greatest mistake is made. We have seen that our makers, far from being ignorant of their business, have gone to its very root, but in the quest after compositions the efforts made have been less successful, not to say entirely negative. Consequently, the fault is not, properly speaking, to be laid at the door of the glassmaker, but to that of the cartoonist, to the painter, who does not exert himself, but relies upon the ability of the workman who executes his design to supply any deficiency.

What are the subjects treated in the early examples of stained windows? We find veritable pictures, extensive compositions, opulent scenes teeming with figures full of life and movement. In the humblest churches as well as in the proudest castles we have heroic, rural, martial, pastoral and other scenes. To gratify the vanity of the abbots and of the lords of the manors, the "skies" of their windows were overlaid with the appanages of their nobility; that is to say, with armorial bearings, devices, symbols and emblems.

It should be remarked here, as an interesting detail, although not closely connected with our subject, that the decoration of churches with stained windows was first thought of in the Middle Ages for the purposes of removing the thoughts of simple and pious people from the contemplation of existence. In directing their minds to the attentive contemplation of these pictorial representations of Holy Writ, the trivialness of their daily lives faded before these glimpses of paradise.

But let us return to our theme. Nowadays these lofty compositions are no longer produced. We follow the fashion, that absurd and rickety fashion, which in its eagerness for seeming simplicity, crushes the slightest efforts and stunts all attempts to do something grand and imposing. There was first a great liking for seals and imitations of the small Swiss medallions, but this inclination was of short duration, as is always the case when the sentiment does not rest upon real affection. Then arose a fondness for affected bucolics full of insipidity—Watteau shepherds and pink little sheep abounded, without the appearance of one single meritorious work to justify this infatuation. The wind next blew from the East, and there was a sudden run upon things Japanese. But what a ridiculous, spurious, servile copying of imported works! What was chiefly selected for imitation was the hideous, which people have agreed to call the strange. We know that ugliness, when it is positively horrible, almost amounts to beauty. Inspired by this subtlety, ugliness was the one thing aimed at. However, there was another change of fashion, and the "Japaneseries" were sent to join the "Watteaus" in some dark corner.

The artist whose task it is to make the drawings for our domestic stained glass windows—and it is these that we are treating of at present—have never realized the necessity of freeing themselves from imitation of the past, taking care, of course, to avoid seeking inspiration from sources which leave nothing clear, decisive or durable. Stained glass plays such a large part at present in house building that it is requisite to know how to meet the requirements of the case without being concerned about styles and without following any ready-made formulas. The chief thing is to clearly define the complex object to be aimed at. When this is done, its realization becomes easy, for the means of execution are as plentiful as the executants.

Before submitting a few specimens of stained windows, which will give a fair idea of contemporary æsthetics, we think it will be of great interest to describe in a simple and precise manner the conception held by the leading French stained window makers in regard to the ornamentation of private houses. This seems to us all the more desirable, as it establishes a parallel, foreign makers having, if not other styles, at all events other tastes, as much open to discussion as ours.

In the first place, one sees few bold colors, for the very simple reason that these colors, which are necessary in a work of broad scope and large dimensions, would become tiresome if one had them constantly before the eye. It is, therefore, wise to employ, as is the custom, a medium coloration of soft, attenuated tints. This manner of proceeding has also the unquestionable advantage which springs from a necessity, that it allows for the entrance of an abundance of light into our homes.

Among the numerous brands of glass in existence it is best to choose those that are limpid and regular, from which all shades of blue seem to be excluded, and which, on the other hand, abound in warm, pleasant shades of yellow and red. This is owing to the fact that blue and its compounds have in them something melancholy which renders them unsuitable for the decoration of any room except an oratory.

In order to avoid the monotony that attaches to even the most beautiful objects, and especially to colored windows which more or less resemble each other, it is the practice to introduce opal and dichroic glasses, which, by the effect of various lights, change their tints in a very agreeable manner. These glasses, which are largely used in France, impart a delicious animation to the compositions of which they form a portion and seem to make them quiver with life.

Furthermore, for certain stained windows of the first order, milky and opaline glasses have been adopted, which suit the purpose very well, especially in cases where it is only a question of ornaments. With these milky or opaline glasses, the use of which is extending, it will be possible to constitute decorative arrangements of the most interesting character, very transparent inside and appearing from the outside like mosaics and frescoes, producing a soft and charming effect. This may be regarded as some sort of palliative to those immense glazed bays, which, instead of brightening the halls where they are placed, give them a dull, disagreeable aspect, so much so that one anxiously asks himself whether the medley of colors and lead which he sees before him is a masterpiece or a horror.

In Paris the flats are so arranged that in many cases long corridors and subsidiary rooms, vestibules or closets, have to be lighted by means of dormer-windows. The latter are easily transformed into really decorative pictures in which the eye is charmed with foliage, arabesques, twine, accentuated by the silvering, or in some instances the gilding of the lead, etc., which appear as beautiful in the artificial light of lamps and candles as during daylight.

Attention is also paid at the present time to a special kind of work of which we will say a few words, as it has acquired a right to a place

Designed by Grasset.   Figure 1.   Executed by Gaudin.
(In Chateau. Chalons-sur-Saône.)

in the art of glass staining. We refer to what can be done by embedding pieces of stained glass in plaster or cement suitably pierced. This is the only way the Arabs have of decorating their mosques, and they have in this curious and not unartistic manner acquired the faculty of transforming common lanterns into sparkling lustres.

By combining these same glasses with forged iron, which, we may say, is an efficient substitute for lead, our modern house decorators produce large transparent enamels with inlaid metal divisions, forming a very artistic and inexpensive decoration for gratings, frames, imposts, etc. From the outside as well as from within, the appearance is pleasing, and this method of decoration has the great advantage that it is not necessary to double with plain glass.

Speaking generally, it can be said that, although glass is called into requisition nowadays for many purposes in connection with housebuilding, it is not yet put to all the uses to which it might be applied. In France we are not innovators. We strive with great energy to amplify what foreigners, especially Englishmen and Americans, bring to us, but we rarely act upon our own initiative. It is on this account that we Frenchmen are not yet accustomed to the use of bricks of blown glass, which, being elegant and strong, offer great advantages and could be utilized in manifold ways, nor to the use of glass for transforming pavements, steps and raisers into illuminating surfaces, which would give the cellars of our buildings a value they certainly do not possess at present.

The series of artistic stained windows which we shall illustrate in the course of this article have been chosen with great care. All the styles now in favor in France are represented, from the return to the classic cartoon up to the most disheveled, the latter specimen being of a design that the new schools admire and the old ones decry, without any decisive argument, either for or against the new art, resulting from the dispute. The future, in this as in everything, will tell what value there is in these peculiar designs, made up of symbols and so simple in appearance.

Fig. 1 represents a magnificent dining-room window. It was designed by Grasset, who is the painter most in favor with our chief makers. He has so thoroughly assimilated the art of glass staining that even those of his colored drawings which have not stained window making as their objective seem to be stained windows themselves, shedding around a hieratic, majestic brightness wholly their own. The window here shown represents Spring and Autumn. It was made by the master glass-stainer Gaudin, whose name will recur repeatedly in the course of this article, and is in the château of Mr. L. C.——, at Châlons-sur-Saône. When one looks at this window a delicate poetry seems to emanate from it. The perfection of the image and the finish of the detail enhance the charm of the subject, and certainly anyone seated in the room lighted by such a window might well fancy himself transported towards those bright heavenly regions of which poets have sung, where the fruits are delicious, the women lovely and the flowers full of perfume.

This double window, so eloquent and so graceful, is the brightest jewel in the crown of modern French art.

We now come to Fig. 2, executed by the same maker. It is a most inconceivable arrangement. The cartoon is by the eminent French painter, Luc Olivier Merson. It represents a hunt, a fantastic scene in which cavaliers, hunters and lances cross each other in fabulous gallops, distracted flights and brusque leaps. In the distance, within range of the arrows launched by the longbows, is seen a forest whose leafy trees intermingle their branches; and still further away, as if dominating the combat, impassable upon its rocky foundations,

Designed by Luc Olivier Merson.   Figure 2.   Executed by Gaudin.

(In the Gallery of M. Pector, Nicaraguan Consul, Paris.)

stands an old castle with queer shaped turrets, in defense of which, perhaps, the fight is being waged, for the hunt we see may well be a man-hunt. In any case, man-hunt or hunt after beasts, the work is perfect in its realism, its animation, and its bits of stirring strife.

In Fig. 3 we have a very graceful allegory of Photography, that

Figure 3.   Figure 4.

comparatively new factor in the world's industry. This personification of Niepce's art, with all the appliances thereof tastefully arranged around her, is truly charming. The makers of this window are MM. Hubert & Martineau, and its fortunate possessor is Mr. Pector, Nicaraguan Consul at Paris. It ornaments his gallery in the Rue Lincoln.

In the same line of thought, we have next a personification of the

Press, that wonderful propagator of ideas (Fig. 4). The star shining on the brow of the figure indicates its usefulness and its glory. This window embellishes the hall of a leading Paris journal and was produced by the expert hands of MM. Hubert & Martineau.

We now come to a window of an entirely decorative character, but which is none the less a genuinely artistic conception of the purest and clearest kind, in spite of its apparent obscurity (Fig. 5). It is a double window and is placed over a door in the house of M. Paul

Designed by Grasset.   Figure 5.   Executed by Gaudin.
(In the residence of M. Paul Robert.)

Robert. Grasset, who designed it, pictures in a corner of the "sky" a radiant sun which vivifies a majestic specimen of the plant which bears his name and which emerges upright and lifelike with its bright green leaves and yellow petals. This work is by Gaudin, as also the following one (Fig. 6), which is a portion of ceiling eminently artistic in its simplicity of detail.

In Fig. 7 is shown a very fine production by the cartoonist, Grasset. It represents Music, and is intended for the decoration of a concert hall. This conception is so beautifully soft, so mystic, so ethereal and so celestial that it is difficult to describe it well. Only the eye can appreciate it, so much imagination is there in the charm which

Figure C.

Figure 7.

Designed by Grasset.   Executed by Gaudin.

it breathes. In gazing upon this work one seems to hear a slow, sweet violoncello melody, and there steals over one the ineffable feeling of content experienced in the silence of a calm evening. Everything contributes to this effect, from the enigmatical moon behind the trees to those unknown flowers which one imagines to be beauti-

Designed by Luc Olivier Merson.   Figure 8.   Executed by M. E. Oudinot.
(Made for M. Chandon, of Moet & Chandon, Epernay.)

ful and odorous with a dream-inspiring perfume. It is M. Gaudin who, in this rapturous work, has interpreted M. Grasset's fine conception.

We next come to something exceedingly delicate and graceful, intended to serve for the ornamentation of a nursery. The subject is extracted from a collection of popular French songs (Fig. 8).

Sur le pont d'Avignon
Tout le monde danse, danse;
Sur le pont d'Avignon
Tout le monde danse en rond.

Figure 9.
(Detail in lower part of Fig. S.)

We see pretty children dancing a sort of minuet, full of salutes and reverences, reminding one of the olden times. We also see the bridge, that historical bridge, over which the Popes used to pass, with its massive gateway and frail lantern. At the bottom of the window appears the music of the roundelay, while an angel of deliciously frank and merry expression beats the measure on a tambourine. We have thought well to reproduce separately (Fig. 9) the corner of the window containing this angel. The author of the cartoon for this

Figure 10.
Designed by M. P. Verneuil.

work is M. Luc Olivier Merson, and the window itself is by M. E. Oudinot. It has been made for M. Chandon, of the firm of Moët & Chandon, champagne growers at Epernay.

In Fig. 10 we give an illustration of a curious window for a sitting room. There is a shy tenderness about this design, which is by M. P. Verneuil. This female visage, bust and arm, entwined with flowers and surmounted by a sky in which little birds are flying, have something mystic in them, made up of quietude and old memories. The work is entitled "The Woman and the Poppies."

In the course of this study we have shown the different conceptions formed by our stained window makers in regard to their art. We now give a series which will serve as an example. In the four or five windows of which we are about to speak, painting on glass has in several places been substituted for mosaic work. The effect produced is certainly very fine, and the painter is able to indulge in a luxury of

Figure 11.

detail which, in all likelihood, would be impossible to the glass worker, however expert his fingers might be. But, although the effect is fine, such work is not so durable, a point worthy of consideration.

Fig. 11. Springtime, is an allegory full of grace and lightness. This window is for a conservatory. The scantily clothed figure personifying Spring, with iris blossoms at her feet and a bunch of flowers on her knees, has her eyes fixed on the sky, enraptured with the bright, smiling display of nature around her.

The rapid increase, in France generally and at Paris in particular, of those establishments called brasseries (breweries), although they supply many other beverages besides beer, which, moreover, is not brewed there, has been a godsend to the stained window trade. Fashion demanded that all these brasseries should be installed in the same style. There has consequently been a great run on stained windows during the last five years or so. Naturally, for one good window a score of worthless ones were put up. The fantastical names given to these brasseries suggested vitrified decorations in the worst possible taste and at the same time of the most comic character. Gambrinus, Heralds-at-Arms, allegories of Coffee, Beer, Absinthe and a host of other beverages more or less adulterated, were the usual and by no means complicated subjects depicted on these windows. French soldiers and Russian sailors were also immensely popular for a short time, but, like all things which become the rage merely through the caprice of the hour, these ornamentations are already beginning to go out of fashion.

Far more interesting is the subject illustrated in Fig. 12. It decorates the large room of the Café de la Paix, in Paris. It is a faithful picture of the grand staircase of the Paris Opera House on the night

Figure 12.
In the Café de la Paix, Paris.

After Hyppolyte Berteaux.   Figure 13.
A Luminous Ceiling in the Hall of Festivities, Firm of Dufayel, Paris.

Figure 14.
Executed by Hubert & Martineau.

Cartoon by Besnard.   Figure 15.
("The Woman at the Spring.")
"Symbolist" School.

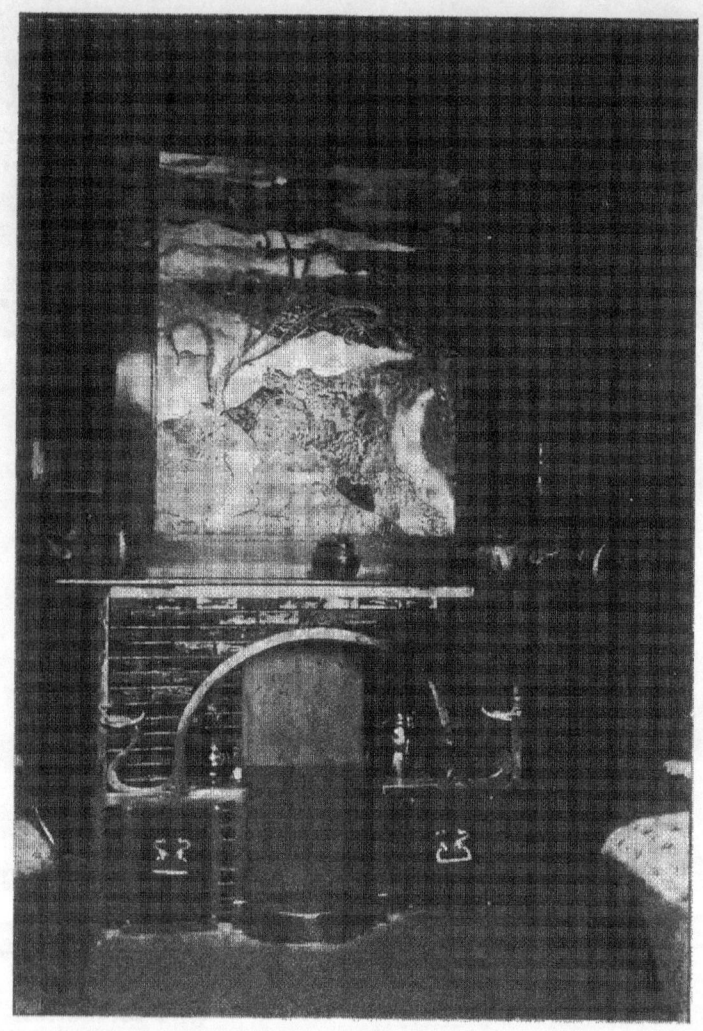

Figure 16.

Figure 17.

Figure 18.

of a masked ball. The steps are crowded with a moving mass of people on pleasure bent; clowns, columbines, musketeers, etc., are whispering soft nothings to each other, while a Watteau shepherdess is seen in the act of falling fainting into the arms of a noble wearing a Henri III. costume. In the foreground, as if leader of the mad frolic, stands a man in a mask and disguised as Mephistopheles, who invites those present to the pleasure of the dance and the joys of nocturnal revels. This window has a very curious effect.

Another interesting specimen is the luminous ceiling called The Arts (Fig. 13), after Hippolyte Berteaux, which decorates the Hall of Festivities of the firm of Dufayel, at Paris, and into which MM. Hubert & Martineau have introduced shades that are admirably clear and mellow.

The triptych (Fig. 14), executed by the same artists for the firm of Vaissier, of Roubaix, is, as can be seen, very cleverly conceived. The three Hindoo scenes which it represents are perfect in their interest of subject, richness of costumes and delicacy of execution. One can easily imagine that this painting on glass would be very difficult, if not impossible, to render in adjusted stained glass.

Our promenade among modern colored windows of French production would be incomplete if we failed to cite a few specimens of that symbolist school which has been so highly praised by some and decried by others during the few years since it was first heard of. Let us, at the outset, express our indebtedness to M. Bing, who has obligingly allowed us to reproduce them. Whilst they are not beautiful in the absolute meaning of the word, they are certainly interesting on several grounds.

In Fig. 15 we have "The Woman at the Spring," the cartoon for which is by the painter Besnard. A young woman with florescent hair is drinking at a spring which falls in a cataract. At her feet is a lake into which the water flows and on which a swan is gliding. In the distance, a plain, some brown mountains and a pale sky.

Fig. 16 shows us a mantelpiece consisting of some queer vegetation and marine animals all twisted and twined. Above, one perceives a vague, stormy sky. Although it is rather difficult to grasp the painter's meaning, the effect is nevertheless very striking, thanks to an ingenious method of lighting from behind.

Fig. 17 comprises two enfantine pictures in one. The decoration is not at all complicated—a few trees, a chair and a small boy. The design is very primitive, but the artlessness of the impression felt makes one smile and forgive.

Much the same may be said of the window illustrated in Fig. 18, which represents, perhaps, the courtyard of a boarding school, shaded by big trees. One observes an indefinite sort of house, the figures of some pupils and, in the distance, the cap of a sister of mercy, who is praying against the doorway, heedless of the laughter and the gambols of the girls under her charge.

The two last windows here pictured (Fig. 19 and 20) are by M Ibels, the most "modernist" painter that exists, even though by modernism we mean the widest possible conception of the art of drawing. These two curious landscapes are fantastical to a degree, and only of very relative interest. It would be unwise on our part to make any great effort to fathom the allegory of these productions : not only would it be a tough task, but one would run a serious risk of not correctly interpreting the artist's idea. We, therefore, leave full latitude to our readers' imaginations.

Does any conclusion force itself upon us after this survey of the present state of the art of colored window making in France? Perhaps so. It seems to us that, with the mass of examples accumulated, instead of wishing to innovate, as appears to be the aim of the lastnamed artists of whom we have spoken, eminently satisfactory applications might have been made of the said examples, and this without adhering rigidly, as is generally done, to a sobriety of tone which almost amounts to the absolute exclusion of color. It is very evident that, with the resources of ancient works, which furnish the best of teaching, old methods might have been utilized with success, provided that the rational study of the discoveries and weakness of our forefathers allowed of the formation of a clear idea of the art of glass staining and the extraction of precise definitions concerning the absolute accord of the composition as a whole, the harmony and power of the coloration, the simplicity and fidelity of the design. It is, in fact in this direction that we must turn. The creation of the cartoons should be confided only to artists who are thoroughly aware of the difficulties as well as of the resources peculiar to the art. Knowing that lead emphasizes and exaggerates the least imperfections in the design, we can form an idea of the true cause of the singular appearance of some of the specimens referred to in this article.

As the master glassmaker Gaudin tells us, the cartoon is the veritable soul of the work, and he adds that "to an excellent cartoon, to a brilliant coloration, must be united an able interpretation to obtain a perfect stained window. This is beyond doubt. But this science of execution becomes a dead letter from the moment it ceases to rest upon necessary and constitutive qualities, and the cleverest man in the world, if he tries to rehabilitate by force of virtuousity a poor design of an unfortunate coloring, will certainly waste his time, and in most cases only succeed in accentuating the faults he would have liked to remove."

This, then, is the logical conclusion which flows from our brief examination of this subject. In France the art of stained window making is brilliant. The glassmakers have acquired a high degree of skill,

Figure 19

Designed by Ibels.

Figure 20.

Designed by Ibels.

but we are lacking in artists whose care and duty it is to prepare the cartoons. Apart from two or three men of first-rate talent whose names recur again and again, there are only mediocrities and some who are able men, but do not know how to give their ability the suppleness necessary for vitrified interpretation.

Yet we must not be too dissatisfied. France, if she does not hold the first place in this branch of art and industry, is at all events well to the front, and happily our artists have not said their last word. Art is the intellectual life of a people, and ours is not by any means at its last gasp.

René de Cuers.

ON THE GRAND APPROACH.

THE NEW YORK CAPITOL BUILDING.

THE completion of the New York State Capitol building was a theme which the tourist was prone to ridicule for more than a score of years. Travelers from Europe came to Albany and returned there again only to find another story added to the edifice, whereas it was expected to find it finished. Although the construction of so large a building was in other ages the work of centuries, as the history of many a cathedral shows, still thirty years in these days is considered a long time, in the face of the modern mechanical arts and the money of a rich state with its seven million inhabitants to boot. The building is now practically completed, but although it is so considered, in reality it remains to be finished by the erection of a tower or dome. Nearly thirty million dollars have been spent upon the edifice since the first shovelful of earth was turned that number of years ago, or to be accurate, July 7, 1868, and as the building has all the parts needed for practical purposes, no new governor will feel like spending money during his administration upon the adorning parts. The erection of the tower, a necessary feature to complete the ensemble, is, therefore, never mentioned.

At least ten governors and as many legislatures have had a hand in the erection of New York's Capitol, each finding it in turn a bank of patronage upon which to draw; but with the incoming of Governor Theodore Roosevelt this was ended, for Governor Frank S. Black directed the last operations upon the building, and by his en-

NEW YORK STATE CAPITOL, ALBANY, N. Y.

ergy pressed the work with more noticeable alacrity than any of his predecessors. It was during his term that the magnificent eastern, or front approach was rapidly completed, rows of hideous sheds removed, a beautiful state park laid out. The work of the two sides and the rear façade, large affairs in construction, were started and ended by continuing the work during the winter under housing carried upwards forty feet, and by working a second gang at night. Sunday work was suddenly prohibited when certain societies raised objections. No matter how much patronage the building afforded to state officials, no investigation commission ever found that the money was misused, save in connection with the ceilings of one or two rooms, so that with the handling of close to $30,000,000 and the almost constant employment of 1,200 men for that long term the record stands without that sort of blemish.

A scandal connected with a building does not necessarily interfere with the fine appearance of a building, so that considered as one of the world's works of art there may be something that interferes far more with an edifice than the robbery of its funds. In this instance such has been the case to a greater degree than has been agreeable. For art, it might have been better had it been a scandal instead. The memory of a scandal may die at some date, and during all that time and forever after the building will stand as a high representation of a work of art; but when a series of architects handle the one large building, and each in turn cannot overcome the inclination to stamp his own individualistic idea upon it, then there is something the matter that may never be eradicated by time. This happened to some extent in the building of this capitol, and the best critics condemn it accordingly, yet find any number of features which deserve the highest praise. Taken apart, these individual conceptions would be creditable to any architect, but, viewed together, the effect is disastrous.

Were one to consider this building along with others, its cost would place it among the foremost were the valuation of contents disregarded, for a state building does not permit the same amount of elaborateness of decoration as does a secular institution, or the palace of a king, where fabulous prices may be paid for objects not necessarily included in the design. Thus it is that a contemplation of building alone places this one among the few that have cost over twenty-five million dollars. As it has been said, that the Capitol represents to a fair degree the vast sums appropriated, it stands as a fact that the new Capitol is a building of exceptional interest.

One hundred and two years ago Albany was designated the state capital, and the centennial was fittingly celebrated on January 6, 1897, according to a legislative act, and a ball was given in the state armory on an elaborate scale that evening. The first provision for the state's capitol building was made in 1803, when the Common Council of Albany adopted a resolution requesting the legislature to pass an act authorizing the erection of a state house. A committee composed of John Cuyler, Charles D. Cooper and John V. Yates, was named to prepare maps and a petition, to report the estimated cost, etc. Their report was submitted March 7, 1803, and the building was authorized by the act of April 6, 1804. The capitol commissioners named in this act were Philip Schuyler Van Rensselaer, John Taylor, Nicholas N. Quackenbush, Simeon De Witt and Daniel Hale. These names appear upon a tablet of stone which now forms part of the highest part of the wall in the grand western staircase, though the lettering is nigh illegible from age.

The act passed was characteristic of the peculiar proceedings of those days. The bill for the erection of the Capitol was entitled: An act Making Provisions for the Improvement of Hudson River Below Albany and for Other Purposes. After providing for some minor improvements in the river at Troy and Waterford (above Albany) it appointed those above-mentioned as a commission, and further enacted that $12,000 be raised by lottery, which was a common thing in those days, and a popular method for raising funds instead of resorting to taxes, until the practice became corrupt and was abolished by the act of Legislature in 1821.

The first building cost $110,688.42. Albany city paid $34,200; the county paid $3,000, and the state appropriated $73,485.42. The site chosen, now Capitol Hill, was then known as Pinkster Hill. The corner stone was laid on April 23, 1806, Philip Schuyler Van Rensselaer, then the mayor, being master of ceremonies as mason. The edifice was equal to the finest in the state in those days, and was first used on November 1, 1808, on the occasion of a special session.

As the growth of the state had rendered the capitol building of 1808 too limited, and as it did not afford a single committee meeting-room, the subject of a new one commenced to be actively agitated about 1850; but no action was taken until April 24, 1863, when on motion of Hon. James A. Bell (senator from Jefferson county) the subject was referred to the Capitol trustees and the Committee on Public Buildings. In 1865 the senate appointed a committee of three to report propositions as to whether to remove from Albany, and great was the discussion engendered by the feeling in various sections of the state. Albany decided to contribute Congress Hall (hotel) block. This offer was accepted, and an act of May 1, 1865, authorized the erection of the new capitol. Excavation was commenced on July 7, 1869, and on June 24, 1871, the corner-stone was laid with imposing ceremonial. Addresses were made by the Hon. Hamilton Harris (now living in Albany, and counsel for the N. Y. C. & H. R. R.) and Governor John T. Hoffman, while the Hon. William A. Rice read aloud a list of the articles placed in the copper box. The masonic part of the ceremonial was conducted by Most Worshipful John Anton, Grand Master of the Grand Lodge of the State.

The plans submitted by Thomas Fuller were chosen on August 12, 1868, and they have been partially carried out. His original model of the building was an elaborate affair, with its dome towering higher from the floor than a man's head, and was perfect in its details. It called for a building in a rather free French Renaissance style the dimensions of the base nearly square, a front elevation of three full stories and a high dormer, with an exposed basement to the rear, although the land slopes to the extent of showing a sub-basement. The building was to be built of the best of granite, and a high tower was to arise over the central front, with four abbreviated towers at the corners. About the time that the building was carried to the second story Mr. Fuller removed to Canada, and on Sept. 12, 1876, Cyrus L. W. Eidlitz was named as his successor.

The plans were allowed to be changed to conform to the desire of Mr. Eidlitz, and he modified the exterior as far as he might without departing from harmony in treatment. The part constructed under his supervision was highly ornamental (and he planned a different style of approach), which included the construction to the highest point of the front elevation. The noted Richardson was the third architect to exert an influence. At the time of his appointment, associated with Eidlitz in the work, he was regarded as the great rising genius in architectural matters. His advice was advantageous, as he left an imprint most estimable on all that he had to do. It was while they were in charge that the two main rooms were under discussion. Mr. Eidlitz devoted himself to the northern side of the building, where is situated the Assembly Chamber, while Mr. Richardson worked out the plans for the southern side, containing the Senate Chamber, a work that will stand among the fine monuments to the glory of his achievement in this country. The grand western staircase, the finest of the kind in America, was the conception of Richardson, and his reputation would be safe if based on this alone, for it is a noble piece of work.

On March 30, 1883, Governor Grover Cleveland, under a new Act, appointed Isaac G. Perry as commissioner of construction, he being the sole one in charge. The position was equivalent to that of state architect, for under him plans for nearly forty armories and a variety of state buildings have been drawn. Politics failed to interfere with him for sixteen years, for though he was a Democrat he continued to act under Governors Morton and Black. He modified the design of Richardson and added many features. To him may be attributed the eastern (front) approach, a work which required nearly eight years to construct and the cost of several million dollars. The

State Library portion is his. Under his charge the greater part of the carving of the interior was executed, for this was left to be done during the last ten years.

In February of 1899 George Lewis Heins, of the well-known and respected firm of Heins & La Farge, of New York city, was nominated by Governor Roosevelt to succeed Mr. Perry. The same was hotly debated in the Senate up to Washington's birthday, when by a strict party vote of 26 to 21 the nomination was confirmed. The governor's chief reason was to obtain the services of a younger man, for it was a cause for marvel for some years how Mr. Perry could perform his arduous duties so thoroughly at his advanced age.

The soil at some depth below the Capitol is composed of quicksand, and this is one reason why at intervals of a few years there is a hue and cry from New York and other cities deprecating the location of the Capitol, warning its official occupants of danger lurking under ground, and advising abandonment of the building for a new one to be erected in another city. The interior walls have shown some defects in one part, near the staircase located in the northeast corner, but this was not extensive and was due to uneven distribution of weight above. This portion was replaced a few years ago and was an unnecessary cause for alarm, but created the conviction that a stone tower could never be added to the weight borne by the front of the building. The stonework of the tower, which had risen twenty feet above the building, was stopped, and two years ago it was taken down.

In order to provide a foundation suited to the size of the immense building at the crest of the hill leading from the Hudson, a thick concrete bed was formed equal to one large stone underneath the entire building. Excavation was made to the depth of 15 43-100 feet below the sub-basement, which because of the slant of the land at the western end is much below the surface. The concrete formed a bed four feet thick, and directly above it is the sub-basement, with a height of nineteen feet and four inches. This part of the building contains 935,000 cubic feet of stone, and the walls, from 32 inches to five feet thick, contain 11,000,000 brick. The foundation which was prepared for the tower is 110 feet square at the base and tapers to 70 feet square at the basement. In this sub-basement are 144 separate apartments formed by thick broad arches, and it is here that room is provided for electric light machinery. At first the heating plant was operated here, but there was fear of explosion, so adjacent property on a side street was purchased, whence a subterranean conduit conveys the hot air for about four hundred feet. The base of the building is 155 feet above the level of the Hudson, in which direction the ground slopes fifty-one feet in the park until State street is reached, which broad thoroughfare stretches directly from the park

THE ENTRANCE LOBBY.

before the Capitol to the shore of the river. Other buildings of the
city seem to be dwarfed by the Capitol as it is seen from a distance
down the river, and to gain an excellent view the tourist takes the
elevator on the Assembly side to the floor above the Chamber, and
then by mounting 110 steps (8 in. tread) the base of the proposed
tower is reached. This places one at a height of 224 feet, and the
tower, as now planned, will, if built, reach a height of 390 feet, and
be constructed of iron.

The main approach is from the east, the river side, and it extends
in a graceful flight of steps for 175 feet from the building. The long
stretches of balustrade from landing to landing are each made in one
piece of granite. At all advantageous points carving of the finest
kind is to be met. Having ascended 77 steps, one stands upon a
broad plateau before the entrance, almost on a level with the roofs
of handsome brownstone houses on the neighboring avenues. The
lobby ceiling is of groined granite blocks, the walls of polished stone,
and two rows of eight glistening red granite pillars form a noble
sight.

Turning down the corridor, to the left, one reaches the Executive
Chamber, while the corresponding front corner of the building is
occupied by the Secretary of State. The former room is entered
through a private office, except on state occasions. Here two clerks,
appointed in the days of Grover Cleveland, demand the business of
the visitor. Most persons are allowed to enter and stand for a few
moments in the corner of the room, whether the governor is engaged
in business or not, for when private or pressing matters are on
hand he retires to a suite of rooms ranging from the Chamber to
the wall of the entrance lobby. The door to this suite is concealed
by the panel work of the richest mahogany. Ever since the days of
Governor David B. Hill, a private staircase has been in use for the
governor to reach the street without passing through the public way,
where politicians and office-seekers are wont to haunt. The
outer door was originally intended as a window, but it is reported
that the shyness of Governor Hill was accountable for its transfor-
mation into a modest door with the sole key in the pocket of the
executive. No one else has been known to enter here.

Oil portraits of Washington and of Lafayette, measuring about
sixteen feet in height in the frames, grace the walls. A large fireplace, in the centre of the wall opposite to the windows on the front,
is an ornamental feature. The governor's desk is a large affair,
placed at the centre of the front wall, and writing at it he faces the
fireplace, while the door for visitors is diagonally to his left in the
same wall he faces. His secretary has a large desk nearer the south-
east corner, to his left.

The building is to all appearances constructed in a square, but it extends 400 feet from east to west, the length of its side, and measures 300 feet across the front, the north and south line. Approximately in the centre is a court with 92x137 feet for its dimensions. The highest windows overlooking this court are ornamented by carvings of the coat-of-arms of the earliest settlers of the state, among them being those of the Clinton, Jay, Stuyvesant, Livingston, Schuyler and Tompkins families, and over the selection there has been much discussion. The four pavilions ornament the corners of the building and rise to a height of 125 feet above the water-table. They terminate in red terra cotta, with a pinnacle of the same, and the one on the northeast corner was once shattered by lightning. In the southern corner of the building is a fine staircase of Moorish design and one of equally fine appearance, but of Gothic design, corresponds with the former in its location at the front of the Capitol.

The governor's suite of rooms not only reaches along the front to the lobby, but extends to the centre of the building on its left side. Here one finds a room devoted to his military secretary, to his pardon clerk, and other members of a large corps. In the corner of the building back of the Executive Chamber is the department of the Attorney-General and his deputy. Then one comes to the rear entrance, opening upon a park, while directly across the hall is the commencement of the Grand Western Staircase, as it is styled. Near the other rear corner, the northwestern, is the department of the State Board of Health, and in the corner itself and along the side of the building is the Department of Excise. The remaining corner, with a dozen connecting rooms, belongs to the Secretary of State, and here many papers are filed.

Four corridors cut the four sections enclosing the central court, that is, the four main portions of the square building are dissected by a corridor passing through the centre. These corridors originally continued to the exterior, thus obtaining light, but the increase of state commissions crowded the building, and in order to gain room the end of each corridor was made into a room. The result is that these corridors, although tiled elaborately, the sides panelled with marble and stone of various kinds and polished highly, are not attractive stretches, for the light comes from transoms only. The four corridors, arranged similarly on several floors, are therefore simply long, narrow vistas, with numerous doors giving upon them. On the floor just described seven committee rooms open from the corridor on each side of the building and occupy the space to the interior court, where light is derived.

Above this is the principal floor where are located the two legislative halls. The Senate Chamber is on the southern side of the court, and, as was said, was treated by Richardson. It measures 60x100 feet and is fifty feet high. The room presents a square appearance.

The walls of the Chamber are of selected Mexican onyx, highly polished. The ceiling is of carved mahogany, the freize, perhaps twenty feet in depth, is of rich gold, and through the opalescent glass a subdued light falls which adds to the glorious scene, for it is one of the finest rooms in the world.

The balconies, which completely fill the two opposite sides of the Senate Chamber, have balustrades of diminutive onyx pillars. Two arches divide each front of the balcony into three openings and the arches are elaborately carved. On either side of the entrance from the lobby is a fireplace, reaching to nearly the height of the ceiling, or fifty feet, with openings large enough to admit a man standing upright. Opening on the Chamber is the room of the clerk of the Senate and the Lieutenant-Governor's private office. This suite brings one to the corner of the building which is occupied by the senate finance committee. The lobby extending alongside the interior court and forming a hallway from the Senate Chamber, leading to front and rear of the building, was originally a corridor, the broadest and finest in the building, with a row of sandstone columns running through the centre and forming a beautiful vista. This place is used as a lounging room for the senators and visitors. It is richly carpeted, large paintings adorn the walls, and costly curtains moderate the light from the court. The sum of $20,000 was appropriated to furnish this lobby, aside from all constructive work.

Turning out of this lobby to the right and pausing at the centre of the rear of the building, one comes to the State Library. About the doorway one finds the most elaborate carving in the building. The room's dimensions are about the same as those of the Senate Chamber. There is abundant light from the rear, looking out upon a small park. The ceiling is fifty feet above, decorated in the most delicate of coloring, designs of cherubs, floral pieces, and symbolic ornamentation being finely executed by hand, painted upon a sky-blue ground. Two galleries, on the sides between the entrance and rear wall, show that the room has a height of three floors of liberal space. A few marble busts, portraits of men of note in the state fifty or more years ago, and cases containing the rarest of relics in the building, are a few of the features of the room. Adjoining, and occupying the northwest corner of the building, is the law department, containing about 25,000 volumes. In the passage between hang several frames holding priceless Indian wampum belts, not long ago the property of the Six Nations.

Continuing the walk about this floor of the building, one arrives at the Assembly Chamber, corresponding in position to that of the Senate, but a much larger room, for it covers the space from the northern wall to the court, doing away with any corridor or lobby paralleling its side as in the other case. The dimensions are 84x140

GRAND WESTERN STAIRCASE.

IN THE GRAND WESTERN STAIRCASE.

feet, including the area covered by the galleries at the east and west ends. Four great columns of polished red granite, four feet in diameter, sustain the ceiling. Until removed about six years ago, the original ceiling of carved and decorated stone was the largest groined arch in the world, with its keystone 56 feet above the well, as the place where the members sit is termed. On the northern wall was a painting entitled "The Flight of Evil Before Good," and on the south wall was one called "The Discoverer." The position was about fifty feet above the floor, over the higher row of windows. Each measured 15x40 feet, and they were the work of the late William M. Hunt. For their execution he received $15,000. Unfortunately these were painted upon the stone, and when the ceiling of this room was altered they were doomed. Cracks were discovered in the stonework of the ceiling. Everybody became greatly alarmed and the room was practically condemned. For one year, in an effort to obviate the danger threatening, an enormous weight was carried to the attic above the ceiling to balance and keep the pressure even. Water pipes were also placed there to keep the stones at even temperature and moisture. Science could not devise a means to save the handsome ceiling, and at last several hundred thousand dollars were appropriated to remove it and for the construction of a safer one. It was in this instance that a scandal arose. Instead of the carved Mexican mahogany as called for in specifications, a number of papier maché panels were employed, which at the great distance looked about as well as the real—in fact it took an expert to tell the difference. The new ceiling is an eyesore to good taste. Art critics believe that the money would be well expended were another introduced. The four immense columns call for an arched ceiling, and a flat one is decidedly out of place, no matter how much money was paid for it. No amount of money spent on a flat ceiling may make amends from an architectural point of view, for it cuts the arches and so shows on the face that it is a makeshift of the worst description.

Having spoken of the principal rooms, it will not do to overlook the Grand Western Staircase and the carving. It is the delicacy and appropriateness of the carving, its execution and conception, that are objects of much attention. This staircase commences its elaborate detail of design at the basement, which is really one of the principal floors. Two distinct flights of steps ascend to a platform, then divide again at right angles; ascending half way between floors to another staging the staircase is again divided, and thus it is continued, so that at each platform there are two flights ascending and two descending, four flights meeting at each level.

Two or four heads are carved on the capitals. Each column has its distinctive feature, as for instance the military pillar with its head of Gen. Grant and other great officers of the Civil War. Mytho-

logical heads will peer from one capital, while from another the
faces of great inventors look down. Five women are honored by
heads carved in this manner. They are Harriet Beecher Stowe,
Susan B. Anthony, Frances Willard, Clara Barton and Elmira P.
Spencer.

A design carried out in unique manner is the choice of the coat-
of-arms of the oldest cities of the state as ornaments for the columns
of the side porticos. There is hardly any space left upon the main
approach that is not carved. The American eagle and turkey of
life-size are ornaments on the face of two large granite blocks in this
approach, and heads of a buffalo and of a lion, the size of nature, give

ON THE WESTERN STAIRCASE.

dignity to the terminals of the driveway under the front flight of
steps. Some of these stones weigh 26 tons. Mr. George D. Brines,
lately of Providence, R. I., and who sailed the last of 1898 to spend a
year or more in study abroad, was the designing sculptor of a large
proportion of the finest work. Stone carvers were paid at the rate of
twelve dollars a day to execute the same.

The electric system is the finest ever installed to light the exterior
of a building. There are twenty-eight electroliers, and the cost of
many of them was close to $4,000 apiece. In order to have the wires
concealed, borings of 28 feet were made through the stone to reach
those on high pediments. The cost for these exterior lamps was
about $70,000. The designs employed are the state coat-of-arms in
high relief, over a foot in height, and an eagle surmounts a prominent pair, for the designs differ throughout in couples.

The removal of the State Library from the capitol is a question that will be a matter before the public for some years until a proper edifice is completed for the University of the State of New York, to contain the library, all of its many departments, and a fitting state museum, now located in three buildings at Albany. On the night of Jan. 23d of this year, a bill was introduced with this idea in view. The amount asked for was $400,000, but no one believes that this will do more than prepare the way for an edifice in keeping with the Capitol, especially as it is definitely settled that the location for it is directly behind the other, separated by a park of little more than two acres. The two city blocks regarded as necessary for the purpose are in the heart of the best resident section of the city, bordering on State street and Washington avenue. From a close examination of the assessment rolls it is found that this property is valued at $286,-100. It is likely that the new building will be construced as was the Capitol, by expecting to complete it with an appropriation amounting to one-fourth of the amount expended in the end. If the new commissioner, Mr. Heins, is to design it, it will be a shame if he is not given full liberty to make it the finest library building in the country. It may be that this was Governor Roosevelt's idea when he made the appointment in February. It is admitted by politicians on all sides that this new edifice is a necessity, as it is impossible to find room in the Capitol for needed committee rooms and places for many commissions, new ones being added each year. Albany will then have reason to speak of its fine public buildings.

Cuyler Reynolds.

IN THE COURT OF APPEALS.

DOORWAY, HOSPITAL OF SANTA CRUZ.

Toledo, Spain.

MAISON AUX MASQUES

Rome, Italy

ECOLE NORMALE
D'INSTITVTRICES

ECOLE, NORMALE D'INSTITUTRICES AT CLERMONT- FERRAND, FRANCE.
E. Camut, Architect.

DESIGN FOR ST. PETERS CHURCH.

Frankfort.

John Vollmer, Architect.

OSSUARY · CHURCH · OF · S · MILIAU
GUIMILIAU · BRITTANY·

ECOLES SUPERIEURES.

Algieres, Africa.   M. Dauphin, Architect.

HOUSE AT STAPLEFIELD, SUSSEX.

F. T. Baggallay, Architect.

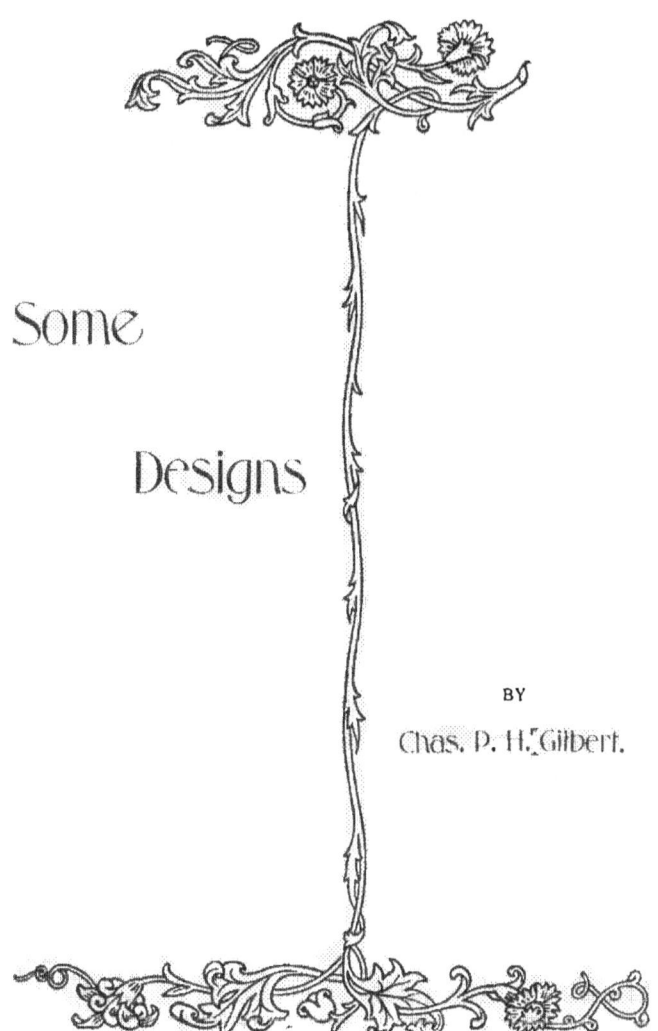

Some

Designs

BY

Chas. P. H. Gilbert.

THE CUSHMAN BUILDING.
North corner Maiden Lane and Broadway, N. Y. City.   C. P. H. Gilbert, Architect.

RESIDENCE.
Seventy-second Street and Riverside Drive, N. Y. City.   C. P. H. Gilbert, Architect.

THE CONVERSE RESIDENCE,
No. 3 East Seventy-eighth Street, N. Y. City.   C. P. H. Gilbert, Architect.

RESIDENCES.
Seventy-seventh Street and Riverside Drive, N. Y. City.   C. P. H. Gilbert, Architect.

RESIDENCE.
Seventy-sixth Street, near Riverside Drive, N. Y. City.   C. P. H. Gilbert, Architect.

RESIDENCE.
Seventy-fifth Street, near Riverside Drive, N. Y. City.   C. P. H. Gilbert, Architect.

Seventy-fifth Street and Riverside Drive, N. Y. City.   RESIDENCES.   C. P. H. Gilbert, Architect.

THE FLETCHER RESIDENCE.

Seventy-ninth Street and Fifth Avenue, N. Y. City.

C. P. H. Gilbert, Architect.

THE place that stone must occupy in our future building, in city and country, must not be measured by the old standard of Fifth Avenue and such like streets and their elegances. The rubbed slab of brown sandstone set up edgewise and attached after a fashion to a wall of brick behind it has been instrumental in developing perhaps the most unintelligent style of street architecture of modern times. Nor was the stupidity of the architecture in question much relieved by the use of the same stone in more solid blocks, as in the retaining walls and facing of areas, in the stoops, or even in the columned porches by which the stoops were crowned. All partook of the same spirit of dull, flat, dusky-brown monotony; and there is no wonder that there was a reaction and that other materials than stone seemed to be identified with any artistic reform. As the character of an architecture must be fixed, first or last, by the treatment of the great wall with its openings—so the universal employment of the smooth, rubbed slab, and moulded strip, set the pace, as it were, for wall surfaces of other material, and the wretched fashion came in of considering the city street-front as being of necessity the insignificant, overworked and underthought contrivance with which we are too familiar. One great reason why other materials than stone have been in demand of late years has been the feeling of architect and employer alike, that so much flat and semi-polished uniformity was a thing out of which no architectural thinking was likely to grow.

All this while the books were telling us that stone ought to be used in a very different way; that, if stratified, it ought to be laid on its quarry-bed, or nearly as nature laid it; and, therefore, in smaller, more diversified and slightly more irregular pieces—irregular in color and in texture, but not of necessity very visibly irregular. And, if igneous rock may be handled and placed more freely, there was, ready at hand, the witness of those minor communities scattered about the country and situated in the neighborhood of stone quarries of importance; a witness which could not have failed to have changed our views of the proper use of stone had we listened to it. Let any-one go to see curious and interesting New Bedford, once the town of whalers, now the town of cotton manufacturing. There the visitor will see big granite monoliths set up on end to serve as gate-posts leading to simple little domestic "dooryards." Moreover, he will see the earth of these same door-yards kept in place by retaining walls, built, each, of two or three courses of really huge blocks of a most beautiful, purplish-red granite, roughly dressed, of course,

but squared neatly enough, and set with a certain accuracy. He will
see the foundation and cellar walls, or, as it is often called in Massachusetts, the "underpinnin'," even of small, low, shingle-covered
houses, faced, and evidently composed, as the retaining walls are
composed, of huge blocks of the same hard and perfect stone. It is
quite clear that the builders of these houses, and the layers-out of
these little front gardens, three-quarters of a century ago, when New
Bedford was still a small town, living mainly by whale oil and sper-
macetti, cannot have had in mind the same architectural ideas which
at the same time and soon after drove the builders of houses on city
avenues towards monotony; and, indeed, we see that it is not monotony which the granite workers obtained. It is really most attractive to see in a simple, not over-rich, and, in a sense, unsophisticated
community, such free and easy use of what is to most people in the
world a somewhat rare and very costly device for building. The
megalithic instinct, which impelled the Imperial Roman builders at
Baalbec to put sixty foot rocks into the retaining wall of a temple-
platform was there, in the New England seaside town; and there was
also present the love of the vari-colored, many-lighted surface itself. The same interesting use of granite will be found in other Massachusetts towns, the names of which occur readily to one's thought.
At Fall River, in the foundation wall of a frame house, there is a
stone thirty-two feet long, if memory is not at fault; but the granite itself is seldom as beautiful in its varying tints as that which is so
common in New Bedford. The granite at Quincy, for instance, is a
bit monotonous in its uniform grayness, and one hesitates over the
question whether it should not be used in a somewhat different way.
How would it be, for instance, if the more uniformly colored granite
were used in smaller pieces—in lower courses or in broken, un-
coursed work, and less smoothly dressed; so as to receive from the
ever-ready tinting of nature's sunlight and shadow an immediate
variety of tint? The more obelisk-like shafts could still be set for gate-
posts, and the love of big stones be satisfied in that way: nor should
we insist upon the dressing of these into any semi-classical or semi-
mediaeval architectural character; the square tapering post, suggestive of Egypt and the highest of all antiquity, is as good a form
as any. The play of light upon its alternating sides is all that can
be asked, and it contrasts perfectly with the grass, the shrubbery, and
the over-hanging trees. The question becomes more difficult, however, when from a granite country we enter a region underlaid everywhere by white marble. Parts of western Massachusetts and parts
of southern Vermont seem to be pretty much made up of white marble beneath the thin cuticle of vegetable soil and the roots of herbage;
and when we pass through one of the towns of that region it is a little doubtful whether the New England bucolic mind has known how

to grapple with the snowy white material. It is a little painful to the eye, that appearance of a long stretch of retaining wall and a carefully worked base for a garden paling when all this substructure is of vivid white and crystalline material, semi-translucent, and reflecting every ray of the sun in apparently a thousand broken lights. And it is to be remembered that the prosperous and seriously minded community, with a strong disposition to assert its dignity and its responsibility by the external aspect of its built walls and its Sunday clothes, will insist always upon keeping its marble white. A beautifully weathered flight of steps is not to be allowed to remain tinted as nature would have it, but it must be scraped rather carefully, washed with acid, and left as glitteringly white as such domestic operations can make it; lucky if the man with the chisel is not called in and a new snowy surface is not worked upon the ancient blocks. The ailment here, as we have said, is less easy to prescribe for. If, indeed, as in some towns, the marble runs bluish in certain veins, then an agreeable variety of color can be got by a very free use of the blue marble. It tends generally to fade in color; or, at least, the weathering of stones of two colors, side by side, is generally found to produce a satisfactory approximation of tint, so that after ten years the blue marble and the white marble are not so noticeably in contrast. None the less, however, do they help one another wonderfully. The eye may not know; the untrained observation may not catch the reason for the comparative charm of certain garden walls, certain house walls even; but the charm exists, and the irregular interspersion of the bluest blocks that can be found with the almost perfectly white ones adds attractiveness to every piece of work which they go to make up. Failing this device, the one thing for the builder to bear in mind is the beauty of the shades and of the shadows upon white marble, which are always of unexpectedly lovely colors. And here a word of what may seem digression. Does the reader happen to have noticed the apparent incongruity of a white marble statue in a gallery of pictures? Has he thought to himself that it was an open question which hurt the other the most, the paintings the statue, or the statue the paintings; whether the color made the statue look cold, or the whiteness of the statue made the color look garish? Let him be reminded of the answer which a great living painter gave many years ago to a question upon this very subject: "There won't be any incongruity," said the artist, "if a statue is good for anything—if it deserves a place in the gallery at all. Nature takes care of that, and invests your statue for you with a clothing of variously tinted grays, so that it is a white object only in name, and in your own failing observation. The question for you to settle is whether the modelling of your statue is so fine that this garment of grays will be in itself a lovely thing; for remember that the difference between good sculpture and bad sculpture is mainly this, that the one has such varieties of surface that the gray shades upon it are lovely severally and collectively, while the other will never have anything but harsh and ugly combinations of shade in whatever light it may chance to stand." Such refinements as the sculptor expects to put into his marble are not for the builder of garden walls, and mounting-blocks, and front-door steps in small towns; but the lesson taught by that wise painter's words remains applicable. What the builder in white marble has to consider is the use of shade, and how he can, without ruinous expense, employ it to diversify the too excessive whiteness of his material when the native color of the stone has little or no variety. Thus, as these marble blocks come easily of uniform height, and coursed masonry is easy to get and inexpensive, let the builder of a three-course wall try the effect of setting his second course with three-quarters of an inch projection beyond the first, the third course three-quarters of an inch projection more, and the coping finally with a projection somewhat greater than either of the others. Such a wall looked at from the point of view of a pedestrian ten feet away, or a rider in a buggy forty feet away, will have a general effect which may be described as follows: Above the short course which separates the foot-path from the wall there will rise a stripe of brilliantly lighted, almost entirely white, surface, roughened only by the irregularities of the axed finish, and divided longitudinally by two narrow and one wider horizontal lines of the most delicate gray, which will be sometimes ruddy through reflection from the walk of pounded earth, sometimes cool from the transmitted color of the grass, sometimes almost pure purple as the sunlight brings with it tints from the sky rather than from the earth: but always beautiful. Now, anyone who has designed or who has bought and enjoyed textile fabrics, mattings, and the like, knows how effective may be three horizontal stripes when their width and the distance by which they are separated one from the other have been rightly considered. A good deal of design goes into that simple device, and it is worthy of the trained intelligence of the Javan or the Persian artificer to regulate those stripes in relative width and in spacing in proportion to their intensity of color. To the stonemason no exact advice can be given. There is one at least in every little town who has the eye and the brain for such work as this, and to see at once just how high his courses had better be; or, if the height of the courses is practically settled for him by economical considerations, to see at once how great his projections must be, in order to produce gray lines of the width which he requires. Moreover, he will find himself free, if he has a little more money allowed him and the chisel in his hand, to diversify each one of these stripes. It has been assumed that the upper course would overhang the lower one with a plain sharp arris and nothing more, but that is altogether

too rash an assumption. There is no reason why the wall should be
built as in A, Fig. 1. Even if the surfaces, here shown as vertical,
are set at a slight inclination so that the point, x, shall be vertically
above the points y, there remains a perhaps crude simplicity about
this design in bars of light and shade which the ambitious stone-
cutter will desire to forego for something finer. He may then very
readily give to his courses of marble the facial profile shown in B and
in this he may vary the slopes and the resulting obtuse angles at o
quite indefinitely. In this case he will have substituted broader, paler
gray stripes for the narrower, darker ones of A, and if this pleases
him, and if he wishes to contrast them decidedly with a very dark

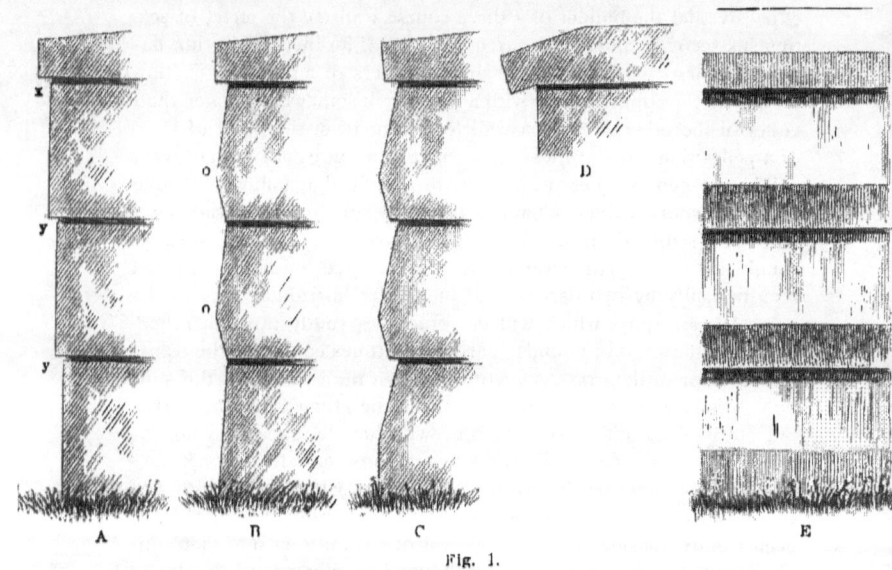

Fig. 1.

stripe indeed at the top, there is nothing to prevent his giving to the
overhanging part of the coping a different and more sharply pronounced section than the one here shown. The coping whose section is shown at D will not (*experto crede*) be an expensive one to
cut, and the slight difference of angle caused by the upward rake of
the overhang will be wonderfully effective in intensifying the color of
the shadow of it on the white wall below; while, at the same time, it
will form an admirable drip. This coping or the simpler one may
then be used to crown the still more elaborate wall of which the profile is shown at C. In this, the pattern drawn by the sun upon the
white surface will be very much more complex than those we have
dealt with previously. There will be the darkest stripe of all at the

top and this may be wider than any of the stripes below, or not so wide, as the mason-designer may elect; but below that he will have an alternation of the broader, paler stripe, one narrower and just seen to be less brilliantly white than the still broader slope of the stone above, and below this what will appear by contrast a very dark stripe indeed, which the designer will prefer to have the narrowest of all, and which the builder will find it the easiest to make so. That is to say, he will have, as is shown in E, a pattern made up of ten stripes or, if the top of the coping be considered, of eleven, in at least four different intensities of brilliancy, extending from the high light of the top of the coping which will be repeated in the stripes below it, to the extreme dark under the coping, and made up of the shadow thrown by that coping upon the uppermost course of the marble.

The relation which such simple decoration bears to the channelling and fluting of Grecian columns, and to the horizontal banding of important buildings, such as, to take a very modern instance, the American Surety Company's gigantic structure in New York City, will occur to everyone. Who was the wiseacre who suggested, as a probable reason for the channelling of Doric pillars, that it was necessary to have a surface which would hold the points of spears when they were leaned up against them? The Greek mind was capable of providing a better receptacle than that for weapons of war; but also, whether his column was to be left white, stained yellow, or painted in two or three bright colors, he loved intensely the delicate vertical bands of soft gradation.

The above is not so much a digression as it looks, for the purpose of this article is to help a little towards the bringing back of architecture to its proper place as one of the decorative arts, and the one especially concerned with the shaping and piling up of solid pieces of material. We have had altogether too much during the last century or two of the architecture of the cabinet and the office—the architecture of lines ruled straight by the T-square and the set-square, and interspersed by pretty figuring. Any mason who will try to handle the stones of his neighboring hillsides as they may be handled by a man of taste and a little independence, will be doing more to restore "the elder days of art" than the designer of a new statehouse, unless that same is a very remarkable statehouse indeed—a thing not to be expected.

But from the question of snowy white stones let us go by a leap even longer than it looks, to the consideration of stones which are full of color. All through middle Connecticut there is a sandstone of a superb deep red. The old locks, retaining walls, and bridge piers of the New Haven and Northampton Canal were built of that noble material, and there the quarried blocks lie in their now unused and abandoned structures, waiting for some right of ownership to be

legally decided before anybody can put them to use a second time.
But the hillsides are full of the same stone, and the wiser people of a
century ago used great slabs of it as the lowermost steps (acting also
as foundations for superstructures) for the wooden flights which led
to their front doors. Thicker and otherwise similar masses of stone
they used for mounting blocks, and to a limited extent they used this
stone, laid up in course walling, for just such purposes as have been
referred to in the case of countries of granite and of marble. It is not
long since the writer was walking through a granite-built, granite-
paved, granite-trimmed, granite-based town, with a man who owns
much property in the sandstone region now under consideration;
and the question was naturally asked of the landowner why he and
his neighbors did not utilize, nowadays, the splendid red sandstone of
their own acres. The expected answer was that the stone was too
soft; and, indeed, it is not as hard as the Portland stone which comes
from the more southern line of counties, nor would it do as well as
that for copings; nor would one willingly build an elaborately
worked, deeply cut, and finely sculptured church tower of it. If it
were put to such unfit uses it would be found untrustworthy; there is
no doubt about that. But it is a perfect stone for use in a wall laid
up according to the admitted and well-understood doctrines for stone
walling. Even if, what is not for one moment probable, it were found
necessary to make the coping of a different material, the face of the
lower wall would be as splendid in the natural play of deeper and
paler red as the art of man could make the gray and white wall which
we have imagined in connection with the marble region. Moreover,
the stone, without selection except that of the roughest and slightest
kind, as of throwing out the seriously defective pieces, is capable of
doing good service in walling even of two-story and three-story buildings; and one is to be envied who can have his own house or his
neighbors' houses built of so beautiful a material. In using such
stone it will be found that the modern tendency, superinduced by the
very high cost of handwork—the modern tendency towards perfectly
unmoulded, unadorned openings cut square through the face of a
wall—would work itself out extremely well. For the local color of
the stone, so to speak; that is to say, the actual tint which its particles
have when seen together, will vary so much between the different
surfaces of different stones and different faces of the same stone that
the need of mouldings and projecting and recessed working of the
material may be thought less obvious. On the other hand, if mouldings are to be cut they must be planned, as to their profiles, with careful thought for the avoidance of projecting beaks, drips, and overhangs which may easily drop away as the soft stone takes the weather.
Thus, in Fig. 2, the courses of stone being assumed to be about ten
inches high and with fairly wide joints, the mortar between them may

be considered safe. The stone will, of course, be laid on its quarry bed, and the edge or side face of each course will gradually weather, sometimes by becoming slightly dished, or hollowed in the middle, sometimes by wearing off above or below, next to the joint. These slight deteriorations will be of no possible injury to the body of the work, to its permanence, or even to its beauty. But with regard to the moulded and worked course forming a somewhat ornamental band running horizontally along the face of the building, an entirely different problem presents itself. The dweller in a city house of brown-stone trim and fittings which has seen half a century of existence, knows well that one of the defects of the hard and assumedly durable sandstone of which his walls, door-steps and stoop are composed, is its disposition to wear by turning into large separate sheets, easily detachable one from another and peel-

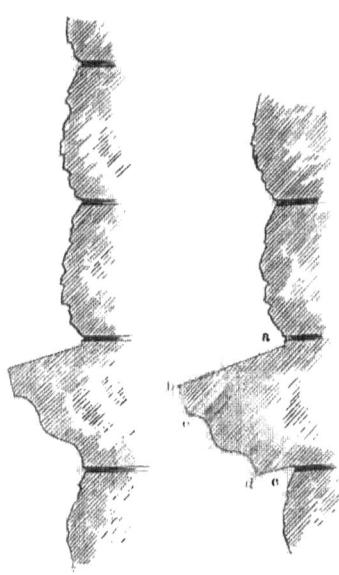

Fig. 2.   Fig. 2 bis.

ing or flaking off to the extent of many square inches at a time. This particular form of decay is not so much to be feared in the soft red stone of which we are speaking; this latter will rather crumble away in smaller parts so that fragments no bigger than an egg will drop from parts of a long continued moulding. The question for the designer is, therefore, what form of moulding will be least liable to be affected in that way, and the section given in Fig. 2 and the bolder one in Fig. 2 bis is offered as one of many which suggest themselves. The surfaces a b and c d are assumed to be parallel, and the surface b c is assumed to be at right angles with them, though, of course, a different disposition may be equally good. The moulded or curved section may be of two coves and a bead, which flow into one another without arrises; it may have its coves cut deeper and its bead more revealed as the stone is thought to be more trustworthy. It is for the local mason to settle the question whether the line, a b, representing the outward slope of the water-table and the general inclination of the projecting sill-course shall itself lie in the direction of the quarry-bed; or whether the quarry-bed had better remain in this course, as in the other courses of the wall, horizontal, while the projecting member is cut out of the block in the more usual way.

Stones whose own special color is less beautiful than the red sandstone of middle Connecticut, are even more effective than that when they are treated rightly—with a proper feeling for modulation of surface. The noble sandstone which only New York of all earthly communities can boast of—the "blue stone" of the Catskill Mountain mass—is known even to most New Yorkers only as an ideal material for foot-pavements, sidewalks, and the like. Indeed, it varies in color and quality, and it is perhaps true that the grade of the stone most in use for flags is less well fitted for decorative wall work, moulding, and carving than for more utilitarian purposes; but there is a dark blue variety which is of all deep-colored stones the most effective. One should notice the monolithic basins of some of our New York fountains, such as the Bethesda Fountain in Central Park, or the foundation and basement wall of the great house at Madison Avenue and East Seventy-second Street, or the highly wrought stoops, approaches, areas, and parapets of the three houses, 4, 6, 8, West Fifty-seventh Street, in order to understand what Catskill Mountain blue-stone is capable of. Used alone, it is sombre enough; and yet its treatment in the cases just mentioned may suggest a simpler handling of it for simpler occasions. What it lacks, however, is a certain refinement of modelling which has more to do with the cut-stone work of which there will be mention by and by than with the rough uses of the country stone mason. It would be well if those surfaces which come most naturally to the stone mason, and which are commonly stained with iron in greater or less degrees of reddish brown, could be avoided altogether, for the tint in question does not well ally itself with the deep blue of the freshly broken or cut material.

That is a curious stone, as limited in its location as the New York blue-stone itself—the peculiar greenish, so-called serpentine, of the neighborhood of Philadelphia. To any person not accustomed to the country churches of that region, their sombre green walls are a novelty, indeed; nor is it wonderful if they bring up in the mind of the travelled student the more varied green of the "Prato" stone which he has learned to know in Italy. The use of all these dark stones as parts of a chromatic architecture; their utility, in short, for such purposes as the Tuscans have always put them to; is not now our subject; we are considering only what is easiest to do with our splendid natural materials, and there must be mention, however brief, of the magnificent hard, red rock which was used so freely by the architect of those ever-to-be-regretted buildings of Columbia College which stood not so long ago in the college grounds at Madison Avenue and Forty-ninth Street. That stone, we were told, was too hard for chiseling, and yet it would have been good fun enough to have tried the experiment of using it for finer purposes than the basement walls in question. It was very like a certain light red sandstone with much coarse gravel in its consistence which was at one time dressed beautifully in New Haven and elsewhere on the Connecticut shore, and which was an ideal material for foundations. The true lover of stone must always, it would seem, be eager to try further experiment with these rocks of admitted excellence but assumed unfitness for delicate work. There is delicacy and delicacy! And he is no true builder who does not long to try all the possible uses of the fine-material, and see whether, indeed, it is as limited as people have been saying.

The splendid light brown and light gray sandstones of the Ohio region require no such experimenting to show how perfect a building material they can furnish. From year to year the colors of the most accessible stone vary too largely for the satisfaction of the careful designer who is, by this fact, thrown off his balance, somewhat; and year by year their names vary also. At least it is so in any market that you can name. As with California wine—as with the textile fabrics which one cares most about for his personal or family use— the wretched habit of appealing to the possible purchaser by the constant changing of names, trade-marks, tricks of presentation of all sorts, prevents anything like a thorough understanding of the whole business of stone work in this country. As every fresh project for a building takes shape, the designer, or superintendent, or owner has to make fresh inquiries and start afresh with his scheme of building and consequent design. There is, for instance, a magnificent light brown, or, if you please, warm, light gray sandstone from the middle west, which is reputed to be more nearly fireproof than any natural material known to us. It is said on good authority that ovens are built of it, or partly built of it, in regions where it abounds. That stone and its quarry should be so well known, at least by every architect, and by every large contractor in our cities, that there would be no more difficulty in procuring it on demand than in procuring Wamsutta shirting cotton. It is so, of course, with the limestones; and peculiarly so with them as they are more newly come into the field and are disputing the right of way with each other a little more fiercely. All this, however, is merely the *obiter dictum*—the brief aside of one who loves to know what he can count upon, and objects to hear verandahs called piazzas, carriage-porches called *porte-cochères*, the name of a good vineyard lost in the announcing name of a company, and the name of a stone quarry lost in that of an agent or a speculating firm. If we knew the quarries we should know what was possible with those quarries which once were famous. How about the stone of which were built, during the same short lapse of time, Trinity Church, New York, and the University Place Presbyterian Church, at the corner of University Place and Tenth Street?

According to all the traditions, this stone, quarried in the years 1846 and thereafter, was carefully examined, and the blocks sorted as for color; the expensive and stately Trinity Church being built of the stone which is least varied in color, while the blocks which run the darkest and the lightest were left out, and could be put somewhat more cheaply for the less sumptuous structure. It is hard to say which of the two buildings is the most successful in this most important matter of the color of the material. Different persons of good taste will differ as to this; the stone is of a lovely color whether in its darkest or its lightest shade, and gradation and contrast between the darkest and the lightest shade is at least worthy of comparison between the nearer approximating middle tints of the larger and more famous building. That quarry was in New Jersey, and not so very far from tide-water; and other quarries were there which were famous not many decades ago. The commercial eagerness to push a stone into the market to the extent of underselling competitors and taking perhaps a price lower than that which will really pay the dealer, is, of course, responsible for the constant substitution of new stone for the old familiar varieties. We are always hearing that an old quarry is exhausted, but on examination it proves continually that the old quarry is as good as new, the stone varying perhaps in its tint, in its grain, in its hardness, but valuable stone still. What we really want is a sort of agreement among the architects, and the formation of a committee of examination which will keep the run of the quarries as far as commercial exigencies allow the facts to be known; and will enable a man to build with a given stone in his youth and to use it again in his maturity.

The assumption in all the cases of stone-working which have been mentioned above, is that the surface of the wall, made up of all these separate courses, shall be of that modified roughness which is produced by hammer-dressing, or, at most, by "pointing," in some of its forms. That is to say, the rough and simple work here contemplated is not assumed to involve the use of the chisel in any of its forms, but only of the simpler tools which knock off larger fragments of stone and leave it in a generally true vertical facing. But now let us consider the value to stone-work of such high finish—of such more delicate manipulation as the tough, durable, and well-compacted stone allow. What is called rock-faced work has been common in America. Among the new buildings of Yale College, Durfee Hall, as it is now called, was built about 1870, with all its larger surfaces treated in this way; and the large and elaborate Battell Chapel, a church costing nearly $200,000, completed about 1873, had its stone walls rock-faced also, although here the large amount of arcading and other ornamental exterior semi-Gothic elaboration diminish the proportionate amount of the rougher surface. This rock-faced work was done by a simple process less easy to describe than

to work. In Fig. 3, let A be a rough block of stone, upon which the
mason has worked the four "beds," namely, the vertical faces a and
its opposite, and the horizontal faces b, the top bed, and the unseen
bottom bed parallel to this last. Upon these four beds he has drawn

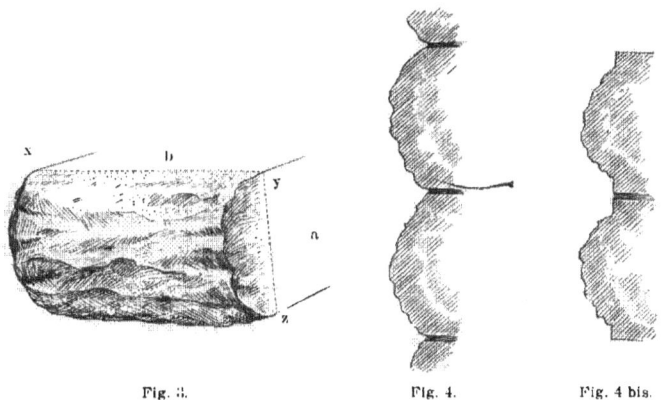

Fig. 3.   Fig. 4.   Fig. 4 bis.

in, in pigment, or by common rough lead pencil, the lines xy and yz,
and corresponding lines on the other two beds. These lines are carefully squared with one another, and are kept "out of wind" (wind to
rhyme with mind). The next and the final step is to put the edge of
your broadest "drove" chisel at one point on any one of those lines,
to strike it with the mallet and let all come away that will—and to repeat this process continuously all around the line. In other words, all
that naturally flakes or splinters away as the chisel cuts into it from
above is allowed to break away; but the chisel is allowed to go no
further, nor to alter the natural cleavage of any part of the face, which
is required to have everywhere the look of the naturally broken stone.
When a wall is composed entirely of pieces of stone of this character,
its section will be as in Fig. 4. It will be seen that the mortar will remain at home within its own proper place; that is to say, the joint
between each two blocks. No stray splashes and no "ponds" or
large receptacles for the mortar will appear anywhere on the face
of the wall. The mortar joints are as thin as the actual distance between the upper bed of the lower stone and the lower bed of the upper
stone, nor does the pointing which may be applied after the laying up
of the wall in any way increase the apparent width of these joints,
which, indeed, are kept as narrow as is at all practicable. Such work
as this was afterwards used very freely by H. H. Richardson in the
Romanesque buildings which he erected between 1876 and the time
of his death, ten years later. There is one obvious and irresistibly

strong reason for its common use, and that is its cheapness, for the
contractors will generally undertake to do such work at a much
lower rate to the square yard of surface than they could accept for
work done with any of the tools commonly in use. The broken surface is cheaper than the worked surface. That appears to be obvious.
On the other hand, many architects who know something of the way
in which stone work was faced by the most careful builders in sandstone and limestone of whom we know anything—French, English,
and German workmen of the thirteenth and following centuries—
would reject the rock-faced surface as denying all possibility of the
delicate manipulation of the masses. It is hard to put into words the
scorn with which some of the few modern artistic designers in exterior architecture speak of the rock-faced work around them.

The truth, if there be a general truth, lies somewhere between the
too common practice and the complete rejection of this way of facing
stone walls. No one who is denouncing modern rock-faced work
ought to ignore altogether such a splendid proof of the possibilities
contained in this method as is afforded by the Palazzo Vecchio at
Florence. Every stone in that great structure has a rock-faced surface except those which are delicately worked in moulded and otherwise wrought string-courses and similar architectural features. In
the contrast suggested by the last sentence lies perhaps the whole secret of the charm of this building and of the lack of charm in buildings
which have not been treated in the same intelligent way. Fig. 5
shows a small part of this building, the purpose of the view being to
express the very peculiar and powerful effect produced by such very
minute architectural members when contrasted with large surfaces of
the naturally broken stone. It is evident that the firmly outlined
shades and shadows of the moulded, dentilled or sculptured courses
and bands carries it over the looser, the unorganized, the thicker light
and shade of the rock-faced wall. To work in this way requires more

Fig. 6. Part of basement of Pitti Palace, Florence.   The blocks though classed as
rock-faced are not left entirely as the stone first broke away, but have been worked to
a somewhat rounded form.   Those of the retaining walls below are much bolder.

boldness than our architects, unaccustomed to designing where the
books of authorities have not shown them just how to lay down their
lines, are in the habit of undertaking. The titanic effects produced
in the basement of the Pitti Palace, as seen in Fig. 6, or in the still
more monstrous overhangs of the rocks piled together in the re-

FIG. 5. Part of the Palazzo Vecchio, Florence.

Fig. 5 bis. Detail of the Palazzo Vecchio, Florence: rock-faced work contrasting with tooled mouldings, which yet are effective by contrast of their sharp-edged and distinctly marked lights and darks with the irregular lighting on the rough surfaces.

taining walls of the terrace below—some of which project horizontally eighteen inches beyond their joints—need hardly detain us here. Modern architecture is very unlikely to deal much in such grandiose work as that, unless in a piece of frank imitation of the extraordinary building named. Moreover, this is not the every-day simple and familiar architecture with which we are concerned in this paper.

On the whole, then, the surfaces of granite, of sandstone, and of limestone alike (marble being considered here as a modified form of limestone not now requiring separate consideration) may be thought to be at their best when the deepest recess made by the blow of the point of a pick is not more than one-half of an inch deeper than the greatest protuberance. There will be, of course, a vast number of protuberances, and a vast number of hollows, all having approximately the same depth, the same projection. The general surface is in one vertical plane ; that is to say, a long, straight edge can be applied anywhere to the surface and will be found to correspond no matter in what direction it is applied, while a carefully handled rule at right angles to the straight edge will nowhere find a hollow more than half an inch deep. This is not a rule of the books ; nor is it to be formulated as final and positive ; it is intended merely as a form of words expressive of the nature of the roughest surface to be given to stonework when the best effects are to be looked for. It is necessary, however, to point out one common modification of the processes of the rougher facings of stone walls, whether in their least finished form of rock-faced work or in their more highly wrought surfaces, such as are known by the technical names "pointed," "sparrow-billed," "dabbed," "droved," "tooth-chiselled," "patent-hammered," "axed." It is not unusual to see each block of stone framed all around by a

Fig. 7.

flat surface an inch or two in width, and much more smoothly wrought than the other parts. Thus, in Fig. 4 bis and in Fig. 7, the narrow band which surrounds the face is what is called a draft, and this draft is worked much smoother than the rest of the face. In the sketch before us it has been assumed that the draft has been worked by the drove chisel, while the centre is roughly finished with the pointing tool. In a wall where every stone is thus marked off from its neighbors by a draft, which, being repeated on the edge of every separate stone and carried out by the thickness of the joint between the two drafts, makes a very decided flatter band between the two rougher faces— in such a wall, it is evident that, for the best effect of the whole building, a great deal too much is made of the size and shape of each separate block which makes it up. This comes very near to that other trick of "rustication," in which the edges of the stones are chiselled away so as to leave not so much the face of the stones in relief as the joints in intaglio, recessed below the face of the wall. It is nearly always better for the general effect that the walls should be uniform in surface, the joints of the stones comparatively ignored and the individuality of the different blocks emphasized only by their difference in color and their slight, almost imperceptible difference of plane. Such irregularities as these add immeasurably to the charm of the work, but their very effectiveness is diminished greatly by the framing in of each stone by the strongly marked draft. On the other hand, a draft is of almost inestimable value in those numerous parts of the building where an architectural member is to be strongly insisted on. Thus, if we take one corner of a building where a large and bold bead is worked vertically from top to bottom of the wall, which bead may, by the addition of a moulded base and a sculptured cap, become what is known as an angle-shaft, or which may even, by a still more decided deepening of the quirks which separate it from the body of the wall, become what is known as a nook-shaft, it will be seen plainly that the rougher surface of the stone must be tamed down, in a sense, in order that the architectural member may have its due effect. The verticalities of the lines of the angle bead and its quirks cannot be left at the mercy of the irregularities of the hammer-dressed or pointed surface; it is assumed that the work is on too small a scale for that. If, indeed, the bead is two feet in diameter, a different treatment may be possible; but that is not now the assumption. It will be found that as the bead with its accompanying mouldings require to be worked with the chisel, so these features also require to be finely worked and strongly marked by the similar chiselling of the small portion of the flat surface of the wall on either side. A rougher, more cottage-like treatment may be thought of in which such refinements would not be needed; ordinarily, and especially in city work, it will be found quite necessary to give to the doorways and window openings such firmness of outline as will call for the treatment which is here explained. In these cases, so far from each stone being separated from all the other stones by its own firmly outlined draft, the wall may be considered as divided into certain very large tracts or compartments each framed in, or rather bordered by, the architectural members themselves and the peculiar treatment of the surface which combines with the modelling of that surface to give the architectural members their due weight in the structure. The very purpose of the angle-shaft, or pilaster—of the entablature and the stylobate (at least in walled structures), of the sill-course, lintel-course, wall-cornice, and base cornice; their very purpose and significance, is that framing, that expression of the artistic composition of the building, as distinguished from its merely constructional disposition which makes up so much of the art of architecture as relates to walled and roofed exteriors. It is this very organization of the architectural details and the necessity of displaying that organization which makes against the composition of rock-faced stone walling as suggested above, and it is true that those builders who of all men known to us have shown most strongly a sense of the architectural framework of a building, the builders of the great Gothic churches, never show any disposition to make use of rock-faced work in any exposed, adorned, or elaborated part of their structure.

To consider, then, what other methods there are of working the face of stone, methods familiar to all men and in constant use; to consider these and their relative value and their special characteristics, let it be noted that the tendency is towards a certain grooving or reeding of the surface of stone which may be very objectionable indeed—more objectionable by far than the most ill-managed, the

Fig. 8A.   Fig. 8B.

roughest and most exaggerated rock-faced work. Fig. 8 gives at A a section through a piece of stone which has been finished by the drove chisel, and at B a section through a similar piece of stone which has been finished by the tooth chisel. The fact that surface A is worked sidewise, and surface B endwise; or at least that they are worked in different ways, each blow of the chisel in A working across the groove which it cuts and producing a sort of wave form with a long downward and a shorter upward slope; whereas, in B, each tooth of the chisel cuts its own groove lengthwise, producing a V-shaped groove not very deep, but very sharp at the bottom, the stone between the two adjoining grooves breaking away in an approximately rounded surface and resulting in a section which has been compared aptly enough to "the corduroy of the stone cutter's trousers,"—that fact is inessential to our present purpose. A stone which is in process of being finished by either of these methods, or by both of them combined, is a stone that is being spoiled in nine cases out of ten. The grooved or ribbed pattern drawn over the whole surface of the stone, or over so much of its surface as is enclosed within the draft, is as nearly ugly as the surface of a fair block of cut sandstone can possibly be. The ribs are, of course, almost inevitably carried continuously from top to bottom, or end to end horizontally, and it will become as a matter of course the object and the pride of the workman to make these ribs parallel and beautifully regular from edge to edge. The drove chisel is used with perhaps a little more reason and moderation, but that also is a tool liable to serious abuse. When we see a bead two inches in diameter or thereabout, and therefore a somewhat delicate member—when we see such a bead cut by the drove chisel into a series of hollow channels, so that from a bead the member in question has been brought to a somewhat irregular and unseemly polygon, then we feel the full force of the objection to the drove chisel and the danger of its employment; see Fig. 9. By

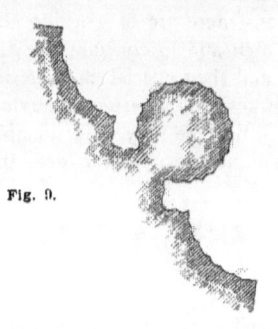

Fig. 9.

either of these methods carried to the extreme which we are now supposing, the beauty of the stone is almost wholly destroyed. This is a very serious consideration; for the superiority of stone over other materials—the one thing which keeps it in the front of all materials for walling which the world knows, and which makes stone building in the universal estimation of mankind the noblest that exists—is the beauty of the material itself no matter how its surface may be treated. From the rough block to the most elaborately carved panel, the surface of stone is lovely if it has only half a chance allowed it! And the surface which we ought to study, to imitate which we ought to strive, is the surface of a stone which has lain for two hundred years in a wall and which has weathered perfectly well. That is to say, if we knew the trick we would all of us reproduce the weather-worn surface of a stone upon which the weather has had no radically disintegrating or otherwise destructive effect. Go to the limestone wall of Rheims Cathedral, or the sandstone wall of Strasburg Cathedral, or the granite wall of Dol Cathedral, selecting sections of the building which are known not to have been rebuilt or refaced, and where the stone has met the weather for six hundred years, and you will see a surface which is the most beautiful that man can devise. In color and in texture, if that word may be employed; that is to say, in grain, in roughness and in smoothness, that stone will have the ideal face for the decorative building of the future, if only we could reproduce that face. Older buildings than these it is hardly safe to examine, for those of classical antiquity have been despoiled of their surfaces by the violence of man during the Dark Ages, or, if in better condition, have been saved only by partial interment; or else, finally, they are known or suspected to have been so far shielded by paint or by surfaces of stucco covered with paint that the full effect of weathering has not been felt by them. Still, however, marble is to be seen in the highest possible perfection in the ruins of Greece; peperino and travertine are also splendid among the ruins of Roman monuments, and these especially in the warmer and less rainy climates of what was once the Roman world. The stone-built châteaux and churches of the northern Renaissance in Europe, and of the Roman palaces of the seventeenth century were once equally worthy of study with the earlier monuments; but there is to be feared a certain watchful care, during the last forty years, on the part of their guardians and custodians which has kept the stone from weathering naturally and maintained it always in a condition of high finish incompatible with the true growing old, with the true ripening of the surface.

This surface when found and examined will prove to be somewhat of the nature of a solid and well-made paper of coarse grain, but not in a perfectly true plane; that is to say, there will be little wavy irregularities, slight and shallow hollows, slight and imperceptible ridges, or mound-like projections with which the whole surface is modulated, while every part of this so modulated surface is more minutely diversified by the grain which has been already compared to that of paper. In short, the stone will be found to be something like the surface of water which the wind has raised into waves, every great wave rippled into a million little ones; but then the waves of the stone are so slight and gradual that the eye does not detect them except in the general effect of causing a charming modulation over the whole surface of the wall. It may be impossible to give this general modulation to newly-faced work, but the slightly diversified, the grained and the roughened flat surface is within our reach, and there are different ways of producing it. What is called sparrow-billed or picked work would be excellent but that the blow of each separate point of the many which strike the stone makes not only a depression in the stone but also a broken or bruised spot which is unpleasant at first and does not lose, sometimes for thirty years, the appearance of an injury—a jar, or disintegrated patch—an effect the very opposite of the strong and enduring character which the stonework should always retain. If it were possible to finish the surface of stone with minute depressions without those bruised or shaken appearances, this would be a good method to resort to. Even as it is it is defensible. Pointed work, that is to say, the preparation of a surface by means of the steel chisel which has a square, blunt point instead of the long and thin cutting edge, is open to the same objection of seeming to bruise the stone. It is and must be in continual use for the second step in the preparation of stone. That is to say, that after the stone has been brought approximately to its surface, either by the hammer or by the broad smooth chisel used as described above in what was

said about rock-faced work, the pointing tool is then used with a
vigorous swing of the mallet to drive it to bring the stone nearer to
a smooth and uniform surface. At this point the work often stops,
and, as has been said, the pointed surface is not apt to look bad. But
then it is this bruised and shaken look to which such strong objection has been taken.

As for the tooth-chisel, there is one way in which it
can be used to great effect. It was tried in a very elaborate piece of stonework in 1873, and with results so good
that it is safe to urge its further adoption. Suppose that
the tooth-chisel is struck once along the surface of an approximately smooth stone. The look of the small surface so struck will be,
of course, that of a series of very slightly emphasized ribs or reeds
parallel to each other. Suppose that the surface so prepared is of the
width of the chisel, perhaps, an inch and a half, and, in length, about
an inch. Suppose, now, that the chisel is set upon the stone again at
a very slight angle with the position it occupied before, and that again
it be struck along the surface for the distance of about an inch. Let
this be repeated constantly over and over again ; every new inch long
patch of ribbed surface invading a little the one last made, so that no
one of these patches shall remain a parallelogram an inch wide by the
width of the chisel in length, but that all shall overlap and invade one
another. The surface so produced may, perhaps, be expressed by the
sketch, Fig. 10, which, of course, does not really represent it—as, indeed, nothing but a photograph, and that of the full size, could really

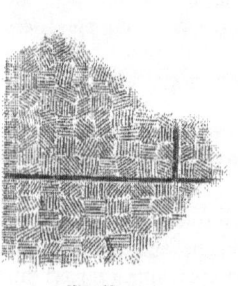

Fig. 10.

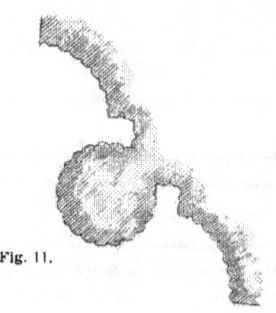

Fig. 11.

do. If now, as in the illustration, such a surface be bounded by a
carefully cut draft worked with the drove chisel, but this only on the
side adjoining the jamb of the door or window opening, or the outside angle of the building, or a part of it, then your wall-surface is
what you will like best, in the long run. In the diagram, Fig. 11,
the difference between the drove work and the toothed work is in-

adequately rendered; the former being comparatively smooth with hardly any perceptible variety of shade caused by the shallow scoops, whereas the latter forming a greater part of the surface of the wall is covered everywhere with fine, hair-like shadows drawn by the ridges left beneath the teeth of the chisel. The drafts, then, are, or seem to be essentially smooth, whereas the smoothness of the body of the wall is rather that produced by an infinitely varied hatching of short dark lines breaking each other at all angles. On the other hand, the diagram exaggerates the emphasis of the joints. If they are pointed in a judicious way they will not catch the eye noticeably.

From coarser to finer we have been approaching the conditions under which stone has to be handled in the most delicate way; that is to say, when it is to be carved into ornamental patterns. An approach to this refinement of work is essential in the case of ornamental mouldings, such as those which enter into the entablature of a classical building, or into the window jambs and door cheeks of a decorative structure of any epoch. The more elaborate the groups of mouldings, as in English Gothic arcades, as between nave and aisles in a fourteenth century cathedral, the more essential it is that the touch of the chisel upon each rounded surface should be the more subtle and delicate, and at the same time the most effective possible. If, indeed, we had an uninjured, unbroken group of fourteenth century mouldings to study we should probably find the highest possible expressiveness and vigor in French work, and the particular cut by which that expressiveness was produced should be the subject of our thoughtful study. Consider, for instance, the case of a rounded moulding, either of a bead or of one of those surfaces of double curvature— those whose profile is expressed by the familiar term, an S curve; the tool by which such a surface is cut nowadays will generally be a narrow, flat chisel, and it appears that the same tool must have been used in ancient times that is used to-day. It is doubtful if the gauge or chisel of curved edge was ever in use for stone-cutting on a large scale. The flat chisel then being the tool used, a good surface of rounded section will tend to approximate only to these rounded surfaces and to make of a bead not a true cylinder but rather a polygon of an indefinite and varying number of sides. This is not to be regretted so long as the non-circular character of the supposed cylinder is not too visible. Thus, in Figs. 9 and 11 the two extremes of ugly work are seen, the one having been produced by the drove-chisel, the other by the tooth-chisel; the one fluted, the other reeded. Which of the two is the uglier in actual execution it is difficult to say; probably the reeded one. Fig. 11 is apt to be the most detestable, because the reeds are gloried in by the stone-cutters who seem to think their work is the better, the more strongly and viciously these ridges manifest themselves. But if in place of these exaggerations, the bead,

16-22 William Street and another.

The left-hand building, drove-work or machine-tooling in imitation of that. The right-hand building has the large panelled pilaster, the deep recess, and the draft around the rusticated blocks, all drove or machine-worked in imitation of drove-work. The projecting parts of the rusticated blocks are sparrow-billed or pecked. The mouldings of carved surface are also drove. The lines of the tooling are carried in different directions, and are of different degrees of fineness, and this would add greatly to the effect if the tooling were done delicately by hand.

33 Wall Street.

Courses of stone alternately tooled (probably machine-tooled) and roughly pecked or sparrow-billed, with a tooled draft about each stone so treated.

PORCH OF DELMONICO'S.
Beaver St.

Shaft of column finished in drove-work, or a machine-wrought imitation of it. The surface has been lowered or cut away so little that some of the pits left from the original pointing of the block are still visible. This adds greatly to the effect of the shaft.

45 and 47 Wall Street.

Rock-faced work in the archivolts between the carved hood-moulding and the mould-ings of the intrados; also in lintel of windows below or in filling between that lintel and sill above; also in upper story. The remainder tooled in different ways. Stone of two colors used

46 Wall Street

Rock-faced work in piers, contrasting with tooled work of inner jambs of windows and of moulded base-course a little above the side walk.

46 Wall Street.

Rock-faced work in a pier, each stone of the full width of the pier; contrasted with roughly tooled moulded watertable.

large or small in diameter, is cut as closely to the cylinder as the flat chisel can do it with reasonable speed and facility, the ideal surface is probably reached. It would be a feeble and uninteresting building, indeed, in which every bead were cut as true to the curve as if it had been turned! The coves, too, and the mouldings of double and of complex curvature, are all better if they are off the curve a little. One reason why carved work is better than cast work, and hand-wrought work generally better than struck, stamped, or otherwise machine-made work, is that the hand does not give absolutely correct curvature to its products. And this same state of conditions apply perfectly to the question of sculpture as it is applied to architectural matters. With statuary added to buildings—set up on the top of parapets or in niches in the wall, we are not now concerned, but architectural sculpture, so-called, that which is as it were a development of the architectural members themselves, is to be treated with the chisel exactly as delicately moulded work is to be treated, and left from the cutting tool without the invasion of sandpaper or of any smoothing process whatever.

Russell Sturgis.

THE RETURN TO STONE.

EVEN the wayfarer must have noticed lately that more stone buildings have been erected in New York and in other large centers of the country than formerly. A few years ago all or nearly all the buildings the wayfarer saw in course of construction were of brick and terra cotta. Perhaps even he might then have marvelled at this, particularly if his memory were sufficiently long to reach back twenty-five years or more to the time when every considerable residence, and still more every commercial building of note was erected of stone—either the brown-stone of those rows of becolumned and bestooped "fronts" that still give an air of sad sobriety to many of our streets, or the white marble of those "survivals" which may be encountered even to this day here and there, such as the Park National Bank, the old Stewart mansion, or the still older Fifth Avenue Hotel.

The older generation that put up and "put up with" these structures no doubt were poor artists and even poorer constructors, but it is perfectly clear they hankered after stone, or to speak more correctly a surface of that material, when they attempted to do anything fine. In this they were right. Probably it may be said that no architect who has not a "sense" for stone rises above the subordinate grades of his profession. Certainly no nation that has not possessed that sense has attained to the monumental rank in the history of architecture. Stone is the "epic" material, and the choice of any other has in all times and places acted as a bar to work of the highest character.

THE NEW COURT HOUSE
(Of Marble).

Baltimore, Md.

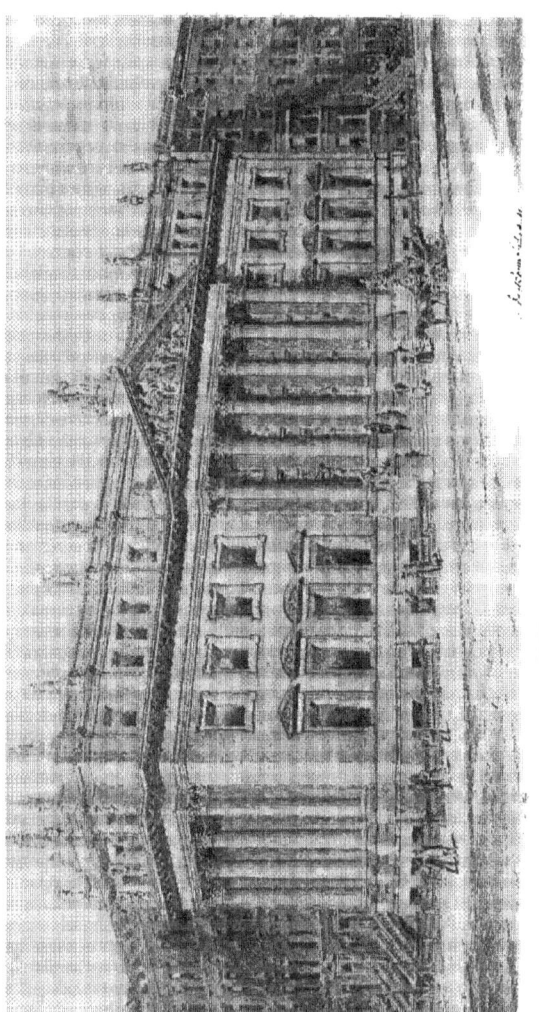

APPELLATE COURT BUILDING
(Of Dover Marble).

Madison Ave. and 25th St., New York City.

James Brown Lord, Architect.

NEW OFFICE BUILDING
(Of Indiana Limestone),
N. W. Cor. Waverly Place and Broadway, N. Y.   Clarence L. Sefert, Architect.

RESIDENCE OF HENRY T. SLOANE

(Of Indiana Limestone),

Carrere & Hastings, Architects.

9 East 72d St., New York City.

I have no distaste for the humbler materials. One cannot deny the charm of old Dutch or English brick-work, or fail to appreciate the beauty and fitness of Swiss and Scandinavian timber buildings. But they are not of the first order. Even as more modern things go there is much to admire in the terra cotta work of the "eighties" that covers this country from Maine to California. But in my judgment, and I believe in the opinion of others, the material was over-worked. Cheapness and facility, two of the dangerous qualities of plastic clay, led architects and public astray. It was so easy to do the "excessive," and, as Dr. Johnson pointed out long ago, there is something in human nature that delights in making people stare. Terra cotta just suited this instinct, and many of the buildings in which it was used seemed to have been designed with this object in view.

I think, therefore, that the increasing favor which stone is now finding in the estimation of our architects and our public is an encouraging sign, and the "return" ought to be furthered by everybody. In architecture, I know, choice is mostly dictated by fad and fashion. Terra cotta had its day, and after a time a change of some kind becomes desirable. I believe, however, that the return to stone is founded on something deeper than the modish taste of the hour. Every year our architects are being called upon to do work of greater importance than before. Our commercial buildings become huger piles, and our private residences of a more sumptuous and palatial character. For this reason the choice of stone is in a sense imposed upon us. The twenty-story office building in brick cannot be saved, even by great care in design, from a certain thinness and cheap look. If anyone doubts this, let him compare, for instance, the Park Row Building with its towering neighbor the St. Paul Building. The eye can almost take in both at a glance. One is brick, the other stone, speaking of the façades. How much more substantial and monumental the stone building appears. There is not much to boast of in either of the designs. They are both rather meagre, but in the brick building, such design as there is seems to be almost killed by the material, whereas in the stone building, the material decidedly strengthens and emphasizes whatever there is of design.

Left to themselves, architects probably would always choose the nobler material. They cannot, however, ignore the owner with his desire for economy, but, under present conditions, the saving effected by discarding stone is so comparatively slight and amounts to so much less than it used to, that we doubt whether it pays to accept it.

By employing a good architect the owner practically confesses that there is a certain monetary value in a handsome well-appearing building. Actual experience shows this to be a fact, and every real estate agent knows that tenants are attracted by a handsome front. To build in stone is only to carry out this idea to the fullest.

Moreover, the stone building "lasts" longer. I am not speaking, of course, of physical durability, but of those "wearing" qualities to the eye which keep a building from taking on an old-fashioned appearance. This is a very important matter for an owner to consider. It figures in his rent roll, for people, especially the American people, object to antiquated looking things. After standing twenty years a stone building will look very much more modern than a building of other material. To make this plain, consider how very much more ancient the old Custom House on Wall Street, or the old Astor House would appear if they were constructed of brick, or, compare, for example, the Park National Building with the Evening Post Building. Nine passers-by out of ten, I judge, would regard the older building as the more recent, unless their judgment were influenced by the greater height of the one than the other. Considerations of this sort, I think, would outweigh with most owners the bill for the extra cost of stone.

And let it not be forgotten this extra cost amounts to less than it did. The application of machinery to nearly all the operations of quarrying and dressing, as well as cheaper transportation, more economical methods of handling, have greatly reduced the cost of stone work. Stone carving, moreover, is a craft very much better understood than it was twenty years ago. There are more firms in the business, and they are all equipped with large plants and are provided with abundance of labor.

The illustrations accompanying these remarks exhibit some of the recent buildings in which stone has been used. They are not given primarily for the artistic value of their design, but rather "pour encourager les autres," and to show how in all classes of buildings alike, public, commercial, and private, our architects are returning to stone.

W. S. Adams.

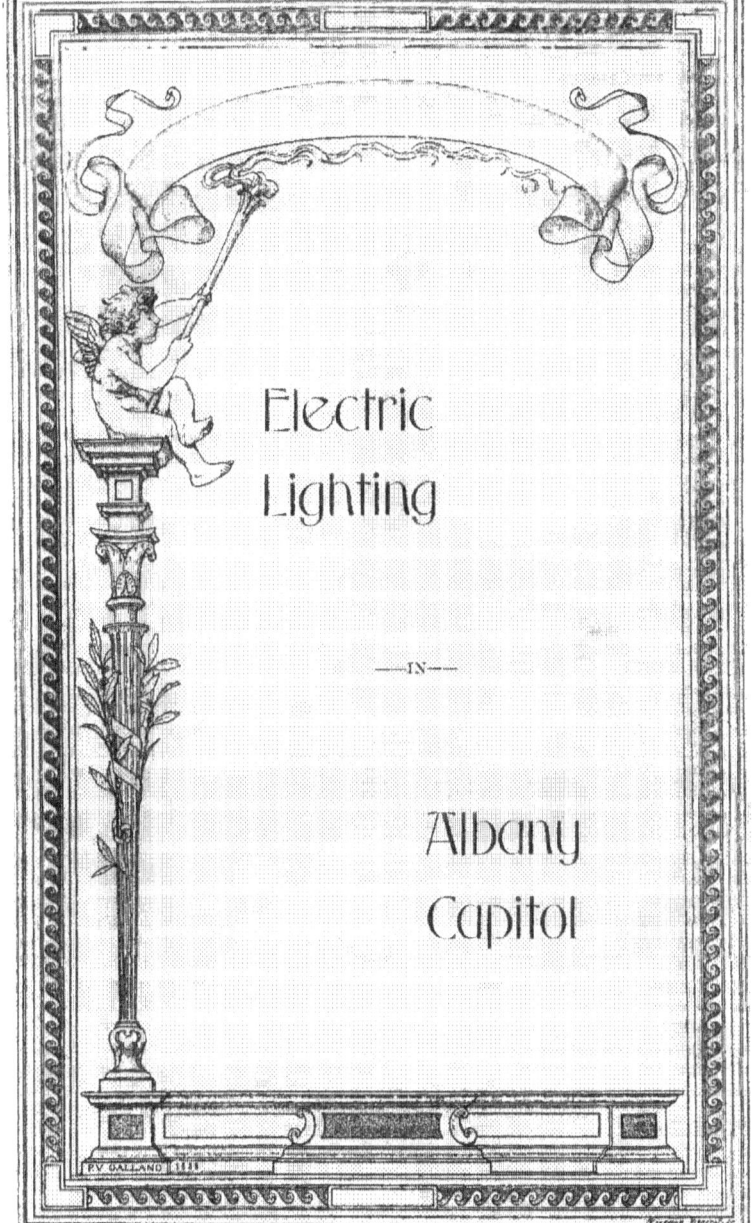

Electric

Lighting

—IN—

Albany

Capitol

ON THE EASTERN APPROACH.
CAPITOL, ALBANY, N. Y.

ON THE EASTERN APPROACH.
CAPITOL, ALBANY, N. Y.

ON THE EASTERN APPROACH.
CAPITOL, ALBANY, N. Y.

ON THE EAST TERRACE.
CAPITOL, ALBANY, N. Y.

THE EASTERN POST OF THE NORTH ENTRANCE DRIVEWAY.
CAPITOL, ALBANY, N. Y.

ON THE WESTERN ENTRANCE.
CAPITOL, ALBANY, N. Y.

ON THE TERRACE OF THE DRIVEWAY.
CAPITOL, ALBANY, N. Y.

INTERIOR ELECTRIC LIGHT FIXTURES.
CAPITOL, ALBANY, N. Y.

INTERIOR ELECTRIC LIGHT FIXTURES.
CAPITOL, ALBANY, N. Y.

INTERIOR ELECTRIC LIGHT FIXTURES.
CAPITOL, ALBANY, N. Y.

ELECTRIC LIGHTING IN THE ALBANY CAPITOL.

IN this age, more than at any other previous time, science leads the way only to be closely followed by art. In the olden days art was most frequently conceived by the master mind and then the object was wrought principally for the sake of art, applying the idea mainly to buildings and a few household utensils, while scientific discoveries led to nothing save their practical application and that in the plainest sort of way. Science and art were infrequently combined then; but now art finds a means to link itself with scientific productions shortly after the announcement of the discovery. The two are linked more closely day by day, and, as one person has remarked: "America will shortly prove itself the Louvre of the world," so it is that to attain the beautiful in all things is a chief desideratum of the educated persons living in this country; that is, perfection is the object to be attained and perfection is art, for is not art represented by the perfection in building, in stone-cutting, in the printing of a book, or in the correct completion of any minor objects.

Following this line of thought, the artistic treatment of the new electric lamps at the Capitol Building of the Empire State are presented as an example, being fine illustrations of artistic designing and mechanical construction, and they add materially to the appearance of the imposing structure. In designing them prejudices had to be overcome, for it is not so easy to conceive the form for a lamp which, by its modern conception, is distinctly removed from the types in use ages ago, those which, when serving to burn candles or oil, frequently offered the artisan a form linked to mythology, and such popular conceptions as the flame of the torch of victory, of the sacrificial fire, or else symbolizing literature. Lamps of the ancients are accepted as beautiful forms for decorative designs in carving, but it is hard to regard the electric lamp in the same category. The work imposed upon the designer of these lamps was, therefore, much more difficult than had science presented him with some other form of lighting.

There is no other building in this country which has such an effective system of lighting, or that has such a massive, dignified and elegant electrolier system for distributing its light to the entire building. When all the fixtures are giving forth their rays there is presented the most beautiful exhibition of electric lighting that has ever been produced. They are grouped about the edifice, each with its many globes of light which in the darkness of night appear as "numerous as glittering gems of morning dew." The impression is that of a view conjured from the land of elves.

The effect of the lighting of the Western Staircase is perfection. An absence of all shadow is noted, demonstrating the thought that had been given to the location of the fixtures in order to avoid the usual defects encountered, and which in this case results in a more perfect light being thrown upon the elegant carvings than can be obtained upon the most brilliant, sunny day. All the outside posts and the portico fixtures are made of real bronze of the United States Government standard, exposure to the weather adding beauty to this metal, and age producing the rich, greenish effect peculiar only to high grade real bronze.

The architecture of the building has been closely followed in the designing of all the fixtures; the modern Romanesque detail has been worked out in a most graceful manner, and they represent strikingly perfect examples of art work in bronze. The enormous size and weight of several of these posts, and their perfect construction, give to them an additional value of merit, in so much that large pieces of this kind are very rarely produced without defects, whereas there are few, if any, defects to be noted by a critical examination. Credit for this skill in casting, as well as for the cleverness of the designs, is due entirely to The Mitchell-Vance Company of New York City, and these lamps illustrate the progress and ability of Americans.

The large post, designated for convenience as No. 1, is the first fixture encountered at the foot of the steps to the Eastern Approach. The total weight of this fixture, as it appears upon the post, is over one ton. It is supplied with fifty 16-candle power electric lamps, giving a total of eight hundred candle power. Design No. 2 is the large three-post standard at the head of the first run of the steps to the Eastern Approach. It is the largest of all the fixtures, and is readily recognized by the beautiful detail of work shown upon its base; the coat-of-arms of the State is here represented, and it has been admitted by experts that the modelling of this coat-of-arms is the most perfect that has ever been executed. It is unquestionably a most beautiful work of art, and will be appreciated by the many competent critics who will pass upon it. The general effect of the fixture is admirable and it is entirely appropriate to its location. There are fifty lights within the globe of this fixture with a capacity similar to that of post No. 1, but its power is capable of being increased at any time. The total height of this fixture is nine feet and a half, and the weight about 3,000 pounds.

Design No. 3 is the third post on the stairs of the same approach, and in the opinion of many it is considered the most artistic of all the posts. It certainly is novel and yet graceful in design, denoting a bold, yet consistent, departure from the conventional patterns of post lights. Following this is Design No. 4 of the 30-light large standards, which are to be seen on the terraces of the driveway, the design of which is so appropriate to their locations that it is evident that their form was in the eye of the architect when creating the design of the stone-work for their foundation.

The fifth design represents the fifteen-light small standards on the east, north and south terraces, and, like the preceding design, shows the thought of the designer in constructing them so as to be in entire harmony with the surroundings of their location. Design No. 6 represents the large fixture on the eastern post of the north and south entrance driveway. Design No. 7 represents the fifty-light massive standards at either side of the western entrance steps. They differ in general design from any of the other lamp posts of the building, and are perfect specimens of Romanesque lamps, executed with great mechanical skill. Their weight is about one ton each.

The interior fixtures are made of brass, finished in a satin effect, great care having been taken in the construction to have nothing save the heaviest grade of metal in all the parts.

A comparison of the new fixtures with the old ones in the same building, or with those in some of the finest edifices in this country or abroad particularly, demonstrates to the most casual observer the superiority in design and construction of those recently supplied, and particularly pleasing is their suitability to the location. Some of these lamps cost three or four thousand dollars apiece, and the total cost of the work was about $60,000.

The entire contract was constructed and placed in position complete within seventy-five days, which is a phenomenally short time for such a great amount of work. No factory abroad and doubtless none other in America could have accomplished such a feat, and this stands among the few examples of large undertakings accomplished at the time set. There are no doubt fine lamps abroad, but in electric illumination there are no superiors to the ones described.

While the preceding article illustrates the progress of an important American industry, and records the wonderful achievements of The Mitchell-Vance Company in that branch of electric light fixture construction which demands the accomplishment of great artistic and mechanical results, yet the excellency of their goods is not confined alone to works of such magnitude: a similar, perhaps greater proficiency, characterizes their varied productions of electric light and gas fixtures of the more conventional kind, which are used in residences, churches, club houses and theatres. Of this class of goods their patterns and styles are legion, each one bearing the imprint of the artist's knowledge of its proper fitness for the condition it is designed to meet. In this particular, The Mitchell-Vance Company appear to have made special study, as the demands of the architects and decorators of to-day are that in modern buildings the fixture producing the artificial light must needs be a consistent, yet not too important feature of the surrounding decorations.

For many years this Company has enjoyed the distinction of being the largest manufacturers of these goods in the world, and under the present progressive management of the organization, they are continually adding to its reputation by reason of the high artistic quality and construction of their productions. In the execution of their work, one striking feature is always manifested, that whether tne fixture be an intricate and costly one for the adornment of a mansion, or of the simpler and less expensive kind for the moderate dwelling, the same care is exercised in the correctness of its design and a uniform consistency is shown in the completeness and finish of its detail. This distinctive feature is largely responsible for their success.

In addition to the manufacture of lighting fixtures, The Mitchell-Vance Company execute all descriptions of ornamental cast and wrought bronze work for stairs and office rails, gates, doors, posts, tablets, and clock frames, in accordance with architects' and decorators' own designs and suggestions. This branch of manufacture has been followed in a moderate way during the fifty years that the concern has been established, but within the past year or two, this department has been enlarged and made an important and successful feature of their business.

With their extensive equipment and plant, there is no undertaking too great for their resources, and the thorough business-like policy of the concern is demonstrated in its careful and courteous attention to the smallest wants and desires of its patrons.

STAIRCASE AT FRANKFORT, GERMANY.

STAIRCASE AT RIOM. PUY DE DOME, FRANCE.

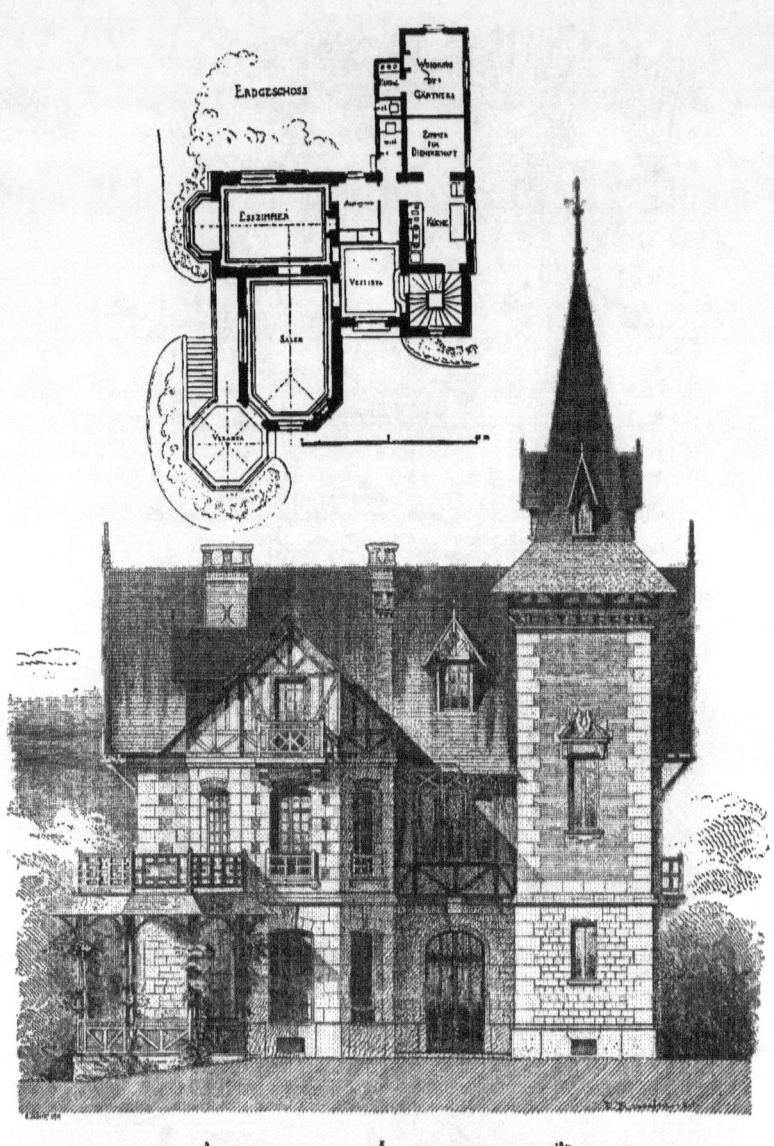

ERDGESCHOSS

FRENCH VILLA.

J. Guette, Paris.

The

Architectural Record.

VOL. IX.   JANUARY, 1900.   No. 3.

An Unscientific Enquiry Into Fireproof Building.

WHEN we congratulate ourselves on modern advance in humanity, we are apt to think of theological and other burnings alive as the type and culmination of all the horrors of the past. And yet we burn each other alive in large, elegant, and costly modern hotels; offering only the alternative of deliberate suicide by the always frightful leap from a height.

As this is written it is four months since the hideous catastrophe, in which a hotel only a quarter of a century old and carefully built, for a hotel—kept up in good style—inhabited by wealthy and critical people—managed always by well-known hotel men—was destroyed in an hour with two score of its inmates. Such are, however, our municipal and our national characteristics that no full or authentic account of it has ever been made public, or, so far as is known, brought together. The hasty and generally mistrusted accounts of next morning's newspapers are all that there is for the public in general to build upon. It is, therefore, not altogether surprising that the memory of this horrible incident grows dim, and that there is visible no new, no unusual demand, resulting from it, for protection against such incidents in the future. Sagacious New Yorkers walk their avenues and streets, looking up at this hotel or that, and saying to each other with anticipatory distress: "It is a mere question of months or of days when this hotel goes, and that—which do you say will go first?—they are all fire-traps together, and the next great burning may be worse than the last." It is not, however, apparent that the travelling public avoid the houses which are notoriously structures of carpentry work skilfully combined to form combustible flues, horizontal and vertical, along which fire may run swiftly and effectively. It does not appear that the travelers' books of such hotels as these are left blank while those of the newer and less combustible buildings are filled with travelers' names. The very New Yorker who has counted up in his mind the carpenter-built hotels which will burn brilliantly when next a curtain takes fire, will call upon his out-of-town friend residing in one of them, and will never think of calling to his attention the well-known character of the building he is in.

And yet let the reader think for a moment of the scene in the fifth and in the sixth story corridors of that hotel on the 17th of March, 1899. Let him picture the scenes that have been described and the other scenes which it requires but little imagination to picture to one's self. The woman standing at a window and waving at brief intervals a white handkerchief to attract the attention of the managers of the very few extension ladders which were on the spot; the woman who, having gained the assurance that she was seen, deliberately shut down the window in front of her to stop the draught; the woman who is described by one who escaped, going on her hands and knees along the fifth story corridor, thus keeping her face below the stratum of smoke and feeling blindly in that noon-day darkness for some means of descent to the street; the women who, as is known from the part of the hotel which they occupied and the point in the cellar where their bodies were found, went wandering about those corridors of the sixth story hoping to find a fire-escape at the southern end since that at the northern end was impassable and the stairs were already destroyed; the woman who escaped from the building by the aid of outsiders, and who died within a few days of her burns, as a trustworthy physician has stated. Put out of sight, if you choose, the more merciful deaths, those by suffocation from smoke, those by falls upon the ground, or the railing, or the stone paved areas; though these also, with their accompaniment of anxious expectancy, of fright, of bewilderment and of long continued anticipation, are not what most people would consider easy deaths; put these out of sight: think only of the deaths by fire, and then try to answer the question whether our material civilization is all that we imagine it to be. People of European stock living in America have six thousand years of tolerably unbroken building traditions behind them; and in the new country they have wealth at their disposal and an absolutely unlimited choice of material; with the result that there are not twenty buildings in New York in which one may sleep secure.

It is not long since there was a fire in one of the rooms in the long and narrow building which fronts on the garden of the Palais Royal and separates it from the Rue Valois. Americans sitting in the garden at the table of their café watched the fire, the primitive means adopted for extinguishing it, the increase in the jets of flame and smoke which burst from the windows, and anticipated a conflagration on a scale to which they were accustomed at home—when, suddenly, one of them noticed the inhabitants of the apartment immediately above, looking out of the window and thus enjoying the sight just so far as the rising smoke and heat would allow them. Indeed, the little garden engines employed did the work, or the work was done for them by pails of water, and the fire went out. One of these Americans was a scientific man, and, therefore, accustomed to enquire into things; although he was by no means primarily interested in matters of building. He enquired into the structures of the floors in this and other Parisian buildings—not of the most recent date nor of the most sumptuous character, nor of the most approved modern construction. He found that floors and walls alike were commonly devoid of combustible material. He found that when the burning curtain had communicated fire to the wooden dado and to some pieces of furniture, there was nothing left for the fire to do, and that it died down. He found that the flame which burst out of the window and looked so furious, was as brief and hardly hotter than that which one can make with a pile of newspapers; he found, in short, that Paris had not been so built up that accident or carelessness can burn it down again, and that the municipality may, perhaps, be right in spending no time or thought in organizing a fire department on American principles. But also he found that the materials used were inexpensive and the construction adopted was simple, familiar to the masons and to the fitters of light ironwork, and quickly put into place. He found moreover (and this is what surprised him, the American, most) that all of this incombustible construction was light. As he himself expressed it, afterwards, to an American architect of his acquaintance: "It is a light and cheap construction—why do you fellows insist on a heavy and expensive construction?" It is, indeed, the curse of American building that it draws its traditional inspiration not from the continent of Europe but from Great Britain, and that it is not familiar wih masonry. The devices to which our builders resort to make a structure that will not catch fire are something ludicrous when their monstrous cost is compared with the cheap and matter-of-course expedients resorted to in France and Italy. Cast iron first and wrought iron afterwards—these novel materials, and not the simple traditions of sixty centuries in the way of masonry, are what our carpenter-taught builders resorted to when they were told to build fireproof buildings.

It is due to James Bogardus to say that he always asserted the resisting power of cast iron when exposed to the heat of a conflagration. He it was who, in the first half of this century, when rolled and wrought iron as a practical part of a building was not known, insisted upon the value of cast iron as a building material; who built a four-story building in Centre Street, about 1847, with two outside faces made up of it; and who circulated a pamphlet showing that same building in a diagram as it would have appeared had many of the uprights and many of the interties been taken away. He was eager to prove the value of a construction of posts and ties all firmly bolted together, and which would themselves provide what he thought would meet modern requirements, namely, a very tenacious and economical system of building which, in most cases, fire would hardly affect. Moreover, he and his assistants were extremely uncompromising, and the writer well remembers in 1856, or thereabouts, the violent protest of one of these, a mathematician named Thompson, he being told that cast iron might do for shop fronts. The whole or none, was the Bogardus cry at this time. The cast iron façades which were so commonly built in New York from 1860 to 1875 were really originated by the inventor whom we have named.

Bogardus was so far right that the jeremiads of those who feared fire more than they trusted metal were largely disproved by the event. When the Boston fire swept away acres of wooden buildings with cut granite exteriors, its work was done thoroughly. A week later nothing stood erect in the burnt district except towering and tottering angles where two brick walls mutually sustained one another, and a number of cast iron shop fronts. Undoubtedly, these latter would have shown distortion, warpings, and twistings had they been carefully measured and aligned, but they stood, and there seemed no reason why the superincumbent walls should have fallen from them except that the burning floors dragged them down. Wooden beams anchored to the walls may help to hold those slender walls in place when all goes well, but they also serve to tear them from their places and to crumble them into ruin when there is a fire.

Since that time the test has been applied many times, and both wrought iron and cast iron have shown their power of resistance to heat to be greater than was anticipated. The same lesson seems now to have been learned in regard to steel. It is not the purpose of this paper to apply statistics at all; the general admission is that, while it is altogether advisable to protect the iron or steel of the framework in every possible way, by terra cotta, or the like, it is still evident that there remain large powers of resistance in the metal framework itself. So far as this goes, the skyscrapers may still be built twenty-five stories high without unreasonable risk.

There still remains the question, not very easy to answer: What is the utility of such resisting powers in the framework, if the building, apart from the framework, is so combustible as to be destroyed, within; or its costly outside to be hopelessly defaced, by a not very formidable conflagration?

It has been shown very recently that a small, old-fashioned building burning hotly by the side of a modern office building, or opposite to it across the street, may send such jets of flame to lick the windowed fronts of its neighbor that glass gives way, sash takes fire, wooden flooring as it is often laid leads the flames horizontally along it, dados and door trims blaze up, and the furniture in the room joins in the burning, until a new blast of flame is generated within the building sufficient to rush furiously through open doors, and to beat down and sweep away those light partitions of wood and plate glass and to render nugatory those of light plaster blocks which separate offices. This is under the supposition that we are dealing with what is called a "fireproof building." It is commonly said, when the scoffer ridicules structures of this sort, and points out the immense amount of wood which is allowed within them, that this wood is so isolated piece from piece, and so fixed upon incombustible walls and floors that it may be counted out. It is evident that it will not take fire very readily; and from this the assumption is made that it will not burn at all, and is not to be feared. It is true, of course, that wooden flooring, if laid as it ought to be without air spaces and close against the solid bed of cement—that a wooden dado planted close against a brick wall, or with mortar filled in behind it, and connected with no other wood except the flooring and the window trims—that neither of these will burn readily. An accidental match thrown down before it is extinguished, a coal of fire snapping out of the grate, even a jet of flame from a gas fixture will fail to start a bad fire in the building. Window shades or light curtains may catch fire and burn up and such a room as we are imagining would be injured by smoke, but in no other way. Overheated or defective flues are not to be much feared in buildings of the modern type, because the flues are pretty sure not to be in close contact with anything that will burn. Granted all this, the possibility of a furious and very hot fire attacking the building from the outside has still to be reckoned with; and, if, as in a recent notable instance in New York, many of the above-named conditions of safety have been neglected, that attack may be nearly fatal to the structure. Against this danger there is nothing to be set up, except the substitution of that material which minds heat but little for those materials which cannot resist it for any length of time, together with the substitution inside the building of stuff that will not burn for that which will.

Let us then consider the thing in the abstract, and imagine ourselves for the moment public-spirited citizens, building for our own purposes but still public-spirited, having the spending of a deal of money in the "erection and completion," as the specifications say, of a big office building of the usual American type. That class of building is associated, at present, with more provision for fire-resistance than any other. Little as they deserve the name of being proof against fire, what has been done to make them so shows, well enough, what more may be done in the same direction.

Let us suppose that our building is to front on two of the narrower streets of that city; that is to say, that its windows will open upon a space from sixty to eighty feet in width to the opposite windows, rather than upon a great open square, or a street like Broad Street in New

York of quite unusual amplitude. As the building is to be high, it will probably rise above its immediate neighbors, and a few windows will be opened in the gable wall, helping to light the upper stories. The rear windows will look out upon an open yard of no great size which separates the building from its next neighbor in that direction; so that on the whole no window will be nearer than sixty feet to the opposite window, and none much more distant than that from such opposite window. Under these circumstances the very first question to settle will be: Shall there be iron shutters to the windows? In old times it was quite the rule to put up iron shutters in the front as well as in the rear of the simple buildings of the by-streets, and the fire department authorities used to object to these shutters until a fastening was introduced which could be opened easily from the exterior by a man on a ladder. Now they have pretty much disappeared from the fronts. The demand for a very large percentage of surface opened up in window space and filled with glass, has been the chief cause for the abandonment of these projections; and with this is to be counted the unmistakeable trend toward a certain elegance of aspect, in the courtyard wall as well as in the wall fronting on the street. Let anyone go into the Equitable Building, or the Mutual Life Insurance Company's building, or Aldrich Court, or the Metropolitan Life Insurance Company's building, in New York, and look out of the rear window upon the court surrounded everywhere with creamy white enamelled brick and treated with a good deal of elegance, and let him notice also how large a proportion of the masonry has been cut out for the sake of admitting light and how little there remains to receive shutters if thrown back against the wall. It will be hardly possible to force the builders of such buildings to add iron shutters of the usual hinged type. It will be felt that they disfigure the building too much, and also that there is no room for them, that they will be terribly in the way and can only be handled at all by means of some long iron hook or strip, some "blind adjuster" or "slide bar," which would hold them in a position nearly perpendicular to the face of the wall—which arrangement would be more disfiguring than any other. If, indeed, the piers could be so deep—or, in other words, if the wall screen where the windows are could be so deeply recessed—that the shutters could rest against the reveals or sides of these piers! This plan is impracticable, because such shutters, to be of any use in the way of protection against fire, must be in one fold or valve, so as to avoid the joint between two folds in the middle. Such shutters ought, indeed, to be received when closed in a large rebate, as shown in Fig. 1. In this manner alone can the joints between the shutter and the frame, or the sill, lintel and jamb, be made tolerably proof against the effects of heat which first warps the shutters and opens the joint, and then passes through that joint to destroy what is within. The "Underwriters'" shutter of wood covered with tin is really better than any iron shutter can be; but for exterior look it is not more likely to commend itself to the building or renting public. And it is to be remembered that, where such shutters overhang adjoining property, its owner has a right to object to and remove them. On the whole, therefore, it is really useless to consider as a practical possibility such shutters as these. The only protective shutters which can be supposed available under the circumstances are sliding or rolling shutters of some pattern. With the first, that is to say with shutters which slide horizontally into pockets reserved for them in the wall or pier, the difficulty is that the protection required by law for the steel column which forms the main upright of the building is seriously interfered with. In the more usual construction of the piers of such a building as we have in hand no such groove or pocket as would be necessary for the shutters could be reserved, without endangering the whole structure. There is also the difficulty that everywhere the piers would have to be a little wider than the windows which they separate, and

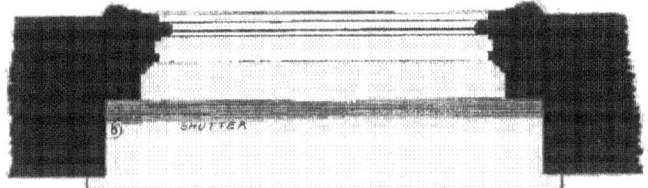

Fig. 1.--Tin-Covered Wooden Shutter, Hung in a Deep Rebate in the Outer Wall.

this is a serious difficulty. Granted that on the whole the total horizontal dimensions of the exterior wall in any story are divisible nearly equally between solids and openings, it still remains a serious hindrance to our design that we are compelled everywhere to couple a window with a pier a little wider than itself. It is not our possible artistic design alone that is affected. The required arrangement of windows in a given office may at any time be such that this disposition of sliding shutters will not succeed. Let us proceed to consider another one, namely, rolling shutters, such as are common in the fronts of shops opening directly on the street. The only difficulty with these is their cost. In other respects they are convenient enough. They are well out of the way when open and rolled up, and are easy to open and shut; moreover, they form an excellent protection against fire from the exterior, and in no respect more than in this, that they run in grooves and so make close connections with the jambs. In this respect they are superior to any hinged shutters now in use. They need no bolts nor catches; and there is no serious difficulty to the fire department in opening them from the outside. The pocket in which is situated the roller is removed from the constructional piers of the building and is contained in the panel between each pair of windows, that is to say, it is above the head of each window in its turn. The cost, however, is very heavy indeed, and it is extremely unlikely that any legislature will pass and obtain the governor's consent to a bill making such shutters compulsory. For skylights, indeed, such shutters should be made compulsory, nor would it be a hardship to anybody to so protect his roof, which is likely to prove one of the most vulnerable parts of the building in the case of a fire in an adjoining building of the same or a greater height.

In the absence of shutters, then, what is the proper expedient? How is fire raging in an opposite or adjoining building to be kept out of the interior of our own building? There is the device of wire glass, by which a sheet of glass has in its very substance a system of netted wire work with meshes so large that they do not obstruct the light to any perceptible extent. Experiment seems to have proved that such glass will resist a very intense heat without giving away. It will be defaced and disfigured, and its transparent quality pretty much destroyed wherever a sheet of flame strikes it for a moment, but probably only in these exceptional cases. The mere radiant heat coming from even a very furious conflagration will hardly affect it so much as that, and the tendency of such heat to throw the lights of glass out of their frames by causing them to expand and break away from their setting may be disregarded in the case of this wire glass. The tenant of a handsome office, for which he pays a handsome rent, expects certainly clear glass through which to look into the street; but he may easily consent to having only the lower lights of his window of polished plate glass, so that two-thirds of the window space may be filled with the wire glass in question. If, then, such glass of the two kinds mentioned, the one above, the other below, be set in an iron sash swung on hinges or on a pivot in an iron frame, the arrangement will undoubtedly be found proof against almost every conceivable attack of the heat of a fire on the outside. For tenants who prefer the old-fashioned sash sliding in its own plane, new patents offer themselves—devices not yet wholly approved by use.

Now, it must be urged without further postponement of the crucial point, that wood needs to be absolutely excluded from the buildings of the future, except in the case of which there must be question in the next paragraph. Except in that case, wood should be prohibited by law, and should have been banished long ago by our architects, our contracting builders and our owners of property, all acting together in harmony. Nothing but the old traditions of the American house builder in favor of wood has kept that material in use so long for what are called fireproof buildings. It is an anomaly, a monstrous piece of careless indifference, that even in so-called fireproof buildings there should still be wooden doors, wooden door trims, wooden window sash, wooden panelled backs, wooden dados and wooden flooring, together with all the outfit of furring strips, stops, grounds and loose mouldings which are needed to complete the job.

The case supposed in the last paragraph, in which wood may be kept in use in good buildings, is the possibility of making it completely and safely fireproof. It is hardly enough that it should not kindle easily and conduct flame readily; it must also be able to hold its inserted clear glass or wire glass in place without crumbling or wasting away before the flame, in suchwise as to leave to it an opening to do further mischief. We are told now, at the middle of the year 1899, of the perfect solution of the long-studied problem of how to make wood incombustible, and we are assured that the success attained is so great that the warships of Great Britain and the United States are to be supplied with it for their interior finishings. If, indeed, wood as used in house carpentry may come to be considered as no longer a combustible material, then the case is altered, and our window frames and sash might continue to be of that material as so modified, if architects were not so handicapped by the ever-accursed demand to make a cheap house look like a costly one! What architect dares try to call his employer's attention to the hideous danger which attends building in the old-fashioned way? What architect can afford to beg for the addition of twenty-five per cent to the amount of the carpenter's contract (that is to say, of six or eight per cent to the total cost), in order that his employer's family or his tenants may avoid the danger of sudden death by fire or by more merciful asphyxiation? The architect finds it already so very hard to get the needed appropriation for sufficient walls, solid foundations and enduring floors and roof that to ask for incombustible material besides would be —he feels and knows—to import into the already confused situation a new element of confusion. Still, the non-inflammable wood is there, it appears, for people who care to reduce to nothing the risk of being burned alive; and we have at all events, the right to assume that the glass of our windows will hereafter be set in frames which will not catch fire by heat applied externally.

There is now to be considered the exterior surface of the walls, its material and design. If we were satisfied to use brick, well and solidly laid up, and terra cotta, with every hollow filled with concrete made with broken brick and cement, with tile in its appropriate place, all would be well. We should have done what is possible, in the present state of civilization, to resist the attacks of fire from without, by the omission of the traditional ashlar, which so far from being fire-resisting, is commonly most readily affected by fire and water.

In the heat of a conflagration granite will crack, and at the points of projection and of salient angles, great pieces separate themselves from the mass; it will even crumble to an unrecognizable heap capable of being shoveled up. Sandstone is often safer than granite, and will bear a great deal of heat without losing more than a spall or a chip here and there. Limestone is the most treacherous of all; it is speedily reduced to powder, and this effect of the heat is enhanced and hastened by the stream of water from the fire engines. Artificial stone is commonly like sandstone, and often with more cohesion. A wall built solidly of plain blocks of it might do well under trial, but projecting, ornamental cornices and the like have little power of bearing heat and none of resisting, when in very heated condition, the impact of a stream of water. There still remains to be tried, in any serious way, the monolithic system of building by concrete, or its equivalent, cast in wooden molds, set up on the spot, and so taking shape for the first time in the mass of the wall in which it is to remain. There may be in this material unexpected safety for the future. One thing only we know which is really proof against fire, which we have the right to call in ordinary parlance proof against fire, and that is baked clay. Heat affects it only by sudden expansion; and sudden contraction when cold water strikes it; it seems that this may be disregarded. Brick and terra cotta are our standby, with tiles of different sorts and sizes for roof-covering and for wall-sheathing on occasion. Buildings exist which have been so conceived and so carried out. The most interesting and useful lesson for any beginner in the art of thinking for himself is to be found in the two fronts of the Union Trust Company. This building has a façade on Broadway which is faced with stone in the orthodox manner, and a façade on New street which is the exact counterpart of the Broadway front, except that it is carried out entirely in yellow brick. It is not now the question whether buildings of brick should have the same system of design as buildings faced with stone; it is notorious that the two materials may be so treated, or may be treated on quite other lines; the thing that is most interesting in the building named is the fact that two fronts, in other respects precisely equivalent, are realized in these two materials—the despised one and the admired and desired one.

The trouble with introducing any improvement in building in this direction is the queer superstitions about dignity and stateliness which possess the popular mind. And it must be observed that the popular mind is that of the millionaire property owner, or millionaire donor of buildings to public institutions, fully as much as it is the mind of the man who rents a small dwelling house. To an architect of rationalistic tendencies there is nothing more comical than to reflect upon the sayings of his clients with respect to the superior dignity of stone as a facing of their walls, and the profound contempt of those same clients for brick. If, under the stress of the architect's personality and knowledge, the owner gives a half smiling assent to pleas for the value of brick work, the contempt underlies this assent, and is in full force again in another instant. The deed of gift to a college of land and money contains the absolute proviso that the building "shall be built of stone"; by which, of course, it is meant that its exterior shall have a stone veneer. The requirement of a church committee is that the exterior "shall be of granite," and this in spite of all persuasion and all warning on the part of the architect and on the part of the two or three members of the Board of Trustees who see things as they are and who point out that the more you spend on the exterior sheathing the less you have for the far more important work of the interior. The owner of property on an avenue, where stately shops abound, assumes the necessity of increasing the amount of his investment by a limestone front above the iron ground story; twenty years ago it was an iron front he built, and that, because each new tenant could have it painted up afresh and make the building look new: but that whim has passed. The wealthy builder of a huge office building assumes, in like manner, the necessity of a street front of stone, and that although for one street front there are three gable walls and courtyard walls, blank and staring in the nudity of plain brick work and square holes in it, towering high above the neighboring buildings and fully as visible as the wrought and elaborated street façade. Nor are there wanting architects against whom the charge can be brought of unreasonable worship of stone. When a firm has completed a paper design for a palladian façade, what can be more annoying than to have to reduce this to the ignominy of brick covered with stucco? Uncovered, unconcealed brick it can hardly be. No, it seems to be thought that the dignity of late classical formal designing is not to be served except in marble or light gray limestone.

Let the reader select the buildings which he likes best in New York, and he will find that all or nearly all of them could be perfectly well carried out in brick. What building is the most approved? Is it the City Hall, or Trinity Chapel, or the Clearing House, or the Metropolitan Club? Each of these is a building of which every feature could be perfectly well rendered in brick and terra cotta without loss of character or even important modification in detail. Is it the Madison Square Garden? That is already of brick and terra cotta, except the granite shafts of the arcade. Is it the Judson Memorial building, its church, campanile and apartment house? That also, exceptis excipiendis, is of brick and terra cotta. Is it the Union Trust Building? That, as has been said above, has one face of stone and the other of brick and no man can tell the two faces apart, in a photograph. Is it the Vanderbilt residence at Fifth avenue and

Fifty-second street, or the Gerry residence at Fifth avenue and Sixty-first street? These two houses, designed by the same artist in the same style, are interesting as subjects for comparison, for one of them is carried out entirely in limestone and the other is of brick with only the usual "trimmings" of stone. Indeed, the reader may hardly be aware how very much building has been done in New York, with baked clay for the whole, even the decorative part of the exterior, until he takes pencil and paper and makes for himself a list. He will find then that the attractive and spirited Goelet Building at Broadway and Twentieth street and the admirable Hotel Imperial, at Broadway and Thirty-second street, the Marquand residence at Madison avenue and Sixty-eighth street, the Union League Club—in a style now out of favor, but a most interesting and spirited design—the interesting house in Madison avenue at the corner of Thirty-ninth street, and many another mansion of size and style not far unlike that one, the imposing residence of Mr. Robb at Park avenue and Thirty-fifth street—and, in short, more important buildings than there is room to enumerate, or time to think of, are already brick buildings in every essential particular. It is therefore useless to argue the question in favor of using the material in part; even in large part: but a word should be said in favor of its exclusive use. The employment of stone in the buildings named above is generally so slight and of so little importance that a hot fire might destroy it all—every piece of stone visible in the outside of the building—crack it to pieces and reduce it to powder, and yet leave the walls standing and tolerably solid; but there is no reason in the world why even that much injury to the walls should not be spared—no reason in the world why terra cotta should not be used for sills, lintels, jamb-blocks, quoins, architraves, archivolts, coping, pilasters, string-courses, parapets and the rest just as much as for the body of the wall. Some of the buildings named above have large masses of stone—columns and entablatures of stone—used in their decorative design if not in their essential construction. That there is nothing to prevent the carrying out in terra cotta of these features, even these, is evident to those who know the resources of the existing American establishments, and, failing these, the facility of importation. There are several "plants" in this country the managers of which ask for nothing better than a much larger and more general employment of their resources than is now given them. As to their capacity of producing first-rate work and that on a large scale an examination of the buildings of the last five years will satisfy anyone; a glance at the Waldorf Hotel, built about five years ago, followed by the Astoria, recently completed, and a glance backward for twenty years at the Morse Building in Nassau street at the corner of Beekman will sufficiently inform the reader who has not thought much about the subject. The Morse Building represents the business building of the earlier "elevator period"; the two hotels, especially the enormous and striking mass of the Astoria, represent the newer steel-cage construction, and that applied to a great building of small sub-divisions, a vastly more trying plan and arrangement to carry out in any material than are the plan and arrangement of any office building conceivable.

Nor is it to be feared that a city built mainly of brick, and adorned with brick and terra cotta will be monotonous or ugly. If the people of our time were to brag, reversing the celebrated *mot* of Augustus, that they proposed to leave New York a brick-built town whereas they had found it mainly of marble and brownstone in its exterior aspect, they would be posing wisely. It is long since the writers upon the abstract question of modern architecture and its requirements first broached the theory of an architecture composed mainly of iron framework with exterior facing of colored tile. This was proposed as a remedy for the action upon exterior walls of the smoke-beclouded air of London; but also was it proposed as the most hopeful prospect for the comparatively sunny air of Northern France. Buildings have been built both in France and England exemplifying this scheme, and more especially in the temporary structures of the great Paris Expositions have designs been carried out according to independent and deliberate planning and building, on rational principles by architects of eminence. As yet but little has been done to carry out such designs in permanent form; but that is in the near future. It takes time for the designers, on their side and those who employ designers, on the other hand, to break loose from their early affiliations, and the same influence which keeps Americans wedded to their ideas of carpenter work, as the prime and essential feature in all buildings, makes them and all the world of European descent doubtful of the possibility of building except as their forefathers built in the seventeenth century. It is for that reason that one is inclined to welcome so heartily a great exterior like the Astoria Hotel, in New York, showing as it does to the most careless observer how great are the resources of modern decorative building in the only material fit for general employment in a modern city.

And yet here the enthusiast checks himself, recollecting that in a city of the Continent of Europe stone would not be banished as rigorously as the maker of an ideal building for New York or Chicago would banish it. It has been pointed out before, in these columns, that on the Continent, where fires of formidable extent are very uncommon, no such universal avoidance of a building material which may suffer from fire has ever been proposed. Even where the right of the community to regulate the actions of the individual is more unquestioned than here and where the "paternal" action of the government is carried far beyond what Americans think of as possible, nobody has seriously proposed to banish stone, or wood either, from the general list of building materials. The constant recurrence of dangerous fires in America comes mainly of the custom of building the whole frame of our structures of wood; but partly also of our disposition to keep our houses very warm, a custom bringing with it a constant use of fires in the cellar and fires above stairs, hot flues and hot stovepipes and fires left burning throughout the night. The future will show whether those restrictions which are proposed in this article as really essential to our future tranquillity, need to be maintained in their full vigor. Let the city once be rebuilt with the use of wood not greater than that in, let us say, Paris, and it may be well that granite and sandstone and even limestone and marble may reappear in our exteriors as no longer greatly objectionable. For fifty years to come we shall have no such privilege. It is our business, now, to exclude from our buildings everything that can burn, even to the smallest pieces of the construction; and to bar out of our external street architecture every material that is not capable of standing a blaze.

An office building nowadays has nearly always a flat roof; and a high parapet wall usually surrounds this and conceals the paraphernalia of skylights, ventilators and the like, which break the roof and rise above it. This is an excellent step toward the completion of our fireproof exterior. It facilitates the protection of the building greatly to have a solid fire wall rising above its roof; and although this is not absolutely required by the law in fireproof structures, yet the openings toward the sky which the modern requirements of light, ventilation, and access make necessary, will find in such a fire wall their first line of defense, so to speak. The suggestion for exterior design which this parapet wall gives to the architect is confirmed and aided by another suggestion, namely, the inappropriateness to the place and the character of the building of a wall-cornice of great projection. There has been recently a controversy in Boston over the cornice projecting, perhaps six feet from the lofty wall of a new business building, and the objection urged against it was chiefly the shadow that it cast, and the darkening of the somewhat narrow street, together with the buildings opposite. This objection ought always to be urged; in every case where a broad spreading cornice is proposed in our narrow streets it ought to be fought by all the influence which the neighboring property owners can bring to bear. An overhanging cornice is an anomaly in our city buildings; worse economically in a low building than in a high one, but bad in all. It is worse in a high building in so far as the architectural effect goes, for nothing has been done yet to prove the possibility of putting a broad spreading wall-cornice upon a very lofty tower-like structure without making it look in a

ludicrous way like a broad-brimmed hat; that is to say, without its
seeming awkward and out of place. What is wanted is, of course,
the vertical and not the horizontal crowning of the structure. The
battlemented parapets of so many buildings of the Middle Ages and
those not military buildings exclusively; the balustered parapets
upon cornices of slight projection during the neo-classic era, and
now, the brick parapet-walls of such buildings as the Judge Building in Fifth avenue, the business building No. 55 Broadway, and

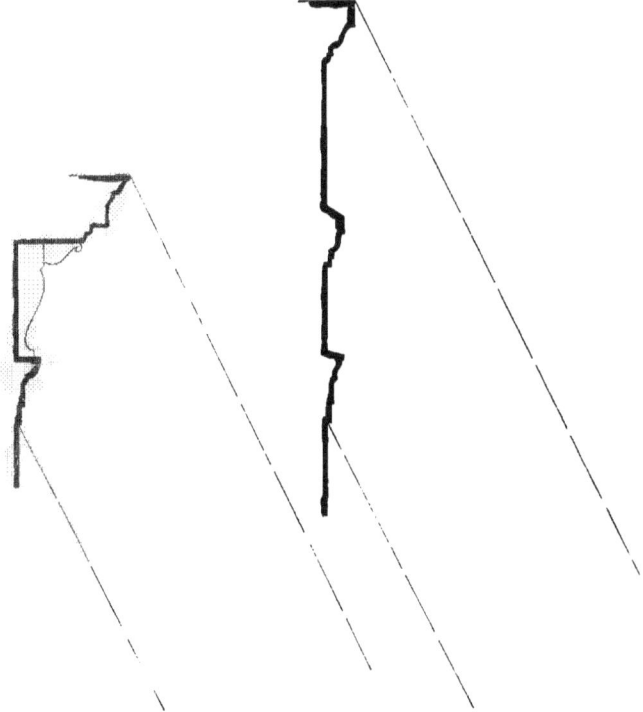

Fig. 2.—A Vertical Cornice-Member, 14 Feet High, Subtending the Same Angle as
a Wall Cornice, 9 Feet High and of 4 Feet Projection.

many a great warehouse which has been treated in the large and
massive way so common of late in New York—all these are wit-
nesses to the vigorous effect which can be obtained by means of a
vertical wall replacing the horizontal overhang. Fig. 2 is intended to show how the arc of vision subtended by the upper story
plus the cornice and by the upper story plus the parapet may
readily be the same. The inference is not far distant that very little
thought and care in the decorative treatment of the vertical wall will

make it as effective as ever the overhanging cornice may have been in the past. The parapet wall need not be so elaborately pierced as to lose its protective value; it need not be so absolutely solid as to be less decorative in effect. In fact, the passing of the light of the sky through openings more or less elaborately shaped is an element of design which cannot be overlooked. It gives the most exquisite counterchange, as a herald might say, which it is possible to imagine, and we all of us felt that the great Surety Building in Broadway, corner of Pine street, had lost a great deal when the circular occuli in its parapet wall were closed up and the blue no longer showed through the sun-lit white.

A business building such as has been pictured above, with iron frames and sash, and wire-glass used as far as practicable; with or without iron shutters; having nothing but brick, terra cotta, ceramic tile and cement to form the exterior face of its wall; having, moreover, a flat roof with a high and somewhat massive parapet wall surrounding it—such a building would be little endangered by the heat of even a most furious conflagration, nor would it suffer, except only from the smoking, scorching, and such disfigurement. But let it be supposed that a jet of flame breaks through the windows in spite of their defensible character. This may always happen, and, therefore, the interior finish must be considered. The question is, therefore, what to substitute for wood in our American interiors, which have hitherto found their chief means of decoration in elaborate joiner's work. If, indeed, wood which has been treated by a chemical process shall prove actually incombustible, this interesting question disappears in an assurance that the old conditions will still prevail. That would be a great relief to the citizen proposing to build, and quite unable to adjust his mind to new conditions; but the student of the nobler class of work common in countries where carpentry and joinery do not leave their proper sphere and invade, so generally, the domain of the higher architecture, may almost regret the interposition into our slowly developing architectural world of wood which cannot be burned. The old requirement of the man who would build an incombustible edifice, the requirement that he should use the materials of the mason and worker in marble, had that of good about it that it required a nobler and more permanent style of decoration than anything which woodwork can ever lead to—at least in the hands of men of European race.

The tenant will have a planked floor. He is sure, in advance of all experiment, that nothing else will be agreeable to the feet. In like manner it seems useless to point out the easy working and the slight additional cost of iron window frames and sash, and useless to bring up European, or the few existing American, examples. It seems useless to urge that doors might be made of something else than wood. Have not doors always been made of wood? Law might, indeed, be invoked in such cases, and law might relieve us of our difficulty, but Americans know pretty well what to expect of their legislatures, and they have not a profound belief in the possibility of carrying through and putting into enforcement a law which would be very disagreeable to many owners of real estate. The community suffers in silence. It, the community, does not take the trouble to buttonhole members of the legislature, or to appear before committees and to talk more publicly than that in behalf of its requirements; but the owner of property does both, and he does it vigorously and shrewdly. And yet, private money-interests cannot always hold public welfare as of no account, and we are forced to consider the possibility of carrying out every part of our interiors in materials which will not burn, and, in doing so, to study the ways of men who build in other lands than our own. In the South of France nobody feels obliged to hang his light wooden doors to wooden hanging-stiles, which form part of door-frames, themselves made of wood and involving the further use of stops, grounds, nailing strips, trim planted on after the plastering, and loose mouldings to complete the trim. Such work is eliminated from house building of Languedoc and Provence, Auvergne and Gascony by the simple process of building into the solid wall or partition of masonry the tongue, strap, or more solid block, to which is attached the wall piece of the hinge. In Italy, throughout the peninsula, similar ways of work are common and in all buildings in the towns wood is almost confined to the swinging doors and the swinging window sash themselves—the fixed frames being, if of wood at all, so very light and slight that they are hardly more formidable than an enlargement of the door itself by a few inches in any direction. Rooms too in these lands are vaulted; staircases are solid rooms or compartments, as many stories high as the stair ascends, with walls of masonry, and with no further connection with the rest of the house than by means of the comparatively small doorways. The floors of halls are commonly laid with slabs of stone, which may indeed rest upon wooden beams, but those always left visible from below and practically out of the way of fire. The floors of bedrooms, of sitting rooms, of eating rooms, of kitchens—of every separate "piece" indeed, except in a building especially prepared to tempt foreigners as possible lodgers, are floored with earthenware tiles, and these are set upon a thin coating of cement which rests in its turn upon planking, to be sure, but planking which is tolerably protected by the solid, air-tight and incombustible bed which it carries. In place of the earthenware tiles, terrazzo of some kind is laid, a kind of cement flooring with chips and pebbles of marble or bright colored stones of any sort, not too hard and refractory, let into its surface, so that when the whole has been smoothed, rubbed down and polished a pleasing resemblance to mosaic is the result. No one who has lived for any time in an Italian city but remembers the nervousness which came over him when he first found the wall and floor of one of his rooms growing so hot that he could hardly put hands to it, with the fire in some furnace or stove below, and his feeling of relief when he found that the flue passed through a two-foot wall and behind a solid cradle-vault coming no nearer to anything which could burn than as a table might be set against or near the face of that heated wall. In Venice the houses are lighter and slighter than elsewhere in Italy and that for obvious reasons, and yet no one hears of a fire in Venice and this not merely because the people do not care to keep themselves as warm as we do, but also and to a still greater extent because of the comparative rarity of wood in the construction of the buildings and its complete exclusion from parts that are concealed, covered up and capable of spreading fire before it can be detected or prevented.

All of the above is of the simple, cheap, commonplace building which is traditional in those countries of Europe where wood is not, and has never been common. Those, too, are lands in which the usual rate of expense in the preparation and fitting of a house is as nothing compared to the extravagant proceedings of the United States. With us no immediate imitation of those easy-going, South-of-Europe ways can be looked for; but with us, again, the iron members of all sorts and sizes—the angle iron, the strap iron, the innumerable forms of rolled metal which may be used in connection with cement, terra cotta, brick and the like for floors and partitions have made our work easy to us if not exactly cheap. And there is this to console the owner of a building, which he finds will outrun his estimates in cost, that it will be immeasureably more solid, more durable and therefore very much more agreeable and more capable of elegant finish. Your marble worker will be greatly rejoiced, and will tell you so, when he finds that his ornamental tiling is to be laid upon a floor of iron beams with brick and cement filling, because it will do him credit, he thinks, and need fear nothing but the shock of direct injury from above. The building will be comparatively dust-proof, it will be comparatively soundproof and smellproof as well as fireproof, nor will the dwellers or the temporary occupants of the rooms in such a building suffer from the constant annoyances of the wooden shells in which nearly all of us are compelled to live. Repairs will become a "negligeable quantity" in that owner's future calculations. Plaster will not crack nor partitions shrink and settle;

doors will not bind on the saddles; rats will not gnaw through lead pipe—the occupants will live free of the vexatious visits of the patching workman.

Doors can be made of paper in one form or another, and so almost entirely incombustible. They may be made with light metal frames upon which leather is strained, and the leather if taken in the large sheets of horsehide which are now prepared as "American Russia" or the like, is not very expensive. They may be made in a similar way like the old-fashioned green baize doors with textile of almost any inflammable sort strained upon frames which it would not be difficult to construct of stout wire exactly as the skeletons of our stuffed sofas and arm-chairs are made. The insurance companies recommend doors of wood covered on all sides with tin-plate; and modified forms of these "Underwriters" doors are now made with panels (see Fig. 3), which, together with the rails and

Fig. 3.—Panelled Door for Interiors, Hung Nearly as the Shutter, Fig. 1.

stiles are covered with metal secured by the usual loose mouldings, which alone are uncovered—even these mouldings might be of decorative metal and made very effective. It is found that these will bear a very great heat before yielding in the slightest degree; because, while the wood within may char, it does not burst into flame nor lose the whole of its rigidity. Doors may be made of wire glass, and these will not be unreasonably expensive when they are more constantly in demand.

If such doors be hinged by any simple process well known to all country masons, as of building into the masonry wall one-half of the hinge, the only question left will be the protection and the adornment of the door-casing. This then has to be considered, as well as the window-casing in connection with such windows as were described above when we are considering the exterior of the building in hand. The most effective way, the noblest way is certainly to build the door-casing and jambs with solid blocks of some stone hard enough to bear the ordinary accidents of inhabitation and dressed smooth enough not to be disagreeable as one's woolen garments brush it; or, in place of such stone, its equivalent in terra cotta, filled with concrete. Such a door-casing may be built as shown in Fig. 4, the quoins bonded firmly to the brick wall behind and having just so much projection beyond the face of the brick as to receive the thickness of a coat of plastering. This production may be increased to re-

Fig. 4.—Door Casing of Cut Stone, Projecting Beyond the Brick Enough to Serve as Ground for Plastering.

Fig. 5.—Door Casing of Cut Stone, Flush with the Brick Above, Projecting Below
Enough to Serve as Stop for a Dado of Ceramic Tile.

ceive the thickness of a dado of marble, slate or tile, if,
as is highly expedient, the brick wall itself be exposed and
plaster be foregone. Fig. 5 shows such an arrangement; the jamb
pieces and the lintel flush with the brick face of the wall, except
where the uprights of stone are cut with projection enough to receive the added thickness of the dado. Fig. 6 shows a window
with its surroundings treated in the same general way; but entirely
in brick work and ceramic tiles. Or, the custom more frequently
followed in the South of France is quite within our reach; there
the thick walls are splayed at the door openings in such
a way that the door is hung nearly at the ridge where the two splays

Fig. 6.—Window Casing, etc., Corresponding with Figs. 4 and 5, but Entirely in Brick and Ceramic Tile.

meet, and this door strikes upon a very small and slight trim which may even be of wood, but should by preference be of metal. It is to be observed that the door is not hinged into this light frame, which is merely a striker or buffer, something to keep the shock of the door from tending to disintegrate the rudely built masonry around. Where the walls are very thick, it is customary throughout South-western Europe to divide a doorway even of moderate width into two folds, one of them hinged to the jamb of either side; each fold being then so narrow that it can open into the thickness of the wall. This arrangement allows of portières on either side and is in other ways convenient, but it does not allow of the constant opening and shutting of the door because of the annoyance of fastening, with bolts or the like, the one valve against which the other is to shut. There remains indeed the device of spring hinges keeping each valve in the plane of the wall, but doors hung in that way are not very tight nor proof against the eaves-dropper. The one thing which is not to be allowed or thought of for a moment is the device sometimes followed where buildings in this country have been made fireproof and that is the copying of carpenter work in cast-iron. We

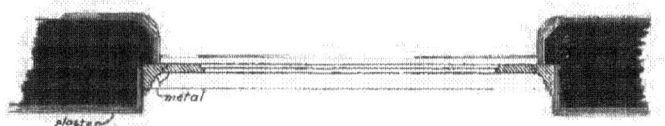

Fig. 7.

have all of us seen whole buildings in which a door trim of joinery has been closely imitated in painted and grained metal at great cost and with most unsatisfactory results. Barring that stupid resource all other modifications are open to us and it will not need many years of a determination to avoid woodwork to fill the market with devices for trimming openings and hanging doors and window-shutters, some of which may even allow of truly architectural treatment.

Already hinges of admirable general design are in use in one of the new stations of the Edison Company, in the Salvation Army Building in West 14th Street, and in many others, and used for hanging doors directly upon masonry jambs.

Fig. 7 shows a modification of such a door jamb, in which the plastering is applied directly to the wall of brick or porous terra cotta, or hollow blocks of any fireproof material; the door frame is of wood covered with tin, and metal mouldings are used to cover the joints. There is no opportunity here to complete the study of design possible to these or other possible doorways, nor of their co-relative and corresponding window-work: but it may be noted that the plastering is no part of the necessary finishing of the job—it is merely a cheaper expedient.   The uncovered brick is immeasureably more dignified.

The walls themselves of our office rooms will be more agreeable if laid up of hard bricks than people are apt to imagine who have not had experience of such walls.   There are buildings in which the whole chimney-breast is faced with brick; and the mantel, elaborately carried out in terra cotta, forms one architectural mass with the breast.   The bricks may have enameled surfaces; there is no difficulty about that, for, though the cost per thousand is high, so very few bricks are needed for the lining of a room that the actual outlay would not be great.   It is not, however, at all essential, except from a somewhat fantastical belief in favor of the non-porous surface as being more healthful, that enameled or glazed bricks should be used; the selected hard baked brick of our markets is amply sufficient for all purposes and it can be got of many different tints allowing of pretty variety in the laying up of the wall face.   Admirable instances of such work were to be seen in the old buildings of Columbia College—which are now falling in piles of rubbish. Friezes of moulded or patterned bricks, in the cornice at the top of the room or bands at the level of the chair-rail or elsewhere may also be made with excellent effect.   This, however, is to be said, that brick is not agreeable to brush against— as indeed was suggested above with reference to sandstone used for door trims.   To guard against this, dados of marble or slate are excellent and may be of any height from three feet six to seven feet or higher.   Nor should the abundant supply of natural and artificial decorated marble with the grave and sedate colors of slate to contrast with it or to substitute for it, cause us to forget the ready device of ceramic tiles.   There is no room here to dwell upon the brilliancy of effect so easy to produce by this means.   The very ugly tiles commonly offered us are not to be allowed to blind us for a moment to the beauty of a few of those already in the market nor to the extreme ease with which the most beautiful patterns that can be invented by man may be transferred, either in color or in low relief to the surface of tiles which need not be costly beyond our means. Tile can be painted as canvas or panel can be painted at any price up to the fee asked by a master of the masters in sculpture or in painting; but, also, tiles of such beauty that we buy them for our museums and such as have been for centuries made throughout half the world may be studied, and the resulting studies sold at such prices that every house-builder might enrich his dwelling with them.

Where the wall surface is smoother, whether from use of enamelled bricks, of tiles, or of plastering of a superior quality, the familiar old baseboards may still be copied in a better material: or the dado, three or four feet high, may be made inexpensively.   Fireproofing companies there are which undertake to run mouldings and to execute panellings in many kinds of hard cement and plaster; and metal mouldings are at hand for the reinforcement of these, the protection of their arrises, and for their adornment. There are, too, a multiplicity of patent contrivances in the way of papier maché and similar compositions. And it is to be noted that, once the true uses of color-decoration understood, these inexpensive devices are not unworthy. The architect of spirit may well despise pilasters and entablatures of stucco; but color-effects may be got upon a plaster or a paper background as well as in ceramic ware and in marble.

As for the floor surface, there is no remedy for the whim that none but that of planks is agreeable, except the simple expedient of living where no plank floors are to be had. When one has spent two successive winters—that is to say, all of two years except the summer vacation—in an apartment of twenty pieces, unconscious of the fact that not a square foot of plank flooring existed, and then finds, to his surprise, that underneath the carpets and the rugs there is everywhere mosaic, terrazzo, earthen tile or cement, and this in an apartment near the top of a big house, an apartment of comparatively low ceilings and undignified appearance; then he makes progress in the knowledge of interior fittings. Such progress as that is what this article pleads for. The desideratum is that the occupants of offices, like the occupants of dwellings, should think for themselves a little more freely than they are apt to do in this country, cut off by such breadths of sea, of language and of custom from the nations of older tradition and frequently wiser habits of life. We cannot learn so much from England in this matter, except in the matter of inexpensive and beautiful stairs of white stone, with which stairs all dwellings of any pretensions are fitted, in London; but the Continent of Europe contains endless stores of suggestion for those who would build better than we are in the habit of building, and these suggestions, worked up by the American readiness at taking a hint when there seems to be an inducement, will give us all that we need in the way of incombustible appliances. Nor should the owner of a new and costly office building be satisfied unless his architect can say to him, when the last workman leaves the building, There is not in the building itself, its walls, floors or fittings of all sorts, as much wood as would make a lead pencil! That is the standard which, in spite of the assurances of a wood which will not burn, each owner and architect should set up for himself. They will assuredly have more beautiful buildings if they work in this way: and that fact is hereby offered as an additional inducement to those who would fain have buildings that will not burn.

Russell Sturgis.

EXPRESSION IN ARCHITECTURE.

ALL who are interested in architectural practice, either directly or indirectly, are familiar with a doctrine, which has much currency in our day, that buildings must express their purpose, and their structural qualities in their design, if they are to be looked upon as works of architecture. Not a few readers, indeed, who have been influenced perchance by Ruskin's fascinating writings, may have come to look upon this dogma as a recognized cardinal principle of the Art of Architecture.

But if one has thus accepted this dogma, and in connection therewith has taken the trouble to study with care the work of contemporaneous builders, he can scarcely have avoided the somewhat depressing conclusion that architecture is for us a lost art. Indeed, one may go much further than this; for a student who has followed with critical bent the historical development of what is usually called architecture in the past, and who has at the same time kept this dogma always in mind, must surely have found himself forced to the position, which is apparently held by some of our most prominent architectural critics, that architecture ceased to exist at least 3,000 years B. C., and long before any buildings were constructed of which any examples are now extant.

It is apparent from the words above written that the validity of the dogma above referred to is to be questioned in what follows. Nevertheless the reader must not look for an argument to prove it utterly valueless, rather will he find reason, after all is said, to trust to it in a way, as the architect will find reason to work by it; but this not because the dogma will appear in the end to be true in itself, but because it will be seen to veil a real truth. What this real truth is we will consider briefly at the start, that we may be the better prepared to speak of special examples later on.

We most easily grasp the truth which is back of, and veiled by, this dogma if we first come to realize that it is only a special adaptation of what has long been held to be a general æsthetic principle. It is but an interpretation of the general dogma of artistic realism in terms of the art of which we speak specially in this article, and to this general dogma of realism we may well direct our attention for a moment, before considering its special architectural adaptation.

This general dogma of realism may be stated thus: "Fine art is the expression of the true essence, of the real nature, of the subject presented by the artist." This is a dogma with which we are all made reasonably familiar by the teachings of the literary realists of the day,

of writers like Zola for instance, and our own Howells; and it is a
dogma that is comparatively easy to uphold, so long as we forget,
what we should never forget, that literature is only one form of
artistic expression coördinate with sculpture, painting, music, and
architecture. But when we are asked to broaden the application of
the dogma to all the arts we at once see that it cannot be upheld in its
original form; that it must be qualified, or limited, or restated, if it is
to appear in any way applicable to all the fine arts.

It very obviously does not apply to modern music, for instance,
without such qualification and restatement; and if we but think of it
we find that the same is true in all the arts, to no two of which can this
principle be applied with exactly the same significance. As we have
already noted, the doctrine we are discussing is but a restatement of
this general dogma of realism to make it applicable to architecture,
which we are specially considering in this article.

In order to make the supposititious principle thus applicable to the
work of the artist-architect it has been assumed by its defenders that
the true essence of architecture lies in its constructional and practical
worth, and that true architecture, therefore, consists: 1st, in the expression, in building, of constructional values; and, 2d, in the suggestion, upon the exterior, of the uses which the hidden interior portions of buildings, as wholes, or in their special parts, are intended to
subserve. But it is easy to show that both of these assumptions are
entirely unwarranted.

To consider first the expression of structure. There can be no
doubt of course that there is great æsthetic value in certain expressions of constructional function in the design of a building; but to
claim that the expression of constructional function is *per se* necessarily æsthetic is certainly impossible; for were this true all scientific
engineering would have architectural value, which manifestly is not
the case. Think, for instance, of the ugliness of the ordinary cantilever bridge in which constructional function is most clearly expressed. It is evident in fact without argument that works of engineering must thrill us with their beauty if they are to lay claim to the
possession of architectural values.

We have on the grounds of one of our most important colleges a
building erected by a skillful architect who has long since retired from
practice—but who some time ago told the writer with expressions
of regret that he designed it when he was carried away by the influences of Ruskin's teachings, "and I defy you," he said, "to find a single illogical thing about it. Yet I must confess that it is not beautiful."

If we consider the second assumption of the architectural realist,—
the assumption that the suggestion of the interior uses of a building

in the design of its exterior is of the essence of good architecture, we find it equally unsatisfactory.

It is true indeed that certain indications in the design of the façades of a building which lead one to appreciate the purposes for which the interior is to be used give satisfaction to the beholder, a satisfaction which often adds much to the æsthetic value of the whole mass; but to hold that the indication upon the exterior of the purposes for which the parts of a building are to be used is necessarily æsthetic is manifestly absurd; for such a principle in an ideal building, would require the architect to indicate by appropriate forms or decorations the existence of menial offices which we not only wish to forget, but which we actually must necessarily lose sight of, if we are to enjoy the beauty of a building as a whole. Suppose, for instance, that we felt ourselves called upon to emphasize the kitchens and sculleries of our large mansions, say by decorating the windows with representations of pots and pans, as we use book plates sometimes in the decorative leaded glass in our library windows.

It becomes evident then that while the uses of a building, or of its parts, may be expressed in the forms employed in the design, nevertheless this expression must be beautiful if it is to add to the æsthetic character of the structure. It is apparent that we have discovered no "royal road" to the attainment of beauty in architecture when we have grasped the realistic dogma we are now studying.

And if we examine the general dogma of realism of which this architectural dogma is an adaptation we at once see that it itself is utterly inadequate as a guide to the artist in any field; for it is very easy to show that, far from being given up to the expression of truth, all of the arts are deliberately concerned with, and are based upon the adoption of, conventions that are *per se* inherently untrue.

No art attempts what can, by any stretch of terms, be called a complete expression of truthfulness. In all the arts we find the artist working on the basis of conventionalized falsities; and this is true even in those arts which so clearly deal with realities that they are commonly designated as the imitative arts.

For instance, in sculpture, which is perhaps the most clearly imitative of all the arts, we find the artist expressing his genius by presenting to us beauty of form in all cases, whatever else he does, and in most cases he pictures for us living forms. But note that for this purpose he uses lifeless material; and that, in order to emphasize the beauty of form, he deliberately avoids expression of movement and color; and in this he assumes unreal conventions. And mark how firmly this convention of unrealty has been fastened upon us. Lessing, the reader will remember, makes it a canon of the criticism of sculpture that movement must not be portrayed. And as to color, if any one will take the trouble to speak of this subject with the greatest of sculptors, and the best informed, and most thoughtful of other artists, he will find how deeply rooted is the objection they have to colored sculpture. It is true that some of the best sculptors have, from time to time, attempted to use color in their works, but the coloring has seldom been realistic, and where the sculptor has reached any measure of success in such attempts it has been by adding to his work delicacy and charm rather than that special nobility of beauty which can be impressed upon us by sculpture as by no other art.

The painter goes even further than the sculptor in the direction we are considering by assuming as a necessary convention of his art an added falsity. Form he depicts as does the sculptor, and perspective and even movement, but all "in the flat," upon plane surfaces; and as the sculptor artist in general objects to the use of color in his work, so the painter artist would look upon the painter who might model up his work before applying his brush as something of a trickster; although, mark you, in this modelling the so-called trickster would in fact be assuming less of falsity than the one who works in what we feel to be the legitimate field of the painter's art.

The mural painter has a special convention of his own which demands that the feeling of the flatness of the constructional surface, of its attachment to the wall itself as part and parcel of the building, must never be lost through all his work.

The painter of whom we have been speaking gains his effects by assuming many untruths, and endeavoring to reproduce merely true relations between color masses; but the painter in monochrome, and the draughtsman in black and white, assume still another falsity, and deal merely with relations of mass, and values of light, eliminating all color. Some artists in fact have been most successful in expressing these relations of mass and light value by the deliberate use of color which is impossible to the Nature they are interpreting.

Recall, for instance, the marvellous effects Turner obtained in his water colors in this way. We may differ in our estimate of Turner if we judge him from his work in oil; but no one can deny his great genius who has studied the large number of his water colors gathered together in the National Gallery in London.

But beyond the unrealities in the art of painting thus far mentioned, note furthermore that the highest "key,"—(if we may use the slang of the studio),—that the highest "key" at our command for use on canvas or wall surface is most untrue to nature's "key." Furthermore, size and scale are also both deliberately falsified by the painter and draughtsman.

Perhaps the point we have been considering is made by reference to these two arts alone, but it may be well to go further and mention a few of the unreal conventions assumed by artists in other fields.

The dramatist deliberately assumes unreality of entourage, and untruth in all but the main suggestive relations of active expression. In connection with the development of the earliest drama men have discovered that the repeated story, the written word, will to a great extent produce the full effect of dramatic action, and they have thus again reduced the truthfulness of expression by describing action, instead of acting themselves. The poets have gone still further and have added other conventional unrealities, viz.: those of rhyme and rhythm. We have thus in poetry no real expressions of real activity; in their place we have mere verbal symbols which lead us to imagine or recall activities.

Finally, we have the extreme of falsification by the artist-writer, who, like Stevenson at times, or like Carroll in his "Alice in Wonderland," deals with altogether imaginary lives of imaginary people. Yet this art of literature, which assumes such a wide range of untruth in its technique, is the form of art in which those express themselves who speak loudest to-day in favor of realistic dogma.

Perhaps the strongest corroboration of this argument is furnished by the art of music, as it has developed in modern times; for in music the absence of realism is very marked, while, on the other hand, the musician is dominated by, some indeed will say overburdened by, artificial and unreal conventions of many kinds.

And if we turn to architecture, with which we are most concerned in this article, we find the same characteristics emphasized in a very distinct way; these characteristics, however, need not be dwelt upon at length just here, for in the course of what follows they will be referred to very fully.

At the moment it will be well to mark one conclusion to which we are forced. It is impossible to believe that all the assumptions of unrealities above referred to are irrational; we cannot agree that these unrealities are forced upon man, and that the great artist is ever endeavoring to express truth in and through these unrealities that press him down, as must be the case if the realist is correct. Rather, on the contrary, must we agree that these unrealities have been deliberately assumed by man in the course of his æsthetic development; and this becomes clearer when we discover that this assumption of unrealities by the artist is easily explicable.

The first artists were those who tried to produce beautiful objects which they could contemplate whenever they so desired, that is they had perceived beauty in nature, had mourned its evanescence, and sought in some way to make it permanent. Naturally they attempted to gain this end at first by imitating the beautiful and admired object. But presently they discovered that they were able to make their work more thoroughly beautiful if they assumed certain unrealities in order to enable them to emphasize certain qualities which were necessary to the beauty for which they were in search. And as a matter of fact we find when we come to consider it, that unconsciously they have always assumed these unrealities in some measure.

The artist always does his best when he produces, by the use of any special material or method, effects which cannot be as well, or as economically, produced by any other technique; and this fact forces the artist, who uses any special medium, to emphasize the qualities which this medium enables him to present most effectively, at the expense of others which cannot be so effectively treated; these latter are thus thrown into the background, to the loss of their realty, but to the great gain of æsthetic result.

It is because we accept this principle, though usually unconsciously, that we object, as most of us do, to colored sculpture; for mere color effects can better be produced by the painter than by the sculptor, while beauty of pure form can be better presented in sculpture than upon the painter's canvas. For the same reason critical people have come naturally to object if they find the water colorist using solid, opaque color, as though oil pigment were his medium. They do not object, mark you, because this misuse of material opposes a principle which they have gained by generalization, for few, indeed, are the critics of art who know anything about general æsthetic principles: they object because they have adopted a convention of unreality which makes such technique illegitimate, and they have adopted this convention because they have learned that transparent washes of water color laid upon light reflecting paper enable the artist to produce beauties of relations of light which solid non-transparent oil pigments can never give.

For the same reason again do the musical critics object to "programme music." Why they object they can perhaps not tell you, but it is surely because they appreciate that for the artist who would express himself in this direction literature furnishes a better medium than music does; while the conventions of literature, if applied to music, limit its flow and development in a most unfortunate manner. They realize that reality should be sacrificed, if special beauty is attainable by the sacrifice.

It is thus that we can account for the persistence of the conventions of which we have been speaking, and their existence forever discredits the dogmatism of the realist by showing that thoroughgoing truth is not necessary to the highest forms of beauty, and that the expression of truth and the production of art work are in no sense coördinate.

It may be taken for granted then that the current doctrine of realism is not a sound one; and yet some reader may say to himself as he reads: "It is remarkable that this doctrine of the realist is so very persistent, if there is so little in it; may there not be, nay surely there must be, some basis for the doctrine if it has kept alive, as it has, ever since Aristotle's philosophic ancestors began the discussion of Æsthetics." This objection, indeed, seems to be well taken; but it is not difficult to explain the reason this discredited doctrine keeps everlastingly bobbing up, and in stating this reason we shall indeed find the truth at the base of this supposititious principle of the realist.

We men and women are persistently bad logicians, and when we find that an argument serves us well on the whole we take it for granted that it is valid. We discover that non-X gives us Y, and from that we very commonly draw the illegitimate conclusion that X will give us the opposite of Y.

We say clear sky, no rain; and then not clear skies; that is, cloudy skies, therefore rain. Now this conclusion is not a valid one, and as a matter of fact we know it does not always rain when it is cloudy; nevertheless for practical purposes, the argument serves us very well, for it so often does rain when it is cloudy that most of us go without our umbrellas if it is clear, and take them if it is cloudy; and we should consider ourselves incapable of judging from experience if we did not do so.

It is in accordance with this bad logical habit of ours that we take certain experiences which give us a sense of ugliness, and argue that if we could gain opposite experiences we should gain beauty, which is the contrary of ugliness; but this surely is an entirely illegitimate conclusion.

Men note, for instance, that objects in nature which depart widely from her types are ugly—the monsters of one kind or another; and they, therefore, say "follow nature's types," or "imitate nature," and you will produce beauty. But what right have they to make this statement. It is true, indeed, that we shall not produce ugliness if we follow nature's types; but no arguments from such premises ought to lead us to expect to gain the opposite of ugliness, i. e., beauty, by picturing nature's types; all we can be sure to gain by this means is the absence of ugliness.

Or to take another instance: certain students of Æsthetics have noted that inharmonious relations of color, or form, or tone, are ugly, and they have argued that if we produce harmony we shall gain beauty, and these theorists have raised the doctrine of harmony to the dignity of a basic principle in æsthetics. But a proper argument will surely lead to no such conclusion. All that we can certainly expect if we avoid discord is a lack of ugliness, not necessarily an acquisition of beauty.

Now it is in this same manner that the realists reason. Having noted that unreality, untruth, are essentially disagreeable and hence ugly, they argue that if we gain the opposite of unreality and untruth, that is, if we gain impressions of reality and truth, we shall have obtained beauty, which is the opposite of ugliness. Upon this fallacy is their theory based.

But here again we find the invalidity of the conclusion. If we avoid untruth we shall in fact avoid so much of ugliness as was determined by this untruth, but by no means is it a fact that we shall gain an impression of beauty.

The correct doctrine for us to inculcate then is not the realist's dogma: "Strive to express Truth," but a much more modest doctrine, viz.: "If you would produce Beauty begin by avoiding untruth."

And now if we apply what we have been saying to the art of architecture we find that we have in this principle of truth, of sincerity, of veracity, as applied to the art of architecture, but a half truth; as indeed we have seen that the doctrine of artistic realism in all its modifications expresses but a half truth.

In architecture, as in all the arts, untruth, insincerity, lack of veracity, and pretence, are in general disturbing, unpleasant, and therefore ugly; if a work of architecture, therefore, is to have permanent æsthetic value it must avoid the expression of untruth and pretence.

Now the easiest way for the lazy thinker to manage to avoid this expression of untruth and pretence is to bear in mind, and to some extent to express, the truth. But this mere expression of truth will never make a work of man's hand æsthetic: the æsthetic quality is something which must be superadded.

The aim of every artist should be to produce an object of permanent beauty, in whatever material he expresses his conception: this he cannot well do if he shocks the observer in any way whatever, and one of the worst of shocks is that of unreality. If the artist be an architect, he cannot succeed in producing the effect of permanent beauty in his buildings if he persistently lies about the construction he adopts, or, if he constantly deceives us about the uses of the apartments he erects: but this is due not to the fact that where he succeeds in producing an æsthetic result the truth is expressed, but to the fact that lying and deception are in themselves anti-æsthetic. For mere sincerity, and lack of pretence, in one's architectural work will not make it artistic; to this negative lack of deceit must be added the positive quality of beauty which brings to the masses of cultivated beholders a permanent feeling of pleasure.

It cannot be denied that the architectural student gains a certain practical value from the emphasis of the dogma of truth: wherein this value lies becomes clearer if we take a familiar analogy from our ethical life. It is more effective to teach the child the importance of speaking the truth than it is to correct him for falsehood. Nevertheless in Ethics we practically try to keep in mind general ethical ends, and often quite properly avoid blurting out perfectly certain truths when they are unimportant and inopportune. Correspondingly in Æsthetics, it is easier to emphasize its value of truth than the necessity of avoiding insincerity; nevertheless, it is perfectly legitimate, and often most advantageous, in architecture to avoid emphasizing some special structural truth, some uses of parts of buildings, provided this emphasis would involve the production of forms that are distinctly ugly; and this we do quite properly, as we easily see if we constantly bear in mind that the end for each and every artist, and for the architect as an artist, is the production of a work of beauty.

We have thus far been treating almost altogether of theory, but if the position we have thus taken be correct then the architect, in the guidance of his artistic efforts, may well make certain practical applications of the principles involved, negative though they be; and the reader as a helpful and appreciative critic may well take them to heart as guiding principles in judging of the architect's efforts to attain beauty in the buildings which he erects. There are just two results of our study which there is space here to bring into prominence, and both of these, the reader will find, bear directly upon the subject we have undertaken to consider in this article.

In the first place the architect is taught that he should aim to avoid the pretence of constructional effects which evidently cannot exist; but having done this he must equally avoid the expression of constructional effects which are not beautiful. It may be true, if we may take an analogy from a kindred art by way of illustration, that the human frame is made up of bone and muscle, and the artist-sculptor will certainly not model his figure so that it will appear to be apparently unanatomical—unconstructional, so to speak; nevertheless the most perfect reproduction of anatomical detail will not make a statue beautiful, nor should we consider the sculptor to be in any sense an artist who on principle represented his human subjects as exceptionally thin in order to emphasize the position of bone and muscle which make their attitudes possible. Similarly is it true that buildings could not stand did there not exist certain balancing of forces, certain strain on material parts, certain lines of thrust and pressure; but evidently to strip a building of all beauty in order to express this balancing of strain, and thrusts, and pressures, would be manifestly absurd from an artistic standpoint, and this point critics should not fail to bear in mind; for the critic who so emphasizes the delight he obtains in the architect's expression of these physical forces, that he finds in such expression alone the true essence of architecture, is as abnormally warped in his æsthetic development as is the surgeon who finds beauty in a skeleton, or in a fine piece of dissection, or in a skillful preparation of cancerous tissue.

The architect should aim in all cases to produce a beautiful building; to this end he must avoid obvious constructional untruth which for most intelligent men is ugly. So far as in him lies he should also aim to emphasize the constructional and practical values of the parts of his structure, and he should do this for the simple reason that such emphasis tends to be attractive to the intelligent observer. But he should never emphasize these constructional and practical values at the expense of a loss of beauty; nor need he strive for this emphasis unless it is possible to gain it in a manner which will actually add to the permanent æsthetic value of the building as a whole.

But as the architect should avoid giving the observer the shock which constructional untruth entails, so also should he avoid shocks of all sorts and kinds, for such shocks always involve more or less of ugliness.

And here again appears the value of this negative principle of which we are speaking; for not infrequently the architect finds in practice that by the adoption of some scheme which involves a minor inconsistency of construction he may avoid other shocks of much greater importance; for instance, shocks caused by bad proportion, or lack of symmetry.

Suppose the architect has built a large fireproof hall, across the ceiling of which a heavy girder must cross, dividing the ceiling into unsymmetrical parts. Here he has an ugly ceiling. He may remove this ugliness by furring down the ceiling to the bottom of the girder, so that he may obtain a perfectly flat ceiling of symmetrical form. No one will contend that this is improper, because in order to avoid leaving an ugly ceiling he has masked the ugly girder. But this arrangement compels the architect to lower the whole height of his room, and this may be disadvantageous. Now if this girder is exposed it must be protected against fire by hanging down over it a covering of terra cotta blocks, which are plastered over for further protection. This leaves the ceiling of a very ugly form. There seems no reason why he should not hang down other sets of terra cotta blocks, which do not cover girders, in order to make the ceiling symmetrical, if he is thus able to make a beautiful ceiling instead of an ugly one. This, indeed, will involve a minor inconsistency of construction, which usually nobody but the workmen and architect know of, but, on the other hand, it enables him to avoid a very important shock which would be caused by the lack of symmetry in the ceiling, and gives him an opportunity for decorative treatment of this ceiling which he could not otherwise obtain.

The ideal architect to be sure would, of course, be able to avoid all

shocks of all kinds; but we poor human beings all too often find ourselves called upon to make a choice of the lesser evil; and surely the
architect who is merely human should not be condemned if he asks
us to overlook some inconsiderable untruth of structure, or use, for
the sake of the better æsthetic results he may thus obtain. He may
well argue that at best we can express but partial truth in any art;
the truths which the most thoroughgoing realist is wont to emphasize
are only some of many which he chooses to consider, whilst he
leaves out of sight many others which but for mere convention might
as well be considered as those which he aims to express. The sculptor,
for instance, in general, as we have seen, assumes a conventional falsity of colorlessness which he asks us to overlook in order that he
may the better express certain beauties that are independent of color.
So in architecture there are many other truths than those of structural thrust and strain, or of practical use, which all artistic architects (and even those who labor strenuously to express constructional values) have come to overlook entirely, and this with perfect
propriety in consideration of the fact that the end in view is the production of beauty; e. g., they overlook the expression of the nature of
their foundations, of the filling in behind their finished protective and
ornamental stone facings, of the masonry and furrings back of their
plastered interior wall surfaces. If, then, in the effort to build beautiful buildings, it is permissible for the architect to forget some of
many realities, why should he not occasionally ask us to pass over
some slight structural disingenuousness, provided he is able by such
means to produce a nobler type of beauty than were possible if he
did not disregard this minor inconsistency.

Architecture more than all the other arts is replete with forced
compromises. A symmetrical exterior, for instance, may produce
æsthetic results which could not be gained were all the minor lack of
symmetries in plan emphasized upon the exterior. The artist must
trust to his genius to determine for him how far he can afford to
sacrifice one element of beauty in his effort to gain another; and the
fact that he is an artist is attested by the fact that the structural truths
he fails to express are forgotten by the observer in the beauty of the
results attained.

Let us now consider a second application of the theoretical study
which we made in the beginning.

We have inherited from a long line of our artist ancestors many
architectural forms of great beauty which have arisen in constructional usage, all too often very faulty from our modern scientific
standpoint. Thus it happens that inherited architectural forms, more
or less illogical, have been refined and beautified until they have become in themselves æsthetic elements capable of employment for the

purpose of adding artistic quality to buildings, much as the artist in color adds to the value of his painting by his technique; and there seems to be no manifest reason why the modern architect should not use such elements, as in fact his ancestors always have done, to beautify his work, without too great regard for their constructional worth; only provided he does not use them for purposes of intentional deceit.

We may illustrate this by reference to the types of the arch in general use on the exterior of buildings, and which are accepted by all of us as beautiful in form.

In the ordinary round arch the pressure line runs in a direction which is not concentric with the curve of the arch. Certain parts of the arch stones are, therefore, constructionally valueless, and if we attempt to work quite logically we should build our arches in a strangely ugly form, keeping the line of thrust in the middle of our arch stones and increasing them in width from top to bottom. We should furthermore give up the emphasis of the key stone, for there is no constructional reason why this should be larger in height than the next stones to it. But think what would be our æsthetic loss if logical criticism compelled us to discard the use of all arch forms which do not comply with the logical constructional thrust lines. Not only the round arch would disappear from our exteriors, but all forms of the pointed arch would make the glory of Gothic architecture.

And in this connection it may be well to note that we should to-day be unable to enjoy the beauty of the maze of flying buttresses in the Gothic cathedrals had the medieval architects understood how to calculate thrusts as accurately as we do, and had they expressed these thrusts logically. In the construction of a vaulted roof, held in place by a double set of flying buttresses, such as is seen in the great cathedrals of France, the thrust of the main vaulted roof does not correspond with the form of either of these sets of flying arches, but with a line which cuts through the wall between the height of the two. There is evidence that the first builders of the large vaulted roofs put in only one set of flying buttresses, but finding that when they did so the walls were pushed out at another point they then put in the other set of buttresses to counterbalance this newly-discovered pressure. In subsequent structures they then used the double set of buttresses from the start.

The mass of flying buttresses thus built gave the architects of later cathedrals the type which they developed as we know (yet as we have just seen quite illogically) into the beautiful forms which entrance us as we view their finished works.

It is thus that great architects have invariably used forms developed in constructional practice, as merely decorative features; and if the

beauty of the result is sufficient to arouse our enthusiasm we do not
hesitate to condone the slight inconsistency. It is thus that the Romans
used the Greece-born orders, being content to accept and adopt forms
perfected by long use in other relations than those which were appropriate to their civilization, and while adapting old forms added
elements of grandeur and proportion, which lead us to overlook altogether the illogical usage. It is thus that the Venetians used old constructional forms as purely decorative elements to add to the beauty
of their well-studied compositions; and we forget, and quite properly
forget, the inconsistency in the joy we gain from the entrancing
groupings in their waterside palaces.

It is, of course, to be conceded, as has been suggested above, that
the ideal architect, or race of architects, would avoid such incon-
sistencies, but even in the architectural work of the Greeks, which
reaches to the highest grade of structural consistency, we find, e. g.,
in the triglyphs, the modillions, the dentils, of their masonry temples,
the use of forms which had been perfected æsthetically in wooden
structures, and which were then used decoratively, but from a structural standpoint not truthfully, is stone construction. In the development of the Gothic cathedrals, which many think of as the best examples of an architecture of thoroughly logical construction, we can
easily trace the same practice; for example, in the use of many tiers
of flying buttresses of which we have spoken above; and again when
we note the blundering steps by which the columns of the basilica,
used first as mere columns, were gradually transformed into buttresses where engaged in the walls, or into piers where standing
isolated and free.

Our conclusion then is this, that the expression of constructional
Truth in Architecture is only one element amongst many which are
at the command of the true artist-architect, for use in the production
of beautiful buildings; a most important element, indeed, and one
which if skillfully used must add great satisfaction to the trained observer; one also which cannot be disregarded without great risk of
ruining the beauty of the building in which the architect is expressing his thought. But for all that, we are compelled to agree that in
many cases this constructional and practical worth may quite properly be subordinated to other elements which are incompatible with
it, provided the latter, without it, are capable of producing æsthetic
results which with it would be impossible of achievement.

In closing it will be well to make a practical application of these
contentions to the reader as a critic; and first let us beg him to consider the many difficulties with which the architect has to contend,
and let this thought modify the harsh judgments he is wont to make

on the results they attain. We do not ask him to condone their failures; nor should he be satisfied with ugliness, nor be content unless the buildings they design are beautiful when finished. But it were well if he always looked for the beauties, and not for the faults, and this not for their sakes as much as for his own.

It is so easy for the critic to establish in himself artificial standards which no artist can reach, or in fact ought to try to reach; standards which will prevent him from catching the beauties which the artist intended to present and has succeeded in presenting.

The notion which we have been considering is one of these artificial criteria. If we demand that all structural values, that all uses, shall be expressed to us in a building, and that no forms which have been perfected by past structural usage shall be employed nonstructurally, and merely as ornament; and if we refuse to acknowledge that a building is architecturally noble unless it meets this demand; then certainly we shall find ourselves forced to hold that no truly architectural building has ever been constructed.

But if we agree to gain delight from all forms of beauty which the architect can present to us in his building, (and amongst these we, if we choose, may give pre-eminent place to the expression of structure and usage); if we condemn only ugliness and real failures of taste; then not only shall we aid the artist by higher appreciation of his effort, but we shall add to our own delights, in studying the architectural works of the past and present, joys which will be utterly unknown to us if we fail of such breadth of appreciation as we should surely strive for.

Henry Rutgers Marshall.

COLONIAL · ART · AND · ITS · ADAPTABILITY · TO · MODERN · PIANOS

WHILE the phases of fashionable furniture have run their cycle—Renaissance, Empire and Eastlake—and emerged into the liberty of choice which reigns to-day, the outward appearance of the piano has remained for many years much as we see it now. Colonial art possesses a recognized style which we utilize daily in architecture, furniture and ornamentation; nevertheless the piano, which came into general use toward the end of the last century, has suffered by the neglect of designers to apply the Colonial features which it was created too late to receive in its first inception. Our progress in the development of tone-qualities has closely approached perfection, but the Colonists were further advanced than we in the decoration of their musical instruments.

Colonial Art has been so fully written upon, and illustrated, that I shall only try to show its possible uses in connection with modern pianos.

To-day we seek our ideal in the classical motifs of the Renaissance, now revived in endless variety. Colonial Art is simply the usage of such of our forefathers as possessed refinement, education, and wealth, and were thus able to gratify their tastes and to import labor which brought with it to this country the essential features of its original environment—brought associations with art and applied its ideas to the construction and embellishment of the homes of our early settlers. These homes we must admit are splendid examples for us to work from to-day. The simplicity, dignity and refinement of the details of Colonial Art, together with the unusual amount of good sense shown in it, place it beyond the reach of adverse criticism.

Let us peep through the keyhole into one of those stately Colonial mansions, its broad hall running straight through the house, opening into spacious rooms each furnished in accord, with delicately constructed and carved furniture, spinets or harpsichords; damask draperies, family portraits and quaint old mirrors adorning the walls;

and mantels bordering the great fireplaces. The host in knee-breeches, silken stockings and ruffled shirt, the hostess in loose flowing gown and powdered hair, are dancing the Virginia reel or the minuet to the music of one of their quaint old instruments—a picture artistic and beautiful.

Now suppose the Colonists could have had the modern grand

MODERN COLONIAL PIANO.

piano with its perfection of tone to furnish the music instead of the superficial mandolin-like scratch of the spinets and harpischords, beautifully decorated as they often were; wouldn't it have been a startling revelation of music?

Colonial houses are being built and furnished every day. Is it not incongruous to have the usual piano of to-day, with its massive form and rather severe lines, placed in one of these delicately refined and artistic rooms? Is there not something lacking which the spinets and harpischords generally possessed, such as a lightness and grace of form which was heightened by the legs, carved with great refinement; by cases beautifully decorated either with oil paintings or chaste inlays? Why are the early instruments so sought for by people of culture and admirers of the antique? Certainly not for their superior musical qualities; but most assuredly for the beauty of their

SPINET.

graceful construction, for their picturesqueness and well-balanced lines.

Good taste in furnishing demands that the pianos of to-day should be specially treated and decorated, just as were the harpischords of our forefathers; and demands this even more because we require the best examples of every known style of art in furnishing our houses. We are wider traveled than our forefathers, and thus better able to judge between good and bad art; we have more wealth to gratify artistic tastes. Therefore the artistically-treated piano is no longer a luxury but a necessity; it is just as necessary to have the piano in keeping with the style of the interior to which it appertains as to have the trim of the door like the trim of the window of the same room. The piano is part of the furnishing like the wood work. Suppose we take, for illustration, a pure Colonial room. Compare the spinet or harpischord with the usual piano of to-day; can you not easily judge for yourself which would be the most suitable piece of furniture for such surroundings? Since artists are just as sensitive

COLONIAL HARPSICHORD.

to form, line, and color as musicians are to music, the same keen sense and true appreciation should rule in each mode of artistic expression in which the piano has a part.

Let us see how we can adapt the Colonial style to our modern piano. Particular attention should be given to lessen the width of case by avoiding all lateral lines; by breaking up the surfaces into panels; covering the piano surface with carvings in low relief; also by using the crotch veneers or painting the panels in color. This concentrates the sight, checks the diffusion of the vision, and, by taking away from the entirety of the object at first glance, affords opportunity for examination and comparison, and thus excites the imagination. Such expedients used together diminish the apparent amount of surface.

Legs or supports should be light and graceful; yet a feeling of strength should be given by proper design, and they should grow out from the case, as it were, and become an integral part of it. The arm can take many forms—angular, curved or straight. The lyre should correspond with the legs in exact duplicate or be radically different—no intermediate form! The desk should be light in design, or, if the character of the design be heavy, it should be cut through, or perforated so as to look as light as possible.

The outside about the edge of the top should have a band of ornament, delicate in design; and inside this another, in inlay or color, to detract from its large expanse of surface; still within these borders may be paintings or a cartouche of inlay. It would also be proper to repeat the same treatment on the under side of the top, or to blazon the arms of the family, well manteled. A stretcher may be used to tie the front legs, or a series of legs surrounding the case. Everything should be done to lighten the total effect to the eye.

Architects and designers and their patrons should give this too long neglected piece of furniture more thought and consideration when planning for the furnishing of homes, as there is no limit to the possibilities of making the piano an artistic part of the furnishing.

Piano manufacturers generally seem to have lost sight of the necessity of making their wares objects of beauty as well as of utility. The woods and veneers are, as a rule, to be praised, although used with the ever tiresome piano-polish. But in symmetrical proportions, well-balanced lines, harmonious details, pianos are not what proper thought and study can make them. This is probably due to the lack of demand in the past for artistic pianos; while strong commercial competition has forced the majority of our smaller manufacturers into the same groove, until originality, correctness, and the conception of true artistic principles have been entirely overlooked. Thus the piano in these essential respects has become a pitiable object.

J. Burr Tiffany.

IN THE DUCAL PALACE, NANCY.

ALTAR ST. PATRICK'S CATHEDRAL, NEW YORK CITY.

PALAZZO BONIN GIA THIENE VINCENZA.
Palladio, Architect.

HOUSE IN LEUZE, BELGIUM.

OUR ACQUIRED ARCHITECTURE.

WITHIN the past year, the United States have come into possession of a great number of buildings in widely scattered parts of the planet. It is unlikely that they will exercise any perceptible influence upon our domestic, or "metropolitan," manners and customs of building. Such is not the course of conquests. Rather it is that the conqueror entertains a general contempt for the people he has beaten, and refuses to learn even what they have to teach. This was not quite true of the great conquering nation of antiquity. It is true that the Roman had a great general contempt for the Greeks, which took the form of a special contempt, at least during the conquering and "expanding" period, for the arts in which the Greeks surpassed him. But this never led him to deny, that, in these small and effeminate arts, the conquered did surpass him. Those famous lines of Virgil, in which he allowed that "others" might more tenderly carve the breathing brasses and draw living faces out of marble, while the business of the Romans was to rule peoples and lay down terms of peace, were the real expression of the Roman sentiment, the same sentiment which doubtless now prevails in Berlin with respect to Paris. But modern conquerors have not had so much grace given to them. The British, the Romans of our time, have practically refused to recognize that people they could "lick" had anything at all to teach them, and have proceeded tranquilly to apply to their subjects their own view of the fine as well as of the coarse arts. The old Romans, who to be sure had no architecture of their own when they entered upon their career of expansion, had the modesty to pay to that of the Greeks the sincerest flattery of imitation, although they did apply it, as a system of decoration, to an alien mode of construction, and the Roman monuments, in the provinces as well as in the capital, are still found worthy of study accordingly; of too exclusive a study, a good many people are coming to think. But the English have carried abroad their official architecture as faithfully as their bitter beer or their mixed pickles, and the result is that they have produced very little of any interest. It is more than a century since Burke said: "Every other conqueror, of every other description, has left some monument, either of state or beneficence, behind him. Were we to be driven out of India this day, nothing would remain to tell that it had been possessed, during the inglorious period of our dominion, by anything better than the orang-outang or the tiger."

That is far from being true, or even rhetorically plausible now.

THE QUEEN'S RESIDENCE, HONOLULU.

PACIFIC MAIL SS. CO.'S OFFICE, HONOLULU.

MAIN STREET, HONOLULU.

AN AMERICAN BUILDING, HONOLULU.

The British have left monuments in their railways, if in nothing else, which it would take a long time to reduce to mere oxide of iron. But when we come to compare the artistic merit of what they found and what they have founded, we find a more than Roman insensibility. Compare, for example, the architectural remains in India of the Mahometans and the Christians, the Taje Mehal at Agra, or the Golden Temple at Amritsur, with the "cathedral" or even with the

CATHEDRAL STREET, SANTIAGO, CUBA.

vice-regal palace at Calcutta. The Romans at least refrained from constructing public buildings at Athens or Corinth, to be "to the Greeks foolishness," and to expose themselves to the derision of the conquered.

One of our new possessions has already been architecturally Americanized, much to its injury. That, of course, is Hawaii. The missionaries and the sons of missionaries had their architectural will of Honolulu for two generations, while it was still under a nominally native rule. It was not to be expected that, under the auspices of the missionaries, whose ideas of architectural beauty were derived from the meeting-houses of their native New England, we should even have "sent forth the best we bred," in the way of architecture. The best we bred, when the missionaries were having their way, was not

PANORAMA OF THE PRADO, HAVANA.

THE ROOFS OF HAVANA.

very good, but the missionaries induced the simple Kanaka to believe that the second-best was quite good enough for him. So the
public buildings of Honolulu offer a belated reflection of the modes
of building that prevailed in the States during the period of the the-
ocracy. Unhappily, this coincided with the very nadir of American
architecture, the time when the architecturally protestant carpenter
was exercising his "right of private judgment" in that "fancy" building which was about the most vulgar phase through which architec-

CAPTAIN-GENERAL'S PALACE, HAVANA.

ture ever passed anywhere. Honolulu got the very dregs of it. The
crowning vulgarity of the Mansard roof in the American variation of
it Honolulu escaped, doubtless because the building activity of the
Kanakas antedated its introduction, or at least its journey across the
continent. For it is abundantly evident that the official architecture of the Hawaiian capital was imported directly from "the coast,"
and that architecture, there is nothing invidious in saying now, when
the architecture of "the coast" has been so greatly improved, at the
time when it was exported to Hawaii, was as repulsive, in its combination of incompetency and pretentiousness, as any mode of building the world has ever seen. Chicago before the fire, or Chicago
just after the fire, the spectator of what was built for "the palace" and,
during the brief Republic, became the "Executive Building" is
moved involuntarily to exclaim. It is an example, although the actual material is costly hewn stone, of the American cast-
iron school, meaning, of course, not a style devised for

the material, but a style which imitated profuse ornamentation in stone. And yet the Executive Building does employ, and degrade, actual masonry. Nothing could be more revolting in its cheap pretentiousness than the front of this palace, with the two tiers of stilted segmental arches in the wings, the stilted round arches at the centre, the meaningless keystones and the lavishness of unstudied ornament. The Judiciary Building is like unto it. Rather better, at least much simpler and less pretentious, is the Richardsonian Romanesque of the so-called

CHURCH NEAR GUADALUPE, CUBA.

Kamehameha School. Westward the course of fashion takes its way. Our latest fashion has not arrived at this new possession, but no doubt the Beaux Arts will make its appearance upon the scene in due season, and the simple Kanaka will be edified with pieces of Paris, transported across the American continent "in bond." We may freely admit that it would be better in itself than the civilized architecture he has thus far been privileged to behold, without thereby admitting that it would have any sort of relevancy to his needs. Decidedly, as architectural missionaries, we have not thus far shone in the Pacific. Our architectural procedures have been enough to vitiate the taste of an archipelago.

Meanwhile, the gentle Polynesian, like everybody else who builds

Copyright, 1898, by Harper & Brothers.

GENERAL VIEW OF SANTIAGO DE CUBA.

From Harper's Weekly.

IN THE SPANISH CASINO, HAVANA, CUBA.

SAN CARLOS CLUB, SANTIAGO, CUBA.

for mere necessity, has devised for himself a mode of building which answers and expresses his requirements. In its general features, it is the same all over the South Seas, even to the Philippines, though these are classified as Asiatic and not as Polynesian, and the local difference among the different islands do not affect the general uniformity. In other words, it is the most natural and easy construction

THE CATHEDRAL, SANTIAGO, CUBA.

to which the local needs point and the local materials lend themselves. But one can scarcely call it architecture, for the reason that it does not go beyond the supply of physical needs, and does not aim at monuments, civil or religious. Under our tutelage, the Hawaiians have aimed at monuments, with the discouraging results we have seen. But, upon the whole it may be said that the building of our new possessions, so far as it has become architectural, has become Spanish. Indeed, it seems safe to go further than that. Apparently the readiest materials at hand in the East and in the West Indies are very much alike, and the construction of the cheapest and most quickly constructed shelters are startlingly alike in so far, at least, as photography enables us to judge, in Cuba and Puerto Rico, on the one hand, and in Luzon on the other.' In each case, it is a hut with a light framework, and a pyramidal roof, the walls, if one may call them so, being covered with thatch as well as the roof. Doubtless these are the "houses" of which we read that so many thousands have been destroyed in Puerto Rico. But it must be the least of the damage done by storms in the West Indies, or by battle and fire in the East, that dwellings so easily replaceable should disappear.

When we go a step higher in the scale of costliness and permanency, but still confine ourselves to idiomatic and vernacular structures, we find the resemblances still hold good. The bungalow construction of a spreading roof and light walls of one, or at most two stories, seems to have domesticated itself alike in the suburbs of Manila, and in the coast towns of Cuba and Puerto Rico. There are differences of detail, but the family resemblance is very striking and the differences of detail seem rather individual than geographical. According to the costliness of the dwelling or "godown," the wall may be of thatch or adobe, and the roof of thatch, metal or tile, but the plan is virtually the same, and the larger and more costly edifice merely an expansion of the smaller. Really the chief geographical difference to be noted seems to be that the roof in the Spanish Main is more apt to be in two pitches, with the lower the flatter. There is in this arrangement a picturesqueness all the more effective for being apparently unconscious. This arrangement does not seem to have extended to the Philippines, but there is there another peculiarity of construction which has an equal effect, and comes to very nearly the same thing. Instead of being built in two pitches, the roof is apt to show a gentle concave curve. In many cases, the effect of this is aided by the fact that on the longer axis of the rectangle which seems to be the invariable plan, the roof is not continued upward to the point, or hip joint, but the upper extremity is occupied by a truncated gablet. It is virtually the same arrangement that is so common in Swiss carpentry, and that is so commonly reproduced in modern country houses. There is another peculiarity of such building in the Philippines as is above the mere improvisation of shelter, while yet not making "architecturesque" pretensions, by which it is assimilated to Swiss architecture, and that is the frequent projection of a verandah in the second story from the whole circuit of the building, by means either of posts continued to the ground or of brackets stopped against the lower wall. Some of the details of this arrangement, and especially the curve of the roof, are evidently of Asiatic, and apparently of Chinese origin, and, as we shall see, Chinese details are sometimes mixed with Spanish architecture in more pretentious buildings than those of

the class we are now considering. But it is plain from the illustrations that the common building neither of the Spanish East nor
West Indies is derived from Spain. The similarities in buildings
half the circuit of the planet away from each other, are explained
by the similarities in needs and in materials. The result in each case
may be described as a large, fixed, and more or less permanent um-
brella; that is to say, an erection intended as a shelter, not from cold,

THE CATHEDRAL, CIENFUEGOS, CUBA.

but from sun and rain. These are the requirements of a tropical
abode or of a tropical warehouse, and they are met with equal and
complete exactness, alike in the Spanish and now American possessions off the Southeastern coast of North America and in those off the
Southeastern coast of Asia.

The ordinary town-house of the fairly well-to-do in the Spanish
West Indies is more apt to lack than to have a visible roof. Very
often, indeed commonly, it is but of one story, raised above the
street level by a plain and unbroken base so high as to require at one

or both ends an outside stairway which is a feature of the house and is decorated by a treatment of the iron railings which is often very pretty and effective. The tall openings of the main or the only story give upon a gallery which is another feature. The front is an imitation of masonry in plaster, being almost invariably "masticated," according to the venerable joke that used to prevail when that false pretense was commoner in this country than it is now. It is not a sham in the Antilles, since the coursing and joints of masonry are not imitated, and it exhibits itself merely as a coating; but of course it is not monumental, and it gives the houses to which it is applied a stagey and unreal air, and a collection of them the air of an opera village. This is promoted by the tinting, sometimes in two colors, of the plaster of the front, a process often employed also in the churches..

But, as we have said, this provision of mere shelter cannot properly be described as architecture. It is an interesting and even exemplary mode of building and doubtless a good deal more "sightly" than if it had been done with the recollection, in the minds of the builders, of architectural forms which it seems to be impossible, in that case, to prevent from intruding into structures to which they do not belong. There is this difference; that the common building of the Philippines is really indigenous, while the common building of the Antilles is, historically speaking, exotic, since the extermination of the aborigines was a preliminary to the Spanish settlement. But the common building is as vernacular and straightforward, to all appearance, in the one case as in the other. In each case the "architecturesque" building is, on the other hand, entirely imported, entirely Spanish, and entirely official. This is equally true whether it be ecclesiastical or secular. The church, in a Spanish colony, is the state, the priest as much a part of government as the soldier. When the British captured Manila, it was the archbishop who surrendered the place, and promised for it the ransom that was never paid; and when Cervera took refuge in Santiago de Cuba, it was the archbishop who said that this great victory was not enough, and that it must be followed up by planting the Spanish flag on the capitol at Washington. The convents and the churches in Spanish colonies are just as much "government architecture" as the captain generals' palaces, the forts, the markets or the jails.

This list almost or quite exhausts the classification of "architecturesque" edifices in the late Spanish possessions. It is curious how like they are in all, and how Spanish. The very materials do not seem to vary with the local supplies. Stucco over rough masonry or brickwork has the same effect, and lends itself to the same architectural treatment, as the adobe which is substituted for it in the Spanish-American settlements. The stucco walls and the tile roofs are the marks, wherever they are found, of the Spanish domination. And the uniformity of the treatment is as marked as in the Roman monuments erected in Roman colonies by Roman engineers. It is so marked that one has to look with care for local variations. I have already noted the concave curve of the tile roofs in the buildings of

From Harper's Weekly.—Copyright, 1898, by Harper & Brothers.

CATHEDRAL AT GUAYAMA, PUERTO RICO.

pure utility in the Philippines as an Asiatic and more specfically a Chinese detail. When used architecturally, it may become still more effective. In the Chinese church, near Caloocan, it is used unmistakably as a badge of the nationality of the parishioners. In this case not only has the slope of the roof, but also the ridge, a concave curve, and this latter ends in the unmistakably Chinese upward curving horns. This Chinese roof is dropped between two pavilions of as unmistakably Spanish architecture, with a queer and picturesque as well as with an unmistakably designating and expressive effect. In another case, this time a piece of military architecture, the gate in the wall at Cavite, the Asiatic curve of the roof is introduced, albeit with a straight ridge-line, and over a rich and very Spanish entrance, in a still more artistic way and so as to complete effectively an extremely picturesque piece of architecture. I should very much like to see anything as good as this in the military architecture of the United

PLAZA DE COLON AND CITY HALL, MAYAGUEZ, PUERTO RICO.

States. The best that we can do in that way is the kind of thing we
were doing at the beginning of this century, when even military engineers seem to have had some training in architecture. The entrance to what is now Castle Garden in New York, is a very good
example of what we were doing then. There is an example of very
much the same sort of thing at Manila, in the entrance to Fort San
Antonio, where the American flag was first raised after the surren-
der. This entrance is a round arch between an "order" of banded
columns and under a pediment, and is a conventional and very good
specimen of the architecture which military engineers learned until
well on in the nineteenth century. All the greater is the contrast
between it and the Orientalized Spanish of the gate at Cavite, which
is evidently the individual work of an architectural artist. What
could be prettier, more expressive or more effective than the way in
which the guard-house emerges from the wall falling away on either
side, or than the way in which the portal is projected from the guard-
house and connected with it by the prolonged slope of penthouse
roof, and the upper stage, with its central niched saint, so craftily
punctuated by the plain square holes on each side and the happy little eyebrow in the roof above? In all this there is an art very far
beyond military engineering. One can hardly be mistaken in at-
tributing such a design as this to the influence of the genius of the
place; though indeed Spanish architecture, in the Peninsula itself,
is so Orientalized that it is impossible to be quite sure.

Most important of all the public architecture of the Spanish colonies is, of course, the ecclesiastical. Just as, in Spain itself, the
churches are more numerous and more gorgeous than anywhere
else, except in Italy, and in comparison with civil and domestic
building more important even than in Italy, so in the outlying possessions of Spain. We have not acquired the most important of this
architecture. There is nothing in Cuba, nothing in Puerto Rico and
nothing in the Philippines, to be compared with the churches of
Mexico and Peru in point of magnitude or importance exteriorly
or in georgeousness of interior decoration. And this for the obvious reason that Mexico and Peru are gold and silver bearing countries, and that to strip them of their mineral wealth was the object,
in each case, of the Spanish conquest and remained the object of the
Spanish occupation. It has often enough been pointed out that this
was the original and fatal vice of the Spanish colonization. The
spirit of Cortez and Pizarro continued to animate their successors,
and after the supply of the precious metals "in sight" had been exhausted, the reason of being of Spanish possession reduced itself to
what in China is known as "squeeze;" that is to say, the levying of
official tribute on production and exchange, so that the viceroys were
enriched as the country became impoverished. But meanwhile the

DRINKING FOUNTAIN AT AQUADILLO, PUERTO RICO.

CALLE DE MENDEZ-VIGO, MAYAGUEZ, PUERTO RICO.

tithes of the Church in the argentiferous colonies were of great amount, and a great part of them was devoted to the erection and embellishment of the churches. It is characteristic that the first really systematic investigation of the architecture of Mexico should only just now have been undertaken, and that by an American enterprise. We may expect from this very interesting and important results. Not only does the city of Mexico contain examples of the Spanish Renaissance of the sixteenth and seventeenth centuries which would be noteworthy in the Peninsula itself, but such examples are to be found in the provincial capitals, as witness the illustration of the cathedral church at Saltillo. The "missions" which we acquired from Mexico with California were not only much later in date, but of much less architectural importance. Wherever we find it, however, the Spanish colonial church is almost sure to be an architectural sham. Its effect is scenic rather than that of reality, just as the gorgeous ceremonial that goes on within it and which is more gorgeous in Spain and Spanish possessions than in any other Catholic countries, addresses itself rather to the imagination than to the reason. Adobe, or sun-dried clay, is indeed, a legitimate, though far from a monumental, building material, and it is often used legitimately in the building of Mexico and in what remains of Spanish building, or has been imitated from Spanish building, in our own Southwest. But in churches and public buildings it is not the rule to employ it legitimately, or, indeed, at all. A coating of stucco is applied to cover and conceal a structure of rough stonework or rough brick, with the same scenic effect that was attained in the temporary and avowedly scenic buildings at Chicago, and the impression it makes upon an observer accustomed to a more solid system of building is of something temporary, something theatrical, just as the effect of theatricality is made upon such an observer by the pageantry of the worship which goes on within, or, in processions, without. The cathedral of Havana is scarcely either so important or so favorable a specimen of the style as we should expect to find in a see which, perhaps with the exception of Mexico, has been the greatest seat of the power of the Spanish branch of the Catholic Church on this side of the Atlantic and north of the equator; but it is a highly characteristic specimen. The great expanses of unpierced wall, relieved with a double order of huge and rather clumsy proportions, the niches, the ailerons, the curvilinear gables; all these things are unmistakably Spanish, perhaps one may say unmistakably Spanish-American. There are other churches in Havana which show the style to better advantage, and which, if not in general composition, at least in detail, exhibit a much nicer artistic sensibility. "The regular thing" in a church of more pretension, especially of cathedral pretensions, is a gabled center of rather low pitch between two mas-

THE MAIN STREET, CALLE DE MENDEZ-VIGO, MAYAGUEZ, PUERTO RICO.

sive towers, perhaps with the corners quoined in actual masonry, while the curtain walls are in plaster, relieved with arched openings bull's-eyes, niches and what not, according to the taste and fancy of the architect. Of such is the cathedral at Guayama, in Puerto Rico, and of such the cathedral of Mayaguez in the same island, familiar to most readers from Mr. Zogbaum's well-known drawing of "Schwan's Regulars on the Plaza," of which the cathedral forms the background. And indeed this indicates a feature to which the Spanish churches owe much of their effect. Enough ground is reserved from secular uses in front of them, if not on all sides of them, to enable them to be well seen. That is a precaution equally taken with reference to important civic buildings. It is one which we might with great advantage imitate, not only in such building as we may have occasion to do in our new possessions, which is not likely to be much, our new possessions being already rather over-stocked with public architecture. We might also very well imitate it in our public building at home. Nothing is commoner than to see the effect of a building lost because such a reservation was not made. To take a third off the actual cost of erection and devote it to clearing a space whereby what was left could be seen may often be good architectural economy. "That is a good building," said one eminent architect of the work of another, "it is a pity nobody will ever find it out." Narrow and tortuous as the streets of a Spanish-American or a Spanish-Asiatic town may be, this criticism is in these towns always successfully obviated.

The steeples, when they have been introduced, are by no means always of the grandiose and pretentious treatment shown in those of Mayaguez. Evidently those of Guayama are not complete, and were intended to receive culminating features, presumably in the form of monumental open belfries. It is noticable that all the Spanish steeples follow the treatment of the Romanesque, revived with the Renaissance, of a succession of nearly equal stages, very strongly divided, rather than that of the intermediate pointed Gothic, in which the several stages were more or less merged in each other. The towers of Burgos have made no impression on more recent Spanish architecture. Burgos is, of course, an example rather of German than of Spanish Gothic. But, in the matter of the roofing of the towers, one comes upon erections, doubtless exceptional, in which the likeness to German work is even startling. The tower of the church at Santa Ana, near Manila, would, in the photograph, be taken by any student for that of a German village church. The equal division of strongly marked stages is as characteristic of the German Romanesque as of the Italian, or the Spanish; the polygonal plan much more so; while the steep hood of roof, with its dormers seems evidently a product of the temperate zone and of a Northern

CONGRESSIONAL HALL, MANILA.

(Here Aguinaldo was elected President. One of General MacArthur's
men signalling from the tower.)

THE FASHIONABLE RESIDENCE SECTION, MANILA.

race. It is much more nearly a spire than it is one of the belvideres which in the South of Europe takes the place of the Northern spire. Certainly nobody would take it for a steeple in a tropical island which was a Spanish possession.

The smaller and less pretentious parish churches in the towns and villages, even the little mission churches, show an unmistakable

CALOOCAN CHURCH—THE PHILIPPINES.
(Man on tower signalling to navy.)

family resemblance, scarcely modified at all by local conditions, insomuch that it is impossible to tell from a photograph of one of them whether it is in the Philippines or the Antilles, but impossible not to tell that it is Spanish. In fact, there are examples of the style within the United States, and even in the Atlantic States. The so-called "Cathedral" of St. Augustine in Florida, built about the end of the last century, would be quite at home in Cuba or in Luzon. And there is at Goosecreek, in South Carolina, a curious church nearly a century older, which, to me, is as unmistakably Spanish in its origin, though built, I believe, for the use of the Church of England. The frontispiece of a screen-gable, which is so characteristic of the

Spanish church that is too small to be furnished with flanking towers had not been added, but the preparations for adding it are evident, and the church might be transposed with the church in Caloocan, near Manila, without any sense of incongruity on either side.
Even the smallest and humblest of the churches attached to the
furthest outlying Spanish missions, as in California, Arizona and
Texas bear unmistakable marks of their nationality, and could

ROMAN CATHOLIC CHURCH, MANILA.

change places with such a humble edifice as the church at Agana,
on the island of Guam.

The convent is as marked an expression of the kind of civilization
which Spain has regarded it as her mission to diffuse as the church.
Indeed, the religious orders have had much more to do with the
revolts against Spain in the Philippines than the parochial clergy,
who indeed seem to have gotten on with their flocks very peace-
ably. The convent at Malolos has become suddenly historical as the
capital, so to say, of the Filipino republic. It was in the church of
this convent that Aguinaldo read his message to the first session of
the First Filipino Congress, September 15, 1898, and it was in the
court-yard of the same convent that, on the same day, the crowd
assembled to hear him speak from the balcony.

It must be owned that the interior is both characteristically Spanish and extremely ugly. It shows what Spanish building may come to in bad hands. There is as little correspondence as possible between the exterior and the interior, though an opening does seem to correspond with each bay formed by the posts that divide the nave and the aisles. But there is really no design, no studied relation of parts, no harmony, no rhythm. Nothing could be poorer or meaner than the thin posts with the cornice-capitals that seem to have been nailed on by an American carpenter, unless it be the poverty and

PHILIPPINE SUGAR WAREHOUSE.
(The black spots on the ground are sugar drying on mats.)

meanness of the arches they sustain. In fact, the church is as innocent of art as a New England meeting-house, which it strikingly resembles. It is of no architectural account.

On the other hand, the exterior is of so much account that it seems impossible that the two should have been done by the same person. The court-yard is already secluded from the public road by a considerable withdrawal, outside of which is a covered porch in wood, of nondescript design, which seems to be of indigenous Filipino production, and which is surrounded by lowly thatched cottages that are undoubtedly such. The chief monastic building consists, at the ground level, of a wide loggia, an open arcade behind which is withdrawn the main wall with the actual entrances. A cloister one might call it, though it is open all along at the base, and the effect of it is undoubtedly cloistral. In the second and only remaining story is another loggia, an open gallery consisting, this time, not of arches, but of square piers supporting the architrave which in turn sustains the roof, and provided with a protective railing. This is a description of the centre, which consists of three arches below, and of five or six rectangular openings above, and which is set off from the enclosing ends by a slight but sufficient projection of these. The roof is an unbroken expanse apparently of dark tile, hipped at the ends.

A PHILIPPINE COUNTRY HOUSE.

The great expanse of the building in proportion to its height gives it a repose which is enhanced by the simplicity of the dispositions and by the unbroken spread of the roof. But it is a studied simplicity, and the effect of it is assisted by the design of the detail. The low piers of the arches are very effective in conjunction with the simply treated arches, of which the impost is simply but sufficiently marked, and the intrados emphasized by a chamfer. Distinctly it is a pity that the piers of the upper loggia should not have been arranged, as apparently they might have been, without any practical sacrifice, with reference to the arches of the lower. In fact they seem to have been placed at random, and the crowns of the arches are as likely to be loaded as their abutments. There is, however, such a margin of strength of abutment that this defect is merely injurious and not fa-

tal, as it might easily become. The exterior as a whole is a good example of what seems to be unconscious and instinctive art, since an
artist who had been trained to do so much could scarcely have for-
borne to do more. At any rate, the building is more than merely in-
offensive. It is an expressive and a positively attractive piece of architecture.

The official civic architecture of the Spanish settlements resembles itself as strongly, in the East and in the West Indies, as the ec-

INTERIOR OF THE CATHEDRAL, MANILA.

clesiastical. The Chinese church near Manila, and the picturesque
gate at Cavite are, each in its respective kind, unique, so far as goes
the information the present writer has been able to gather. The rule
is that the builder of a public building, in a Spanish settlement wherever, builds it precisely as he would build it in old Spain. It is one
of the results of the immobility of modern Spain that he built it in the
eighteenth century just as he would have built it in the seventeenth
and that he builds it in the nineteenth just as he would have built it in
the eighteenth. The result is that no Spanish public building "dates
itself," except by the extent of its dilapidation ; and that one has to

resort to external evidence for its antiquity, which evidence is also apt to be hard to obtain. But then it also follows that for the purpose of the merely architectural inquirer, it does not matter when it was built. What could be more different from the state of things here at home, where we live in such a flux of what we always call progress, though in this matter it so often proves to be not so, that one can date a public building within twenty years, and almost infallibly, by merely looking at it? But then also one has to allow that

CAPUCHIN HOUSE IN THE LINE OF ENTRENCHMENTS AT
MAYTORBIG, NEAR MANILA.

the Spanish builder shows a sense of specific appropriateness to the work in hand, which we do not always get from the American builder. If among his works we find "a palace and a prison on each hand," his palace does not look like a prison, nor his prison like a palace, though each of them is apt to have the dignity that ought to distinguish a public from a private building.

The almost or quite invariable habit, in Spanish towns, of grouping the public buildings, ecclesiastical and secular, around a central plaza, of course adds immensely to the effect of the individual buildings composing the group, and gives a grandiose air to the collection, even when the edifices that make it up are of no great individual pretension. Strangers find themselves disappointed in the aspect of the commercial quarter of Manila, by reason of the squat and flimsy look of the commercial buildings. This is no doubt largely due to the fact that the Chinese have so much of the trades of the place in their hands, for though the Chinese nation be even more torpid than the Spanish, the individual Chinaman shines, by contrast with the individual Spaniard, in the matter of commercial

From Harper's Weekly.

Copyright, 1899, by Harper & Brothers.

GATE IN CITADEL, CAVITE, NEAR MANILA.

enterprise, and he has impressed the humble character of his native building upon the commercial quarter. But the public buildings of Manila have their impressiveness. The rich Renaissance of the Governor's Palace at Manila is effective in itself. A flat façade containing what is in effect a continuous arcade, though in fact a row of lintelled openings with bull's-eyes above, could not fail to make its impression, and that impression is aided by the very rich and carefully modelled frieze above punctuated with small openings and crowned

CHURCH AT SANTA ANA, A SUBURB OF MANILA.

with a well-adjusted cornice with its parapet, behind which emerges the slope of the unbroken hipped roof. This is by no means so striking a performance as the Orientalized gate at Cavite, but just compare it with the Executive Building at Honolulu! It is not that it is rich alone, but that it is decorous and well-behaved. Equally decorous and well-behaved, equally appropriate to its purpose, is the prison at Manila, which does not bear a single ornament, of which the windows are rectangular holes, all alike, and which owes all its effectiveness to a general disposition which is also extremely simple. The projection of two polygonal ends from a centre rather wider than both, and the differences of roofing enforced by this disposition suffice to give form and comeliness and dignity to a build-

ing which, if not directly expressive of its uses, shows nothing in-
consistent with them. The roof here, with the two stories of the
wall, makes a proportion which could not have been attained in the
absence of a visible roof and the other two terms of this proportion
are indicated and distinguished by the slight string-course between
the stories, one of those simple subtleties that show the designer of
the plainest building to have designed in the spirit of an artist.

Upon the whole, however, Havana is doubtless a more satisfac-

From Harper's Weekly.   Copyright, 1899, by Harper & Brothers.

BRIDGE NEAR MANILA.

tory town to look at than Manila, doubtless the most picturesque
town within "the disposition, government and control" of the United States. The private building has much more the air or solidity
and permanence, an air which it owes to the common use
of stone, and the very frequent employment of white Italian
marble. Also it flowers out more frequently into decoration which really does decorate. And upon the whole
there is more art about the public buildings. The Peninsular institution of the "patio," ultimately an Oriental institution reminiscent
of the seclusion of the zenana, is an excellent device for tantalizing
the by-passer and keeping his curiosity awake as to what is going on
and what is to be seen behind the dead wall. The dead wall itself is

susceptible of "treatment," and often receives it, which emphasizes
its extent and its massiveness, and such apertures as may be required in it are all the more effective for being thus powerfully
framed, while the apertures themselves are necessarily the objects of
design. The glimpses of greenery caught through the openings or
over the garden wall, are more charming for being but glimpses, and
they suggest a mode of "laying out" a residence which might with
great advantage be adapted and adopted in cities within the temper-

CHURCH, AGANA, PHILIPPINE ISLANDS.

ate zone. Mr. Carnegie, in the plans for his new palace in New
York, is the only multimillionaire who has thus far seen his way thus
to enhance the effect of a town-house, and to take as much ground,
or "grounds" as he needed, even where land was enormously costly.

The seclusion of domestic architecture, the fact that the street
fronts consist so nearly of dead wall, has a great advantage in the
relief and setting which such a mode of private building gives to public architecture. In American cities in which the sky-scraper has
begun to prevail it has become quite out of the question that public
buildings should be signalized "above" private buildings in the most
obvious and unmistakable way, by a superiority in actual altitude.
Trinity spire, for more than a generation the landmark of Manhat-
tan Island from the West, presents now a melancholy aspect, inef-
fectually spindling heavenwards among the huge bulks taller than
itself, by which it has come to be surrounded. The simplicity and

especially the lowness of the private building of Havana, generally of
but one story and almost invariably flat-roofed, makes it feasible and
even easy, by a mere increase of scale, to give relief and detachment
to a public building, even of two stories, and none of the public
buildings of Havana has more. What, in a city of low shops and
houses could be more effective than the bulk and height and expanse of the Columbus Market, or what more rational than its general design, an ample, a more than ample corridor and "ambulatory"
surrounding it, the arcade abutted at the corners by powerful piers
weighted with heavy pavillions and the centre distinguished by the
emergence of a pavillion of an additional story, with a balcony at its
base? If we have any monument in New York of this kind and degree of impressiveness, it is the Madison Square Garden, and note

PRISON AT MANILA.

well that the impression of the Madison Square Garden, even apart
from the tower, is distinctly Spanish, an impression which it owes
less to its detail, though that is Spanish also, than to the general composition with the unbroken extent of the low walls, broken on the
short sides by central "features," and on the long sides not at all,
thus showing a wise and modest belief that to exhibit and emphasize
the mere brute length of such an expanse is more efficacious than
anything the architect can "do with it" by trick and device. The
Columbus Market might have been the prototype of the Madison
Square Garden.

There is another civic building in Havana quite as noteworthy,
perhaps more noteworthy, in its very different way. That is what
was the palace of the Captain-General, and is the headquarters of
the American provisional government. This, again, is of two stories
only, but it has not only the relief of the low building of the city in
general, and a decided distinction of scale. It has also the effectual
detachment of the plaza, which, as has already been said, the Spanish
planners of cities never failed to provide for their public monuments.

Here also the lower story is an open arcade, and here also this feature in a public building gains additional effect in a city in which the basement of the private, at least of the domestic building, consists so almost invariably of dead wall. The difference in the first place emphasizes the publicity of the building which is so accessible in contrast to the privacy of the building of which the access is so jealously guarded, and emphasizes by its infrequency the value and picturesqueness of the feature itself. There is one grave defect in the treatment of the arcade in this building. It is a defect very common in the architecture of the South, including that of Italy as well as that

CHINESE CHURCH NEAR MANILA.

of Spain, though it has been entirely avoided in the design of the Columbus Market. It is the same which constitutes the chief drawback to the complete success of the Doge's Palace in Venice. That is the want of a visibly complete and effective abutment at the ends of a long arcade. Here the terminal piers are scarcely more substantial than the intermediate piers, and are visibly inadequate to the work that is required of them. This is the more remarkable and deplorable because the terminal bays do receive in the upper story the separate treatment which they so urgently need in the lower. A very decided increase both in actual mass and in apparent massiveness is imperatively "indicated" for the ultimate abutments of the arcade. The evident inadequacy of these gives the front a look of weakness which no skill of detail could wholly redeem. But imagine these terminal bays made of a sufficient solidity, and the result would be an extremely effective composition. Indeed, that is what it is now, in spite of its faults, or rather of its fault. It recalls to the New Yorker his own City Hall, though the developed triple or quintuple arrangement of a projecting central portion and projecting wings, connected by recessed curtain walls, is merely indicated by the columns that punctuate the flat front of the upper story of the

From Harper's Weekly.　　　Copyright, 1898, by Harper & Brothers.

ARSENAL AT MANILA.

Cuban edifice, and in the continuous arcade of the lower is not even indicated. In revenge, the palace has the advantage of a much freer and less formal treatment, of a much more indigenous and vernacular air, though in fact each building is an exotic and an importation. An importation, that is to say, as to its general composition, but only the New York building as to its detail, for the detail of the Havanese has a delightful freshness and individuality, as if it had been designed, as it doubtless was not, by the man who made it and who enjoyed making it. It is a national possession of which we ought to be proud and careful.

And of our acquired architecture in general we may say that it sets us a standard to which we shall find it troublesome to "live up." The architecture of the Philippines and of the Spanish West Indies is a great deal better, being Spanish, than it would have been had it been "United States." Whoever doubts that has only to look again at those awful public buildings in Hawaii, of which the architecture was introduced under the unbenign influence of the sons of American missionaries. The intrinsic ugliness of these structures is no more marked than their complete absence of relation to their environment. And one of the excellent points about the building of the Spanish colonies has been its appropriateness to its environment. "Metropolitan" as it is, wherever you find it it seems to fit. It has been modified, as we have seen, in some cases by Oriental influences in the Orient, but it has been modified only by the good sense of the individual architects in the Occident, and yet in either case it equally "belongs." It is true that the Spanish mode of building fits the requirements of the Spanish colonies better than would the American mode of building, if there were any. The sunbeaten plains of New Castile and Estremadura are in summer of a tropical heat, and shelter from the sun is then and there the principal need of shelter. The thin walls impermeable to heat, the long dark open arcades along which one may make his way in the shade, these are features of the architecture of the Peninsula which are equally appropriate, which are even more appropriate in the tropical heats of Cuba and Luzon. And these necessary features are susceptible of a most attractive architectural expression. Some of the most sensitive of our own architects have yielded to the influence of Spanish architecture and tried to reproduce something of its effect. The Madison Square Garden in New York we have already had occasion to mention. Not less noteworthy, in the success with which the essential charm of Spanish work has been preserved in a more individual rendering, is the American theatre in the same city. And everybody is agreed about the brilliant success of the Ponce de Leon, the great hotel in Florida, of which the charm is the reproduction of the charm of Spanish architecture.

Upon the whole, it is a matter for national congratulation that our new possessions seem to be supplied with all the public architecture they are likely to need for a good many years to come. No "thoughtful patriot" could contemplate with equanimity the prospect of having designs for public buildings in Havana, in Manila, or in San Juan de Puerto Rico sent out from the office of the average Supervising Architect to come into competition with the architectural remains of the Spanish occupation. They really could not stand it. It is true that even if we keep American official architecture from appearing in a competition which it cannot sustain with Spanish official architecture, we cannot, if our possessions become commercially prosperous, prevent the American engineer from getting in his deadly work. The "colonies" will need railroads, and the railroads will need bridges and other structures and the American engineer will design and build them. "You must think, look you, that the worm will do his kind." He has already done it to some extent, for the railroads of Cuba are of American construction, and there is a Helotic piece of American engineering on the south coast of Cuba, near Santiago, which shows what we have to expect. The average American engineer, as we know him, would not have the slightest hesitation or remorse in demolishing such a piece of artistic engineering as the bridge of San Juan, near Manila, and sending to Trenton or Pittsburg for a nice trussed girder or lovely cantilever to take its place. Nay, he would be apt to gloat over the ruin he had wrought and, when he came home, to read papers about his work to his fellow-vandals. If we added our official architecture to our unofficial engineering, such Spanish patriots as might be left stranded in their Americanized homes would get, in a way additional to the several ways in which it is to be feared they are getting it already, their entire revenge. Their countrymen would appear to them, and to the judicious among ourselves, as the "others,"—

Excudent alli spirantia mollius æra,
Credo equidem, vivos ducent de marmore vultus:

and the old-fashioned Spanish gentleman would be apt to view his conquerors very much as the old-fashioned Roman gentleman might be supposed, if any of him had been left during the fifth and sixth centuries, to have contemplated the procedures of Attila the "hustling" Hun, or of Alaric, the "up-to-date" Visigoth.

Montgomery Schuyler.

RESIDENCE, No. 9 BLUMENSTRASSE, Hamburg, Germany.

F. A. de Meuron, Architect.

F. A. de Meuron, Architect.   DINING ROOM, No. 9 BLUMENSTRASSE,   Hamburg, Germany.

DRAWING ROOM. No. 9 BLUMENSTRASSE.   Hamburg, Germany.

F. A. de Meuron, Architect.

HALL.

FIRST FLOOR LANDING, No. 9 BLUMENSTRASSE,

F. A. de Meuron, Architect.   Hamburg. Germany.

LOUIS QUINZE RECEPTION ROOM.

LIBRARY AND CONSERVATORY.   No. 9 BLUMENSTRASSE,
F. A. de Meuron, Architect.   Hamburg, Germany.

STONE MANTELPIECE IN AGNES SOREL HOUSE, ORLEANS, FRANCE.

THE FITNESS OF THINGS.

I.

IN the old village of Greenwich, which was, not many years ago, the residence portion of New York City and quite "uptown" by stage along Bleecker street, one of the most familiar occupations in the building line is the renewing of brownstone stoops and fronts. Sometimes one sees the "restoration" of classical details accomplished in a most astonishing fashion. Corinthian capitals, which in their day were the glory of the block, having lost portions of their foliage through the action of frost and sunshine, are "restored" into any "style" or "order" which the artistic instinct of the artisan may suggest, being governed, of course, by the amount of brownstone left in place. Whole stoops are seemingly rebuilt and new faces put on the ashlar, and all by a very skillful use of Portland cement, sand and coloring matter.

There does not seem to be very much which is out of place in all this. The houses themselves served the purpose for which they were built, and for the most part have changed hands and are serving a purpose entirely different from that for which they were intended by their former suburban owners. So also the brownstone had served its day and was no doubt the best material available at the time. It was eminently suited to the purpose and had its color in its favor.

II.

While walking up West End avenue not long ago the attention of the writer was attracted to the northeast corner of Eighty-sixth street, where painters were busily at work, where, to a practical mind, it did not seem that a painter should have any reasonable excuse for being at work at all. But in these days of ever-changing methods and new processes one is never done learning, and it usually pays to

SARATOGA MONUMENT.
"Battle of Saratoga."
(Of Connecticut Granite.)   J. C. Markham, Architect.

keep one's eyes open. The building at this particular corner is a church of some pretensions. The congregation is a wealthy one and had cash when it moved from Twenty-second street and Fourth avenue, where it worshipped in a building which never needed painting to the day it was torn down. But here, where the new structure has not been long occupied, the painters were at work. They did not seem to be painting this pile of masonry to bring out any color effect, as the color of the paint used varied but little from the color of the original material. The building did not seem to need paint because of smoke and soot having blackened it. It was of a light colored material, and there is no smoke in that part of New York.

The wonder of the observer that painters should be at work there, on closer examination is changed to astonishment that such a building should be faced with material that actually needs paint or something else to hold it together.

One is inclined to cry out against such an iniquity, but, of course, he has no right to do so. The congregation probably is satisfied, and it is nobody else's business They just moved out of a substantial structure, which at the time it was torn down was considered so good that it was to be re-erected elsewhere, and moved into a structure of earthenware which needs painting. The critics who have traveled in the East say that we should not paint our woodwork, that we mar its beauty by even varnishing it. What then must be said of us when we get to painting our masonry? This does not seem to be just the same case as the brownstone stoops in the village of Greenwich. This is a case of material entirely unsuited to the purpose. This alleged terra cotta no doubt would be an excellent body for a stucco front in a more genial climate, but is not suitable for a structure which is expected to look decent five years after it is erected.

III.

At the circle intersected by Eighth avenue, Broadway and Fifty-ninth street, stands a shaft, erected some six years ago by Italians resident in the United States, to the memory of their illustrious countryman, Christopher Columbus. In front is a figure emblematic of Discovery. The monument is surmounted by a statue of Columbus himself, both beautiful pieces of workmanship—of marble. The teeth of our climate has already begun to eat into these marble figures, and before long they will appear like faded bunting on the face of the imperishable granite shaft, sad remembrances of a glorious festive day which is almost forgotten. The shaft stands as a never-dying monument of the Discoverer of our Country. The beautiful statuary emblematic of the Discoverer himself must succumb to the ravages of our climate within a comparatively few years.

IV.

It was reported in some of our newspapers that at the Dewey celebrations at Washington the beautiful statue of the Father of His Country, which stands on the Plaza facing the Capitol, had been wrecked by an unscrupulous but patriotic urchin who had used his country's ancestor to further his selfish ends. It was not claimed by the news item that the urchin was the first cause of this inglorious downfall of the immortal George. It was mentioned incidentally that the weather had so disintegrated the marble of the statue that it was ready to come down of its own accord.

V.

At the intersection of Broadway, Fifth avenue and Twenty-fourth street, stands the model, life size, of what one day will be without doubt the most magnificent monumental arch ever erected.

Must we, in our generation, witness this arch go to pieces before it is well completed? Or can we in this practical age meet the question of material for this most glorious of all monuments in a practical way? Can we not learn a lesson from the brownstone stoops in the Greenwich of years gone by, or from the short-sighted church, or from the Italian sculpture on the Columbus monument, or from the perishable monument to the imperishable memory of George Washington?

By all means let us honor not only the American navy, but the talented citizens who gave their time and genious and unflinching energy to the production of this marvelous piece of architecture and entrancing sculpture by building it of a material which will last till the end of time.

MAUSOLEUM FOR V. HENRY ROTHSCHILD.
(Granite.)

Brunner & Tryon, Architects.

RESIDENCE OF MRS. THOMPSON.
(Indiana Limestone.)

Madison Avenue and 41st Street, New York City.   Montrose W. Morris, Architect.

Tbe

Architectural Record.

VOL. IX.   APRIL, 1900.   No. 4.

SOME NOTES FROM THE RHINE VALLEY.

STERNBERG.

SPECTACULARLY the Rhine is a disappointment. A broad and turbid stream, surging slowly along in a fertile plain, with the horizon line utterly unrelieved, or, even in the famous gorge, with the height of the surrounding hills discounted by the great width of the river—is not the equal in the qualities of mysticism and romance of a rushing mountain torrent, such as is common in Scotland or in Wales. But it possesses more of grandeur and of majesty, qualities which are not perceptible at first, but which gradually reveal themselves and eventually overwhelm.

The architecture, too, is disappointing, and more permanently so. Everyone has heard of the Rhenish Castles, and everyone in consequence expects to find much beautiful Gothic building of the sterner sort. The remains of the castles are there, sure enough, in heaps of crumbling ruins on every point of vantage along the gorge, picturesque in their decay, but so utterly decayed that there is nothing architectural left. It might be possible, with great pains to reconstruct the plans of some, but of their details and ornamental features nothing tangible is to be found—for one cannot sketch and measure mouldings and enrichments from rumors and vague legend.

ALTER BURG, BOFFARD.

GATE TOWER, ANDERNACH.

REMAINS OF ROMAN GATE AT ANDERNACH.

WATCH TOWER, ANDERNACH.

THURMBERG.

In the riverside towns, however, architectural and archæological interest are alike awakened. Each one has a history, and though the history of one is very much the history of all, yet the evidences vary in each case. Upon two occasions at least the Rhine has formed the principal route along which civilization has marched northwards from Italy. Almost all the towns were founded by Drusus as carefully selected military posts along the great waterway which formed the line of communication for the Roman legions, and evidences of Roman occupation are tolerably frequent, though naturally ruinous, from the heaps of stones which were once the supporting piers of the Aqueduct at Mainz (Mayence), to the archways at Bofford and Andernach. Then, again, in the early days of the Romanesque, there was activity along the Rhine, and towns were revived and buildings erected, based upon those of that period in Italy but with a strong local individuality, caused by the comparatively small size of the available building stone, and by the high-pitched roof which the climate necessitated; and it is quite doubtful whether the lofty towers and spires of the churches which were built at that time were not demanded for the sake of the towns beneath to serve as watch towers in troublous times. These churches are numerous, and most of them are large out of all proportion, as we should think, to the population which they had to serve; yet even now, on Sundays frequently, and

GATE AND GATE HOUSE, BOFFARD.

on high festivals always, they are crowded to overflowing. Most of them have suffered grievously of late at the hands of the restorer, and the German restorer is worse than any other, in the hard, scientific, and mechanical way in which he goes to work; but yet if the detail has been rendered precise and hard, the old general outline remains, with the lofty nave arcade of semi-circular work, the apsis east and west (and sometimes north and south as well), the doors in the aisle walls as a rule, and almost always minor features, the flat buttresses and the external arcading at triforium level, and often under the eaves as well, at least around the apsis if not round the whole church. The detail, even in its restored state, has its interest—for the restorers have faithfully striven to copy the old work scientifically if they have failed to render its original spirit and "go"—with constant evidence of Byzantine influence in the form of the common acanthus leaves, sharply pointed, and with clumsy lions both among them in the capitals and also introduced occasionally at bases. An example of this is seen in the well-known door of Mainz Cathedral, of which a sketch is given.

During the succeeding centuries the little Rhenish towns seem to have flourished well, though subject to constant attacks from neigh-boring towns and from the castles. They were trading centres, the traffic between the sea and mid-Europe passing by them, almost to the exclusion of any other route. As a result of these circumstances they were strongly fortified against attacks both from land and river, but particularly from the water side; and in most cases the walls still remain, if not complete at least in a sufficiently perfect state for re-construction to be easy to the imagination. Upon the land side are irregular walls provided with bastions and towers at the corners, so that all could be protected by archers stationed at these points; with, of course, the deep moat outside, which could be flooded at will from the Rhine. On the river side there would be the wall without the moat, with strongly guarded gates opening down to the water; sim-ilar to gates guarding the entrances to the one main road which usually passed through the town from end to end. A picturesque and almost universal feature was the high watch tower, placed in such a position as to command a view of long reaches of the river. The walls of the towers were generally tapered with the upper pro-jecting portions carried by slight corbel tables; the heavy machico-bations being confined usually to the main wall and just that portion of the towers which overhung the gateways. Of the remains of all this work it is very difficult to decide the date, even though they are considerable in extent; for military architecture seems to have varied little during the middle ages. There is, as a rule, neither tracery nor moulding to assist the judgment, and even the form of the door or window is little indication of the age of the masonry in which it is inserted; for, harassed as these towns were, attacked and taken time after time, such details necessarily were destroyed again and again, only to be rebuilt as soon as peace prevailed once more. Built originally probably for defensive purposes alone with little thought of picturesqueness, they now, at any rate, impart great charm to the little towns which no longer need them for protection; whose prosperity is passed, and whose trade is confined to the little that is done by the sailing barges the greater proportion of the traffic which still passes down the Rhine Valley hurrying past by steamboat or by railway, from great city to great city, ignoring the little towns.

G. A. T. Middleton, A. R., I. R. A.

GAURHAUSEN AND SCHLOSS KATZ

WOODEN HOUSES IN FRANCE DURING THE MIDDLE AGES.

SOME of our readers will perhaps remember having read an essay in this Magazine on wooden house-building in Switzerland, with a number of illustrations of old châlets which still exist.* In that article we stated that the art of working in wood had been exemplified in Switzerland in one of its most picturesque forms, and we endeavored to indicate the principal causes which have made this art so full of grace and animation, namely, a right comprehension of the qualities and properties of wood and an application of building rules appropriate to the material employed. But the Swiss châlet does not exhaust the uses to which wood can be put. It serves other purposes, and not less interesting ones. The ancient and venerable art of carpentry has taken more than one architectural shape, and those who study its various developments are charmed by beauties which, while simple, evidence great skill.

Following our examination of the Swiss châlets, we should like now to visit the old towns of France and seek out their wooden houses, those precious relics of the domestic architecture of the Middle Ages which reveal, to those who know how to question them, an abundance of curious things concerning the kind of life, and the notions of art, of the people of those distant times. Although we have said "following the Swiss châlets," the wooden houses of France date from the end of the thirteenth century, from the fourteenth, fifteenth, and (less frequently) sixteenth centuries, whereas the châlets belong, a few to the sixteenth century, but the majority to the seventeenth and eighteenth centuries. Thus the Swiss art would seem to be a continuation of the French, to which it is posterior, and that logically these studies should have taken France or Germany as their starting point, and finished with Switzerland. It is worth our while to stop to notice this apparent contradiction, for in explaining it we shall touch upon one of the essential points of our studies on wooden house-building, and accentuate the differences of construction in the various countries.

In the Middle Ages the system of building followed in France was that called pan de bois. A glance at one of the photographs here reproduced will show what is meant by this term. It is a system of framework in which the resistance of the timber, serving in turn as brace, or support, or belting-course, is greatly increased by the multiple combinations of the joinery. The spaces left between the differ-

*See Architectural Record, Vol. VI., No. 4; Vol. VII., No. 1.

ent pieces of the framework are pugged, that is to say, filled in with
materials—old plaster work, bricks, etc., which do not bear, but
simply stop up. The pan de bois constitutes the carcass of the house.
It is, in fact, the present method of building in wood, the only one
that French carpenters know; but the wooden framework is now exclusively employed for attics and upper stories, stone or brick form-

FIG. 1.—LE LOGIS ADAM, ANGERS.

ing the bearing part, whereas in the edifices of the Middle Ages the
pan de bois was systematic and general.

In Switzerland, on the contrary, we find, in most cases, beams piled
one on another, crossed and let into each other at the angles. The
timber is massive. See, for example, the Auberge de Treib, or the
Iseltwaldt châlet (Nos. 1 and 5 Architectural Record, July-Sep-

tember, 1897). All the beams bear equally; no combination of frame-work or any relieving arch or keyed-in support is needed. It is, in fact, the ancient blockbau, or log house, refined by decoration being added. The pan de bois, employed also in Switzerland, comes from Germany; what is peculiarly Swiss is the system of piling.

We have thus two distinctly opposite methods of construction; one consisting of clever combinations, and the other being a simple throwing together of materials. One is refined and the other primitive. Now, the stacking-up system is of ancient origin, although the examples we have are almost modern. It is even probable that it represents the earliest manner of building employed by the Indo-

FIG. 2.—OLD "MAIRIE" AND SCHOOL HOUSE, FONTAINE-EN-SOLOGNE (LOIR-ET CHER).

Germanic races. The Swiss châlets are thus connected with very ancient modes of construction, which they perpetuated at a time when, for several centuries, a more skilful manner of building had been developed in France and countries adjacent thereto.* Had we time to seek for the reasons for this we could find several. Among them would be the different species of timber. In Normandy, for instance, oak is used, a knotty wood, hard to cut up and having irregular shoots. Hence the employment of frames, the pieces composing

*"The construction of châlets (piling) is most interesting to study. It is one of the systems of building which approaches the nearest in Europe to the wooden structures of primitive times."—Viollet le Duc.

which never exceed a moderate size. In Switzerland the fir tree abounds, with its slender stems. It has few gnarls, is easily cut, and furnishes without trouble the long, regular beams required for the blockbau. We have to mention, too, the geographical reasons. It is easy to see how, in the isolated Alpine valleys, unaffected by external influences, old traditions retained their sway, traditions which carry us

FIG. 3.—CHATEAU AT THIERS;—A XV. CENTURY HOUSE.

back to primitive ages ; whereas in northern countries, near those seas on which Normans and Danes passed their adventurous existences, it is natural that the skill necessary for the building of ships should have had an influence on the development of the art of wooden house-building. These comparisons make clear the whole art of working in wood, and justify the order followed by us in beginning with the

Swiss châlets and dealing afterwards with the French houses of the Middle Ages.

One general observation is called for before we proceed with our subject. The Swiss edifices are isolated. Even in the villages each châlet is an entity, with its four sides, and the great majority of the examples given by us were country or mountain dwellings. In France,

FIG. 4.—THE FORTIFIED HOUSE AT ROUEN.

on the contrary, the wooden houses are in towns; we shall meet with scarcely a single country house. Most of them are urban habitations, and have only one face, except when they stand at a corner. The purposes to be served by these two kinds of houses are totally different, and this has given each kind a distinct aspect. In Switzerland, as we have seen, the roof projects considerably and, at the corners, shelters

FIG. 5.—A GOTHIC HOUSE, ROUEN.

the galleries and the staircase, which latter is nearly always outside
the house. On the front, under the roof, one finds a balcony. In the
town houses, however, the staircase is inside, while the sides, of
course, could not have anything on them, being party walls. Besides,
the parochial regulations prescribed a certain width of street, and this
led the architects to put successive projections on every story in order
to gain room. Consequently, in narrow streets the upper parts of the
houses almost touched each other, and there was no place for a balcony. Furthermore, a store usually had to be set up on the ground
floor. At the top we find the gable sometimes in front and sometimes
at one side. Finally, the necessity of utilizing the ground to the fullest

FIG. G.—A XVth CENTURY HOUSE, LA ROCHELLE.

extent possible led to houses of several stories being built. In Switzerland there are no châlets with more than two stories above the ground floor, whereas in French towns there are many houses with five. (See the house at Angers shown in Fig. 1).

We thus see that the conditions of existence were entirely opposite. In fact, no two things could differ more than the châlet and the French house differ from each other, both in arrangement and in decoration. Not only do they not serve the same requirements, but, their type once fixed, they develop under totally different conditions of living; here, in the calm and peace of a mountainous country, without excitements and unstirred by the shocks incidental to artistic progress; there, on the contrary, in commercial towns, where the in-

FIG. 7.—WOODEN HOUSES, PLACE DE LA MAIRIE, AURAY.

creasing demands of luxury develop resources, where the political
struggles of the bourgeoisie against the bishops and the feudal lords
gave formidable strength to the middle class, in centres where arose
the most admirable art movement ever witnessed since that of
Greece, namely, that known as the Gothic movement, but which is
French; in short, in a land which has restored monumental sculpture
to the world. Here, therefore, we find a purely ornamental decoration, and there a figurative one; in Switzerland, the continuation of
neo-Latin traditions; in France, the influence of Gothic statuary.

   *   *   *   *   *   *   *   *   *

The building of houses in wood dates back to remotest antiquity.
The Romans introduced into Gaul the art of stone-working, but stone
did not take the place of wood. It served other purposes—for big

FIG. 8.—WOODEN HOUSES, LES ANDELYS.

edifices such as temples, theatres, arenas, for bridges, aqueducts, and other public works which the Romans executed in the lands colonized by them, and also, no doubt, for the villæ in which the chief officers dwelt. But although the Gauls adopted stone as a building material, they continued to use wood as well, which they knew how to manipulate and turn to the best account. The wood-working tradition retained great vitality in Gaul, as is shown by the fact that when invasions destroyed Roman rule and covered the country with a new flood of barbarians, stone fell into disuse and was replaced almost everywhere by wood, even for important buildings. In the time of the Merovingians the churches, according to Gregory of Tours, were built of wood. They were ornate and, for the period, sumptuous edi-

fices, covered with paintings. It was the same under the Carolingians.
This explains the frequent fires which destroyed houses and churches.
A large number of neo-Latin churches and Gothic cathedrals existed first in wood, and after having been burnt down were rebuilt in
stone.* Nothing remains of the wooden constructions of those

FIG. 9.—RUE AUX FEVES, LISIEUX.
(Houses of the XVIth Century.)

distant times. Besides, stone was never altogether discarded; it certainly was employed concurrently with wood for churches and cathedrals. Under the Carolingians, with the Renaissance of learning which
was promoted by Charlemagne, stone played the leading part for
public edifices, but wood held its own as a material for private houses.

*There exists at Troyes, in the Cancleus quarter, a wooden church, called the
Chapelle Saint-Gilles, which is the only specimen still standing of a kind of building very common in olden times.

In the twelfth century the influence of the great Cistercian and Cluniacensian Orders tended to the replacing of wood by stone nearly everywhere. This is the period when, in France, wood played the least important role in domestic architecture. Wherever the

FIG. 10.—WOODEN HOUSE IN PARIS (AUBE).

monks of Cluny or of Citeaux brought their influence to bear stone was first, even in the countries most deeply impregnated with Northern and barbarian elements. In Normandy stone appeared as a competitor of wood, the result being compromises of the kind shown in the Bayeux Tapestry, namely, a ground floor in masonry with an upper story in wood. Viollet le Duc or M. Courajod would see in these buildings the affirmation, on a Roman survival, of that Northern and barbarian ideal which was designed to triumph on French soil with thirteenth century art.

Wood had its revenge in the middle of the thirteenth century, the way having been prepared therefor by political and social changes.

FIG. 11.—RUE DE LA MANUFACTURE, BEAUVAIS.

This was the period when the *bourgeois* class prevailed in their struggle with the lay and ecclesiastical authorities. Using sometimes lord against bishop and sometimes the king against both, they extorted charters everywhere, and when their rights had been guaranteed they were able to work with a certainty of enjoying the fruits of their labors. It was a rich and hardworking class, attached by its condition and its wealth to the cities and towns. Stone, which had been used chiefly by the nobles for their castles and by the church for its religious edifices, offered fewer advantages for the *bourgeoisie*. Wood could be worked far more rapidly and was much cheaper. Hence it was adopted by the middle class. From the end of the thirteenth

FIG. 12.—WOODEN HOUSE, LISIEUX.

century throughout the fourteenth and fifteenth, and even in the sixteenth before the neo-classic Renaissance had produced its full effects and become absolutely triumphant—a triumph destined to endure who shall say how many centuries—wood was in general use for urban constructions.

Consequently, the buildings we have to examine are town houses, erected for merchants and people in easy circumstances. They are not distributed uniformly over France. The south, where Gallo-Roman culture flourished, and where, also, timber was scarce, retained the habit of using stone, even for the humblest dwellings. We cannot offer a single example of wooden house in Provence or

FIG. 13.—WOODEN HOUSE, RENNES.

Languedoc. As can easily be imagined, the bulk of the types are found in the West—Brittany, Vendée, Normandy—and in the North. There are a few in the Centre and in the East. In Dauphiny and in the mountainous districts there are some châlets which closely approach the type most common in Switzerland—square beams piled one on top of another. Finally, in Normandy there still existed some fifty years ago some houses surmounted by a piece of wood in the shape of a crest, which connects the Norman edifices with the Norwegian and general Northern style.

At Angers, there is a fine corner house (No. 1) which shows in a clear manner a few of the characteristics of urban wooden houses.

FIG. 14.—MAISON DE LA REINE BLANCHE, BOURGES.

It is called *Le Logis Adam*. The *pan de bois* is in lozenges, with the sablière beams strengthened, distinctly marking the division into stories. The corbeling is not pronounced. The walls are divided into panels by vertical beams, which are ornamented and decorated. The house has a picturesque aspect; it is symmetrical and ingenious. At the corner is a *bretèche* with five faces, built corbelwise. Very often the *bretèche* served as a staircase which, as in most houses of the Middle Ages occupied by a single family, was inside and went directly from the hall to the floor above. Sometimes, however, the *bretèche* simply enlarged the hall and formed a pleasant corner nook,

FIG. 15.—WOODEN HOUSE, LUYNES (INDRE-ET-LOIRE).

whence, through a couple of small windows, one could see far up the
street. On one of the fronts is the main door (on the other was also a
door, but it has now disappeared) surmounted by a projecting *pan
de bois* reaching to the roof, which has two gables on one side, a piece
of wall forming the coping on the other front. The roofs are covered
with shingles. We see shingles again over the sablières of the second
floor, to keep off the rain. We have met with the same method of protection, so necessary to wooden constructions, in more than one Swiss
châlet, where it is carried out with a logic that goes to an extreme.
(See the *Auberge de Treib*, in the "Architectural Record" for July-
September, 1897.) The framework is in well-preserved oak. It is to be

FIG. 16.—WOODEN HOUSE, LEVROUX (INDRE).

noted that timber keeps much better when exposed to the open air
than when it is covered with a coating of plaster. The plaster, by pre-
venting the action of the air, keeps the wood in a constant state of
dampness which soon eats into and deteriorates it. The woodwork constructed by those excellent carpenters of the Middle Ages has lasted
several centuries, and would endure still longer if it were not that
these pacific and civilized times of ours are more destructive to the ancient beauties than the most troublous periods of the past. It is to be
feared that the moment is not far distant when there will not remain
a single wooden house to tell us how our forefathers loved to live,
what a taste they had for art (although we often call them barbarians)!
and how well they displayed this taste in matters of everyday life. We
have made art a thing for museums. Our houses are comfortable (not

invariably, though), but by no means artistic, and soon there will be no place, even in the remotest corners of France, for the wooden walls so dear to our ancestors. More than sixty years ago an English artist, A. Welby Pugin, drew some of the old timber houses of France, with details of their decoration.* After a series of fine old models comes the last plate, entitled "The Present." It pictures some intrepid workmen cutting up pieces of beautifully carved timber belonging to old houses. To finish as quickly as possible with the past they are throwing the fragments into an immense fire.

The carved decoration of the house at Angers is thoroughly in keeping with the spirit of the Middle Ages. How well we realize that

FIG. 17.—THE SO-CALLED HOUSE OF FRANCIS I., ABBEVILLE.

we are in a part of the world where wood carving is of all arts the most living, the best known and the most familiar! On the ground floor, under the *bretèche*, the corner is occupied by a tree, and everywhere—on the columns, the beam and window-frame supports—we see angels, old women squatting, grinning heads, beasts and battles, monsters, and, what is really exceptional, a centaur, the whole forming a series of subjects and figures which give an appearance of life and animation to the old house. We do not assert that these carvings

*"Details of ancient timber houses, XVth. and XVIth. centuries, from those existing at Rouen, Caen, Beauvais, etc." By A. Welby Pugin. London, 1836.

FIG. 18.—THE PRESBYTERY AT TREPORT.

are of great artistic merit, but they are in their place, they are not pretentious, they express what they are intended to say, and bear witness to an attention to art which was as common then as it is rare nowadays. Before leaving *"Le Logis Adam"* we must note the fine projections of the sablière beams and the strong accentuation of the window frames. These marked reliefs are quite in accordance with the best traditions of woodworking.

No. 2 is a rustic model, the only one we are able to offer. It is the old town hall of Fontaine-en-Sologne (Loir-et-Cher). The building is the simplest that could be, and the least ornamented, consisting of only one floor, on a level with the ground. The walls are schematic.

Note how ingeniously the big beams of the roof are upheld by a piece of timber resting on a middle beam. It is impossible to fix the date of this house to a couple of centuries. When there are no carvings which will guide one it is often daring to speak positively, as the traditions of a trade remain fundamentally the same for ages. The primitive framework having once been found, it continued to subsist practically unchanged. The only guide to the date of an edifice is the additions made at later periods. In regard to the old town hall of Fontaine-en-Sologne, we would draw attention to the survival of an ornament of the highest antiquity—we mean the decoration in diagonal lathes re-

FIG. 19.—AT SAINT-VALERY-EN-CAUX (SEINE INFRE).

producing the decoration applied to stone or pottery by the Gauls many centuries before the Roman conquest. See, as an example of this, the celebrated Gallic warrior in the museum at Avignon, on whose shield there is the same kind of ornament. We are not aware that it has been remarked before on any building.

Reverting now to urban dwellings, we have here (No. 3) the Château at Thiers, a fifteenth century house with a *pan de bois* of regular arrangement, the traditional corbelings, a shop on the ground floor, and a handsome roof with a shapely gable whose projection is supported by a frame the lines of which are most harmonious. The proportions of this house are excellent, and the roof is exceptionally elegant.

The "Fortified House" at Rouen seen in No. 4 is much more massive. It has a rude aspect. The solid arris, the big horizontal beams of the first floor, protected by boards, the coping and the turret, speak

FIG. 20.—HOUSE NEAR THE CATHEDRAL, RENNES.

of a troubled period and the need of being able to defend one's house in case of an outbreak. Rouen, which is so rich in art, will furnish us with other examples more ornate and delicate. Indeed, in No. 5 we have one of the most richly decorated wooden edifices that has come to our notice.

The method followed in this case differs from what we have seen in the preceding examples. The *pan de bois* is entirely covered with carved boards and the house has the appearance of a richly worked piece of wainscoting. It is the flaming Gothic style, and we can readily fix the fifteenth century as the one in which the house was

FIG. 21.—HOUSE ON THE GRAND PLACE, ROYE: (SOMME).

built. The carvings are most ornamental; the frieze which crowns the first floor has a fine effect, but some people may think that this decoration, rich though it be, is not properly architectural, and that the house lacks the relief which wooden constructions often present.

The houses which follow are of quite another character. The first of them (No. 6) dates from the fifteenth century and is located at La Rochelle. It is distinguished by an arrangement of parallel vertical beams going from one story to another and crossed by a single beam placed diagonally. The intervals are filled with white plaster, from which the dark lines of the beams stand forth strongly. The general

FIG. 22.—WOODEN HOUSE, ROUEN.

decorative effect is very curious. The arrangement has been largely copied in English for modern country houses, probably without any knowledge of its origin. In the "Architectural Record (Vol. V., No. 4), there is a picture of a country house, "The Cedars," at Edgbaston, whose walls are built in this fashion. The ground floor and the entresol of the house at La Rochelle are in stone; then, on a large corbel supported by stone consoles, comes the woodwork.

We have selected a specimen in Brittany which is to a great extent similar (No. 7). These houses are situated at Auray, the celebrated

place of pilgrimage. There is the same kind of vertical arrangement
of the beams, although the house is laid out in a totally different manner from the preceding one. Many other examples might be cited,
but those given are sufficient to illustrate this manner of construction.
We will add, however, on account of its elegant first floor and its fine
crowning frieze, the "*Hotel du Grand Cerf*," at Andelys, whose walls
are relieved, from day to day, by console beams which have a most
happy effect (No. 8).

The succeeding illustrations (Nos. 9, 10 and 11) present a picturesque aspect of the streets of the Middle Ages. The first one shows
some old houses in the. Rue aux Fèves at Lisieux, in Normandy
They belong to the sixteenth century, but were it not for certain
carved details they might just as well be a couple of hundred years
older. We see clearly the idea the builder had of corbeling. In wood
construction it is done in the simplest manner. The beams of each
floor extend from a foot and a half to three feet beyond the line of the
story below. On these ends is placed the sablière beam of the next
story. The whole is strengthened by brackets which support the ends
of the beams. Corbeling was the rule in the Middle Ages. Generally
there are two stories, the upper one overhanging the ground floor to
the extent of several feet. Doubtless this shut off a good deal of air
from the lower part of the houses, but it was necessary to make the
most of the available space, and in town houses the living rooms were
always above, so that it was only the shop, which occupied the ground
floor, that suffered from lack of light and air. From a picturesque
point of view the old street, with its pointed gables, its large dormer
windows, its successive corbelings, the door and window carvings,
and, above all, the individual appearance of each house, with a style
and decoration of its own, evidently presented a picture far more
cheerful, varied and artistic than the modern street offers with its lines
of utilitarian barracks. In the Middle Ages the house was a thing
which a man constructed not only for himself but to be handed down
to his descendants. For this reason it was ornamented and given a
stamp of its own, for it was built for a particular family having its
own style of life, its own traditions, and desiring a dwelling place in
harmony with its tastes.

It will be remarked that there are also at Lisieux some specimens
of the *pan de bois* of which we have spoken above. The following
houses are at Beauvais and Bayeux. The brackets supporting the
corbels afforded an excellent opportunity for carved decoration, and
the clever *ymaigiers* of the fifteenth and sixteenth centuries profited
thereby, as we shall see in detail. But before coming to the more
elaborately ornamented houses let us look at a few simple types of
large houses.

At Lisieux there is a house with two gables on the street. The way in which the attics are sheltered is interesting. It has been much imitated latterly for country houses, especially in England. In this house we see the variety of effect proper to wooden edifices. The employment of crossings of different kinds of wood is in itself a decoration. The Norman roofs are always tall and picturesque.

Here again we must lay stress on that peculiarity of wood construction which we took pains to explain and illustrate in our essay on Swiss Châlets and which consists in taking advantage of the necessary and organic elements of the construction, and, instead of trying to hide them, endeavoring to turn them to account and make them express a decorative theme. What was true of the châlets is equally true with regard to the French houses of the Middle Ages. The big sablière beams, the brackets and the external and visible arrangement of the framework are at the same time a decoration, not accidental but intentional; not haphazard but desired and aimed at.

At Rennes (No. 13) there is a house of very different aspect. Note the curious manner in which the corbels are executed, and the place occupied by the carvings on either side of the door.

In the next house (No. 14), which is to be seen at Bourges, we meet with another spirit and other aims. It is called *"La Maison de la Reine Blanche."* The timber work is reduced to a minimum; only the main lines are visible, the panels being filled in with brickwork. But what rules supreme here is the carved decoration, and being the first really complete example we have, it is worth while to pause and to look into it.

In Switzerland, where we have a standpoint from which to make a comparison, the châlets receive a very rich carved decoration; but it is pure ornamentation, not statuary. It consists of friezes with series of small arcades, and of diamond moulding, awaking in the mind recollections of Romanic decoration, of which the art of the châlets is but a survival. We have remarked how interesting is this tradition, which is seen flourishing again on the Swiss châlets so many centuries after its disappearance from Europe. In France the wooden houses slipped away from the Romanic tradition. Construction in wood was only recommended, as we have seen, at the end of the thirteenth century, when Gothic art had already reached the plentitude of its means and forms. The art of working in wood seems to have remained a stranger to the expansion of thirteenth century art, and even during the following century it furnished no contribution to the artistic work of the century. This is a curious thing, and one which cannot be explained; but it must be noted that while we know certainly that wooden houses were built at the end of the thirteenth century and during the whole of the following one, we have not a single example of wooden houses with thirteenth or fourteenth century carvings thereon. We must come to the fifteenth century to find, in the kind of construction we are dealing with, a current of art similar to that which manifested itself in stone construction. The only houses with carvings are fifteenth and sixteenth century edifices; and we must add that statuary then occupied a far more prominent place than ornamentation.

One sees here without difficulty that one is in a place where the representation of the human face and body is a thing that has been done for a long time past, where the faculty is possessed of expressing in the plastic art the sentiments and passions, and where, too, it was known how to unite carved decoration to the architectural conception.

In the "*Maison de la Reine Blanche*," for instance, where it is found quite natural to figure on the ground floor pillars, scenes from sacred history, such as Christ in the Garden of Olives; there, a kneeling woman playing a viol and wearing the ample robe with heavy folds of which Burgundian sculpture had, at the beginning of the century, produced unforgetable models? Above, there are consoles, supporting heads; here, the large face of a monk; there, a woman's face, wearing a hood. On the brackets of the roof there is the same series of grotesque heads, many of the types of which are to be seen on the stalls of cathedral choirs. Thus, this house, although not a palace nor a grand abode, furnishes a contribution to the statuary treasures of its period.

At Luynes (Indre-et-Loire) there is, on the square of the town, a high-roofed house which has some fine carvings on the big beams of its ground floor (No. 15). On one of the doorposts there is a long-robed Virgin, and on the other a Virgin with the body of Christ on her knees; at the end, on the same side, a Saint Christopher crossing the Waters, and on the other a bearded individual of majestic mien, perhaps a wise man of the East. This splendid series of carvings now ornaments a butcher's store. To us this is not at all displeasing. This art was not a mandarin's art; it was intended to be understood and loved by all, and it is in its right place near the lowly and those who toil. More than one such house could be found in France, although many images taken from Holy Writ were destroyed during the religious wars, during which the Protestants acted with the greatest barbarity whenever they came across scenes dear to Catholic iconography. Besides, a great number of these figures were removed, and very few of them have found their way into our museums.

At Levroux there is a corner house with some curious grotesque figures carved on the capitals. (No. 16.)

The next four houses are interesting in several ways. They carry us towards the sixteenth century. The spirit of the Renaissance shows itself therein, at first in the ornamentation, as is always the case, and afterwards in the construction; and then it is the decay, and speedily the ruin, of the woodworking art.

The house at Abbeville named after François Premier is faithful
to the old-fashioned style of construction. It marks the end of a
Gothic epoch; statuary mingles with the ornamentation, which is still
Gothic. Above the door one sees a Virgin holding the Child Jesus.
(No. 17.)

The presbytery at Treport is a house in which brick and stone combine with wood in the happiest manner possible. Upon a ground
floor in masonry there is an overhanging *pan de bois* with heads in medallions ornamenting the beam ends. (No. 18.) The decorative effect
obtained by the crossing of the timbers and the filling-in of bricks in
two colors is charming.

A large house at Saint-Valery-en-Caux shows us a fine arrangement of timberwork, and gives another example of the old habits of
construction. The new spirit is manifested in the large ornamental
friezes running in three lines along the front. It is the antique ornamentation—masks and garlands; balusters above the doors. The
carvings are much dilapidated, but enough is left to fix the date of the
work. (No. 19.)

At Rennes we have a very pretty entrance of a house dating from
the same period. The crossings, the decoration, and the admirable
proportion of the parts, make it an example of excellent style, and we
think it will be examined with interest. (No. 20.)

The house illustrated in Figure No. 21 is situated at Roye
(Somme), and is also a typical specimen of the class we are now studying. In general appearance it belongs to the Middle Ages. The
shape of its roof, and its bays of joists, which strive to appear ingeniously combined, but are in reality heavy and awkward, might date
the end of the fifteenth century, whereas the carvings on its brackets,
and the decorative spirit of the façade, place it in the middle of the
sixteenth. Note the heads, the foliage, and the brackets, covered with
all the cast-off clothing of Roman antiquity, which surely has no
business on this Middle Age carpentry.

We now reach the completion of the system whose first types we
have here pointed out. Standing before the Renaissance house at
Rouen shown in Fig. 22, we feel we have changed country. Assuredly
if we wished to consider merely the manual dexterity of the sculptor
who has carved this front as one would carve a chest or a coffer, there
would be ground for admiration, and we would be ungrudging in our
praises. The work is rich and of remarkable finish. Every part is
covered with the most elaborate ornamentation. On the brackets are
little genii, who come from afar and speak a foreign tongue; the wide,
plain borders, the false galleries on the several stories (for the pilasters certainly suggest a gallery); the masks on the brackets, and
lastly, the medallions on the upper story—everything combines to
denote a common origin, not French, but antique. It is an adapta-

tion, not an original. But what is more important is that it is not an adaptation of a style of working in wood, but a transposition from one material into another. This system of decoration belongs properly to the art of working in stone; it is in stone that it was created and developed, and one cannot understand it otherwise. In wood it is void of signification. In our article on the Swiss châlets we explained the deep-rooted reasons for the art values of these constructions, namely, that châlet construction is real, not transposed; that it is based on the qualities of the substance, and that it has logically followed the rules of construction imposed by the choice of this material.

French house construction of the Middle Ages, with other needs to satisfy and other kinds of timber at its command (oak, not fir), has obeyed the same logical principles. It was timber-work, and timber-work it has remained, and it has managed to extract from its theme of construction charming decorative effects fully in harmony with this theme. Wooden house-building, as understood at that period, had a long and not unlovely existence. But the Renaissance came. The Renaissance has often been described as a setting free of minds, but it would seem that those who so judged it did not know the Middle Ages and could not trace the results of Humanism. There was more liberty for art in what are called the Dark Ages than in our French seventeenth century. We know people who prefer Rheims, Paris or Amiens to Versailles or the Jesuit churches. These truths, suspected fifty years ago by a few, are now making their way in the world. One is able to hold these ideas without calling down the scorn of those who talk of art.

In the domain we are dealing with, *Antiquity established and demonstrated*, as the erudite seventeenth century humorist said, had the effect of ruining the beautiful and savory forms in which still breathed the life of the nation's past. It subjected Europe to the uniformity of its rule. No more personal interpretation, no more racial sentiment. The antique canons were law.

The French sixteenth century defended itself well. It was robust enough to swallow the foreign food and assimilate it to its temperament. The admirable series of castles of the Loire are thoroughly French, notwithstanding the ornamentation and the evident plagiarisms. But it is the end, and that for a long time to come.

Wooden house construction was also condemned. Antiquity declared that the only art worthy of the name was that of stone, and stone began its reign of absolutism. Wood, when by chance it was employed, endeavored, in order to exalt itself, to imitate stone, as, for instance, in that house at Rouen which we have before us. Such complete forgetfulness of its origin and *raison d'etre* proclaims the end of the art, for it is evident that stone is far superior to timber for this kind of construction and this system of decoration. Wood is not

FIG. 23.—WOODEN HOUSE, BAR-SUR-SEINE, AUBE.

strong enough to struggle here, not being on its own ground. It has nothing to do but disappear. The Rouen house may create an illusion by its carved chest appearance, but look at a *pan de bois* of the seventeenth century; that, for instance, of the house shown in Fig. No. 23, situated at Bar-sur-Seine, in the Aube. There the absurdity is glaring. These fluted pilasters, those composite capitals, those heavy brackets, the ovolos and the palm leaves, the window supports, and, mingled with the whole, a *pan de bois* regularly and wisely arranged—all this makes up an architectural monstrosity, and we feel that we ought to apologize for putting it before our readers.

The *pan de bois*, as understood in the Middle Ages, is of no use now for urban constructions. It has, however, a fairly wide field in rustic architecture. Combined with brickwork, it is still employed with success, and we believe that architects can find in the types here submitted more than one interesting motive, more than one ingenious arrangement which deserve to be revived. As has been seen, the effect of a fine *pan de bois* is picturesque, and, owing to the variety of combinations it allows, it is capable of rendering good service in the hands of a skilful architect. In any case, the ever-powerful charm of these old houses, and the knowledge of their approaching end, are in themselves adequate reasons to justify this backward glance into the past.

Jean Schopfer.

THE AMERICAN TRACT SOCIETY'S BUILDING.
Nassau and Spruce Streets, New York City.   R. H. Robertson, Architect.

Some

Entrances

To the

Skyscraper

ENTRANCE, NEW YORK LIFE INSURANCE CO.'S BUILDING.
Broadway and Leonard Street, New York City.   McKim, Mead & White, Architects.

ENTRANCE TO THE DE VINNE BUILDING,
Lafayette Place, New York City.   Babb, Cook & Willard, Architects.

ENTRANCE TO THE UNITED STATES TRUST CO.'S BUILDING.
Wall Street, New York City.   R. W. Gibson, Architect.

ENTRANCE TO THE MILLS BUILDING,
Broad Street, New York City.   George B. Post, Architect.

ENTRANCE TO THE NATIONAL BANK OF COMMERCE BUILDING.
Nassau Street and Cedar Street, New York City.
James B. Baker, Architect.

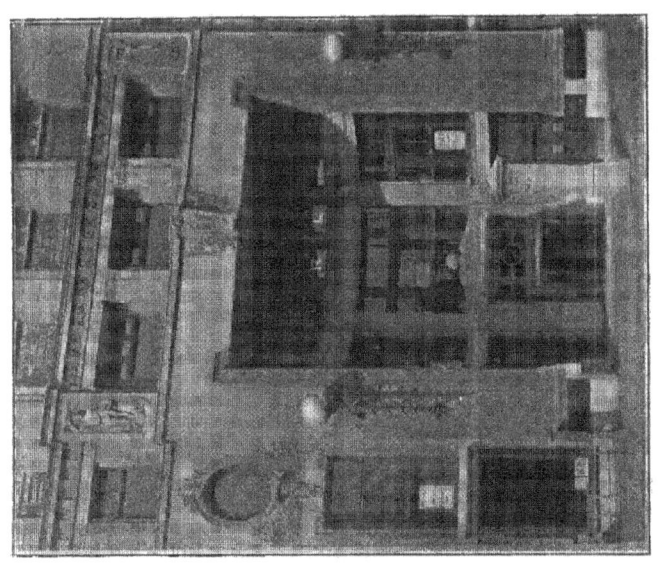

THE POSTAL TELEGRAPH CO.'S BUILDING,
Broadway and Murray Street, New York City.
Geo. Edward Harding & Gooch, Architects.

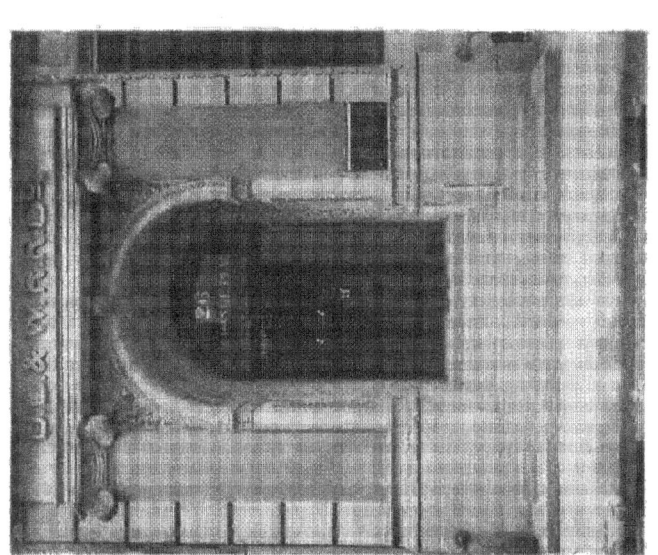

THE D., L. & W. R. R. CO.'S OFFICES,
Exchange Place, New York City.
L. C. Holden, Architect.

56 SOUTH WILLIAM STREET.

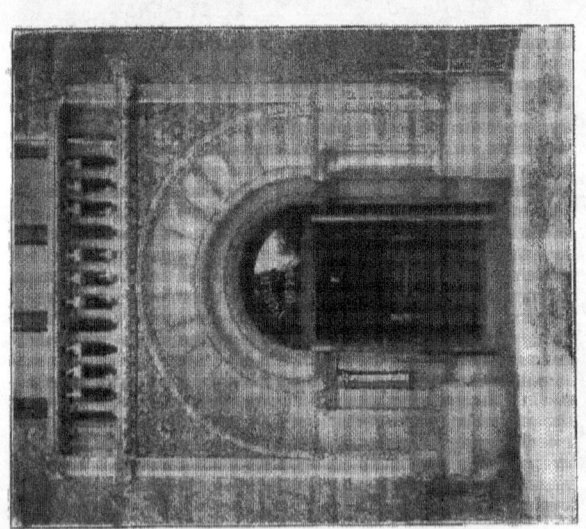

THE NEW YORK TIMES BUILDING.
Park Row, New York City.
George B. Post, Architect.

THE FARMERS' LOAN AND TRUST CO.'S BUILDING,
William Street.
Clinton & Russell, Architects.

THE WOLFE BUILDING,
William Street and Maiden Lane, New York City.
H. J. Hardenbergh, Architect.

THE MORRIS BUILDING,
Broad Street, New York City.
Youngs & Cable, Architects.

DELMONICO'S,
Beaver Street, New York City.
R. H. Robertson, Architect.

THE ENTRANCE TO ALDRICH COURT,
45 Broadway, New York City.   James E. Ware, Architect.

THE GALLATIN BANK BUILDING,
Wall Street, New York City.   Cady, Berg & See, Architects.

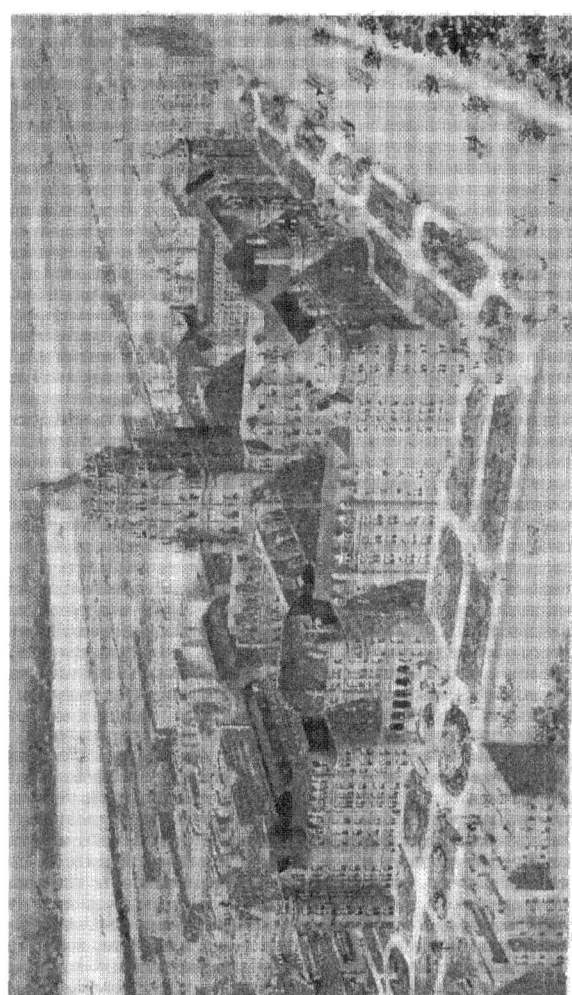

By courtesy of Harper & Bro.

Cady, Berg & See, Architects

BIRDSEYE VIEW OF THE MUSEUM OF NATURAL HISTORY AS IT WILL BE WHEN COMPLETED.

THE MAKING OF A MUSEUM.

REFERENCE in the following pages is made only to Scientific Museums, or Museums of Natural History and Economic Exhibits, and no reference whatever is intended to Art Collections, whose arrangement is based upon different considerations, though in some forms or sections of both Art and Scientific Museums the interests and aims are identical.

In the discussion of the Installation of Museums the subject splits up at once into three groups, of equivalent importance perhaps, but of entirely divergent character. These three are Technique, System, and Effect. Technique relates to or embraces mechanical adjustments, conveniences, receptacles, buildings, and the physical constants, or material. System relates to or embraces scientific sequence, illustration, and information. Effect contains the whole subject of æsthetic presentation.

Technique.

In the widest and apposite use of the term, Technique expresses the artisan phase of installation, reaching from illumination which hints at the construction of the museum itself to the best form of pins for suspension or insertion of specimens. It covers the multivarious details of *how* to exhibit an object, without bearing upon beauty of effect or implications of science. It commends to the curator considerations of stability, of cleanliness, and efficacy. Therefore it relates to the simple elements of construction, including in that term *form* and *material*.

Under *form* it discusses size, shape, and arrangement of a Hall of Exhibition, or the Domiciliary; size, shape and relations of cases, or the Loculus; size, shape and relations of trays, supports, shelves, blocks, standards, pediments, and all accessories of the same, or the Paraphernalia.

Under *material* it discusses or compares the advantages of material entering into the Domiciliary, Loculus or Paraphernalia, as wood, stone, iron, ivory, celluloid, paper, silk, plush, cotton, cork, paint, etc. To resume in a tabular form these distinctions we have:

Form— { Domiciliary. / Loculus. / Paraphernalia.
Material—All useful fabrics.

System.

By System it is not implied that we are entitled to discuss classification of organisms or objects, whether minerals shall be arranged

by formulæ or bases, plants by Gray's or Britton's manual, inverte-
brates by Cuvierian or Huxleyan methods. But there is implied by
System the discussion of such means and ways of display that lead
to certain intended results with reference to a mental impression on
the spectator. Such Systems are quickly comprehended under three
heads—Popular, Philosophical, Scientific—separated most naturally
by the simple implication of the terms. The Popular System informs
the visitor what the objects are, bending on each a discriminating attention. The Philosophical System develops the relations of objects
to each other and to their environment; it may be teleological, it may
be evolutionary, it may be simply spectacular. The Scientific System
tells of objects, their terminology, taxonomy, morphology, biology
and the varied aspects of living things as deciphered by Science.

How these results shall best be attained can be a legitimate consideration under Installation.

Effect.

Effect is quickly understood. The æsthetic quality of a display is
gauged upon inspection. And such effects are numerous; tasteful,
impressive, sensational, sumptuous, plain; but referring always to
visual impressions affecting our sense of beauty, propriety, clearness, etc.

Taking up these separate heads under which it seems possible to
group all questions of Installation, we have a conservative series of
topics which leads us from the basic mechanical structure to the ultimate emotional expression which, issuing from the separate factors,
and from the unity of all factors, pervades the whole Museum.

Technique.

Domiciliary.

The museum building, when many storied, should be rectangular.
It is evident that all curves, irregularities of surface walls, notches,
cones, recesses, disturb the succession of cases, confuse the light and
produce mechanical difficulties in arrangement and construction of
cases. This rectangular building should be shortened in one direction and lengthened in the other in order that the lights falling in on
either side should not lose their intensity by penetration, but somewhat mingle. A square building is objectionable because it is not apt
to be as well illuminated as a narrow one. Such a building should be
placed, in this latitude, and generally, north and south, so that morning and afternoon light could enter it. Its width should be about
fifty feet, and may vary to thirty. Above fifty the illumination is reduced, and below thirty the halls fail to furnish adequate space for
economical exhibition. It is impossible to extend one building indefinitely north and south; additions in some way are imperative.

Their best disposition if the ground is available is in a succession of separated houses arranged *en echelon*, so as not to interfere with each other's light, and connected by terminal halls.

Groupings (Fig. I.) of this character can be indefinitely varied, and they can be made architecturally attractive separately, and their combination distinctly imposing. But such groupings are usually impossible. They occupy too much ground, they involve an expensive duplication in structure, and they are too scattered, failing in massiveness and solidarity. They besides are more exhaustive of effort and energy to visitors. Yet to such a degree as these long merid-

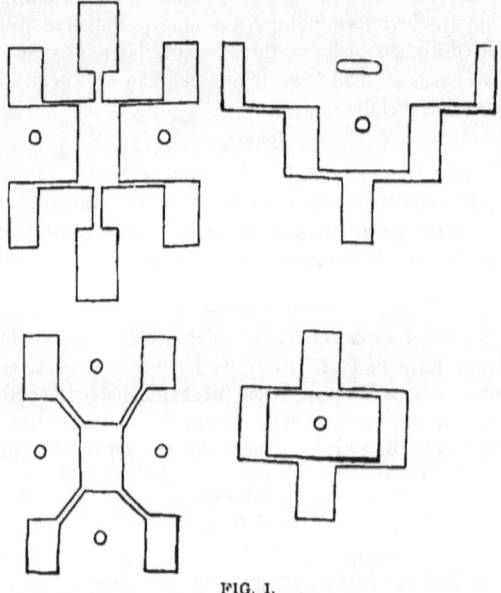

FIG. I.

ional structures can be obtained in connection with a more reasonable disposition of material they should be desired, because their illumination meets usually the most exacting requirements.

In cogency of design, as involving such an arrangement, a wide elongated court, walled in by the continuous museum buildings with axes north and south can be recommended. The width of such a court, however, should scarcely be less than five hundred feet, so that the opposite sides of the court should not prove mutually obstructive of light in the mornings and afternoons. The north and south walls connecting the ends of the long side structures will offer a great deal of room, and cannot, of course, be rejected for exhibition uses, but in order to secure light their ceilings should be high and their width greatly narrowed. In this latitude such east and west buildings, if made deep, lose light greatly along the north interior walls. A better plan as involving less east and west lines are two long buildings connected by a narrow hall of one or many stories, which is a corridor of connection and which can be devoted most attractively to the illustra-

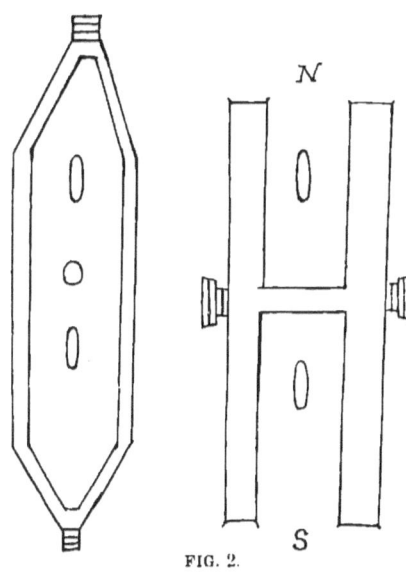

FIG. 2.

tive uses of maps, photographs, and pictures (Fig. 2). A still further modification which provides an almost uninterrupted series of equally lighted halls is the erection of a prow-shaped terminus to the quadrangle of buildings, formed from two inclined wings meeting in a common entrance (Fig. 2). In this case again the dimensions contemplated are rather greater than is usual, and the complete inspection demands a fatiguing journey, and the conveniences of intercommunication is reduced to a minimum. Still ideal conditions only are here regarded, and the human factor must retire into extinction.

A museum building can be erected in the form of a rectangle connected by four arms from a central tower, as is the case with the projected complete structure of the American Museum of Natural History. (Fig. 3). But the criticism to be made here is the great width —500 ft.—of the wings on the south and on the north sides of the rectangle, which are not meant to be connective members simply, but form exhibition halls (the south wing of the A. M. N. H. will soon be completed, and, as the museum stands now, constitutes over three-fourths of the whole edifice) which yield defectively illuminated halls on account of their cardinal position east and west. The same length of building north and south would have been preferable. The National Museum at Washington is in the shape of a Greek cross with a central rotunda. The four main arms or "naves" around this rotunda are 101 feet in length and 62 feet wide, and the rotunda rises 108 feet. The exterior angles are filled in with the "courts," 65 feet square, and these are again flanked by the "ranges," whose

outer walls form the extension of the whole building, which is thus
filled out into a complete square. This plan would be most objectionable as far as illumination is concerned, if it were not that it is

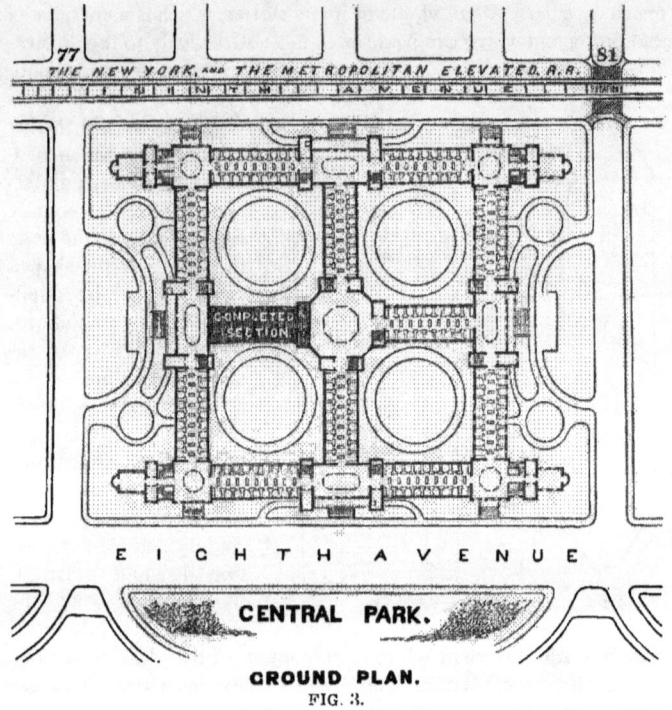

CENTRAL PARK.

GROUND PLAN.

FIG. 3.

carried out on a single level with clear-story windows, which contribute the skylight to the general illumination.

Even under the circumstances given the illumination of the
National Museum is not wholly satisfactory, in fact at points is very
poor. The limits of time in which there is good lighting are shortened in all single-story roof-lighted buildings, where the walls are
very high and the skylight is replaced by clear-story windows, or
the skylight has insufficient slope. In regard to the unfavorable condition produced by the combination of high walls and skylights,
Mr. L. C. Laudy, a most able and experienced photographer, tells
me that from his own experiments he has found that a gradual increasing of the height of the wall greatly diminishes the light. There
are in this connection obvious modifications of the shape of a skylight to be considered, according to the latter's length, for architectural effect, viz, a long skylight should not have too steep a slant, and
a short one not too low.

The light at this latitude varies significantly in the different seasons, and upon the two opposite aspects (north and south) of a building. In summer the sun reaches at the solstice the extreme northern latitude of verticality of $23\frac{1}{2}°$; in winter it is never vertical, and the inclined rays in the morning and evening then issue from a point approaching tangentiality with our latitude. The contrast of the north and south sides of a building in illumination is very noticeable from December until April, and hence the meridional position—the flank exposure—is so much to be preferred. To secure the maximum illumination at all seasons the flat or one-storied museum with skylight, clear story, etc., has been devised. It is always best shown in the great exhibition halls of the different World's Fairs, where the possibility of the largest possible public inspection is desired. This result was very well attained in the Government Building at the Centennial in Philadelphia (1876) and at the Mines and Mining, Transportation and Horticultural Buildings at Chicago. In such buildings extreme height must be avoided.

The Manufacturers' and Liberal Arts Building at Chicago was covered, in its skylight, with eleven acres of glass, but its enormous height of 210 feet precluded the full effect of its upper stories and covering of windows. One-storied canopied buildings, if low, are defective in appearance, and they are diffuse and expanded, covering a good deal of ground while they furnish insufficient wall space, unless cut up into rooms and halls, producing thereby a tangled and confusing labyrinth, and interfering with the aims we shall further consider under System and Effect.

A very tantalizing result of total reflexion occurs also with skylights, unless properly obviated, whereby the glass of flat cases, exposed beneath them, become the mirrors of the roof, and reflections of gratings or sashes are distractingly mingled with the view of shells and minerals.

Material.

The material used in the construction of the Museum building is determined, of course, by taste, resources and convenience. Thick walls form a protection against damp, and stone and fire brick are partial safeguards against fire. Such walls, however, must be provided with a hollow air space, otherwise their thickness is an insuperable obstacle to proper dryness. The most complete defense against the misfortune of fire is an isolated or detached position. Wooden floors are objectionable. They do not admit of complete cleaning, and they accumulate and form dust. The interior of a museum should be austerely plain; mouldings and decorative woodwork, even such purposive decorations in plaster as at the S. Kensington in London, should be repressed or abandoned. All niches, crevices, pits, depressions and traps for dust must be religiously excluded. Artistic effects are to be sought, but by somewhat different paths.

The museum building can be carried upward to any height, and where space cannot be easily obtained in a north and south line, rather than grow sideways let the museum structure rise upward with additional stories. This has never been tried because it interferes with architectural pretense, but it will keep the museum in the best plane for light as explained before. It is perfectly feasible and not necessarily ugly. I believe a sixteen or twenty storied bank of halls would, when the very best position had been selected, form an admirable and almost perfect museum structure. The ascensional possibilities of arrangement would permit a very philosophical development of ideas in System and classification from inorganic through organic to human subjects.

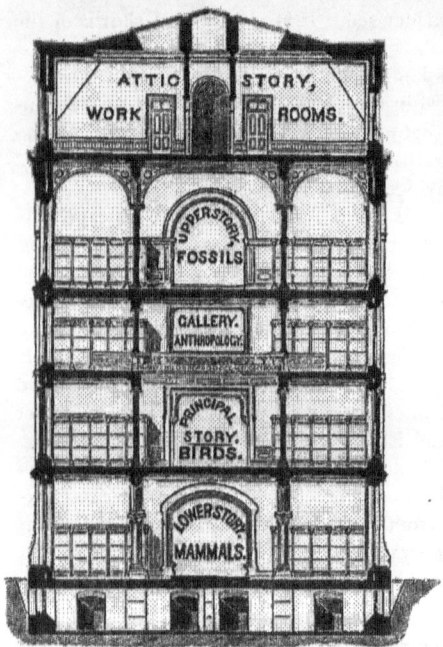

TRANSVERSE SECTION.

FIG. 4.

The material, position and size of the building being fixed, and, considering a four-storied simple rectangular structure as the form contemplated, the windows and the varying heights of the different stories is next to be determined. The proportions of the first section of the American Museum of Natural History in New York are almost ideal. They can be always safely copied. (Fig. 4.)

```
Whole length of building....................................   210 ft.
Tower at north end holding stairway.........................    20  "
Width of building ..........................................    64  "
Height of building .........................................   100  "
Basement floor, above cellar, height........................    22  "
Main floor .................................................    25  "
Gallery floor, surrounding main floor, width................    15  "
Gallery floor, surrounding main floor, height...............    15  "
Fourth floor, height .......................................    22  "
Fifth floor (workrooms, etc.), height.......................    15  "
```
Windows on each floor, nine, opposite.
Basement—Height, 14½ ft.; width, 6½ ft.; rectangular.
Main floor—Height, 12½ ft.; width, 6½ ft.; rectangular.
Gallery floor—Height, 8 ft.; width, 6½ ft.; rectangular.
Fourth floor—Height, 14 ft. at centre; width, 6½ ft.; pointed arch.

Windows on the fifth or attic floor can be modified as desired. Such illumination as this produced was unexcelled. This original section of the New York museum might make a museum *unit*, and every museum be a juxtaposition of such units, or a multiple combination of them. The above dimensions are appropriate. All museum buildings are essentially rectangular, the towers, arms and enlargements being accessory to this initial nucleus, special features of special purposes or structural ornament. Indeed, the *box* is the ultimate museum cell element. The building, the cases, the trays, the labels—one dimension reduced to zero—are boxes, and their multitudinous sizes and ornamentation and positions do not conceal the uniform and necessary form underlying all.

The Domiciliary provided the Loculus comes next under consideration.

The Loculus.

This embraces the cases which are wall, flat, or desk cases, and special or group cases, and turnstiles, drawers, and storerooms.

Cases.—Dr. Goode has remarked that "of all the practical questions which confront the museum administration those relating to the form and construction of cases and the methods of interior fitting are among the most perplexing, and, so far as the relationships of the museum to the public are concerned, the most important. Each well-arranged case, with its display of specimens and labels, is a perpetual lecturer, and the thousands of such constantly on duty in every large museum have their effect upon a much larger number of minds than the individual efforts of the scientific staff, no matter how industrious with their pens or in the lecture room."

In the National Museum a great many forms or sizes of case are in use, and this tendency, the result of a desire to enclose in each case a separate and inter-related group of objects, seems carried too far. It is wiser, especially with reference to Effect, to limit the cases to a few comprehensive forms. There does not seem much reasonableness in forming exhibits separated in a series of differing cases. The mere exposition of an object so that it can be seen, and seen well, and appear most advantageously, does not demand a great variety in the character of cases, nor even such a wide range of dimensions, except, as in "special or group cases," the nature of the contents determines its necessary size.

To begin with, wall cases are of three kinds, though in one the designation is conventional and not literal; wall cases proper, pier cases, and double front cases, or cases with a middle partition affording shelving room on each side. These latter are upright cases, but entirely detached from the walls. Of these various forms of wall cases the pier or alcove case seems most desirable for the larger number of uses. The pier or alcove case springs from the wall between two windows, and thus on either side exposes a surface of illumination to the window. There is always, of course, varying with the time of day and season, an area of shadow at the wall end of the case,

FIG. 5.

which by a device of the late Calvert Vaux can be partially or wholly overcome. Mr. Vaux had lancet windows placed in the wall through which the light entering the middle of the case at its contact with the wall dispersed the shadows formed by the angle of the window. (Fig. 5.)

The introduction of this suggestion leads us to consider a peculiar

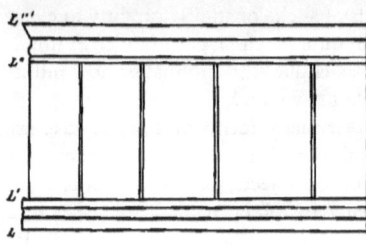

and admirable form of pier or alcove case, developed also by Mr. Vaux, in the first section of the A. M. N. H., our *Unit* museum. This is the T-shaped case designed to form a front upon three sides, those aspects against the alcove itself, and the third upon the hall face of the case. (Fig. 6.)

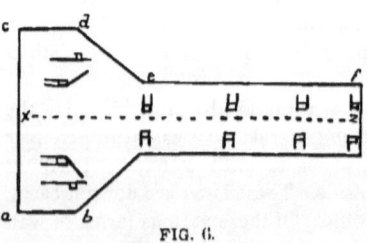

FIG. 6.

In this disposition of course the alcoves are lighted by a window, which should be almost the entire width of the alcove itself. In our unit museum this, however, is lacking. When these cases were first erected the lancet window mentioned above had an illuminating effect but it was found that the cases became confusedly lit by cross lights, and it was necessary to place a partition through the centre of the case, forming a background and reflecting surface for the objects in front. The end or proximal window, however, still is useful. These cases are admirable. By removing the shelving large enough compartments are formed for single large figures, as mammals, while their complete illumination, increased also by the inclined ends, their great capacity, their structural interest, and the room-like effect of the alcoves produced by their approximating distal ends, all combine to give them pre-eminence. Along the main hallway their extended ends form a broad case-like effect quite superior to the narrow end of the ordinary pier cases. The ordinary pier or alcove case is carried out from the wall with two straight sides. The dimensions of these two examples of pier are as follows—compare Fig. 6:

T-shaped pier case a—b, 3 ft.; a—c, 9 ft.; d—e, 4 ft.; e—f, 12 ft.; x—z, 18 ft.; L—L', 1 ft.; L'—L'', 7 ft.; L''—L''', 1 ft.

The mouldings are very simple; the wood black walnut, oiled; the angles in front rounded; the depth of the frame holding the glasses two inches. There are three doors on the front, one on the sloping side and three on the shank of the case.

Box Pier Case.

This, in the instance chosen, is a rectangular case reaching out from the wall twenty-one feet, four feet wide, with a height of eight feet and a few inches (4 or 5), base ten inches, and top moulding of eight inches.

The body of the T cases in the American Museum was of wood sheathed with iron. The doors are of single panes of glass in iron frames swung on iron pins in sockets. They are locked by the bolt or Jenck's lock. The disposition of standards for shelving is seen in Fig. 6, the black squares indicating their position. These standards are of wood on each side of which are screwed racks upon which brackets are gripped. (Fig. 7.)

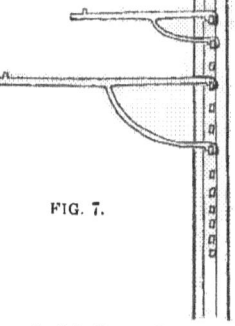

FIG. 7.

This invention of Prof. E. S. Morse, adapted, I believe, from an old fire-side crane shown him by Prof. Putnam, seems absolutely applicable in all shelved cases, and as the brackets can be inclined or blocks can be placed on the brackets so as to tip up the shelf, the

widest range of useful illumination for their inspection is feasible.
Pier cases should be usually divided by a partition through the centre.
Such a partition can be carried from end to end, or, at the free or dis-
tal end cross shelving can be introduced.

It is obvious that the dimensions of the pier wall cases can be much
varied, dependent on the purposes they are to meet and the space,
between windows, which they occupy. Such space should not be
excessive. It should hardly exceed nine feet for all cases holding
shelving and intended for small objects. In many instances where
the wall space is greater, and wide cases can be built, they may be
made into group cases which do not demand extreme illumination
for their inspection. Pier cases can be carried outward from the
walls into the hallways until the hall becomes a succession of alcoves or rooms with a corridor between. Or *vice versa*, as in the

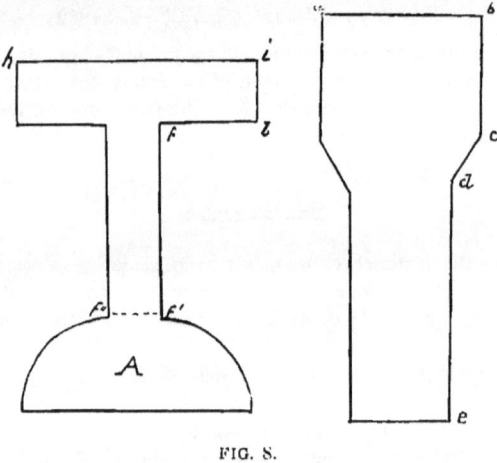

FIG. 8.

German museum, a central partition frame may divide the hall into
two halves, and against this the pier cases can abut, extending out
towards the windows. It is clear that in such a disposition both sides
of the hall must be provided with windows, and preferably as many
windows as alcoves and opposite to them. The extreme length of
the alcove cases is a disagreeable feature, the hall effect is obliterated,
and table cases, so invaluable for many objects, are expelled. As
has been pointed out it serves the purpose of breaking up the hall
into a number of compartments which can be individualized by some
special contents, and so the series of alcoves become involved in a
developmental or pedagogic system. Generally speaking, and re-

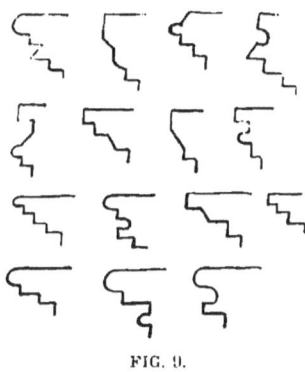

FIG. 9.

ferring again to our *unit* museum, pier cases may reach out in a hall, 60 feet wide, 18 feet.

A peculiar form of pier case has been adopted by Pt. Jesup for his wood collection in the New York Museum. (Fig. 8.)

They are the T-shaped cases mentioned above in the *unit* museum, but in different proportions, and in one instance (Fig. 8-A.) very greatly modified. These are magnificent cases. Their dimensions are as follows—compare Fig. 8: a—b, 9 ft.; b—c, 6 ft.; c—d, 4 ft.; d—e. 12 ft.; h—i, 25 ft.; i—z, 4 ft.; f—f′, 10½ ft.; f′—f″, 4 ft.

The finish and appearance of these cases are surpassingly elegant and chaste. Their bases are completed with a five-inch strip, one-half inch thick, of white marble protecting them against defacement.

Figure 9 gives a variety of bases, mouldings, cornices, etc., which may be used in pier cases, and indeed in any wall case. It seems desirable to repress too much moulding and generally not to have the base mouldings on the pediment of the case over one foot in height.

In figure 10 some working details are depicted (not in scale) of a pier or pavillion case without partition or diaphragm, for which I am indebted to A. R. Strader.

An useful alcove case for displaying cloths, blankets, tapestry, or even implements and flat objects in Natural History is practically a board framed in a sash with two glass

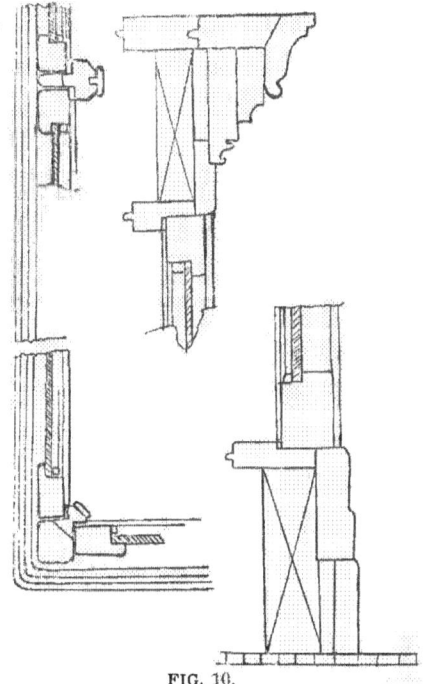

FIG. 10.

doors lifting up. These are narrow cases generally with two doors on each side. They have been used effectively in the New York Museum, and they are employed for the synoptic series in the National Museum.

Wall cases proper are those built up against walls extending considerable distances, in fact, covering all the wall surface of a room or hall as high as the case itself reaches. Such cases are variable in depth, according to uses. Wall cases are frequently poorly lighted when placed between windows. Their best position is east and west, with east or west windows pouring in light along their fronts. The north wall cases of the central south section of the A. M. N. H. are quite defective from poor illumination. In the *unit* museum (the first section of the A. M. N. H.) there are only short wall cases in the north and south alcoves of the halls, and they here receive the lateral illumination of east and west windows. Such wall cases are shelved as the pier cases. But shelving is discussed in some following paragraphs.

The practice of using glass tops to cases, as recommended by Dr. Goode, seems questionable, except in small group cases, where it improves the appearance of the case. Dust soon accumulates on the glass or it becomes otherwise dirty, and it requires frequent cleaning, while when objects are raised above the cases the glass is an obstruction to their manipulation. Dimensions of wall cases of course vary, their depth being adjudicated by the character and size of the objects they are intended to hold. A depth of three feet seems widely serviceable.

The doors of all upright cases should be swing doors, opening outward, for the one sufficient reason that they can be easily cleaned. Dr. Goode's advocacy of doors pushing upward is induced by the broad glass pane, such an arrangement allows, which of course has advantages. But the difficulty of cleaning the whole door properly seems to outweigh all advantages. Such large plates of glass are, however, also feasible in sliding doors moving past each other on tracks.

The double-front cases are rectangular cases detached from the walls, with a diaphragm or back passing from end to end through the centre. They are two wall cases back to back. Such cases are useful and might advantageously replace all wall cases where wall cases cannot be so favorably built as to receive the light from the windows. These double-fronts should be on heavy iron wheels or rollers, hidden by a marginal skirt of wood or stone. And, indeed, all cases, where it is feasible, should be movable. I have seen the most unfortunate strains given to cases, and the most unlucky injuries inflicted on men by the hardship of having them *shoved* into new positions.

The shelving in cases has two objects, provision of room for the specimens exhibited, and favorable positions for their intelligent examination. The second may be considered paramount, except in such instances, as formerly in the building of the Philadelphia Academy of Sciences with the collection of birds, where the exhibition cases become store houses. Probably the best system of shelving involves placing the widest shelf, the first above the bottom of the case, at about two and one-half feet below the level of the eye of the spectator, and carrying the shelves above that in gradually receding order so that the narrower are at the top. The smaller objects should be placed on the lower shelves, the larger above. The shadow of the upper shelves, by the method of progressive shrinkage in width, is less apt to obscure the objects below. Shelves can be slanted by putting sloping blocks on the brackets, or they can be more steeply inclined by carrying up the shelf until its front edge falls within the pin of the bracket, and rests on that, inasmuch as the pin, which fits into a socket or hole on the

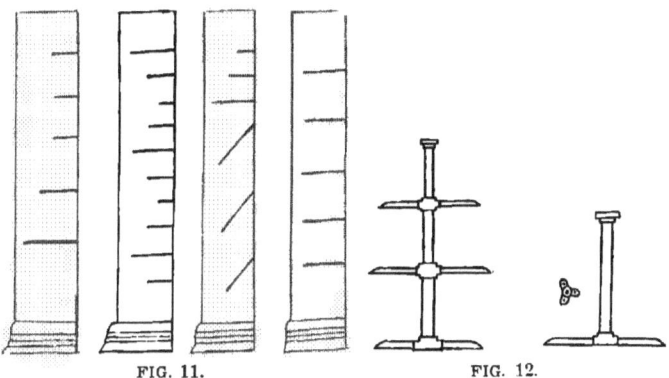

FIG. 11.   FIG. 12.

underside of the shelf, lies from two to four inches behind the front edge of the shelf. This pin can be concealed in many ways, readily suggested by inspection. With large objects the shelves may be tiered directly one above the other, of equal width. Besides tilting in the two ways suggested above, sloped brackets are made which give a less but useful inclination. Shelves brought close to the front of the case exhibit objects nearer the eye of the visitor, and hence for objects of a uniform size, as cubes of building stones, wall cases of the requisite depth with shelves of one width from top to bottom, directly superimposed at equal distances, serve an admirable purpose. The shallow and *appliquée* effect of such cases is sometimes disappointing. The case loses atmosphere, and the receding shelves in deeper cases, from the bottom upward, produce a pleasant impression. The *bay* arrangement of shelving is to alternately widen and narrow the shelving. Figure 11 presents these modes of shelving, with others.

One form of bracket and its manner of insertion in the shelf has been illustrated (Fig. 7.) Besides these bracket supports for shelves the bayonet joint has been tried by Prof. Putnam at the Peabody Museum with reasonable success, though its resistance to strain must be sensibly less. (Fig. 12.)

In regard to shelving, steps can be provided on the shelves which will give the necessary elevation to objects removed from the eye. The appearance of such steps is not always pleasing, and if made too narrow and steeply graded have an impoverished and make-shift expression.

Group or special cases belong to the classes of cases here considered. Such cases can be varied to a very large degree by their external ornamentation, but simplicity seems in all respects desirable.

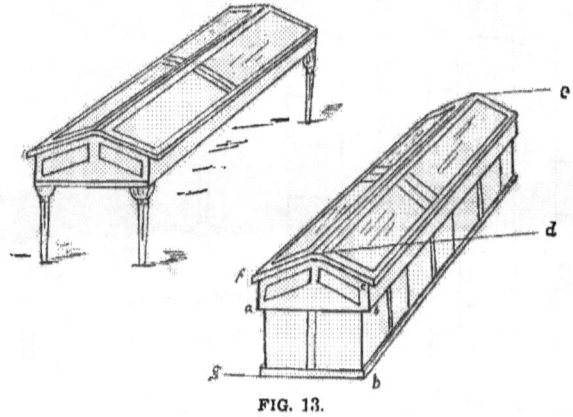

FIG. 13.

Group cases are large or small *boxes* of glass, framed, and provided with the requisite pedestals or bases. Groups not too large, as bird groups, are in the New York Museum placed on tables, which are necessary to bring them within the inspection of visitors. Large mammal groups occupy cases built from the floor, as it is hardly necessary to recall that their realism involves nearly always a life-size treatment of a large scene. The same is true with large mammals.

The table or flat cases embrace two classes, the desk, single or double, and the inverted V case on legs. Desk cases of great beauty have been prepared in numbers in the New York Museum, and it would be difficult to suggest anything more propitious for its objects than these. They are made usually with three sashes, giving them a length of some eighteen feet, and have two sloping sides—one inch in seven—and are fitted on the bearings of the lids with green plush as a dust prevention. Some of these cases are a trifle broad, and the objects at the back of the case are indifferently seen. The best dimensions using the lettering in figure thirteen are as follows: a—b, 5 ft.; b—c, 8 ins.; d—e, 12 ft.; d—f, 2½ ft.; f—g, 3 ft. 2 ins.; g—h, 4 ft. 4 ins.; g—a, 2 ft. 5 in.

Details are given in Fig. 14, for which I am indebted to A. R. Strader.

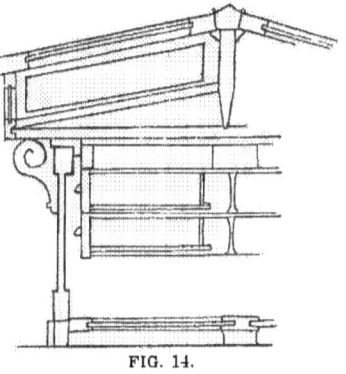

FIG. 14.

These cases, of course, can have these dimensions changed indefinitely by slight alterations, but the example given will meet all requirements. Such flat cases can be raised on legs (Fig. 13), or they can be put on bodies or stacks of drawers which are to be used for putting away duplicate or unnecessary material, or overflows, or specimens unfitted for public exhibition (Fig. 13.) As a convenience to curators they are invaluable. The artistic effect of these "bodies" is certainly unfortunate. The desk cases on legs forming no interruption to the untramelled view of the floor of the hall conduce to the effect of size, and are distinctly more elegant. The flat, or desk case, is sometimes modified by an upright addition in which larger objects

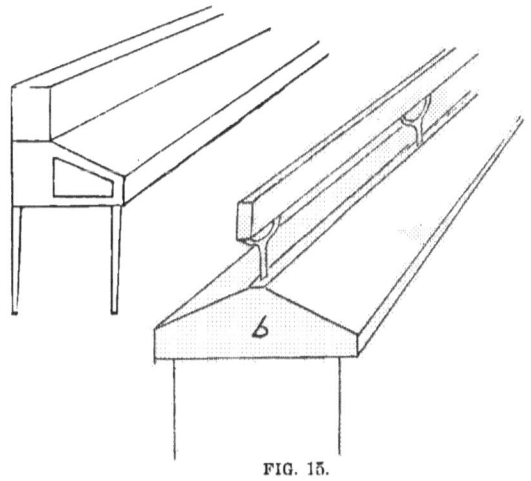

FIG. 15.

can be placed, and which may serve to break the depressed look—squattiness—of the desk cases themselves. (Fig. 15.)

These are really seldom successful. They cannot always be used appropriately, and, unless the objects are large, they serve no useful purpose. They are better replaced by a long narrow box, divided by a partition, and opening on top by lids and supported on metallic standards. (Fig. 15b.) In these receptacles, photographs, maps, sections, separate objects, dissections, etc., can be placed, and made illustrative or explanatory of the exhibit of objects in the flat case below.

The inverted V, or A case, is a useful and sometimes attractive form of case. (Fig. 16.)

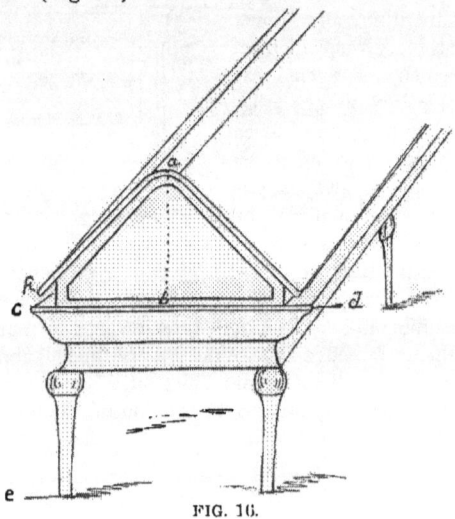

FIG. 16.

They can be filled within by a core or not. This core takes the shape of a smooth or stepped pyramid. If the latter, the series of steps form shelves, upon which the objects are placed ascending upward. If smooth, the core can be covered with baize, cloth, plush, etc., and the objects in some way attached. The white plaster cells holding lepidoptera are in this way arranged very strikingly in these cases in the A. M. N. H., by pins holding up the white blocks. Or these A cases may be used for skeletons, animals, vases, etc., without cores. In this latter case the effect is poor, and the case is evidently constrained to a purpose for which it is unadapted.

The A cases are constructed of a metal frame, stiffening a wooden sheath, the doors on the side may be one or two, they open upward, are hinged at the top, and in the top a "light" is inserted. Dimensions for a typical case are as follows: Compare Fig. 16, a—b, 2 ft.

9 ins.; c—d, 3 ft. 4 in.; e—c, 2½ ft.; f—a, 3 ft. Length, eight feet, eleven inches.

Relief maps, geological features, as mud flowage, tracks, ripple-marks, etc., can be framed in low flat cases, on legs, glass tops and sides, or simply framed, face exposed, and fastened to walls, or left on the floor on rollers.

The material for all cases should be wood in the frames, black walnut, ash, chestnut, oak, or mahogany, or in case of necessary economy pine stained, and the glass should be plate, American or French. Of all these mahogany, or the Honduras Bay wood, forms the most beautiful material, its rich and durable tint affording the most attractive color effects. Rose wood can be used with great elegance

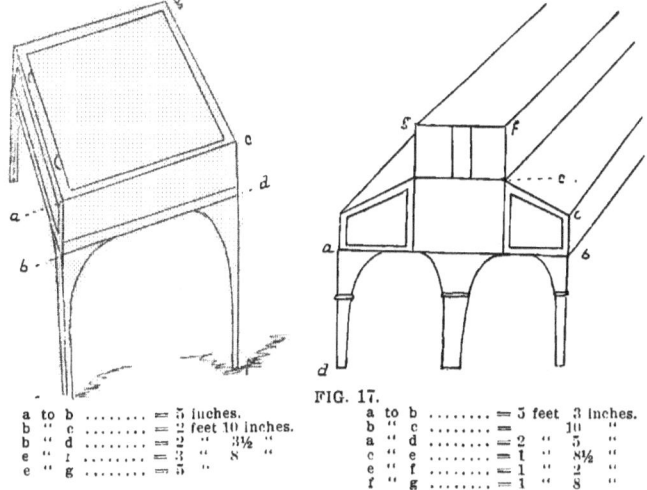

FIG. 17.

a to b	....	= 5 inches.
b " c	....	= 2 feet 10 inches.
b " d	....	= 2 " 3½ "
e " f	....	= 3 " 8 "
e " g	....	= 5 "

a to b	....	= 5 feet 3 inches.
b " c	....	= 10 "
a " d	....	= 2 " 5 "
c " e	....	= 1 " 8½ "
e " f	....	= 1 " 2 "
f " g	....	= 1 " 8 "

in special cases, but of course exacts some unusual concessions from the treasury. Iron should be expelled. It is hideous, and its strength and lightness can make no compensation for its intolerable ugliness. Examples of some of the best iron cases are given in Fig. 17.

Besides the cases we have enumerated, which embrace practically all the kinds really desirable in a museum, many small cases hanging on or fastened to the wall can be employed, in which single or unique groups of objects can be shown. Such cases can also be supported by brackets, and, if judiciously introduced, may form a most admirable feature in a hall. They should not be, however, interminably varied in size and treatment. Their uniformity, at least in each hall, contributes to their aggregate interest.

Glass shelves in cases have been adopted in some museums. They are distinctly objectionable. They do not prevent shadows, for the objects on them cast shadows, the bottoms or undersides of objects discerned through them are unpleasant, and they break.

Their is, however, a need in every museum of establishing a system of convertible interchangeable drawers. This is most important. and Dr. Goode's emphasis of the "unit drawer" is fully justified. The size of the "unit drawer" being fixed, the stacks into which they are thrust consist of runways of such a height as to bring the top of the drawer on a level with the next succeeding runway. The runway may be preferably one-half the height of the drawers. Every other drawer in the stack can always be varied in a multiple proportion of the unit drawer, or can be the same as it. The dimensions of the unit drawers as designed in the National Museum is 24 by 30 inches.

This or any other size can be adopted. The manner of the stack formation is shown, with drawer, in Fig. 18.

Such stacks and drawers are used in the storage of specimens, and

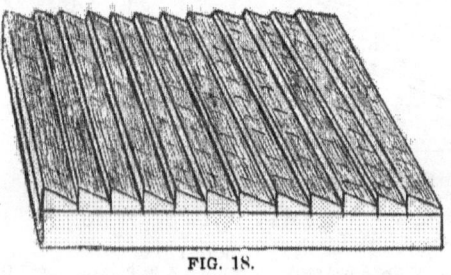

FIG. 18.

for the keeping of specimens which have been removed from the cases. Allusion to it seems warranted in a paper on installation, although it perhaps belongs more properly to questions of Museum Security, Curing and Storage of Specimens, which are not herein considered.

The dust-proofness of cases publicly exhibited is most important. The exposure of these cases to a bombardment of dust particles, continued through years, almost invariably results in an entrance of this defacing material, and a consequent deterioration of the display. It, however, in most cases effects its entrance far sooner, and the unsightly presence of dirt in the cases mars the exhibit of many museums very quickly. A necessary prevention is, of course, cleanliness, the mopping of the floors and a wiping of the glasses daily. The mechanical preventions are plush or felt strips on the bearings of the cover or sash with the case, or a tongue and groove in the cover and case. The latter is the more effective, in fact, it seems perfect.

Turnstiles (Fig. 19) are invaluable adjuncts to cases, and for some objects or exhibits are absolutely indispensable.

In the British Museum such turn-stiles contain the mounted specimens of local herbaria, and Dr. Britton will put them to an identical use in the Museum of Botany in the Botanical Gardens in New York. For photographs, illustrative plates —as once employed by Pt. Jesup for his wood collection—they form the only convenient means of accomodation for a large series of planular objects. They should be simple and strong. Such monstrosities as are seen in the German museums should be shunned. The turnstile of German museums consists in a heavy iron post, around which a circular series

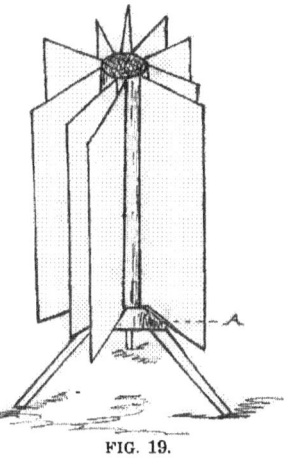

FIG. 19.

of perpendicular wires are stretched. These wires can be released and passed through staples in the frames of pictures, etc., which are thus suspended. The general effect of these is cumbersome, un-gainly and awkward. A better, because more simple and effective style, and more comely as well, is shown in Figure 20. The central post is on ball-bearings, enclosed in the box A, so that the visitor can at will revolve the post and bring the object examined into the best light. Many flat objects can be mounted in frames on walls, and a very notable effect could be produced by arranging the wall space of narrow connecting halls for the exhibition, in this way, of vertebrate fossils, slabs of crinoids, etc. The frame work should always relieve, by contrast, the color of the objects.

Paraphernalia.

The many contrivances by which objects of various sorts are held in position, or the numerous receptacles for them, and the manner in which they are labelled, constitute paraphernalia. Trays, labels, supports, stands, pins, blocks, plaster cells, rods, backings, covers, etc., etc., all make up paraphernalia.

Trays.

More diversity than would be considered probable, may exist in trays; their sizes, heights, colors, and attachments all offering points of difference. A form of exhibition tray has been in use in the Na-tional Museum for a long time, which receives some praise, but can hardly be recommended with enthusiasm. These are made with rather high sides and with a bevel front, upon which the label of the specimen in the tray rests. They are black, and may have the bottom covered with paper or colored fabric. In the British Museum the minerals are laid on jewellers wool, which is packed into the edges of a rabbeted block, whose edges form a black frame. This method for the purpose has met with unqualified approval. A similar or identical effect can be attained by covering the bottoms of shallow paper trays with jewellers wool, which is fastened down by very thin black strips of black wood, fitting inside the tray. The cotton rises or puffs slightly, the frame of black gives individualism and elegance, and the effect is very attractive. In these cases the label is fastened to a sloping block placed within the tray so that the edges of the trays come in close contact. Such trays are made in an ascending series of dimensions, the longer side of one tray forming the shorter side of the tray next above it in size, as 2x3, 3x4, 4x6, 6x8, 8x12, etc., with occasional use of square trays and odd dimensions. These trays have sides three eights of an inch in height. Plaster of Paris trays with bevelled edges have been applied to the exhibition of shells, but they are very poor, their white porous surfaces absorbing dirt and dust, and soon showing a sullied and repulsive surface. Porcelain trays have also been suggested, but they are expensive, and present a cup and saucer tea-service effect which is slightly ludicrous. Dr. Schuchert, of the National Museum, has put in use a terra cotta tile for holding fossils, but its results are doubtful. The best or most attractive method of exhibiting fossils has yet to be discovered. An attempt will be made to solve this by the use of backgrounds and vertical screens for the tabular pieces, containing fossils, while the detached individual specimens can be arranged in trays or on boards of strikingly contrasted color, as ebony or ivory white.

Trays should not be too deep, simulating boxes; their sides should not exceed one-half an inch, and that usually is too high.

Labels.

Dr. Goode has drawn the attention of museum curators and authorities to the importance of labels, and in his report on the National Museum has feelingly expounded the whole subject. It really does seem that the acute and critical position of the label writer is somewhat overstated, and the extreme altitude of lexicographical excellence assumed for him rather exaggerated.

But with that we are hardly concerned. The technique of labels involves their colors and disposition; the size of type, etc., fall under System and Effect. A blue-gray has been for a long time used in the American Museum in New York. It is unsatisfactory. It fades and is soon discolored. A terra cotta seems preferable. It does not fade, and is a warmer tint. In the Mineralogical Cabinet in the

New York Museum red paint on a gray ground has a striking effect. These labels are called *Rubrics.*

Besides these colors, Royal Wooster, maroon, brown, various grays, black with gold or silver letters for large labels, have been adopted. Large outside labels of thin mahogany board with gold lettering are admirable. A label, for separate cases, of black ebonized wood, with gold letters, is excellent and effective. Dark brown leather labels, with gold letters, are also attractive, and can be used to distinguish important gifts. On the whole, in the card board labels on the inside of the cases the plain border label is to be preferred to the label with a line frame around it. It is more chaste. But, if the expense and labor can be afforded, the card board label sunk into, or attached to, a black or mahogany strip of wood, so large as to make a frame around it, is very elegant. The larger general labels in card board should all be framed in narrow bead frames of wood. The outside wood labels of black or mahogany, if on wall cases, are attached by picture moulding hooks, and if on desk cases are supported by brass rods.

Supports, Stands, Blocks, Pins.

To be clearly seen many small crystals and sometimes small shells demand a support, which lifts them into individual prominence, while large groups of crystals and coral masses, as well as all taxidermical specimens, need stands and pedestals as an artistic embellishment. Small black pedestals of wood can be bought from dealers which will serve for mounting crystals, upon which the crystals can be attached by black wax. Glass rods are also in use, and frequently shells or other flat objects are attached to them by wax in such a way as to appear unsupported. In the mounting of skulls and the large fossil remains of the mamalia from the west, Mr. Herrman has used, with splendid results, brass rods socketed in mahogany blocks. For mineral masses, stands of ebonized wood and mahogany are superior, but oak, chestnut and black walnut can be favorably used. On steeply slanting shelves the label block can be used as a support to the object, or, in the case of large shells, a V-shaped collar. Devices are innumerable for meeting such problems, and the skill and taste of the exhibitor can be indefinitely exercised. A pin is a form of support, whether it transfixes an insect, or holds up the end of a chinook blanket, or restrains a clam shell from sliding off an inclined board, or exhibits poster-like a label, or, more differentiated still, with three clamps, grasps a gem. Pin, therefore, is a generic term for metal appurtenances so modified as to meet these different uses. Rods run along the tops of cases, form a convenient rack for the suspension of pictures, maps, etc. The rods are held by staples.

Jars, Plaster and Glass Cells.

The plaster cells of Jencks for lepidoptera are probably one of the most notable inventions in museum installation proposed in the last ten years. They consist in a white plaster block, with a depressed pit holding the body of the insect, whose wings are outstretched, the whole sealed in by a glass cover. Glass cells for food products, medicines, herb preparations, etc., can be formed from five glass plates cemented together by soluble glass, and covered by a glass slide moving on vaseline. A more elaborate form consists of four glass plates socketed in wood, with a glass cover held on by metal pins, which pass through the glass, and can be unscrewed, their ends being driven in the wooden frame at the bottom of the cell.

Glass jars for alcoholics should almost invariably be flat with black painted backs, so that the bleached or diaphanous objects contained in them can be clearly seen. Flat glass jars are expensive, but it seems likely that some experiments, now in progress, will enable the less munificent managements to make their own jars from glass panes held together by a new waterproof cement, buttressed possibly at the angles by a mixture of hydraulic cement and plaster of Paris.

Backings, Covers, Etc.

Backgrounds may be made to play a most important part in the exhibition of specimens. The congruous contrast of colors between the object and the surface on which it is displayed heightens to an almost spectacular intensity a museum installation. Backgrounds can be painted surfaces or fabrics. Painted surfaces are blue grays, the color so lavishly employed in the A. M. N. H. of New York, and for most purposes very effective, or buffs, even reds, while in fabrics black for white objects, as corals, and green for shells, and an ivory white or maroon for fossils, are a good general selection.

Velvet covering cork tablets have been used for gem collections, the gem being laid on the velvet pad or fixed into the underlying cork through the velvet, by a pin. This is quite attractive, though perhaps an olive green would, as one color, better replace the patchwork of white and black. The installation of gems, so as to bring out their peculiar beauty, is not, at any rate in museums, solved. The jewellers do better, and their methods deserve study, possibly imitation.

System.

It has been pointed out that three systems of display which may "lead to certain intended results with reference to a mental impression on the spectator" are possible, the Popular, the Philosophical, and the Scientific. It is also to be inferred that these do not exclude each other, that they may be partially blended, or that they may co-

exist in the same exhibit. And it can also be insisted that these three
systems are applicable distinctions in the arrangement of an entire
museum, as well as of its separate parts.

The Popular system involves naturally an obvious use of striking,
even sensational features, brilliant effects, simple phraseology and
profuse and intelligible comments and directions. It aims to lead
the visitor with continuous interest from hall to hall, to punctuate
his delight with distinct and delightful impressions, and to leave on
his mind a sum of recognizable recollections. Its instructions are of
the dictionary type, each object is clearly defined in and for itself;
its relations are less accented and less evident. The Popular system
of the Scientific Museum is the system of the Dime Museum greatly
elevated, dignified, and replenished with culture, but still a practical
appeal to the sensory centers of the spectator. The Museum building in a Popular system appeals to the eye, and has architectural
beauty; its halls are large, and form attractive vistas, prominent and
beautiful objects are set off with strong features of color and mounting, and in collections the remarkable and beautiful are selected, and
the obscure and homely displaced. Thus, in shells, the large and
showy only would be exhibited, the rest repressed; in minerals, the
fine crystallizations, rare and dull species omitted; in birds, the
magnificent and sumptuous, the plain and gray and dull neglected;
in fossils, perfectly preserved and entire specimens, or those in good
relief, broken and shadowy things consigned to drawers. The label-
ling would not be comprehensive or systematic, but special. Each
exhibit would be well explained, its relations ignored. You might
learn much about the giant squid, you would not be shown its classification, congeners and physiology. You would see wonderful examples of quartz, you would scarcely realize its position amongst the
other oxides. You would read of the habits of the bat, you would
not understand the homologies of its limbs. You might admire the
size of a whale's skeleton, you would not realize its position amongst
the mammalia. Of course, no Museum of Natural History to-day
defers entirely to a system so juvenile and fractional, although all
museums are increasing their respect for its appreciation of *effect*,
its evident intention to make the visitors stop and admire. The
Popular system is a subdominant note in the chord struck by the
whole administrative faculty of a museum.

The Philosophical system aims at unfolding an idea. It is less
concerned with a multitudinous display of species than with developing the regimen those species illustrate. This treatment is well
illustrated in the Main Central Hall of the British Museum of Natural History, where a series of cases present formative principles in
animal life. Thus the group of pigeons, showing the variation of a
species under domestication as the derived varieties from the Wild

Rock Dove (*Columba livia*.) Again the modifications of the Jungle Fowl of India, where extreme changes may be noted, as in the Japanese longtailed fowls, and the fowls of the woods of the Fiji Islands. Also the group of Ruff and Reeves, illustrating external variation, according to sex and season. Demonstrations of color adaptation, Protective Mimicry, Albinism, Melanism, etc., all present the Philosophical System; while the same, carried still further, beyond the limits of mere teleological considerations, converts the museum into an embodyment of an evolutionary thesis. In this way from the inorganic through the first phases of organic life to its crowning development in man with all the related phases of ascending civilization what a transcendent picture of cosmology the museum may become. It is perhaps realized nowhere to-day because the opportunity and the governing mind are not anywhere associated. The Philosophical System in Anthropology and Ethnology affords a field of more than surpassing dimensions. It is exhilirating to consider how a really profound and learned exhaustion of these subjects, with the extraordinary and increasing facilities for a complete compendium, afforded by this day's research and exploration, would exemplify the Philosophical System! To start from Prehistoric Man, to unfold the dawning cults, the nomadic and sedentary strains and to trace their divergences, the origin of race metropoles, and the slow emergence of metaphysical military and industrial civilizations; to take, in fact, Spencer's studies in sociology and give them an illustrated imaginal realism.

The Philosophical System has but a slender regard for systematists, and exults rather in revealing relations, sequences and operations in nature, homologies and analogies, influence of environment, problems of philogeny and those aspects of animal life which elucidate the principles of organic variation. It can, of course, be made most attractive, and has a more popular character than the Scientific System. Its instructions are for the most part quite readily apprehended, or can be made so, and in the larger subjects its demonstrations admit of a considerable pictorial effectiveness.

The Scientific System.

The Scientific System aims at an exhaustive display of species arranged, in Botany and Zoology, according to their biological affinities, and in Palæontology according to biology and position, while in inorganic life it illustrates the entire range of mineral science. This is the more common, the more generally insisted upon form of museum installation. It is well understood; cases filled with examples of all the known or obtainable specimens of species. At its best, when it takes on, more and more, a philosophical expression, the Scientific System, uses diagrams, photographs and maps, to illustrate anatomy, habits and distribution, and it does not hesitate to involve popular features in its work, describing special things with clearness and interest. Indeed an enlightened Scientific treatment tries to alleviate the dryness of its terminology with popular and informing features. The curator who thinks his science is invalidated by entertaining instruction to the public is certainly deceived.

The cosmopolitan museum will make use of all these systems, building up from the Scientific, as a basic method, and introducing the Philosophical at all necessary points, while the Popular treatment would prevail like a dominant influence over each.

In this connection and before passing to effect, I beg to introduce the remarks of Dr. G. Brown Goode, concerning *Labels*. Dr. Goode has remarked that "the art of label writing is in its infancy, and there are doubtless possibilities of educational results through the agency of labels and specimens which are not as yet at all understood." He further says the label must:

"(1) Tell the name of the object; its exact and technical name always, and if there be one, its common name.

(2) It must call attention to the features which it is important for the visitor to notice.

(3) It must explain its meaning and its relations to the other objects in the series. If it accompanies a natural history specimen, it should explain its geographical distribution, which, if possible, should be plotted on a small map, forming part of the label and mentioning peculiarities of structure or habit.

(4) The exact locality, date of collection and source of the specimen exhibited should be mentioned.

(5) For the convenience of visitors it is well, in many cases, to give the dimensions or weight of the specimen."

Dr. Goode has not, however, drawn sufficient attention to the use of General Labels, or pointed out their extreme efficacy in giving useful information. A group of objects, closely related, as a family of birds or shells, can be described *en masse*, as it were, and interesting instruction imparted by such a description, while Synoptical Groups should be preceded by a manual—like diagnosis of class or phyla features.

Effect.

Impressions made upon the eye are of the utmost importance in museum installation. There may be some atrophied and stagnant temperaments to whom a beautiful or tasteful or impressive installation seems at war with the terribly serious considerations of science, but a very little attention to the facts of the case would entirely relieve them of these fears. Because a specimen looks well, it is no

less the same specimen than when it looks poorly, and all cultivated
instinct aims to achieve, in making it look well, is to make it more
easily seen, make it more conspicuous. There certainly is no desire,
in those who strive for effect, to surround objects with decorations
which defeat their own purpose, and bring more attention to the
embellishment than to the object. The most refined appreciation
of effect sees that the different departments of a museum may need
differing treatments and that severity of arrangement better accords
with a display of Building Stones or Ores than ornament, while the
lavish beauty of birds may demand foils and reliefs to their beauty
to even make it more apparent.

In effect, arrangement, and color, contrasts count for everything.
Proper spacing, selection of material, and backgrounds of good for-
tifying colors make notable improvements in the appearance of the
specimens. Besides the painting of the cases and shelves, the use
of cloth plush and paper can be utilized. It is certainly undesirable
to attempt harlequin effects, and usually a few selected colors meet
every requirement.

There is room for much conflict of opinion upon the fitness of wall
decoration, wall painting in Natural History Museums. I am inclined to believe it should not be tolerated; that all pictorial illustration should be in the form of framed painting. They are invariably
better done, less subject to injury and can be conveniently changed
in position. There is certainly an attraction in the grandiose idea of
a panorama about the walls of a room showing scenes and the objects related to them, associated together, in a great mural picture. It
would be splendid if it could be realized, but can it be? To paint a
mural decoration (on canvas) really colossal and appropriate would
demand a master, and a small fortune. How can these requirements
be met?

The public museum has entered into the life of European cities,
and it is becoming apparent here how interested the public become in
their development. Their installation, and the ideas governing it,
cannot be too closely considered.

L. P. Gratacap.

No. 9 Blumenstrasse, Hamburg, Germany.   RESIDENCE,   F. A. de Meuren, Architect.

CENTRAL NATIONAL BANK BUILDING,
Pearl Street and Broadway, New York City.   John Williams, Architect.

SOME HANDICAPS OF PROVINCIAL ARCHITECTURE

Prefatory Note.

BY "Provincial Architecture" is meant all architecture that originates outside of Boston and New York in the East, and a few of the largest cities in other parts of the country.

In this discussion of the subject, domestic buildings are not critically considered, because such criticism would be a sort of invasion of private rights, including the right of every man who builds himself a house to make it as ugly and illogical as he pleases, and because it would be necessary to prepare a special dictionary of terms before an intelligible line could be drawn between the utilitarian art of house building and the fine art of architecture.

Concerning the illustrations ,it may be explained that they are not given as especially depraved examples of contemporary architecture, to be classed with the striking series of "Aberrations," published in this journal a few years since. It is needless to say that they are not, on the other hand, presented as examples to be followed. The most of them are the familiar, largely imitative, and drearily common-place buildings to be found everywhere. They have been achieved by the individual, or combined efforts of architects, considered "successful" in their local fields, and of enterprising business men who are able and willing to leave their "stamp" on the community which educated them, of shrewd business committees whose prominent qualification for their position is a supposed ability to buy the value of three dollars with an expenditure of two, and of public servants who for the time of their official life are called upon to decide affairs of which they are more or less ignorant, and for which, under other circumstances the training of half a lifetime would be thought necessary. Sources, from which, instead of platitudes with occasional nightmare attachments, something of permanent dignity and beauty should have enriched the time and place in which they have been produced.

Although actual and recent buildings, they are not verbally identified, in fact, that is a matter of no consequence, but the accompanying titles will indicate their relation to the text. The alternatives, labeled "What might have been," are introduced by way of contrast.

The permanent residents of each provincial city in the older portions of the country have certain characteristic social customs and manners, certain modes of speech, certain business habits, and other external peculiarities, easily perceived but not easily described, which give a local flavor and coloring to each community. These include fashions and tastes in building. But aside from such minor variations, there is no important difference in the architecture of provincial cities of a certain class, say those ranging from 50 to 250 thousand inhabitants; and in them all it is, as a whole, so poor, so devoid of the merit that entitles a work of art to respectful admiration and careful preservation, that if it were known that all the buildings in any one of them were about to be annihilated, it would be difficult to select a dozen, which any person having even a rudimentary knowledge of architecture, would care to have re-built in its present form. That is to say, apart from association and other sentimental motives, there would be found almost nothing worth saving for its architectural excellence. I believe that is true of at least nine-tenths of our provincial cities.

When we consider the liberality, not to say the extravagance of our large business blocks; the ample, not to say wasteful appropriations for school houses and other public buildings; the enormous sums given to churches, educational and philanthropical institutions; the increasing number of educated architects; and especially when we consider the almost unlimited resources in the way of instruction, investigation and imitation afforded by travel, by literature, and by the completeness with which all the best architecture of the world from the time that architecture began to be to the present time has been photographed and brought within our easy reach—when we consider all these things, the general worthlessness of the architecture by which we are surrounded, furnishes a most amazing instance of the failure of apparently adequate means to reach a desired end.

Remembering what a permanent and conspicuous influence architecture has had upon national character, how from time immemorial it has been the one art that both reveals and determines the character of its creators and contemporaries at any period, it is certain that no greater service could be rendered to the age we live in, than the cure or mitigation of this extraordinary and discreditable state of affairs.

As regards general influences, vanity is perhaps our most ponderous handicap. This appears to be of the deplorable variety which makes us unwilling to confess our ignorance, even to ourselves; unwilling to admit that what we posses, what we invent, what we preach and practice, is not the very best that has ever been done in the way of possessing, inventing, preaching and practicing. Of course this painful accusation applies only to architecture. In all other respects we are doubtless the most modest people on the face of the earth, always excepting our English cousins. This is not implying that everybody is in the darkness of ignorance and the fog of vanity. There are conspicuous exceptions even among laymen; but in the knowledge of architecture it is certainly true of the great majority. Any doubt on this point may be effectually dispelled by a few hours of intelligent observation along the principal streets of any provincial city, the "taste" therein manifested doubtless indicating something above the average intelligence of the entire population.

Leaving ignorance and vanity out of the question as being practically incurable except by the slow processes of evolution, there are several nearer and possibly preventible causes of our architectural poverty. One of the most serious and discouraging is the attitude of the local newspapers. I have never seen or heard of a newspaper, however high its journalistic standards, however earnestly it strives to be impartial, however faithfully and without regard to profit or

FOR PRESENT PROFIT AND A JOY FOREVER. '

popularity it espouses what it conceives to be the right side of questions that have a right and a wrong side, however valiantly it tells the truth in other matters of public and private concern—I have never seen or heard of a paper whose influence upon the architecture of its local field was not damaging rather than beneficial. That isn't the worst of it. For the life of me I don't see how it can be otherwise.

Nothing is more essential to the healthful development of art in all forms that intelligent public criticism; judicious commendation of the good and frank, explicit, detailed condemnation of the bad. Not dogmatic assertions, but impartial judgments, sustained by clearly stated and well-established principles. Music, the drama, landscape architecture, painting and monumental statuary are criticised wisely and often most helpfully by the competent writers employed by the best provincial journals. But the moment they touch the architecture that lies nearest them, and of which simple but uncompromising criticism would be valuable, their pens are dipped in oil. As I have just remarked, they must be; because here questions of taste and professional ability are entangled with private personal rights and interests. It will not answer to declare in good set terms that the new bank of Mr. A. is an extravagant monstrosity; that the new church of the United States is an abortion; that the forty tenement flats on Blank street is a hodge-podge in its external design, a small Ghetto and a large fire trap within; it would be a strange piece of insolence and ingratitude to suggest that the Library, Museum, Gymnasium, or Casino that our liberal fellow citizen has presented to the city or town, is, from the architectural point of view a monument of ignorance and ugliness. On the contrary, each and all of these buildings are sure to be described as fine examples of the skill of the architect, especially if he is a new-comer in town, and of the owner's or donor's wisdom. The reporter's vocabulary is ransacked for suitable adjectives to describe them, both in the main body of his "copy" and in the still more conspicuous and misleading headlines.

Now, it is undoubtedly true, whether happily or otherwise, that the opinions of the great majority of people in all matters esthetical, are largely determined by the comments and intimations of the public journals. So it happens that in architecture whatever the newspapers approve, (and to an extent they are obliged to approve every new growth, even if it is a parasite or a mushroom, or be accused of a lack of proper public spirit), is accepted as good, and, woe the day, is sure of imitation. Even if we leave the owners and the donors out of the case, what would the young architect who is just entering upon a career of usefulness say, if the work of his budding genius, which may be truly original, should be characterized in the daily papers as both original and ridiculous? How would the old architects whose "ear marks" appear on all the streets of the city until, through long familiarity they have become agreeable, as the odor of the stable is agreeable to the hostler—how would these faithful but helpless old architects like to be told that they were never anyhing but builders of average intelligence, who learned to wield the T-square in their youth and to copy some of the mouldings that are shown in the reputable old books on the "Orders," or to appropriate the disreputable details of the "middle ages" between 1850 and 1870?

A complete lifting of this journalistic handicap seems impracticable. A partial mitigation of the evil could possibly be accomplished if the papers which maintain a fairly just and able criticism of other forms of art, a criticism that is instructive to laymen and stimulating to the

FOR THE ENCOURAGEMENT OF TAXPAYERS.

artists, would refrain from all mention of unworthy architecture, commending cordially and in detail whatever is really worthy of imitation and commendation.

The enormous preponderance of poor, or at best negative architecture (which is perhaps the same thing), and our inevitable familiarity with it is another conspicuous obstacle in the way of architectural reform. This familiarity is not of the kind that breeds contempt; it rather tends to respectful tolerance and ignorant admiration. A common instance of this is found in the prevalence of certain characteristics in dwellings of the medium class in different cities. The res-

THE "ORDERS" ARE THE ARCHITECTS' FIRST LAW.

idents of other cities find them unattractive if not positively disagreeable. Those who see them every day find them pleasant and homelike. Familiar examples of this are the flat-headed two-story-and-attic houses, with "cellar windows in the top"; the two-story buildings with the so-called French roof; the chuckle-headed gambrel roofed houses, covered from sill to ridge pole with an eruption of shingles; the rectangular red brick block with solid white shutters, of Philadelphian suburbs. All these and many more are types of what may be called local fashions. (If Philadelphia is not strictly provincial at present, it has a traditional reputation to that effect).

Now, a house or anything else may be interesting and pleasing to

THE PUBLIC SPIRIT OF ITS CITIZENS DETERMINES THE
DEVELOPMENT OF A CITY.

a great number of people simply because it conforms to a prevailing and familiar mode; but art has no more concern with custom and fashion, than it has with politics and sanitation. In minor matters fashions change quickly and their influence for good or bad is of short duration. But in architecture the eccentricities and vagaries which result from the prevalence of some passing vogue, are obtrusively permanent above ground long after the only reason for their existence has been dead and buried. The effect of this is as though all the women who ever wore poke bonnets, hoop skirts or "mutton-leg" sleeves, must continue to wear them to the end of the chapter

EVERY MAN'S INALIENABLE RIGHT.

and only the rising generation be permitted to invent and follow new fashions. This might lead to a picturesque assortment of costumes, but it would not be more incongruous, variegated and uncouth than the domestic architecture of a modern city and its suburbs.

(Having disclaimed any intention of criticising domestic architecture, I ought to say that the above is introduced simply as the most convenient illustration of the influence of fashion in building, an influence that prevails in all classes of buildings but is the most conspicuous in dwellings.)

The effect of this thoughtless and more or less unconscious preference for what is familiar, is distinctly obstructive to such advance

ART IS THE HANDMAID OF RELIGION.

in architecture as ought to follow the vast resources and still vaster
ambitions of the time in which we live. It throws into popular dis-
favor everything, however excellent, that is not actually common-
place. It is obvious that any general and substantial improvement in
architecture must depend on the right cultivation and direction of
popular taste, and this is always guided by what is conspicuously displayed rather than by a knowledge of what is really good. The improvement in architecture that has followed great conflagrations in
the last half century shows how much more rapid this popular education would be if this load of vicious example and precedent could
be lifted, even if it has to go up in smoke. Now, this form of handi-

FOR THE STUDY OF LITERATURE, SCIENCE AND—ART.

cap is relatively far more serious in the cities which I have classed as
"provincial" than in those of more cosmopolitan character, because
in the former, individual instances of departure from established precedent stand out more conspicuously. This is also illustrated in matters of dress, equipages, and in all minor social customs and conventions.

Undoubtedly, the best architecture the world has known in the
past has been devoted to the service of religion, either of the kind
known to us as Christian or pagan. At the present time the most important, if not the most admirable architectural monuments that can
claim any originality are probably found, not among ecclesiastical

THE COMMITTEE WANTED " SOMETHING RICHARDSONESQUE."

buildings, which, when not absolutely bad are mainly imitative in spirit if not in actual form, but among those intended for municipal, or other public and corporate purposes. It is for such public buildings that the most logical plea for thoroughness, dignity and elegance can be made; upon these the most lavish outlay is expected. We say with great propriety that it is fitting for a rich and intelligent people—I put the short adjective first advisedly—to manifest its wealth and intelligence in the character of its public buildings, whether they are for local or national use.

Far be it from me to depreciate the wisdom of our public ser-

THE FINE ROMAN HAND.

vants. There is no reason to suppose that the members of city governments, the common councilmen and the boards of aldermen from among whom the city property committees, or whatever their official titles may be, are chosen, are either more or less ignorant of good architecture and of art, than other average laymen although their ignorance may be more damaging, because more stubborn and aggressive, a generous conceit of his own wisdom and a pachydermatous insensibility to criticism being essential to political success. But the fountain must not be asked to rise higher than its source, and it is futile to expect the best in municipal architecture until its selection is determined by some more trained judgment, by some more special education in the most complex and difficult of all the arts, than the accidental knowledge and "taste" of the ordinary "public servant." Even when "experts" are invited to assist in making a decision between rival designs, their recommendations are seldom regarded unless they happen to agree with the opinions already formed by the officials who "know what they like" even when they can give no intelligent reason for their preferences, and who are not apt to be altogether pleased by the implied doubt of their wisdom.

It is one of the unsolved puzzles why an otherwise intelligent community should entrust one of its most important functions, one requiring for its wise administration the highest degree of technical skill and special training, to men who know no more of architecture than an unlettered boor knows of astronomy; they have seen buildings ever since they were born, and he has seen the stars. It would hardly be more absurd to appoint from the members of a city government, a committee to write medical prescriptions for the patients at the city hospital.

Nearly related to this obstacle is the fact that in small cities there is no proper inducement for the most competent architects to give their services to public work. I am well aware of the ignorance, the vanity, the jealousy, the fantastic notions, the often stupidity and occasional vulgarity of architects; they are mortal men and I may speak of this form of handicap later; but it is also true that there never was a time in the history of the world when there were such ample opportunities for invention, such vast facilities in the way of construction and materials, such a high degree of cultivation among so large a number of architects and such disinterested devotion to lofty ideals as at present. Artistically our country may be behind certain nations of Europe for the moment, but there is no excuse for our remaining so, since everything from the tops of the highest mountains to the innermost recesses of the art schools is accessible to us. But, as I have said, there is no proper inducement in provincial cities for the best architects to undertake public commissions, for the simple reason that architects are rarely selected for public work on account of the excellence of their plans or of their established reputation for rectitude and ability. The city in which it is my happy lot to reside is not more culpable, less righteously governed, or more indifferent to good architecture than other cities of its class; but I am confident that there has not been a public building of any sort erected by this municipality since it became the custom to employ architects, the plans for which have been adopted solely for their architectural merit. Various degrees of personal and political influence have been exerted. It is undoubtedly true in cases of competition that the best plans have sometimes been selected, but when that has occurred it has not been on account of their excellence alone; the verdict has been

ASPIRATION.

affected by some other motive, not, perhaps, of sufficient weight to have led to the adoption of the least meritorious among several plans, but quite sufficient to have brought in the second or third best if the same influence had happened to go towards them.

It would seem possible to mitigate if not entirely to remove this difficulty by the adoption of such competitive conditions as would make sinister influence impossible, but who shall insure the faithful observance of the conditions? So, after all, the matter comes back to the old, old story of upright men in public places.

An apparent cause of the poverty of provincial architecture is the incapacity of provincial architects. This is not as serious as it seems for the reason that there are few cities in which there is not at least one thoroughly trained architect, who only needs the opportunity afforded by the larger wealth and enterprise of the great cities to do as good work as can be found where those favorable conditions exist. But there does also appear to be in the smaller cities a larger proportion of nondescript "Practical Architects and Builders" who, for personal and supposed economical reasons are liable to be employed as architects by men who care little and know less of what might be done in the way of excellent design even for the most simple

and inexpensive structures. Especially do personal motives enter into the question of selecting the architect. A man who would not think of employing a friend or relative to paint his portrait for the edification of his posterity, or even to take his photograph, still less

PLAINNESS AND DIGNITY ARE NOT INCOMPATIBLE.

ROMANESQUE AS SHE IS SPOKE.

to set a broken bone on account of his friendship or relationship, does not hesitate to give him a "job" in architecture in order to help him in business. The consequence of this kind of personal favor is conspicuous and abundant. It is common enough in great cities, but in them it is less marked and has less influence upon public taste.

Another marked condition in the subject under discussion is the prevalent custom of entrusting important work to some architect away from home. Instead of improving the local architecture by exciting a healthy emulation, this is more likely to have an opposite effect. Fifty, or perhaps in some sections thirty, years ago, there were few but "Home-made" architects, evolved from lazy or ambi-

A CORNER IDEA.

tious carpenters, in the small cities. Then it was inevitable that really good work must be obtained out of town. At the present time, as I have said, there is scarcely a city even among the smaller ones in which at least one architect with as good training as the best schools in this country and Europe can give, has not hung out his shingle. If the work that really calls for superior professional skill is sent away from such a competent resident architect he soon decides that there is neither honor nor reward for the prophet who stays at home. Naturally he abandons the field to the second and third rate men who always stand ready to rush in, and who never rise above the dead level of mediocrity. Owing to this same sort of prejudice, if local architects are liable to compete with those from outside there is likely to be a decided bias in favor of the outsiders. This is commonly disavowed, especially by public officials who have political ambitions, but not always. In a recent competition for an important public building in a New England city one of the building commissioners who was to assist in the selection of the plans that were to be submitted openly declared before his appointment was confirmed that he should surely oppose the acceptance of any plan presented by any local architect, regardless of its merit. It is difficult to say which was the most amazing; the fact that local architects should have been willing to compete under such circumstances, or that the man should have been appointed to serve on a commission whose members would be gravely compromised by any deviation from strict impartiality. But then his official position was not obtained by popular

THE "BROWNIES" IN ARCHITECTURE.

franchise, and he was himself a local architect. I mention this as a clear and, I believe, a by no means unusual instance of the lack of high ethical standards in the business relations of architects and their possible clients, as well as one of the forms of handicap to which provincial architecture is peculiarly subject.

On the other hand, a more serious blight sometimes comes from the small politicians who endeavor to increase their own chances of popular favor by a pretence of public spirit in the employment of so-called "home talent." This handicap prevails most disastrously in the large towns and small cities whose local business is not sufficient to tempt men of more than mediocre ability. This is all the more deplorable because the best sites for the display of good architecture are found where land is abundant and inexpensive, and where there is an opportunity for the skillful adaptation of the architectural design to natural surroundings, which, though not always grand, may at least be striking, picturesque and generous.

To give one more instance in a list that might be considerably extended, I think it is true that in provincial cities of the middle and larger class there is, in comparison with the great cosmopolitan cities (perhaps on account of the lower cost of living) an

A "SUCCESSFUL" TREATMENT OF ROOFS.

increased proportion of untrained, incompetent and unprincipled architects, men who try to obtain work by dishonest means, who seek and accept illicit commissions, and, alas for poor humanity, who fancy it is possible to exalt their own work by disparaging their contemporaries. And it is not alone the local irregularities and rascalities that must be encountered, but work that might be expected to be done by the resident architects of the smaller cities seems to be considered fair plunder by the dishonorable practitioners and professional drummers of the big ones. Men whose reputation at home is still comparatively undamaged, and who would shrink from unprofessional practice where they are well known, appear to feel that any means of thrusting their hands into the public crib of the smaller cities is permissible. That is to say, the line that separates honorable business enterprise from unprincipled wire-pulling and sinister scheming seems to be more easily crossed among strangers.

It is hardly necessary to say that some of these obstacles in the way of good architecture exist everywhere. The only reason for including them in this category is that in "provincial" regions they are greatly exaggerated.

E. C. Gardner.

THE INTERNATIONAL BANKING AND TRUST CO.'S BUILDING.
Cedar Street and Broadway.   Bruce Price, Architect.

137 BROADWAY.

THE architect of a new and just externally completed tall building at the northwest corner of Cedar street and Broadway, has
been trying some experiments in design, with results that are of some
interest. The employment, the particular employment, of color is
one of these. The relation between the parts is another, though the
novelty of this pertains entirely to the treatment of the crown and its
relation to the shaft, the relation between base and shaft being quite
conventional. But the experiments are at any rate numerous and
striking enough to arrest attention, and to challenge inquiry how far
they repay it.

The building is some forty feet on Broadway by 150 on the side
street, and the total height is of fourteen stories. With these dimensions, a tower-like treatment of the narrower front would seem to
"impose itself," although the designer does not fully admit that, as
will be seen. A circumstance, too, of which it seems that he had to
take notice was the proximity of the Washington Life. The two of
them occupy the whole block front on Broadway, excepting a melancholy relic in the shape of a cast-iron front, of five stories and twenty-
five or thirty feet of frontage, dated 1863, which is absurdly left
between them. Evidently, it is not left for long, but only
till a meeting of minds occurs between the owner and some
purchaser, or the owner concludes to "improve" on his
own account. A conformity of design in the present building to its larger predecessor would have put a constraint
upon the owner of the interval to conform also, and we might have a
block front at unity with itself, which would, or might, be an impressive piece of street architecture with a frontage greater than that
of any but a very few of the skyscrapers. But here comes in the
curse of commercial architecture, which almost compels the architect of an office building of which the owner is a commercial corpo-
ration and also one of the tenants, to signalize it by singularizing
it, to make it assert itself by difference, instead of conforming in the
interest of the total effect. Very likely, in such a case, the architect
cannot help himself, and prays, like the judicious spectator, for a pre-
fect or aedile to make him behave himself in spite of his employer.
We seem to be making some progress in New York towards this
pitch of civilization ; but we have not reached it yet by a long way.
And, indeed, in the present case conformity would have been difficult
with ever so good a will. The new building is not only distinctly narrower than the older, but it is four stories lower, not to count the

steep roof which is the chief ornament and distinction of the older.
At the back, the two join, and occupy between them the whole block
front, but there is no view to be had, Temple street being more properly describable as an alley.

Conformity would, therefore, have been a puzzling problem. At
any rate, there is no conformity, except in the material of the basement, which is in each case a light limestone. In the work under notice, this is of two stories and in front of it is placed the most conspicuous, architectural feature of the building. This is the portico that
marks the entrance. It is a tetrastyle of Roman Doric, Roman Doric
of the Renaissance, be it understood, and not of the empire, for the
columns are banded with vermiculated stripes. As this banding was
used by the architects of the French Renaissance, it was connected
with the masonry of the wall with which the columns were engaged,
and had the effect of modelled projections of the mass. When it is
applied, as here and as in the basement of the Post Office, to columns
standing entirely free, it loses most of its effectiveness in losing all its
meaning. And, indeed, the effect of a portico detached like this and
not incorporated is apt to be of a feature irrelevant and separable, and
that is the effect it has in this instance. The flank of the basement is
a series of quite plain piers, running through the two stories, with
plain transoms marking the floor line, the whole as unpretentious,
and, indeed, as unnoticeable, as possible.

The decoration of the front of the basement is carried above it into
the superstructure. At the centre of this, and running through the two
lower stories, the third and fourth of the building, is a monumentally
treated opening, flanked by a pair of pilasters carrying a broken pediment, all in white terra cotta, with the enclosed windows, respectively, flat arched and pedimented. And the central window of the
story above, the fifth, is also signalized by the decoration which here
dies into the shaft. But for this, the five stories from the fifth to the
ninth, inclusive, would be quite identical.

The material of the shaft is white brick, red brick and white terra
cotta, the red brick used in the alternate voussoirs, if bunches of bricks
may be called so, and in the quoins of the flat-arched windows. These
are three in number in each story. The uppermost story of the shaft,
the tenth of the building, shows round arches. Above this is a not
very emphatic string course, a string course distinctly not emphatic
enough, which serves as a necking, and divides the shaft from the
capital. This is of three stories, the openings aligned over those below, but running through the three and closed above by round
arches.

The abacus is a single story of square holes, made noteworthy or
noticeable only by the roof treatment. The roof is flat, but umbrageous eaves are boldly projected from it to a distance of several feet

in sheet copper. Of the same material are the pairs of corbels that seem to carry this curious cornice. There is no disguise of the material, but the forms are imitated from a corbelled construction in masonry, even to the reproduction of projecting courses which have a structural significance in stonework. This is, of course, quite lost, and the whole arrangement is meaningless with a flat roof which cannot pretend to shed water by eaves dropping. But it gives occasion for a rather picturesque treatment of the return of the wall on the north side, with crowsteps descending and projecting to the cornice line, a treatment which one can imagine to be very effective in rural surroundings, or in a building in which the character of quaintness was persistently aimed at throughout, as, of course, is not at all the case here.

The longer but less conspicuous front on Cedar street shows an entirely different motive and arrangement, with a general conformity of detail. Each end is occupied by a pavilion, distinguished not by projection, but by a separateness of treatment, marked by comparative plainness and conveying as much sense of solidity as the conditions will allow. The treatment of the openings in these corresponds to that of the Broadway front. Between them, the curtain wall is divided into bays by pilasters running from the basement to the capital and terminating in heavy corbels, which in turn support what might for its projection be almost a "practical balcony," although no signs of such a use appear. But the horizontal feature thus formed is at all events much more adequate and appropriate, as a division between shaft and capital, than the evidently inadequate string course of the narrower front. The stories in each of the included bays alternate pairs of flat arches, with voussoirs and quoins of white and red, as before, with fully developed round arches, the top of the actual opening being horizontal, and the tympana solid, giving rise to speculation about the occurrence of the floor lines which are not marked, and which apparently come in the space occupied by the arch heads. The panels are decorated with a circle inscribed in a parallelogram of red brick on a field of white brick, and the tympana filled with red brick. The capital of this flank continues the division into bays, but each bay is here occupied by a single arch running through the three stories and including two sets of openings over the pairs below. The division is maintained by the emergence of the pilasters which cease at the spring of the arches.

There are undoubtedly "evidences of design" in the variations here attempted upon the conventional type of skyscraper. But upon the whole one has to own that they are ineffectual. The employment of color is logical enough. The stronger tint is used to accentuate the stress of structure and the weaker for the unemphatic intervals. But the logic does not vindicate itself. A pupil in composition at a German music school submitted an essay which he undertook to defend against the condemnation of his professor by showing how he had observed the rules. "But it doesn't kling," replied the unsympathetic critic. Decidedly this color treatment does not "kling." And so with the other variations. The relation of the shaft to the capital, with the identity of material and the similarity of treatment, is entirely un-rhythmical. There is no felicity in it. The umbrageous cornice is a novelty which, as has been pointed out, quite fails to justify itself even on logical grounds. Given the general division, which is the postulate of all the designers, and the eye demands a clearer and more emphatic differentiation of the parts, above all a more harmonious proportion than is to be found in this building. There are suggestions in it, especially about the use of color which its author, or some other designer, may yet work out into an effective and attractive result. But decidedly they are not worked out to such a result in this unsuccessful experiment.

The
New
Appellate
Court
House

New York City

❧❧

JAMES BROWN LORD
Architect

MAIN HALL—LOOKING NORTH AND WEST.

COURT ROOM—LOOKING EAST.

COURT ROOM—LOOKING TOWARD JUSTICES' BENCH.

COURT ROOM—JUSTICES' BENCH.

CONSULTATION ROOM AND LIBRARY.

CLERK'S OFFICE.

COAT ROOM.

COURT ROOM—LOOKING TOWARD ENTRANCE FROM MAIN HALL.

BETZ BUILDING.
Will H. Decker, Architect.

GIRARD TRUST BUILDING.
Addison Hutton, Architect.

PHILADELPHIA, PA.

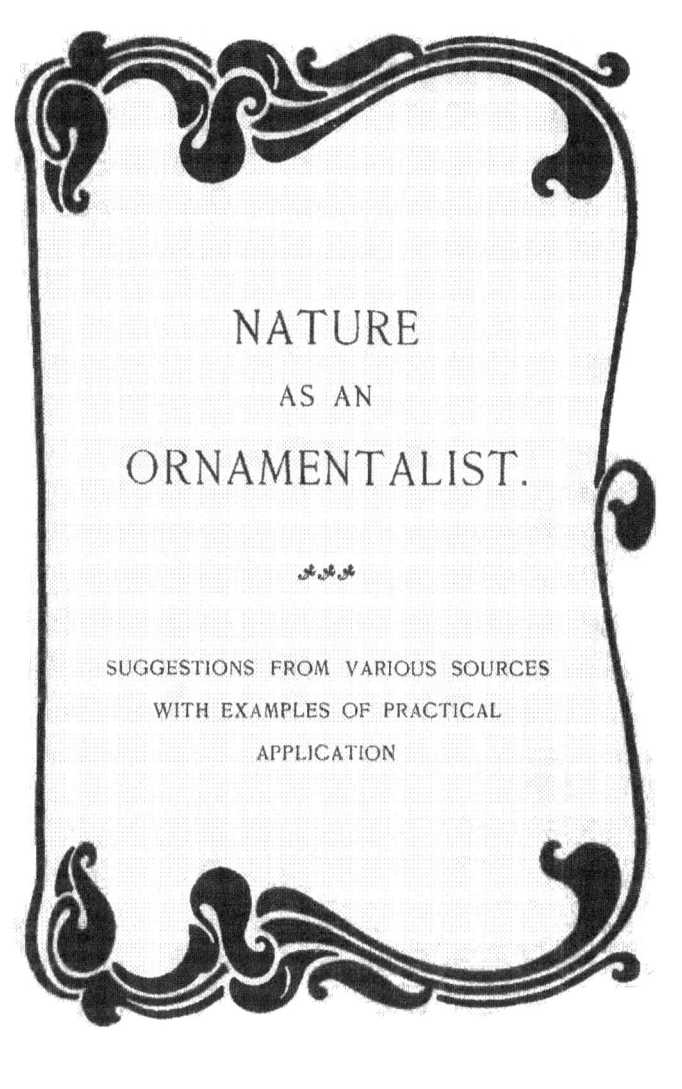

NATURE

AS AN

ORNAMENTALIST.

❊ ❊ ❊

SUGGESTIONS FROM VARIOUS SOURCES
WITH EXAMPLES OF PRACTICAL
APPLICATION

SNOW CRYSTALS.

The fitness of these natural forms to iron and other metallic work hardly needs to be pointed out. A comparison of these figures with Mr. Louis Sullivan's famous gates of the Getty Tomb, represented on the page opposite, is both interesting and instructive. See also the page following that.

TERRA COTTA FRIEZE.

Louis Sullivan, Architect.

THE GATES OF THE GETTY TOMB.

Louis Sullivan, Architect.

The lower of these two figures is given not as an implication that Mr. Sullivan was indebted to nature for his motif, but to show how closely a great designer may approximate to nature's work without copying.

SNOW CRYSTALS.

FROST.

CALCISPONGIAE.

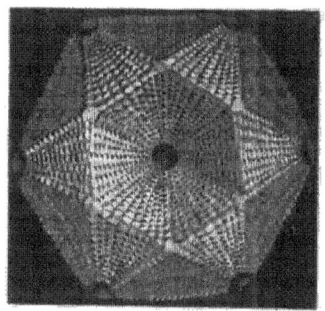

HEXACORRALLA.

DIATOM, MAGNIFIED.

HEXACORRALLA.

HEXACORRALLA.

DESIGNS BY LOUIS SULLIVAN.

DESIGNS BY LOUIS SULLIVAN.

BOOK REVIEWS.

SCIENCE AND ART DRAWING (Britannia Series).—J. Humphrey Spanton. New York: The Macmillan Co.

MANUALA DI ARCHITETURA ITALIANA: Antica e Moderna. Alfredo Melani. 3d Edition. Milan: U Hoepli.

MANUALE DI SCULTURA ITALIANA; Antica e Moderna. Alfredo Melani. Milan: U. Hoepli.

MODERN AMERICAN SCHOOL BUILDINGS. Warren Richard Briggs, F. A. I. A. New York: John Wiley & Sons.

TOLEDO (Mediaeval Town Series). Hannah Lynch. Illustrated by Helen M. James. London: J. M. Dent & Co.

DEVELOPMENT AND CHARACTER OF GOTHIC ARCHITECTURE. Charles Herbert Moore. 2d Edition, Rewritten and Enlarged. New York: The Macmillan Co. $4.50.

SANITARY ENGINEERING OF BUILDINGS. William Paul Gerhard, C. E. New York: William T. Comstock.

CHIMNEY DESIGN AND THEORY. William Wallace Christie. New York: D. Van Nostrand Co. $3.00.

PLASTER CASTS AND HOW THEY ARE MADE. Frank Forrest Frederick. New York: William T. Comstock.

VOYAGE IDEAL EN ITALIE: L'Art Ancien et l'Art Moderne. Jean Schopfer. Paris Libraire Academique Didier: Perrin et Cie.

OBSERVATIONAL GEOMETRY. William T. Campbell, A. M. New York: Harper & Bros.

PEN DRAWING.—An Illustrated Treatise. By Charles D. Maginnis. Boston: Bates & Guild. 1900.

OLD COLONIAL HOUSES OF THE CAPE OF GOOD HOPE. Illustrated and described by Alys Fane Trotter, with a chapter on the origin of old Cape architecture by Herbert Baker, A. R. I. B. A. New York: Chas. Scribner's Sons (imported). 1900. $4.50.

A MANUAL OF HISTORIC ORNAMENT, treating upon the evolution, tradition and development of architecture and other applied arts. Prepared for the use of students and craftsmen by Richard Glazier. 470 illustrations. New York: Chas. Scribner's Sons (imported). 1900. $2.50.

ESTIMATING FRAME AND BRICK HOUSES, by F. T. Hodgson (David Williams Co., publishers), is a useful and comprehensive little volume, which will be found of great value not only by students and laymen generally, but by architects and builders who desire to have in mind some quick, ready rules and methods for estimating costs and quantities in building. The author shows a thorough comprehension of the problem he has taken in hand, and both by the illustrations he has used and the arrangement he has adopted greatly facilitates the reader's task. The book is up-to-date and advocates sound construction.

THE LOGGIA DEI LANZI.

There has been sent to The Architectural Record by Signor Ginevri, the proposer and probably the designer, a pamphlet concerning a great library building which it is desired to erect in Florence. The pamphlet contains a site-plan and elevations showing two alternative schemes for the front on the Piazza della Signoria and the Via Vacchereccia. According to these drawings the building in either of its proposed forms would be backed close against the westernmost wall of the Uffizi building where the archives are and where the postoffice used to be, and would extend westward, including within itself the location of several narrow streets and across to the Via Porta S. Maria which leads straight to the Ponte Vecchio. According to the complete scheme this building would be carried to the quay on the river, the Lungarno Archibusieri, but at present the purpose is to build but half of this. The question of more or less is, however, of the least importance, because we do not learn that the design is positively adopted, or even that the project of putting a library building in this place is definitely approved. This is not the important matter; foreign lovers of Florence need not begrudge the city a fine library building, nor should the proposed destruction of the church of S. Stefano seem to them a great sacrilege, considering the difficulty of obtaining an adequate site for a probably needed public building in the heart of Florence. Foreign lovers of Florence and her treasures of art may indeed fear that any protest on their part would be as badly received as were the appeals of the English lovers of St. Mark's Church at Venice when the cruel restorations of that church were carried out seventeen years ago. Such appeals were called interference then and would be called interference now. Still, everyone who loves the Loggia dei Lanzi, that most unique building, that gem of original Italian architecture, that embodiment of the pure Italian spirit free from domination by the pointed Gothic of the north or by the Graeco-Roman orders and all that was to come with them a century later, that building which more than any other structure shows what Italian building might have been had the Italians been gifted with that building instinct which at a few epochs in the world's history a single nation has displayed, that building which, except that it had no consequences, one might call the most important decorative construction in all Italy, the Loggia dei Lanzi is threatened with the complete destruction of its value as a work of art.

One of the two schemes shows a triple arcade to the west of it and on the same line and at a distance so slight that only a single archway with heavier abutments is interposed between the newer and older structure. A second archway, similar to the last named, is erected at the western extremity. In other words, there would be attached to the western face of the Loggia dei Lanzi a new structure containing five great arches, of which three, with their piers and spandrels, would be exactly copied from the three of the Loggia dei Lanzi and the two others flanking the triplet would be enclosed between more massive piers, so that these divisions of the library-front, each 50 feet wide or thereabouts, may probably be intended to advance t little into the Piazza or the street. The whole new front, then, of about 220 feet, facing nearly northward, would consist of five great arches on the lower story and upon these would be reared a wall with a single row of windows so immense in scale as to have between the stone jambs a width of about 21 feet. The great wall which is pierced with these five giant windows and by no other openings whatever, is shown as crowned by exactly the same cornice and parapet as those which belong to the present Loggia dei Lanzi. In the absence of an illustration before him, the reader must really look into his memory and use his imagination, and try to realize the ruinous effect upon the beautiful monument which now stands in the Piazza Signoria of having attached to it a prolongation of its own arcade used to carry a superstructure of great size and mass. The hoisting of the cornice, which is now nearly 80 feet above the street, to a point 140 feet above the street, is only a small part of the violation of all good taste which this design implies. What would become of the perfect proportion, scale, fitness—exactly repeating the Loggia dei Lanzi erected therefore, what would become of the charm—of the Loggia dei Lanzi if it were parodied by the juxtaposition of its own arcade repeated and used as the substructure of such a building as the one we have tried to describe?

The alternative design is less incongruous, but is, perhaps, equally objectionable. In this the Loggia dei Lanzi is copied by a precisely similar building further to the west, while between the existing and the proposed structure a sort of tower is carried up with one great archway in its lower story. This tower and the copy of the Loggia dei Lanzi are to serve as mere facings or masks for a very plain library building which shows behind and beyond them. To this design the objection would be twofold. First, the mockery of the old and valued building by an exact copy of it erected close at hand; and, second, a vice which this design shares with the other—the hiding of the western face of the Loggia dei Lanzi. Enough has been said to show the extreme impropriety of each of the proposed designs.

THE NEW DICTIONARY OF ARCHITECTURE.

The Dictionary of Architecture which has been in preparation for some time is so near to completion that definite information about it can be obtained. The first volume will be issued by the Macmillan Company, of 66 Fifth Avenue, New York, within a short time, and the remainder of the work is complete so far as the more important contributions are concerned.

These contributions are all likely to prove very remarkable in their character, and unique in their value. Sixty persons selected by the editor as especially expert in the subjects proposed to them have furnished these articles, varying in length from 500 to 10,000 words, and, in the case of this or that continued article, divided into several parts, reaching perhaps 20,000 words. Thus, the remarkable series of papers on the architecture of Italy, divided geographically into its more important divisions, will reach a total sum of more than 20,000 words. This is the work of John S. Fiske, of Alassio on the Rivierra, so far as concerns Lombardy, Piedmont, and Liguria; while, for the rest of Italy, Professor Arthur L. Frothingham, Jr., of Princeton, has contributed unique and thorough studies, as of Umbria, of Tuscany, and especially of Lazio (Latium) and Rome itself. These geographical articles are like guide-books, in that they tell the would-be student of a country's art what he should look for especially. If he would buy photographs and books, or if he would travel, alike he needs to know those buildings, if he neglects all others. Among these geographical articles is the remarkable study of England, by R. Clipston Sturgis, of Boston. Germany is the work of H. W. Brewer, of London. R. Phené Spiers, editor of the newest and best edition of Fergusson's books, is the author of the studies of Asia Minor and Syria, of which ancient lands he has a special knowledge. In like manner, Alexander Graham, of London, the author of "Travels in Tunisia," writes on a geographical district which few know as well as he, the north African states, the Roman remains in which lands have of late formed the subject of special archaeological research. Mr. Spiers has also furnished the article on the ancient architecture of Persia, including the Parthian dominion, and the article on Roman Imperial architecture considered as the pervading style throughout the Mediterranean lands. Portugal, Spain, and Belgium have been treated by Mr. C. H. Blackall, of Boston. Japan has been treated by Mr. R. A. Cram, of Boston, who has made a special study of her ancient architecture; Scotland, by Professor A. D. F. Hamlin, of Columbia University; Greece, by Edward Tilton, now of New York, but for several years of Athens; but this latter article is not to be confounded with that on Grecian Architecture as a general study, which is by Professor Allan Marquand, of Princeton. France and some of the smaller lands of Europe have been handled by the editor himself. The article on the United States is by Montgomery Schuyler, of New York; that on the ancient ruins of Mexico, by F. S. Dellenbaugh, of New York, and that on modern Mexico by T. F. Turner, of New York.

Space does not allow of describing the other branches of the work so fully; but it should be stated that the engineering expert is W. Rich Hutton, of New York, he who built the Washington Bridge across the Harlem River; that plumbing and drainage and sanitation are the province of W. P. Gerhard, of New York, and that the extraordinary paper on Acoustics, perhaps the first explicit and intelligently scientific examination of the subject which has been printed, is by Professor W. C. Sabine, of Harvard University. Drafting, Perspective, Shades and Shadows, and such like preparatory arts, have been treated by the managers of the School of Architecture at Columbia University, Professor W. R.

Ware, Mr. F. D. Sherman and Mr. W. T. Partridge. Refinements in Design, such as have been the study of Professor Goodyear in this country, and of Penrose in England, have been treated for the Dictionary by George L. Heins, one of the architects of the Cathedral of St. John the Divine; for Mr. Heins has always made a practical study of these little noted possibilities in the way of delicate modifications of line and mass.

As for the great styles of architecture, that of Egypt conterminous with the country has been treated by Professor A. D. F. Hamlin, as has been the Mohammedan architecture in all its varieties. Roman Imperial and Grecian architecture have been named above; Romanesque is by W. P. P. Longfellow, of Boston, who has also treated the revised classical styles, and their relation to antiquity, under the terms Greco-Roman, Neo-Classic and Pseudo-Classic. Gothic architecture is by the editor, and there is an additional chapter on the special subject of English Gothic by R. Clipston Sturgis, of Boston.

These, and many such longer articles, are in a way the natural outgrowth of the definition which each term receives. The business of the technical dictionary is mainly to define, and accordingly the term Antefix and the term Annunciator, the very ancient and the very modern device, are defined each under its own caption, and so are palace, palais, palazzo, with distinction between the proper and the popular use of those terms. Such definitions may be 25 words long or may require several hundred words to express them properly, and it is evident from this how a definition swells into an encyclopaedic article when the necessary statements cannot be given in a smaller space. In connection with this we should speak of the sub-titles, for under the term Arch there are some 75 special varieties of arch defined and described, and these are arranged alphabetically under the general head. There are many instances such as this, though none quite as remarkable.

Finally, it should be stated that biographical notices have been written of architects ancient and modern, well known and little known, and of some important architectural writers as well. All of this biographical work has been done by Mr. Edward R. Smith, Custodian of the Avery Architectural Library.